BROTHERS OF WAR

The Iron Brigade at Gettysburg

A Historical Novel by

Michael Eisenhut

This book is a work of historical fiction. Although the story takes place during actual events in the American Civil War and often involves real people, some of the characters in this book are fictional or are used fictitiously. Any unfavorable or inaccurate description or harm to any person's name or reputation is unintentional.

Fulton Books, Inc.
Meadville, PA

Published by Fulton Books 2021

ISBN 978-1-64952-519-2 (paperback)
ISBN 978-1-64952-589-5 (hardcover)
ISBN 978-1-64952-520-8 (digital)

Printed in the United States of America

...Days turn to weeks and then to seasons. Winds blow, and leaves fall. And long winters cover them in snow, but spring always brings warm sunshine, leaves, grass, and flowers. As we walk this field...those honorable men's final bivouac...their stories must be told...by our generations and those not yet born. While souls linger, entire lifetimes pass. And this hallowed ground changes, but still, the memory of what they did here shall endure forever.

—M.E.

-1-

Herbst Woods, West of Gettysburg
July 1, 1863, 10:30 p.m.

Stirred by chaotic dreams, he trembled in a restless sleep.

The pain erupted from his shoulder again, and he woke with a cold shiver. He opened his eyes, but surprised at seeing only darkness, he quickly closed them. Then he heard the trickling water he had heard in his dreams.

The little stream...

Now he remembered...it seemed closer now.

Scared of what he would see, James slowly opened his eyes again. But, again, there was only darkness. Still, though, he could feel the trees and their canopy towering above him. It was nighttime now, and the musty, cool smell of the woods surrounded him.

And other smells too...

Smoke? Campfires?

How long have I been here?

His mind was muddled, and he tried to focus. In the distance, he heard noises in every direction. He tried listening closely, but the sounds quickly faded. Then he heard the trickling of the stream again.

Where is it?

James strained to see. Fighting darkness, he rubbed his eyes and face and tasted dirty sweat. Through the weeds and toward the sound of the trickling water, he could finally see the stream's reflection a few feet away.

Stirring a little more, he tried to sit up, but the pain shot through him again, reminding him of the Rebel's bayonet. The memory of the day's battle flashed through his consciousness and gave him a frightening shudder. He tried to shake it off but couldn't.

So long ago it seemed…the gray soldiers charging into me.
Was Sol there then?

He tried to remember more but could only think of the angry Rebel and his bayonet piercing into the back of his shoulder…and of the tortuous pain as the blade was mercilessly yanked away, tearing even more muscle and flesh on its way out.

The entire gray screaming line of Rebels was then upon him as he was lying there in agony. And then they were past, and he was suddenly behind enemy lines. It had been daylight then, and his world had turned into a blur. Then lying helpless in the weeds and badly wounded, he remembered wanting to stay awake, but he had quickly succumbed to the pain and then to the shock.

Now trying to think back to what happened, he was even more confused. He remembered that, while it was still light, he had crawled…down a slope and away from Rebels who were scavenging the wounded. Most had been lying lifeless among the weeds, but some had cried out with hellish shrills. Others, weaker, could only moan.

Trying to block out the nightmarish scene, James closed his eyes, but then he felt another pain, this time from his leg. Reaching down, he felt the wet bandage around his thigh.

My leg…
Ahhh, that was earlier…

It was when he was running…out past the creek. The bullet had sent him tumbling.

He remembered being down on the ground and then…

What else?

Yes, yes…he was down in the grass, and there were yells and screams just ahead. The rest of the regiment…he could see them across the creek.

Almost there.

He struggled to get up but couldn't. There were more yells, then suddenly, he heard the blast of hundreds of muzzles…

James shuddered, and as he opened his eyes again, a distant scream in the dark startled him. Then it was quiet once more, just the stillness of the dark woods.

He thought of God and then began a prayer. But he was too dizzy and weak, and the words wouldn't come.

With pain surging through him again, he felt himself drifting away.

For several minutes, he slipped in and out of consciousness. And then, he slept.

*****

"Sir?" someone murmured.

The voice was close, but James, thinking it was part of a dream, tried blocking it out.

"Sir, sir," the man quietly said again. James still didn't think the voice was real, but then he could sense someone shaking his arm.

Who…who…?

Then suddenly, he felt the splash of water on his face.

"Here," the man whispered. The woods were still quiet, just the voice. As James struggled to open his eyes, the man's face began to take shape just a few inches away.

7

A soldier?… Enemy?

James squirmed helplessly.

Or Union?

His eyes wrestled with the darkness, fought to see. He trembled, and his heart surged, until finally, he made out the letters *"US"* on the man's cartridge box. The dark figure was also a Union soldier.

The whites of the man's eyes stood out in contrast to his powder-blackened, muddy face. Then James felt the pain, the burning in his shoulder and arm. Wincing and groaning, he started to scream.

"Shhhhh…," the man whispered, shoving his hand down on James's mouth to block the sound. James could smell the stench of the soldier's breath and body odor as he leaned in close.

James was in a panic. His thoughts raced, and he wanted to scream but couldn't.

Where am I?

The last thing he remembered was waking up near the tiny stream. James didn't know how long ago that was and remembered he was by himself then. He put up his other hand and nodded to the man, surrendering to be silent. James, trembling in fear, stared pleadingly into the man's eyes.

The soldier slowly began to release his hand from James's mouth. *"Shhhh…"*

James, desperate, nodded.

"Easy…easy…"

The man's voice was soft, gentle, but still, James's eyes darted, and he nodded again, pleading.

"Real quiet, soldier," the man said, finally taking his hand away and reaching for a small flask.

James felt his panic slowly fade, but his heart still raced.

The man whispered, "Here, take this…whiskey."

James stared. The flask was only inches from his face. Time stood still, and fiery pain flashed through him again. The man nodded, smiled. He understood. *"It's okay,"* the soldier seemed to say.

James thought of his wounds and knew he could be dying. And then he thought of heaven…and of hell. Thoughts of blackness and eternal nothingness struck him with fear. He shuddered. *Oh, God…*

He closed his eyes, but only for a second.

"Here," the soldier whispered.

James looked at the flask and clasped it. After two years of this horrible war, any previous remorse about drinking alcohol had all but disappeared. Whiskey was part of soldiering now, especially for the wounded or the sick. God would approve, James knew.

James nodded a *thank-you* to the man and poured the whiskey into his mouth. It burned at first, then he savored the taste and wanted more. He took another gulp and tried to raise himself up, but the pain in his shoulder shot through him again. With a painful grimace, he downed another swig from the flask before handing it back to the soldier.

James was more awake now, his mind clearer. He looked through the darkness beyond the man in front of him. The blackness of the trees and canopies of their massive branches were silhouetted against the moonlit starry sky above. The little trickling stream he heard while dreaming was still there, lazily wandering through the underbrush and darkness before disappearing around a corner. Farther off, he could see the faintest glow of distant fires. *Campfires?*

"My name's *William*," the man quietly said. "Twenty-Fourth Michigan. Call me *Will*."

"James." He tried to say more, but the pain surged through him again. It was worse now, even more so in his leg than his shoulder. He tried to test his leg by raising it slightly, but the pain was too intense. The bullet was sure to still be inside. Giving up, he lowered his leg back down.

"Your leg looks pretty bad."

"Yeah, I bandaged it up in a hurry before the line fell back," James replied.

"You with the Nineteenth Indiana?" Will asked.

"Yeah…" James paused and tried to think. "How'd ya know?"

Before James had completed the question, Will was pointing at James's hat lying in the weeds a few feet away.

"Oh, my hat…I forgot I still had it."

Seeing his well-worn hat made James think of the rest of the brave men of the Nineteenth who suffered so horribly here in these woods. He especially thought of his younger brother Solomon. James volunteered to fight two years ago not only as a sense of duty, but also to look after his younger brother. Ironically, it was James who ended up needing more brotherly help than Solomon.

Prior to today's fight, James had already suffered two major wounds during the war, one of which resulted in a long convalescence in a hospital. The other severe wound left him nearly lifeless on a battlefield and led to his eventual capture by Confederates. Now badly wounded again, he was fighting for his life and would need the help of a miracle from God to escape the battlefield alive.

He leaned his head back down against the log of a fallen tree and looked up at the night sky. The moonlight peeked through the clouds and the tops of the trees, allowing just enough light to barely see. James examined his surroundings and tried to collect his thoughts. The whiskey seemed to help give him an all-around numbness, but still, he felt the intense pain in his shoulder and leg, and the cool night air along with his wet clothes caused a shiver.

"We have to get you help," Will said.

James looked over at Will and saw he was wearing a bandage around his head that was covered in blood. When Will turned around and looked through the woods, James could see his face was coated with a black crust of mud, gunpowder, and dried blood.

"There's Johnnies all over the place," Will whispered, looking the other direction and paying extra attention to the glows of the distant campfires. Will turned toward James again and asked, "Can you move?"

James's reply was a painful grunt. He rolled onto his side and tried lifting his head to speak. "Maybe some…but not far," James said.

"For now, you're safe here in the woods, at least until daylight. I've only seen a few Rebs come through the woods here, but they're everywhere out in them fields."

"It hurts bad, Will," James said.

"I know. I heard you moaning in your sleep. Thought I might help some, so I crawled over." The Michigan man looked down at James's blood-soaked bandage on his shoulder. "I put that on you when you were sleeping…to slow the blood."

"Thanks."

"We got to get you out of these woods and to a doc."

"My leg…I can't move it," James responded.

"Just rest a little bit." Will was looking around the woods more nervously than before.

James felt light-headed, ready to drift off again. "I'm not gonna make it, Will."

"Take another drink…here…" Will handed him the flask and helped him raise it to his mouth.

"Where are we?" James asked.

"Behind the Rebel lines," the Michigan soldier said quietly, lifting his head again to peer through the woods. "The brigade retreated into the town a few hours before dark. There's gonna be a lot more fighting here tomorrow, James. All night, the whole Rebel Army has been movin' up that pike over there."

"The town…is that Gettysburg?" James asked.

"Yeah, Gettysburg."

Will, apparently hearing something, had turned in the other direction. Grabbing James's arm with one hand, he put his other hand up in the air signaling James to stay quiet. "Stay here… I'll be right back."

He then quietly crept up the embankment on all fours. For the first time, James noticed Will's shoeless ankle was bandaged and that he was limping badly. He watched closely as Will stopped near the top of the small rise nearby and was now totally motionless.

The faint sound of voices beyond the hill toward the edge of the woods sent a tremor of fear through James's body. Will quickly scurried back down the slope to James's side. By the time Will reached him, James could clearly hear the sounds getting closer…at least a dozen soldiers with deep Southern drawls.

The two wounded Iron Brigade soldiers listened carefully as the men approached through the brush. The men were so close now, James could hear twigs and branches breaking beneath their shoes.

"Stay down, James," Will whispered.

James held his breath.

"Rebs…they're coming this way."

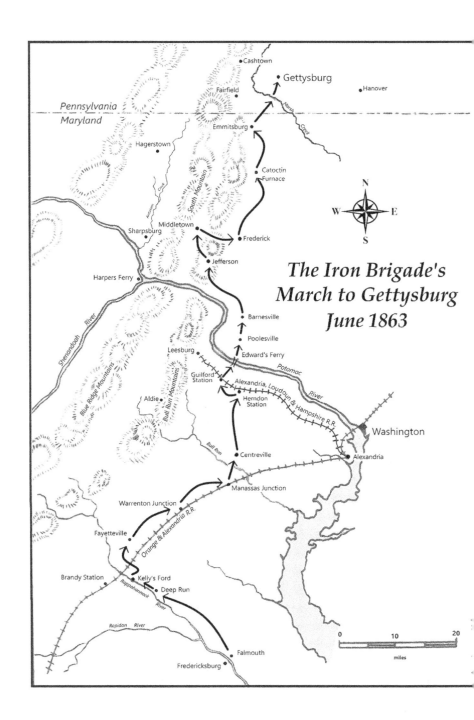

The Iron Brigade's
March to Gettysburg
June 1863

-2-

Two weeks earlier…

Near Herndon Station, Virginia
Union First Corps Army Camp
June 18, 1863, 7:30 a.m.

Solomon woke to the sound of voices just outside. With his clothes still damp, he pulled his blanket back over his legs and looked around the small, open tent. Seeing his wet socks and shoes hanging from the tent's opening made him think of yesterday's grueling march all the way up from Centreville.

They'd marched all day yesterday on hot, dusty roads. But late in the afternoon, the weather had changed and brought a welcomed rain shower. The rain didn't stop, however, and the roads quickly turned to boot-swallowing mud several inches deep. It was well past dark and in a driving thunderstorm when the front of the rain-soaked, staggering column had finally begun dragging itself into camp. Even the toughest sergeants had said the generals may have pushed too hard. The army was in a hurry, Solomon knew.

Slipping his sore feet out from the blanket, Solomon looked down. The blisters had worn thin and now exposed red flesh underneath. Reaching down with his finger, he lightly touched them. The flesh stung, and he quickly let go. With his mind filled with curses directed at faceless generals, he gritted his teeth and looked away.

Next to him, Henry's blanket was empty. Solomon knew it had been another restless night for his tentmate. Henry had said the devil himself seemed to take over his dreams some nights. The war had been hard on Henry, as it had been on almost all the men of the regiment. Henry had been enthusiastic after enlisting and had always performed proudly and bravely, but after "seeing the elephant" for the first time at Brawner's Farm, something had changed inside. That was a long, long year ago. But Henry still prayed…he hadn't given up on that.

The conversation outside the tent had become loud again and had apparently turned into an argument about a local farmer's hens and eggs. Solomon sat up and watched. He could tell that Henry was angry, infuriated even more by Hawk's laugh.

Solomon slid out of his blanket and crawled outside. After stepping barefoot in the moist, trampled grass, he sat down on a cracker box on the far side of the fire. Around them, most of the exhausted army was still quiet, although dozens of smoldering campfires blanketed the fields in smoke.

Hawk and Henry sat on logs only a few feet from the fire, both poking sticks into a pan being balanced on rocks. Seeing Solomon join them, they put their argument on hold and looked up from the fire.

"Hawk stole us some eggs last night," Henry said, his voice bitter. Hawk nodded to the pan with a proud smile that exposed stained teeth.

"Help yourself, Sol," Hawk said, then spat out an ugly chaw mess of tobacco juice, eggs, and bacon fat. While Hawk enjoyed the moment, Solomon stared, disgusted, wondering why anyone would eat and chew tobacco at the same time. But even more amazing was how Hawk had been able to go out foraging after yesterday's grueling march. The heat was the worst they had experienced and left thousands of stragglers suffering alongside the dusty roads. Going into camp in the rain only made things worse.

"Thanks, Hawk," Solomon finally said. Hawk seemed pleased with Solomon's response and chuckled before giving Henry an I-told-ya-so glance.

"Got us some bacon too, Sol," Hawk said, smiling even wider now and proudly boasting of his overnight foraging raid.

Henry had been quiet but finally looked up and said, "That food belonged to a farmer's family, Hawk. It's stealin'."

"You'll eat it though, won't ya?"

Hawk, obviously enjoying his one-sided banter at Henry's expense, laughed and then wiped brown spit from his chin's week-old beard. "Ahhh, come on, Henry… Why do you care about some Reb farmer anyway?"

Henry, with his stick still poking around the pan of eggs and bacon, ignored Hawk's goading and stared into the fire.

"Leave him alone, Hawk," Solomon said, finally coming to Henry's defense.

Henry looked up, his eyes meeting Solomon's and showing thanks… but only for a second before returning his gaze to the fire.

Hawk still stared, smiling.

Henry brooded for several long moments before reaching for his canteen and taking a long swig of water. After clearing his throat, he looked directly at Hawk and finally spoke up again. "We're not fighting the families of Virginia, Hawk."

Hawk, who had been trying to pull Henry into an argument, knew he'd finally succeeded. "No, we're just eatin' their eggs."

"It's wrong," Henry said. "And if the provost finds out you been pillaging farmers' chicken coops, you'll be payin' the devil himself… Or even worse, if the sarge finds…"

"The *ssssarrrrge… Hah!*" Hawk scoffed and spat another mess, this time toward the fire and landing with a sizzle on glowing embers and hot ashes.

Henry looked away but knew mentioning the sergeant would send Hawk into an angry rant. Hawk's smile had already faded, quicker even than the fizzling chaw he'd spat in the fire. "Besides, Henry, they're *Rebs*. You don't hafta eat. Hell, the food wagons are probably gonna be gettin' unstuck from the mud in a few hours…then you can have some more hardtack 'n' maggots…like we had last night."

Henry's stick jerked and jabbed in the pan with irritated twitches now. Solomon recognized Henry's inflamed silence… and his eyes too, searing, staring straight ahead. Hawk had gotten to him—their argument had been much deeper than stolen eggs and pork, that was for sure. Solomon knew he should let it go and let the fires cool some before asking Henry about it later.

In the meantime, Solomon smiled and chuckled out loud. Reaching out with his empty food plate, he said, "Slide me some of them eggs on here, wouldya, Henry?"

Henry, still angry, glanced at Solomon's plate. But instead of filling it, he grabbed his own plate and reached for the eggs and bacon. "Get yur own."

"There ya go, Henry!" Hawk exclaimed with a laugh while reaching over and slapping Henry on the back. After filling his plate, Henry paused and shook his head. He was hungry but also unable to hide the guilt of eating food stolen from a poor Virginia family…even if they were Rebels.

Watching Henry closely, Solomon also slid some of the eggs and bacon from the pan. "It's alright, Henry," Solomon said. "The army oughta feed us better."

"Yeah, suppose you're right," Henry said, taking his first bite.

Hawk stared at Henry and waited for him to look in his direction. When Henry finally did, Hawk gave him a wink and a playful grin.

"Well?" Hawk asked, his hands out wide and waiting for praise.

Henry's glare lasted a few seconds, but then he gave in. "Poor Billy is missin' a good meal," he finally said with a smile and nodding toward the empty tent behind them.

"Where is Billy anyway?" Solomon asked.

"He's over with his cousin," Hawk said.

"Billy's showing Grear how to play *Hawk's* harmonica," Henry said. It was Henry who laughed out loud this time.

"*Greeeear…*" Hawk scoffed.

"Do you like *anybody*, Hawk?" Henry asked.

"I like you guys…and James…and I guess I like Billy now too. And that's about it. Guess you're right, Henry…I don't like nobody else."

Solomon and Henry both knew that was the truth. It seemed that *truth* was about all that Private Elijah "Hawk" Hawkins knew. And he would always speak it too. Many an officer from other companies and even other regiments had stomped off angrily shaking their heads after talking to Private Hawkins. Hawk hadn't ever been shy around a bad officer, and there had been plenty of those. The men of the squad, though… that was different for Hawk. Despite all the banter and irritating teasing, Hawk protected and cared about his comrades in the squad more than anything. Even more than himself sometimes, it seemed to Solomon.

"I hear Grear Williams playin' your harmonica now, Hawk." It was Henry doing the goading now.

"I couldn't play the damned thing anyway," Hawk said. "At least Billy can play it."

"Why did ya carry that thing around for nine months anyways?" Henry asked. "You never even played it, and then ya went and gave it to Billy."

Henry and Solomon both stared at Hawk, waiting for him to respond. They both knew the story but wanted to hear Hawk admit it. When Private William Williams had joined the squad to replace Solomon's older brother James, all three of them, especially Hawk, resented Billy at first.

"I felt bad…you know…for picking on Billy because he took James's place and all."

"You didn't feel bad for pickin' on him, Hawk," Henry said. "You felt bad 'cause Billy landed a right hook on yur lip."

They all knew Henry was right.

Hawk, despite trying not to, finally grinned. When he did, Solomon and Henry both laughed.

"Lucky punch," Hawk said, speaking of Billy's right hook.

"Where *did* Billy learn that anyhow?" Solomon asked, still laughing.

Hawk had proven to be the toughest fighter they had ever seen, on the battlefield and in camp. But Billy's punch a month ago had surprised them all. By the time Hawk had staggered back to his feet and then approached Billy again, Hawk was smiling and more impressed than angry.

Hawk had already given Billy an approving nod by the time Sergeant Boller had walked up and asked why Hawk's lip was bleeding. If Hawk had been caught in another fight, he'd be in trouble for sure.

In Hawk's eyes, Billy's response after their scuffle was his final confirmation into the squad. "Hawk decided to go pee in a sticker bush, Sarge…in the dark," Billy had told the sergeant. Everyone there had laughed, and as usual around Hawk, Sergeant Boller had stormed off.

It was only a few days later that they all had learned that Billy's wife back home had just given birth to a baby boy. Between Billy's "lucky" punch and learning about Billy's newborn child whom he wouldn't be able to see, Billy suddenly had all their respect.

Still thinking about that day Billy had punched Hawk, the three army veterans from Indiana sat around the smoky fire and enjoyed their "stolen" breakfast. All around them, the large army camp slowly came to life. Off to the east, the faint sound of a distant train whistle echoed across the fields. Solomon glanced over at Hawk, who had apparently also heard it and was now staring in that direction too. But the train's whistle had faded, and Hawk looked back down to his meal.

The train made Solomon think of his older brother James, whom he hadn't seen for over six weeks. He clearly remembered saying goodbye to James, who had boarded a train headed to a hospital in Alexandria, Virginia. He wondered if Hawk, who had been James's tentmate and squad partner, was also thinking of their absent comrade. Hawk and James had grown close during the two difficult years since enlisting with the newly formed Nineteenth in Richmond, Indiana, in July of 1861. Everyone in the company assumed James would have been back by now.

It had happened on April 29th at Fitzhugh's Crossing, just south of Fredericksburg. The Nineteenth Indiana had watched from the bank as the Sixth Wisconsin and Twenty-Fourth Michigan men led the brigade across the Rappahannock River while under Confederate sniper fire from the hills on the other side. After those first two regiments crossed the river, the Nineteenth Indiana was ordered up and into the pontoon boats. Splashing into the water, James, Solomon, and the rest of Company B jumped aboard their boat and began frantically rowing as Confederate bullets filled the air.

James was just in front of Solomon when the minie ball had pierced the wood and sent the splinters through the thin, worn leather of James's shoe and into his heel. With the adrenaline caused by the river crossing and flying bullets, James was initially unaware of the wound. Once he clambered out of the boat onto the other bank, however, he felt a searing pain in his foot. Still under enemy fire and hurrying toward the tree line with the rest of the regiment, James had no time to bother with checking on the wound. Later that day and after thinking the damage was only minor, James had the heel of his foot bandaged at a nearby aid station. He had then quickly returned to the regiment's ranks and remained with them throughout the battle at Chancellorsville. Eventually, however, his foot became badly infected and forced him out of action. Solomon was with him when he was taken to a field hospital a few days prior to being boarded onto the train departing for Alexandria.

While still thinking back to the day James had left the regiment, Solomon suddenly heard Billy's harmonica. Quickly looking up, Solomon saw Billy playing the harmonica and walking toward their camp.

"Speaking of Billy," Hawk said, also seeing Billy approaching.

"Well, at least that harmonica is finally getting played," Henry said. "Billy's gotten pretty good at it, hadn't he, Sol?"

But Hawk, not done with his banter with Henry, interrupted and answered for Solomon. "I bet Billy ain't as good as that Georgia boy that had it 'fore him. You know the one, Henry. The Reb that's buried in the mud along the side of the Hagerstown Road…right where we left him. I bet his mother taught him to play it."

"Let it go, Hawk," Solomon said.

But it was too late. Hawk had crossed the line, and Henry was already up and turned away. Solomon didn't blame him. Neither one of them wanted to hear nor even think about Antietam again.

"Why ya gotta do that, Hawk?" Solomon asked, watching Henry disappear beyond rows of tents.

Before Hawk had a chance to answer, Billy walked up to the fire and asked, "What'd ya do now, Hawk?"

"Just tellin' Henry 'bout that dead Georgian that used to play that harmonica I gave ya. You still got it?"

"Right here," Billy said, smiling wide and raising the harmonica in the air for them all to see.

"Hawk was worried, Billy," Solomon said as Billy sat down where Henry had been. "…Worried that you'd given *the thing* to Grear."

Almost as if on cue, Billy had the harmonica up to his lips and gently blew a soft, long note. Then as it faded, Billy played another. The note was lower. It was a 'C', Solomon remembered Billy saying earlier.

Solomon looked up. Around the camp, there was movement now, but Billy's tune drowned it all out—most of it anyway. The call of a distant bugle somehow found their ears, but the three of them ignored it. The Georgian's harmonica made it all seem peaceful almost. *So ironic*, Solomon thought.

Off in the distance, Solomon heard another bugle, and more men stirred. The army was busily coming to life now but still seemed quiet, just the harmonica. It crooned even lower and smoother now, not a dirge but still somber, yet amazingly pleasant.

Solomon noticed Hawk had lowered his head slightly, just enough that the front of his black Hardee hat covered his eyes. Then Solomon glanced over at Billy. His cheeks seesawed in and out, and his fingers danced as he slid the harmonica slowly back and forth.

Solomon suddenly wondered where Henry had gone. Turning and looking, he saw that Henry still hadn't returned. He would soon, though, Solomon knew. He always did come back…just needed to let his mind escape the camp for a few precious moments. Then Solomon looked away and up at the morning's overcast sky. Now thinking of his brother James, Solomon wondered if James would *ever* return. Solomon looked back down at the dwindling fire and then glanced over at Billy still gently playing, even softer now. Hawk still had his head down, staring at the last of the embers, his hat even lower and hiding most of his face.

All the while, the tune flowed out and beautifully swallowed up all the other sounds around them. A few minutes ago, they had been joking around…small talk, banter, and teasing. But now, they all three thought of their comrades whom they had lost. Camp life was like that.

They'd lost some of their squad first at Brawner's Farm, then Manassas, South Mountain, and Antietam…and so many other places too. Solomon thought of the Addleman brothers he'd known since before he was a teenager, both killed at Antietam…and of the farm kid who lived down the road, Pete Bruner. They never did find his body in that bloody cornfield. Solomon thought of Jimmy Mills who had just died of typhoid a few months ago, and of Corporal Thornburg who died of the same disease like so many others.

There were so, so many more too. Solomon looked around the fire. It struck Solomon sadly that just *three* of them were sitting there right now. Early on in the war, there had been twelve of them in the squad.

Billy's harmonica finally stopped, and the loud sounds of the army camp had returned. Not far away, officers were shouting out orders, and squads of men were scrambling into groups. But Solomon still couldn't get the memories of his long-gone squadmates out of his mind, nor the nightmarish sights and sounds of battles that seemed like just yesterday.

"Thanks, Hawk," Solomon finally said before standing up, his voice reeking of sarcasm.

For once, Hawk didn't dare look up. Even he knew he'd pushed Henry too far.

"I'm gonna go find Henry," Solomon said.

-3-

Alexandria, Virginia
June 18, 1863, Early Morning

The torrential rain had kept him up most of the night in the house's upstairs bedroom. Now, a little after dawn, he finally gave up on sleep and propped himself up in the bed. Leaning sideways toward the window, James looked down to the already busy street below. Down on the sidewalk beneath him, two black men were noisily helping a nurse unload wooden boxes from a wagon parked next to the mansion's side door.

James turned away from the window and looked around the room. He had spent the past month in the house—a large three-story, red brick, corner mansion which had been converted to a hospital for wounded soldiers. He now thought of those other men he'd spent the past several weeks with. James was sure he would always remember them and, unfortunately, also their painful moans and cries for help. The hospital's nurses and doctors did all they could even for the most hopeless and desperate patients. Still, though, James had seen many men die here. James now considered himself one of the fortunate ones, although he himself had already been wounded twice during the war.

The first wound occurred just over a year ago during the Iron Brigade's horrible fighting at Brawner's Farm at the beginning of the Second Battle of Bull Run. Despite a serious and bloody head wound and being left for dead on the battlefield, he healed and was able to return to his battered regiment fairly quickly. He'd blocked most of that from his memory, but occasionally, flashbacks and nightmares still haunted him. Although that bloody battle near Manassas, Virginia, was ten long months ago, its horrors would last a lifetime for most of the men of the Iron Brigade who fought there.

James's second wound, which led to the current hospital stay here in Alexandria, however, required a much longer convalescence. The damage done to his foot at Fitzhugh's Crossing at the end of April seemed minor initially. He'd even stayed with the regiment through Chancellorsville. Infection had set in, however, and resulted in a long recovery. Now, nearly six weeks later, his foot had finally healed, and he felt ready to rejoin the army out in the field. The nurses, still worried about his foot and the grueling marching he was sure to be doing, urged him to stay at the house. But, knowing he had a responsibility to be with his regiment, he insisted on them letting him go.

After slowly getting up, James quietly stepped between the other beds. The wounded and sick men around him were much worse off than he was, James knew. And some of them, he was afraid, probably wouldn't ever make it out alive.

James dressed, and after gathering his extra socks, shirt, and undergarments into his knapsack, he crept across the room toward the stairs. He tried to block out the other patients but could still feel their eyes watching him. James even heard his name and wanted to look…maybe even speak to them one last time. He knew it was best not to though.

Finally, he turned around and met their stares. Some had sat up, others couldn't. James received several friendly nods.

One wounded man, Al, even smiled. James nodded too and forced a smile—but only for a second before quickly turning and starting down the stairs.

Outside, James breathed in the fresh morning air. It was cooler this morning with gray clouds scattered in the pink morning sky. He looked back toward the house one last time and thought of those men inside. Saying a quick prayer and then taking a deep breath, he turned around, paused, and then stared off into the distance. Then finally, he started down the sidewalk, feeling a vivacity he hadn't felt since before being wounded just prior to Chancellorsville.

James reached into his pocket and felt the two pieces of paper, making sure they were still there. One of the papers was an unexpected note that had come yesterday, a message from his older brother John, who was in Washington City and hoping to see James. John, a lieutenant from the Third Indiana Cavalry regiment, had been reassigned to the War Department in Washington City several months ago. Along with the note from his brother was a forty-eight-hour pass for James to travel to the city before rejoining the Nineteenth Indiana in the field.

James walked down the street cautiously at first before settling into a steady stroll. Although a little stiff, his foot wound seemed to be completely healed and wasn't giving him any pain as he walked along Alexandria's bustling sidewalks. Horses, wagons, and boots plodded through the puddled and muddy streets. As he turned toward the east and worked his way through the crowd, James could see flags flying from the masts of several ships on the Potomac River and along the wharf a few blocks ahead.

Pausing at the next street, he waited while a regiment of soldiers passed through the intersection. They were all wearing fresh, blue uniforms and carrying new Springfield rifled muskets. Despite the new uniforms, the soldiers' boots and legs were covered in mud from the sloppy, wet city streets. Near the rear of the column, a captain wearing shiny brass had just finished barking out commands to his greenhorn troops as he marched past James standing at the corner. Upon noticing James's salute and well-worn uniform, the captain returned the gesture and gave a respectful nod before disappearing beyond the crowd.

After crossing the muddy street, James weaved his way through the throngs of people on the sidewalk. Alexandria had turned into a busy hub for the Union Army at the onset of the war. In addition to being a seaport on the Potomac River and an important railway junction, Alexandria was a hospital and supply depot for the massive Union Army. Besides the military presence, the city also had a large population of civilians, including both freed blacks and slaves. The city's population had doubled in the first year of the war and remained busy both day and night.

Ahead in the morning sun, James could see dozens of boats with their giant sails and the sparkling water of the wide Potomac River. He saw the railroad tracks running down the middle of the next street and parallel to the water. Approaching the tracks, he searched in both directions before seeing a locomotive waiting at a station several blocks to the south. As he followed the tracks and approached the boardwalk, he could see the words *Alexandria and Washington Railroad* on the locomotive's tender. The black, eight-wheeled American 4-4-0 locomotive was emitting a low hiss as a cloud of smoke rose from its large stack.

Several provost guards wearing blue sack coats and holding rifles on their shoulders patrolled the boardwalk along the tracks. James knew from conversations inside the hospital that the Federal forces in the city had been on high alert. He had heard firsthand of the Confederate sympathies among the Alexandria residents. Rumors of spying, sabotage, and collaboration with Rebel forces ran rampant among the civilians in and around the city.

James nodded courteously as he wove his way between the vigilant guards and down the planks along the tracks. Walking past the locomotive and toward the rear of the train, James showed his papers to the corporal standing guard at the third passenger car's steps.

"What's your destination and purpose for travel, Private?" the guard asked.

"The War Department building...in the city, sir. Here is a pass from Lieutenant Whitlow, sir." With a stiff nod, the corporal stepped back and allowed James to board. After climbing the steps, James turned to the right and started down the aisle of the nearly empty train car.

Approaching the second row, he casually tipped his hat as he passed an officer seated with a lady wearing a yellow dress and matching hat. A few rows farther back, a corporal missing his right leg with his pants knotted just above the knee was sitting with his crutch leaning against the seat in front of him. James smiled sympathetically as he passed and, after walking back a few more rows, took a seat against the window on the train's right side. After placing his hat and knapsack next to him on the padded bench seat, he took a deep breath and tried to relax.

As he looked out the window at a passing ship on the river, he noticed the sun shining brightly through the morning clouds and into his window. He felt tired and blinked several times, almost nodding off. Leaning his head against the window, he fought off sleep and thought of his brothers...and of the other men in the regiment out there in camp. He, too, would be there soon, he knew. Finally, despite his best efforts, he fell asleep.

Twenty-three-year-old James Whitlow had served almost two years in the army since volunteering with his younger brother

Solomon in 1861. The two brothers had fought side by side with the Army of the Potomac in every battle until James was wounded in April, just prior to the Battle of Chancellorsville. They were part of the Nineteenth Indiana, a volunteer infantry regiment and one of five regiments of the famed western Iron Brigade.

James remembered fondly that July morning two years ago when he and Solomon walked into town to volunteer to fight. Although the Whitlow family had spent many years in Kentucky, they moved in 1853 to Preble County, Ohio, just across the state line from nearby Richmond, Indiana. It was in Richmond that the boys of Company B volunteered in July of 1861 before taking a train to Indianapolis and being organized into the Nineteenth Indiana Volunteers.

Their older brother John, whom James was going to visit now, had also volunteered to fight for the Union. John, however, had enlisted with the Third Indiana Cavalry regiment, most of which had been fighting out west in Kentucky, Tennessee, and Mississippi. John, an outstanding horseman having grown up on a horse farm, had proven to be an excellent soldier and eventually earned an officer's field commission to lieutenant. To James, the two long years since he had seen his older brother seemed like an eternity.

"Good mornin', Private."

The voice next to him startled James awake, and he quickly looked over.

"Sorry…I must've fallen asleep," James replied as he rubbed his eyes. "Good morning, sir."

Although the train was still at the station, he didn't know for how long he had nodded off. Still groggy, he shook his head a few times and stretched out his neck to escape the headache he felt coming on. As he looked around, he saw the train car was now almost completely full. A shout from the train's conductor was followed by the sounds of the locomotive roaring to life. With a giant billowing of steam and smoke and the clamor of metal couplings and wheels, the train made a sudden lurch forward before slowly accelerating northward.

The man seated on the bench beside him was in his mid-fifties, James assumed, and dressed in civilian clothes with a tan, felt dress hat. He had with him two editions of the *Alexandria Gazette*. The top newspaper, which the man was currently reading, was dated June 17, 1863.

"Here. Help yourself," the man said, handing James the other newspaper after noticing James was awake and had been looking in his direction.

James looked at the top and saw it was dated June 16th, two days ago.

"The Rebs have captured Winchester," the man said, pointing. "It says so right there."

James looked down at the paper and read the headlines. *"Rebels capture Winchester! General Milroy surrenders 8,000 troops!"* Farther down the page, James saw another article with the title reading, *"Invasion! Confederates cross Potomac River, invade Maryland, threaten Pennsylvania."*

"This damned war," the man said, pointing at the newspaper. "Did you see this?"

"Yes, sir. I heard about Winchester yesterday… from one of the nurses at the hospital."

"If Fighting Joe doesn't stop General Lee before he invades Pennsylvania, Ole Abe will fire him too."

James didn't respond to the civilian's comment while he thought of a way to change the subject. He had learned early on in the war that discussing military politics with others often turned into heated arguments.

"Where you headed, sir?" James asked the man.

"Into the city…to talk to Representative Duncan. The blockade's keeping my shipments down. This war has cost us all a great deal. How 'bout you, soldier?"

"I'm meeting my brother at the War Department."

"Oh, I see. He in the Army too?"

"Yeah, he's in the cavalry. On detached duty here in Washington now. Says he works at the telegraph office. I haven't seen him for almost two years."

"How 'bout yourself?" the man asked, nodding at James.

"Infantry...Nineteenth Indiana."

"Ahhh, yes. The *Black Hat Brigade*." He'd said it slowly... with reverence. "I see your hat now."

"Yes, sir."

"God bless you, son," the man replied out of admiration. "You took on Stonewall Jackson all by yourselves at Manassas last year."

"That sure was horrible for us, sir. We turned off the turnpike thinking we was just gonna scare off some cavalry. But Jackson's entire division was up on that ridge...hidden down in a railroad cut."

"That worthless General Pope almost lost the war there," the man said, shaking his head in disgust.

James just stared out the window for a few minutes as the train loudly rattled on. It followed a slight bend in the tracks to the left as it left the city, offering a beautiful view of the river out the window. Ahead in the distance, James could see some of the buildings of Washington.

"You pushed back General Longstreet at South Mountain, though," the man said, bringing James's mind back into the train car.

"Yeah...guess we did," James quickly replied and then turned his attention forward again. Trying to avoid discussing the horrible battle which occurred three days later at Sharpsburg, Maryland, James stared straight ahead and didn't say anything else. Two soldiers a few rows ahead were arguing over a newspaper they had spread out in front of them. Over the noise of the train, James could hear one of the soldiers angrily talking about General Hooker, while the other one suddenly yelled something about President Lincoln and General Halleck.

The man beside James was also listening to the soldiers' conversation and waited for a pause in their arguing before continuing. "I hope General Hooker can fight Lee out of Maryland like Li'l Mac did last year."

James wasn't sure how to answer. It was at Antietam last year that the Union Army was able to fight General Lee to a tactical draw and eventually force the Confederates to retreat from Maryland and back into Virginia. And now General Lee was back up in Maryland. James closed his eyes and dropped his head slightly as he thought of all his fellow soldiers killed and wounded during those few weeks in August and September of 1862.

"Our regiment lost almost half of our men in Maryland last September," James finally said. "I hope we don't fight them *there* again."

The man's face wrinkled into a painful grimace. "*Antietam…* the pictures of those poor boys," he said as he shook his head back and forth. "Lying along that road and in that field."

"Yes, sir. It was dreadful. I'll never forget the fighting in that cornfield and across that pike." Even just talking about that foggy, horrible morning last September sent a chill down his spine.

"Hmmm…the *Iron* Brigade, they call you, right?"

"That's right. I'm not sure if it's a blessing or a curse…but that's what they call us." Although James was very proud of his regiment and the brigade, he felt awkward discussing the name with the stranger. "General Hooker said, 'We fight like we're made of iron'…or something like that."

"I bet you gonna be doing some more fighting from the looks of this." The man was pointing at the newspaper. James just nodded and thought of his younger brother Solomon, still out in the field, somewhere west of here in Virginia.

"Yes, sir. I'll be rejoining the regiment tomorrow." The papers in James's pocket stated that he was to report to the provost marshal at the First Corps headquarters by June 20th and that the First Corps would be somewhere near Centreville, Virginia.

The man was focusing on the paper again, shaking his head in disgust as he read. "General Ewell is in Martinsburg and has forced General Tyler across the Potomac," the man said, angrily pointing at the paper. James didn't respond as the man went back to reading in silence.

"Oh my," the man said, leaving his mouth open to say more. But the words failed him. James watched as the man cleared his throat and then finally muttered out the words. "There's…there's Rebel cavalry in Pennsylvania."

"Oh," James said. He started to say more but went silent, thinking about what the man had said. And what it would mean for him and for his brothers.

The man read on before speaking again. "It says right here that one of Lee's cavalry brigades…Jenkins…is all the way up in Chambersburg. They're saying General Lee might even threaten Harrisburg…the state capital!"

James sat in silence and let the words sink in. The news about the Confederate invasion into Maryland and Pennsylvania caused James to want to see John even more. James knew that he'd know about all those military matters.

James hadn't seen John since August of 1861. John, still dressed in civilian clothes, still hadn't enlisted by then. That was when the train carrying the newly-formed Nineteenth Indiana regiment, including James and his youngest brother Solomon, was on its way from Indianapolis to Washington. Along the route, the regiment had been off-loaded at Bellefontaine, Ohio, to switch trains and allow the patriotic local citizens to give the new soldiers a quick meal and an appreciative send-off. The stop was long enough for James and Solomon to say their good-byes to the rest of the Whitlow family who had all made the long wagon ride for the celebration at the rail station.

That was the last time James had seen the entire family together. Despite being two long years ago, James still clearly remembered standing on the station's wooden platform next to the idling train. Since then, James and Solomon had talked about those precious moments several times. Before the next leg of that journey eastward in the late summer of 1861, there were tearful hugs and goodbyes with Ma, Pa, John, and their three younger sisters.

John, the oldest of the three brothers, was also the best horseman and hunter in the family. They had all known John would make a great soldier, but John had always felt he needed to stay home to help with the family farm. But that feeling only lasted a few months after his two brothers had gone east to fight. At the end of that summer's growing season, John finally succumbed to the pressures of not fighting and joined the Third Indiana Cavalry.

James heard loud voices again and realized he'd been day-dreaming. Shaking his head awake, he quickly sat up. The soldiers' argument a few rows ahead had heated up again.

"I ain't fightin' to free no slaves," one of the soldiers said. James heard the word *emancipation*, then something about England and France, but he couldn't make out the details. The lady in yellow in the second row and seated with the officer had turned around and given the soldiers an annoyed look. The soldiers stopped for only a moment, however. The topic was too heavy to be hindered by a pretty lady and her fancy-clad officer boyfriend whose ears had probably never felt whistling lead.

"Where were you wounded?" the man asked, bringing James's attention away from the quarreling soldiers.

"In the foot. A minie ball went through my shoe as we were crossing the Rappahannock…just before Chancellorsville."

"It seems okay now." It was more of a question than a statement. The man had glanced down at James's shoes, which were new from the quartermaster only a few days ago.

"Yeah. I hope so," James said.

The conversation was interrupted by the rumbling of the car's wheels as the train crossed a wooden bridge over a small harbor. Tied along a pier below the bridge were several boats being off-loaded with large bails of straw and wooden crates. Horse teams and their wagons waited nearby as hundreds of workers sweated in the morning sun while they moved cargo from the boats. After crossing the bridge, the noisy train settled back into its normal cadence and continued northward.

The train followed a gradual turn to the right and then slowed as it passed through a series of heavily guarded redoubts. It then came to a stop along a long row of wooden planks where a stern-faced provost guard boarded the car. James watched as the guard passed down the aisle, carefully looking at each passenger before exiting from the rear door. The train idled for a few minutes just inside the line of redoubts while several soldiers watched from the boardwalk. After several shouts from the guards, the locomotive roared to life again, lurching the train forward toward the long bridge just ahead.

James looked out the window in awe at the railroad bridge as the train began the trek across the Potomac River. As they headed toward the city, he could see even more piers, all bustling with dock workers loading and unloading cargo from dozens of boats.

He'd never seen such a busy place. Through the window on the other side of the train, he saw the unfinished Washington Monument and, beyond that, the President's Executive Mansion. Ahead he could see the red brick Smithsonian Castle, surrounded by a massive tent city and thousands of its inhabitants milling about. The train crossed over dry land now and angled across several streets and through the long rows of tents and campfires.

On the right, the massive Capitol Building and its unfinished dome towered over the city. The train jerked through a series of turnouts in the track as it slowed and came to a stop at the station just north of the Capitol Building.

As the passengers got up to leave, James turned to his seatmate and extended his hand. The civilian man smiled and gave James a firm and friendly handshake. He seemed to be studying James as he looked at him. His smile then turned into a look of deep, sympathetic concern. James felt as if the man was noticing his scars and haggard look for the first time. The man's eyes showed a glint of moisture before he spoke. "May God bless you, soldier, and thank you for fighting for the cause."

"The *cause?*" An awkward pause hung in the air before James continued. "I'm not sure exactly what the *cause* is nowadays or if the bloodshed and suffering I've seen in this war…is worth any cause."

The man nodded in agreement. "This awful sea of blood… it must recede…or God help us all. You boys…the misery…I'm so sorry." The man's voice trailed off as they looked at each other.

"Thank you, sir," James replied. "Good luck with the congressman, sir."

"Thank you, soldier."

The friendly stranger then slowly turned, grabbed his small case from the overhead rack, and walked up the aisle and out the forward exit. James was the last one off the car and onto the station's busy boardwalk. As he stopped and looked around to get his directions straight, he pulled the note from his coat pocket to read the address.

"James! James!"

The voice echoed above the sounds of the crowded station. As he looked up, he saw his older brother John approaching with outstretched arms.

"John!" James shouted.

James couldn't believe how much John had changed. He looked at least ten years older now and was wearing a clean but well-worn, faded cavalry uniform with gold shoulder boards indicating the rank of lieutenant. He had a broad smile as he approached and reached out to shake James's hand.

After a quick handshake, the two brothers embraced in a long-awaited and jubilant hug.

-4-

Near Herndon Station, Virginia
First Corps Army Camp
June 18, 1863, 8:00 a.m.

The seemingly endless rows of tents followed the slope up the ridge and then disappeared on the other side. Assembled in the dark by exhausted and footsore men, the camp's tent lines were anything but perfect. Working his way between tents and small clusters of bloodshot-eyed soldiers hovering over struggling campfires, Solomon rounded a corner and finally saw Henry just ahead. Henry was talking with a corporal at a supply wagon and was just turning to leave as Solomon approached.

"What ya got there, Henry?"

"Hey, Sol. Here…take a pair of new socks," Henry said, reaching out and handing Solomon a pair. "The quartermaster gave me some extras."

"Dang, Henry. That's nice of ya."

Henry didn't answer but smiled proudly.

"My feet are killin' me, Henry. These socks are gonna help a lot. Thanks. What else ya got?" Solomon asked, pointing at the tied bundle tucked under Henry's other arm.

Henry hesitated slightly, modestly, then said, "I got some for Billy too…and Hawk."

Solomon laughed. "For Hawk? That's really nice after all *his* poppycockin' this morning."

"Nah, Hawk's alright."

"No, he ain't, Henry," Solomon said with another laugh.

"Lord, forgive me for lyin'. I guess you're right. Just figured I owe him for the eggs 'n' all."

"Gotta admit, though, Henry...there's times I wouldn't want anyone else right there next to me other than Hawk."

"Suppose so," Henry said, then hesitated before continuing. "Some people, like Hawk...they're just made for the army...and the war, ain't they?"

"Hawk was, for sure," Solomon quickly replied. "But that ain't me. I just wish this war was over."

Henry was silent, and when Solomon glanced over at him, the solemn look on Henry's face showed that he felt the same way. But even more so. Solomon had known Henry not only for the past two brutal years in the same squad together, but for several years before the war too.

Henry Schultz's family lived only a few miles from the Whitlows, and as teenagers, Solomon and Henry had become good friends. The Schultzes were Quakers, and it was Henry who had talked Solomon into attending the Quaker college on the west side of Richmond, Indiana, several years ago. Earlham College had been established in 1847, only a few years prior to Henry and Solomon enrolling in the fall of 1859. Although Solomon had been slow to convert to all the ideas of the Quaker school, he eventually embraced both the religion and their way of life.

The start of the war in 1861 was a difficult time for the two friends. Solomon had always disagreed with the Quakers' passive attitude to both the war and politics. The entire Whitlow family, ever since moving north from the politically torn state of Kentucky, were devout patriots and strong believers in the government's efforts to preserve the Union—even before the first shots were fired on Fort Sumter on April 12th.

Henry, on the other hand, was raised as a Quaker and didn't believe in war of any kind. The Quakers' strong opposition to slavery and the patriotic fever sweeping the northern states, however, caused Henry's views of war to soften. Finally, in July of 1861, with persuasion from the Whitlow brothers and others, Henry decided to volunteer with the local infantry unit, Company B of the Nineteenth Indiana regiment.

Throughout the first two years of the war, Henry, James, and Solomon were all three in the same squad within Company B of the Nineteenth. Ever since the end of April, when James went absent convalescing his foot wound, Henry and Solomon had become even closer.

Now walking past one of the brigade's Wisconsin regiments, Solomon and Henry were almost back to their own camp. One of the soldiers they passed, a man from the Sixth Wisconsin, looked up from his coffee and nodded. He was bearing a scar similar to the one his brother James wore ever since the Second Battle of Bull Run. It made him think of James, and turning toward Henry, Solomon asked, "Henry, you happen to see any mail wagons back there?"

Henry had read his mind. "No, I was hoping to hear from James too."

Just as Solomon opened his mouth to respond, a bugle up ahead sounded, and an unseen officer called men to attention. It seemed odd, Solomon thought...men drilling after yesterday's grueling march. Thinking of his sore feet and hoping the rain would hold off today, Solomon looked up to the partly overcast sky.

It was muggy and hot already but didn't look like rain. And hopefully, they wouldn't be marching today anyway. As they rounded a bend in the row of tents, Solomon realized he'd hoped wrong. Just ahead at their camp, officers had gathered, and men were assembling. Billy, Hawk, and the rest of Company B were collapsing tents, rolling up blankets, and packing knapsacks.

"What's happening, Hawk?" Solomon asked as he approached.

"We're moving soon," Hawk said, nodding at the cluster of officers.

"Billy, you'll need these," Henry said, tossing him his pair of new socks. Billy, surprised, caught them and smiled. Henry then turned toward Hawk and tossed him a pair too. "Here, Hawk, you probably need 'em even worse than the rest of us."

"Thanks, Henry," Hawk said.

"I figured your socks couldn't have dried last night…you know, with all the…*wanderin' about* you did in the dark 'n' all."

Hawk wanted to hide his grin but couldn't.

Solomon, who'd sat down on the ground to change his socks, had already slipped off his brogans. While he put on the new socks, he watched his squadmates and laughed. He enjoyed seeing Hawk speechless; they all did. But not nearly as much as seeing Henry beaming after having helped somebody else. Solomon learned several years ago that Henry was like that… nothing made Henry smile inside like doing someone else a favor.

Hawk was still grinning and watching Henry too, measuring, judging. Hawk, smiling wide, finally said, "You're a damned fine lad, Henry…damned fine."

All four of them chuckled, then returned their attention to changing shoes and socks and packing knapsacks. They looked up quickly again, however, when a thundering of hooves approached from the north. Several teams of horses pulling wagons raced down the road and turned across the fields to the east. They'd seen riders and wagon teams come and go in that direction all morning, but these latest teamsters worked the reins more vigorously than the others.

"Where they comin' from?" Solomon asked no one in particular.

"I don't know," Henry said, his voice hinting a nervous edge. "But something's going on in that direction."

"That's the train station up that way, ain't it?" Solomon asked.

"I think so," Billy said. "But the tracks are all ripped up now. Reb cavalry did it. Trains used to run past there from Washington…then out to Leesburg. West of there is Winchester, Virginia. That's where the big fight was a few days ago. And the Rebs won it. At least that's what they said anyway."

"How you always know stuff like that, Billy?" Hawk asked.

"Grear told me. Some Company A boys had a newspaper, and they told him this morning." Billy paused and pointed to the west before continuing. "And see right there?"

Solomon looked toward the mountains where Billy was pointing and noticed Hawk and Henry looking that direction too.

"Just past them mountains," Billy said, still pointing, "that's where General Lee's army is. And they're moving *north*."

Solomon saw that Billy's finger had moved north too… first toward Maryland and now Pennsylvania. None of them spoke.

Finally, Hawk scoffed and spat out another wad of mess into the ashes. He cackled at the sizzling sound it made, then turned toward Billy. "What else they say?"

"Said that there's Reb cavalry all over the valley around these parts…right here close…raidin' parties. *Mosby's Raiders*, they call 'em. The paper said *our* cavalry is spread out over them mountains too…looking for the Reb Army…and following 'em."

"*Our cavalry?*" Hawk asked mockingly.

"Our cavalry's different now," Solomon quickly shot back. He was thinking of his brother John and had stood up, maybe a little too confrontationally, he realized. "You saw it in the papers last week, Hawk. Jeb Stuart got himself surprised at Brandy Station. Our cavalry's as good as the Rebs now…ridin' right with 'em…and fightin' saber to saber with 'em too."

Hawk laughed and said, "Like they say…who ever saw a dead cavalryman?"

Solomon glared at Hawk and said, "They take their share of lead too, Hawk. They're just like us. John has lost a lot of good friends out in Kentucky and Tennessee."

"Alright, Sol," Hawk said, smiling and thinking about the many talks between Solomon and James bragging about their oldest brother in the cavalry. Hawk put his hands up in a mock surrender and said, "I take it back. I heard John's a helluva cavalryman."

"*Attention, Company!*"

The voice boomed, and all four of the squadmates looked up and saw Lieutenant Schlagle, the ranking officer of Company B.

"Attention, Company!" the twenty-six-year-old lieutenant shouted again, his sword clanging in its scabbard as he approached. "Form up!"

"You heard him, men!" Sergeant Boller shouted, appearing from the other side of the tents. "We're moving out!"

The Company B men around the campfires stood up and quickly began retrieving their coats, rifles, and ammunition boxes. Officers in Company E near the next row of tents were also now shouting out orders and assembling their men.

"Where are we going?" Henry nervously asked Solomon as they pulled their knapsacks over their shoulders.

"I dunno," Solomon said. "But I hope it ain't far. My feet are still killin' me."

"Sergeant! Have the men assemble right over there at the edge of camp."

"Yes sir, Lieutenant," Sergeant Boller replied.

Lieutenant Schlagle turned away and walked toward the men in Company E. "Looks like it's just us and Company E," Solomon whispered to Henry.

"What's this all about, Sarge?" Hawk asked while buttoning his jacket.

"Just be ready to move, Hawkins."

"We walked fifteen miles yesterday and twenty the day before. If these fools keep marchin' us like this, we won't be able to fight nobody."

"Guess maybe you shoulda stayed in camp last night, Hawkins," the sergeant shot back, but just loud enough for only Hawk to hear.

Hawk, surprised at the sergeant's comment about last night's foraging, opened his mouth to respond but decided not to. Hawk glanced around the other men and wondered how Boller knew he'd slipped out of camp.

Nearly all of Company E had joined them now, and the sixty men of the two companies began assembling in the field. Only Company B and E had been ordered to move, and Hawk thought it strange that the rest of the regiment was remaining in camp.

"Sarge, where we going?" Hawk asked.

"Wherever you're told, Private," Sergeant Boller responded.

Hawk's mind raced, and he wanted to test Boller. "Maybe we're going to get some food, Sarge?"

But Sergeant Boller, avoiding a conversation with Hawk, had already turned and left. The two of them and their conflicting personalities never had gotten along well, and lately, Boller had become combative with the entire squad. Hawk, however, hardly ever backed down from the sergeant, and now was no exception. Seeing Boller walk away caused Hawk to smile, satisfied the sergeant wouldn't dare cause trouble over Hawk's latest foraging.

"Attention, Battalion!" shouted Lieutenant Schlagle, returning from the nearby gathering of officers. "Fall in!"

The sixty soldiers of Company B and Company E quickly formed into two long rows. Waiting and contemplating where they would be going, the men paid close attention as the Nineteenth's colonel strode up and briefly spoke with their lieutenant before stepping to their front.

"At ease!" Colonel Williams shouted. "Men, we have asked a lot from you these past few days." Williams paused and looked into the eyes of his men before continuing.

"God, not a speech," Hawk murmured. Solomon silently agreed. Speeches were the worst.

"I am afraid," the thirty-two-year-old colonel from Selma, Indiana, continued, "that duty will demand even more in the coming weeks. General Lee is on the move, men. No one here or in Washington is sure of his objective. He may take his army north into Pennsylvania. Or they may turn toward Baltimore… or even Washington. There *will* be another battle, gentlemen. But make no mistake…we will be ready. We may be defending our own land this time…maybe even our capital. The fate of the Old Flag may depend on us, men. The entire Union…*our country*!" He paused, realizing he was preaching to the men, hardly necessary to the seasoned veterans at this point in the war.

"Our army has marched nearly eighty miles in the past week," Colonel Williams continued. "General Lee has taken his army into Maryland and even some of his army into Pennsylvania beyond those mountains. We must stay between them and Washington. But the army must rest too, and hopefully, we will do that here."

The veterans grasped the subtle hint that the marching might finally ease up, and a collective sigh of relief, barely audible, murmured among the ranks. Colonel Williams paused again. He smiled briefly, appreciatively…these men deserved at least that. He knew respect flowed both ways.

Williams looked into their eyes again and said, "Today's mission, however, is a short one. We've been ordered to picket just beyond a railroad depot to the north and assist with the supply wagons there. It's not far, men…only a mile away, but we cannot let our guard down, even here. We are not far from the enemy. Enemy cavalry…raiders…have been operating in these valleys, deep inside our lines. They have targeted bridges, telegraph lines, train tracks, and railway depots, including this one…*twice*. They've ripped up the tracks there, but the Rebs are still around, men."

Solomon shot a glance toward the right and noticed Henry's hand was shaking. Billy stood dutifully, ramrod straight. Solomon noticed Hawk scanning the horizon ahead… and smiling.

Mosby's Raiders…Solomon remembered Hawk talking about them a few days ago. The *Gray Ghost*, he'd called them. *"You don't believe in ghosts, do ya, Henry?"* Hawk had asked. Apparently, Henry did.

"You'll have to keep your eyes on the horizon, men. Your relief will arrive at the station soon. We plan to remain in camp for at least a day when you return." Before turning and walking away, Colonel Williams looked to Lieutenant Schlagle and nodded, signaling that the men were now under Schlagle's command again. Lieutenant Schlagle then stepped forward and looked up and down the lines of soldiers, still in two rows facing forward with their rifles at their sides.

"Attention, Battalion!"

The men shifted quickly and rigidly to attention.

"Shoulder arms!"

Sixty rifles were raised simultaneously and came to rest on the men's right shoulders.

"Left face!"

Almost automatically, the two companies of experienced soldiers abruptly pivoted to the left and paused.

"Forwaarrrd! …Maaarrch!"

As if by instinct, as they had done for two long years, the hardened veterans stepped off in perfect unison.

-5-

Washington City
Baltimore and Ohio Railroad Station
June 18, 1863, 12:00 Noon

John let go of his younger brother and, with a giant grin, took a step back. Now looking at James for the first time in nearly two years, John felt a sense of joy fall over him like he had never felt. James looked much older now, a seasoned veteran. The endless marches, long campaigns in harsh weather, and bloody battles had hardened James into a rugged-looking soldier. The scar spanning from the bottom of his chin all the way up to his right eyebrow gave James a tougher appearance than the twenty-one-year-old farm boy John had remembered in 1861.

"You look great, James!" John exclaimed. He said it seriously. But after a few seconds and thinking of the physical effects the war had had on them, they both laughed.

"Ya like my little scrape?" James asked in jest, pointing at the scar on his face. "Bull Run."

"The ladies are gonna love it, James."

"Ya look real good too, John," James said, shaking his head in amazement at his brother, now proudly wearing the yellow-trimmed blue uniform of a cavalry lieutenant. "Dang!... an officer in Washington City! Ya doin' somethin' right, big brother."

John quickly shook off the compliment and smiled. "It's good to see you, James," he said, reaching out and hugging his brother again.

"You too."

"You hungry?" John asked.

Grinning, James said, "I'm in the army, John…I'm always hungry."

"We can go over to the boarding house where I'm staying and get something to eat."

James held his hand out, pushing away the offer. "Oh, no. Thanks, John, but I'm okay now. Got some bread with me. I've been eating better in Alexandria than I have since I left home two years ago. Nurses take good care of us there. It's not like them field hospitals."

John noticed James had turned serious.

"And I've been in some of those," James added, his face descending into a frown.

"You sure you don't wanna eat now?" John asked, quickly changing the subject.

"Yeah, I'm fine."

"Okay, let me show you what I do here in the city…down at the War Department."

"Sure, I'd like that."

"But lemme carry that for ya," John said, reaching down and grabbing James's knapsack before turning and pointing toward the street.

John led them away from the throngs of people at the train station, and as they approached the street, he stopped and turned toward James. John's brow had wrinkled into a concerned frown. "You okay to walk very far?" he asked.

John's inadvertent glance down toward James's foot told James why he was asking.

"My foot? Yeah, John. It's okay now…healed up a couple weeks ago. The nurses, though…they wouldn't lemme leave until they were sure."

John stood and watched James carefully. "Ya sure you're okay? I got a letter couple weeks back…from Ma. She said yur foot was worse than we thought."

"Ahh…nah," James said. "It's nothin' now. Damned splinter from a pontoon boat is all." The look on John's face showed James he still didn't know whether to believe him.

"Really, I'm good, John."

"It's just that…well, with the hospitals the way they are around here 'n' all, we were all really worried 'bout you."

James smiled but didn't respond.

"Let's go then?"

James laughed and, extending his arm forward up the muddy street as if to show his brother the way, said, "Let's go."

"Okay, it's this way, about a mile," John said, finally satisfied his brother's foot wound was really healed. "Gonna be muddy with all the rain last night." John felt awkward as soon as he'd said it…he knew James had walked in lots of mud before.

"You heard from Sol?" James asked as they started walking down the street to the west.

John smiled. "Yeah, about a week ago or so… I got a letter. He was down 'round Fredericksburg then. I always keep a pretty good eye on the Nineteenth…from the telegraph office. With you and Sol in the regiment 'n' all, I been watchin' over you since I got to Washington."

"Where are they now?" James quickly asked.

"Well, the whole army's been movin' north…followin' Lee. The First Corps was in Centreville yesterday…just north of Manassas."

Manassas… James shuddered as soon as John had said the word. Last August, the Nineteenth Indiana suffered 259 casualties there in just one day. James was one of them. That was where James received the horrible wound to his head, the scar still disfiguring the right side of his face.

"But they were to move north yesterday, up near the Potomac," John went on. "I haven't seen anything today. The telegraph line is down again. Rebel raiders have been raising hell on our logistics, James. They've been cutting down telegraph lines, burning bridges, and breaking dams. They've even stopped some of the trains, taken over rail stations…and the C&O Canal is unpassable again."

John stopped talking and slowed down as they approached a marching column of soldiers crossing the street just ahead.

"Vermont men," John said, waiting for the regiment to pass. James looked around and saw the streets were busy with both civilians and soldiers. Looking ahead and to the left, James saw the unfinished monument to George Washington. Never having been in a city this large before, he thought about how different the world was here than the farming life back home… and the army life he'd been living the past two years.

"So, what happened?" John asked, interrupting James's thoughts and changing the subject.

"Huh?"

"You've been in the hospital…in Alexandria. What happened exactly?"

"Little freak accident in a skirmish…that's all." James still couldn't believe how long the recovery had taken from the foot wound at Fitzhugh's Crossing. It was almost embarrassing to him, and he felt he'd been away from the regiment for way too long. Making it seem even worse was that he was one of only a few of the regiment's men wounded during that river crossing.

"Not what I read," John said. "Sounds like the whole Reb army was across the Rappahannock shooting at you."

"The Sixth Wisconsin and the Michigan boys took most of it. The Nineteenth was the third regiment to get in the boats to cross. One of our company sergeants, Sergeant Petty, got shot right before we started across the river. But yeah, the lead was flyin' pretty bad until we got all the way to the other bank."

He paused as they watched another group of soldiers crossing the street just in front of them.

"Sorry, busy place, James. Go on."

"This little wound in my foot," James said, pointing down, "it seemed like nothing at first compared to the head wound I got at Manassas last year. That almost did me in there. It's probably a good thing I don't remember much of it. The Rebs left me for dead. Next thing I know, I'm in a Union hospital…and then marchin' and fightin' again a few days later up in Maryland."

"Antietam?"

"Yeah. And the battle at South Mountain too, couple days before Antietam…at a place called Turner's Gap."

"I read that's where you got your name *Iron Brigade*," John said with a smile, obviously proud of his two younger brothers. "General McClellan himself named your brigade that, right?"

"Yeah, I think so. McClellan told General Hooker that we fight like we're made of iron. Or that's what I heard anyway."

"You know they write about your brigade in the papers here? They call you the Black Hat Brigade, the Western Boys, Iron Brigade of the West…all kinds of things."

James chuckled. "Well, it's not worth it, John. What we been through…no name in the world is worth that. And I don't see what dyin' and being made of iron got much to do with each other." James paused, then said, "All them dead and maimed boys…they're just *boys*, John."

James and John were both quiet for a moment as they turned the corner. The street was even busier here. *Pennsylvania*

Avenue, the sign said. James marveled at the throngs of people on both sides of the street. Dozens of horses and carriages were tied to hitching posts outside buildings.

John, noticing James awed by the grandeur of the large buildings, said, "Not much farther."

"Wow, this is quite a bit different than back home."

John laughed and said, "Yes, it is. Little busier than the horse farm, huh? The War Department building is just ahead."

James looked to the left through a crowd of people and, astonished at what he saw, said, "That...*that* building..."

"That's the President's mansion...the White House."

James stopped and stared. Even though he'd seen the President's mansion from the train, standing in front of it now suddenly made him think of President Lincoln and the enormous burden that he must feel...the weight of the country placed on one individual man...*one man*. James shook his head, then said, "It makes me feel so...*small* and...*unimportant*."

"Oh no, James. You and me and Solomon...we're the ones wearing the uniforms and fighting." John's brow had wrinkled as if he wanted to say more, but instead, he turned away.

James wanted to ask what he had meant, what else he wanted to say. But John had already taken a step toward the War Department building...and away from whatever troubled him about the President's mansion.

"Come on, James," John said, finally coercing his younger brother away from his gaze at Abe Lincoln's home.

James quickly caught up to John and was even more impressed by the War Department's giant, white block building. "Wow," he mumbled barely loud enough for his older brother to hear.

"Amazing, isn't it?" John asked. Noticing James was speechless and still staring in awe at his surroundings, John continued, "Just wait 'til we get inside. It's even more impressive. But remember, I'm only a lowly lieutenant, and you're just a private, so keep your head low in there among the brass."

"I'm good at that," James replied, thinking of the several occasions he'd witnessed privates, corporals, and even sergeants being disciplined for insubordination or merely not showing enough deference to a senior officer. Despite disagreeing with the way officers did things sometimes, James knew it was always best to stay quiet and out of trouble. As the two brothers neared the War Department building, James saw a distinguished-looking civilian walking down the steps and out toward the front gate. The heavyset man was much shorter than the two sentries who saluted him at their gate. His long black-and-silver beard made the man look intelligent, important. James realized he'd been staring and looked at John who was also watching the man approaching his awaiting carriage.

"Who is that?" James asked as the man removed his tall hat and pulled his coat tight to maneuver into the small buggy.

"That's the Secretary of War himself."

"Stanton?"

"Yep, that's him," John said. "Glad he's leaving. He rules that place like it's his castle. Even the President has to go through Stanton to see reports from battlefields."

After watching the Secretary's carriage disappear among the crowd on Pennsylvania Avenue, John led James along the wrought iron fence and toward the sentries standing on each side of the gate.

"I'm Lieutenant Whitlow, and this is Private Whitlow," John said with a casual salute to the guards. The sentries waved them past with hardly more than a glance.

Awestruck while climbing the steps under the massive columns, James felt not only the enormous power of the building, but also of the nation itself. The building itself looked impregnable, and suddenly, the entire Union seemed invincible.

Here, it all seemed so different than all those fragile lives lost in the fields and forests of unnamed battlefields…and in the hospitals too. He'd seen so many men die, their young lives pass wispily, tragically. Lately, after the defeats at Manassas, Fredericksburg, and Chancellorsville, the war had felt unwinnable, but here, walking into this unconquerable stone fortress, he could sense an inevitable triumph and Union victory.

Inside, cigar smoke filled the musty, humid air. After passing a group of officers and men in the corridor, John led James across the hall and around the corner. Just a few feet ahead, James saw the top of a wide stairway.

"Come on, James. Down this way. This is it…the telegraph room." James followed John down the steps reluctantly at first, and then John said, "I'll show you where Solomon is now… with the Nineteenth."

"And where I'm going tomorrow," James eagerly added.

After descending the stairs, they entered a large, busy room containing dozens of tables and desks with telegraph machines. At several of the machines, soldiers busily took notes, deciphering coded messages onto paper. As the two Indiana brothers passed between rows of desks, James noticed a staff officer wearing lieutenant's bars impatiently waiting for one of the telegraph operators to finish scribbling a message.

"Here, sir," the nervous operator said, turning toward the lieutenant. "It's from General Hooker, sir." The staffer quickly ripped the note from the nervous private's hand and scurried up the stairs.

James caught himself staring and quickly looked away.

"Follow me, James…this way," John said, nodding in the other direction and then leading them toward the far corner of the room. They stopped at a cluttered wooden table against the wall. Stepping between two chairs and up to the edge of the table, James leaned over and examined the map tacked to the wall above it.

John had stepped up behind him and pointed at a blue mark toward the left half of the map. "Tennessee, that's where my regiment is now, James. Half the Third Indiana Cav is out here in the east with Hooker. But my company, Company I, has been fighting out west…in Tennessee, even down in Mississippi. Right now, they're here…'bout halfway between Murfreesboro and Chattanooga."

"What's this?" James asked, pointing farther down the map to a cluster of red marks.

"Ahhh…Vicksburg," John said. "The last major Rebel holdout along the Mississippi…" He stopped suddenly when he heard loud bootsteps approach from behind them.

As the two brothers turned, they saw a gray-haired officer smiling and striding toward them. "Lieutenant Whitlow," the older officer said with an outstretched hand. His greeting was loud but friendly. James tried to smile as he uncomfortably watched his brother shake the major's hand.

"Major, hello, sir," John said.

"Is this…Private Whitlow?" the major asked, his broad smile now focused on James. He had released John's hand and now reached and shook hands with James.

"Uhhh, yes sir," James said nervously. "I'm Private Whitlow…James, sir."

The major's grip was tight as he vigorously shook James's hand. His eyes studied James carefully, but his friendly smile showed compassion. "We've heard much about you, James. Your brother is very proud…as we all are…of your service."

"Thank you, sir."

"James," John said, "this is Major Stephens, Army of the Cumberland."

"Good to meet you, sir."

"The honor is all mine, James. I hear you're in the Nineteenth Indiana?"

"Uhhh, yes sir. Thank you, sir. Yes, the Nineteenth Indiana."

"The lieutenant—your brother here—has been quite worried about you these past several weeks. He's told me all about you. He's obviously quite proud…with all the fighting you've done out in the field."

"Yes, sir. I'll be rejoining the regiment tomorrow, sir."

"How you getting along?"

"I think fine, sir," James responded. "Just a little foot wound, is all. I'm ready to get back into the fight, sir."

"You're a good soldier, Private," the major said, his smile still showing sincerity. "As is your lieutenant brother."

"Thank you, sir."

"How'd you get the scar?" the major asked, pointing at the long red scar spanning the entire right side of James's face.

"At Bull Run, sir…last August. The Rebs left me for dead, sir."

The major's face wrinkled into a frown. "Ahh…Second Bull Run. That was a horrible ordeal." He quickly looked over his shoulder toward the center of the giant room before turning back to the brothers and speaking again. "I'm not so sure McClellan didn't leave General Pope out there by himself on purpose…just to teach the President and *Old Brains* Halleck a lesson."

The major scoffed quietly then chuckled. James and John, feeling awkward, waited for him to continue and, hopefully, to change the subject.

"Lincoln has sent our good General Pope out to Minnesota of all places…to fight all the Indians, of course," the major said with a subtle laugh before turning to the map on the wall behind them. Both brothers stayed silent for a few seconds before John finally spoke up.

"I was just showing James the Mississippi River, sir."

"Oh, yes…Vicksburg. The war seems to be going better out west. Grant fights, give him that."

"That's for sure," John said, daring to agree.

The major opened his mouth to speak again but, instead, paused.

James noticed the major wanted to say something more. *About Grant or Vicksburg? Some other general? Lincoln?* James wasn't sure, but the major's face had turned serious.

After a few seconds, the major's frown faded, and with a smile, he looked over toward James again.

"We're sure glad to have your lieutenant brother here with us, James," the major said. "His experience with the cavalry in the field has been most helpful to us rear echelon types here in the city. Your brother is a true soldier, Private."

"Uhhh, thank you, sir," John said, somewhat embarrassed by the compliment. "But pardon me, Major, you haven't exactly always been a rear echelon staffer yourself."

"Ahhh, that was all a lifetime ago, Lieutenant. Gentlemen, it's soldiers like you, both of you, that we call upon to save the Union in this great crisis."

"Thank you, sir," James said. "We're just doing our duty, sir," James continued modestly. "We're hoping to go home soon and back to the farm when this is all over, sir."

"Indeed, son. You're doing a great duty that will be remembered forever."

Watching his brother speak with the major, John felt proud. Ever since James had first mentioned enlisting in the army, John knew James would be a brave soldier. Growing up together in rural Kentucky and Ohio, the Whitlow brothers had always been close. John had always cherished their childhood adventures together, some proving more dangerous than any of them had understood at the time. That same bold attitude had apparently carried over to soldiering. James's wounds told him that.

The major was a brave soldier too, John knew. Although the major never boasted, John could tell from his stories of places like Shiloh, Corinth, and Stones River that he'd rather be out fighting again.

"Right now, there's almost a hundred thousand Rebs movin' north," the major continued, glancing toward the eastern part of the map around Virginia, Maryland, and Pennsylvania. "The next few weeks will be the greatest test for this army yet."

Thinking of the right words, John hesitated before finally responding. "I think we'll be ready, sir."

"Yes, Lieutenant. I hope so. The nation depends on it now."

The major paused and stared at the two brothers for several seconds, then picked up his hat from the table. "God bless you, Private Whitlow," he said to James, extending his hand.

"Thank you, sir."

Turning to John, the major said, "And you, too, Lieutenant. I'll leave you two to yourselves." Placing his hat on his head with a smile, he shook John's hand, then turned and walked away.

After watching the major leave, the two brothers didn't speak. Most of the room was empty by now, with only a few soldiers huddled over a table at the far side of the room. James could hear a few snippets of their conversation, a heated discussion about telegraph lines along the Chesapeake and Ohio Canal. Seeing that they were paying no attention to the two Whitlows, James turned back toward John and then looked at the map.

"A hundred thousand Rebels invading?" James asked, finally breaking the silence and feeling a lump in his throat.

"I'm afraid so, James. Lee's been moving his entire army north. There's reports all up and down the Shenandoah Valley… other side of these mountains here," John said, pointing.

James leaned in and studied the map closer. "What's this here?" he asked, pointing toward a cluttered area of the map labeled *Bull Run Mtns.*

"That's where General Pleasonton's cavalry has been skirmishing with Jeb Stuart. Every time we probe a gap in the
mountains, we run into Lee's cavalry." John paused and shook
his head as if deep in thought.

"How you know all this, John?"

"I've been exchanging dispatches out west for the past few
months. And the Reb cavalry's been making it tougher by cutting our telegraph lines. We spend a lot of time in front of these
maps, James." John paused again, and after seeing James nodding, he continued.

"General Hooker's movin' north too, following Lee, but
the army's all strung out from Fredericksburg to Leesburg."

"Where is the Nineteenth now?" James asked. "My orders
were to report to the First Corps headquarters near Centreville."

"Oh, they're not there anymore. They've marched north.
Last I saw yesterday morning, they were up here," John said,
pausing to point.

James stared, trying to understand.

"The First Corps is up along the railroad...what used to
be the railroad anyway, that runs out to Leesburg." John slid
his hand down the map to Alexandria then moved his finger
northward and westward to trace the railroad on the map. "It's
called the Alexandria, Loudoun, and Hampshire Railroad, but
the tracks are torn up beyond Vienna...here. And the railroad
bridge is out over this stream here, so the wagons probably will
head up to the Leesburg and Alexandria Pike."

James followed John's finger and asked, "So, I'll take the
train out of Alexandria north and west, not down towards
Centerville?"

"Yes. Take the train as far as you can, probably Vienna.
Then join up with a wagon train which should take you out
to the First Corps camp from there. You'll probably join 'em
here at Herndon...or Guilford...or maybe all the way out in

Leesburg…right here. Depends how hard General Hooker continues chasing northward after Lee…and where he places the First Corps in the marching order."

They both stared at the map for several moments before James finally spoke up again. Changing the subject, he said, "Kinda strange, John, but I miss being out there with the regiment. I don't miss the bad weather in the camps and the marching. And definitely not the battles…but the men. Most of 'em are good people, John. Farm boys, like us."

"I understand, James."

"The army…it becomes your life after a while…after all you go through with 'em. They're almost family. I don't miss *everybody*, for sure…but I miss most of 'em. Especially Sol and Henry…and even Hawk sometimes."

"Hawk?" John asked with a laugh. "Haven't heard about him for a while. I can't believe he's still alive."

"The Rebs won't kill Hawk," James said, laughing too. "It's us that wanna kill him…the guys that have to listen to him every day. I gotta say, though, he does keep some of our officers on their toes."

"Still always speaks his mind, huh?"

"Even more than ever."

"I won't forget when you and Sol brought him from Richmond to our house for the first time." They both laughed, forgetting about the war map staring down at them. "I thought Pa was gonna run his fork through him."

"I don't think Ma had heard some of those words before," James said.

"No, I'm not sure any of us had," John chuckled. "It's all kinda funny in a way now."

"He's a mean one in a fight, though, John." James's smile began to fade, and he said, "Never met anyone like him before. This war…and the army…Hawk was made for it. I never have really understood Hawk. He's never mentioned anyone from back home. Never gets mail in camp either."

"An orphan, wasn't he?" John asked.

"Yeah, but he doesn't talk about it. You'd think there would be *somebody* he'd talk about from before the war...either from Richmond or wherever he came from 'fore that."

"Some guys, James...the army's all they got."

Thinking again of the Nineteenth Indiana out in the field along that railroad John had pointed out, James glanced back toward the map.

"How's the rest of the guys from back home doing?" John asked, seeing James staring at the map again.

Without looking away from the map, James said, "Well, several are gone now. Sergeant McCown, Randy Fort, Joey Pike, and a bunch others all got killed at Manassas. Pete Baughan and the Addleman brothers at Antietam..."

"Both of them?" John interrupted.

"Yeah, Jacob ended up dyin' in a hospital, but I think Joe died right where he went down along the Hagerstown Pike."

"I didn't know," John said, shaking his head. He looked down. He'd been friends with Joe and Jake Addleman.

"So many of the wounded have gone home, John. Some have lost a leg or an arm. And a lot of 'em are still laid up in hospitals. You knew 'bout Jimmy Grunden? Shot off his own finger?"

"Read about it in a letter from Ma...she told me. Told me Billy Williams signed up to fight too, along with Grear."

"Yeah, Billy and Grear are doing fine. Grear and Hawk go at it some, though. For some reason, Hawk doesn't seem to like Grear... didn't like Billy at first either when he first joined our squad."

"Ma's letter said Billy's wife had a baby boy," John said.

"Yeah, I saw Billy readin' a letter from home one night in camp. That's gotta be hard." James paused and then changed the subject. "The Nineteenth…they're all men now, John. The last two years have made us all a lot tougher…at least those of us still left."

"How's Henry doing?" John asked, knowing that their brother Solomon and Henry were good friends.

James started to speak, but his mouth drooped into a frown. Realizing John was watching closely, he finally spoke. "Henry's struggling some, John. The war has been hard on him…all the killin' and the bloodshed. It's takin' its toll, ya know. Sergeant Boller doesn't help either."

"Boller…Sawyer Boller?" John asked. John had known Boller from back home and hadn't ever been shy about expressing his dislike for him. "The wretched mongrel that moved in from out east?"

James nodded and then frowned.

"He's a sergeant now?"

James's frown deepened, and he said, "I'm not sure Hawk's not gonna kill him though…or someone else will."

John laughed at first but then noticed James wasn't kidding. John turned serious again, and they both stared at the map in silence for several moments before James spoke up.

"It'll be good to get back out there…to do my part again."

John looked over to his brother and slapped him on the back. "You really are a good soldier, James."

James stood and stared straight ahead at the map. Finally, he cleared his throat and said, "Thanks, John. When I get back to camp, I'll tell Sol you said 'hello'."

"You'll be with 'em again tomorrow, James…tomorrow."

John then turned around and took a step away from the map.

"Come on…let's go."

-6-

Herndon Station, Virginia
June 18, 1863, 10:00 a.m.

Lieutenant Colonel Dudley, riding his bay-colored saddlebred, had led the small two-company battalion since leaving camp. The column had followed a muddy wagon trail for the past mile and was now approaching the village just ahead. Dudley pulled his horse off the path and waited for half the column to pass before shouting, "Battalion! Halt!"

As the men of Company B and Company E stopped, Solomon looked up at the sky. The clouds had turned into a gray overcast, and darker, more ominous clouds loomed to the west. Despite the mud from last night's rain, today's cloudy weather was a cool blessing.

The past week's brutal heat and sun had caused hundreds of men to fall out of line during the long forced marches on the hot and dusty roads. And those weren't just the usual stragglers either, but hardened veterans with lungs choked full of hot dust stirred up from thousands of brogans trudging ahead of them.

Dudley was convening with the lieutenants, and after a few moments, he called over for the sergeants too.

"What are they doing?" Billy asked, staring toward Dudley and the other officers. They were all looking to the north, toward an apparent fuss of some sort up ahead at the rail station.

"Dunno," Solomon said, "but I heard something about a tree line beyond the train station...and pickets."

"And cavalry," Billy added.

"Union?" Henry asked, hoping.

"I couldn't hear."

Hawk, leaning against his rifle just behind Solomon and Henry, chuckled and then tilted his head toward Henry. "Wouldn't be surprised if we get in a little scrap today, Sol."

Solomon ignored the comment, knowing it was directed not at him, but at Henry. Hawk sure loved tormenting poor Henry, Solomon knew.

"You're always wanting a fight, ain't ya, Hawk?" Henry finally said.

Hawk chuckled again and started to speak but was suddenly interrupted by a pounding of hooves coming from the north.

"Look," Solomon said, pointing. "Riders."

"Cavalry," Billy said, also turning and looking. "They're ours...Union."

There were six of them, and as they approached, Dudley gently pulled his reins and turned his horse to meet the riders. He stopped and waited casually, confidently. Lieutenants Greene and Schlagle were next to him now and watched as the half dozen Union cavalrymen veered off the path and headed toward them.

The column of Indiana infantrymen, Springfields resting at their sides, watched closely and waited.

The riders saluted as they reined in their horses and steadied their mounts...masterfully too, they all noticed. The cavalrymen were now just in front of Dudley and the rest of the Indiana men. The horsemen looked haggard, and layers of gray dust coated their uniforms and their sweaty, sun-worn, blistered faces.

They had a serious appearance about them too, with their dinged-up, dirty scabbards. Their swords weren't just for show either, like the shiny ones some of the infantry officers carried. And their pistols and carbines, although holstered and sheathed, looked even more lethal—only a nervous flinch away from bloodstained gauntlets and trigger fingers.

The cavalry lieutenant's horse neighed laboriously and gleamed with sweat as its master brought him in close to Dudley's.

"Guh' mornin', Colonel!" the lieutenant shouted to Dudley with another salute, his accent heavy with New York or Jersey.

"Mornin' to you as well, Lieutenant," Dudley said, returning the salute. With an accommodating smile, he leaned forward in his saddle and asked, "And how, Lieutenant, can we be of help to our fine cavalry this morning?"

The officers' conversation turned quieter but more animated. The cavalry lieutenant pointed...toward the station first, then to the tree line beyond. Dudley and his two lieutenants, Greene and Schlagle, watched. Their faces tightened, showed tension, and Dudley frowned too, all the while watching, listening, and nodding. The cavalrymen turned their mounts, focusing on the station to the north. The lieutenant and Dudley were discussing something important apparently. Heads nodded agreeably. Then Dudley said something to Lieutenant Greene sending him and his sergeants back toward his Company E men. Urgently too, Solomon noticed.

Hawk snickered and whispered, "Sol, ya hear that? Cavalry needs our help again."

Solomon ignored him and, instead, tried to listen to the officers' conversation. It was just Lieutenant Colonel Dudley and the New York cavalry lieutenant now. The other riders had hurriedly spurred their horses northward from where they had come, and Lieutenant Schlagle had returned to the column along with the sergeants.

"There's trouble," Solomon whispered.

"Reb cavalry?" Henry asked with another worried glance toward the station.

"Maybe," Hawk replied in a voice that sounded more hopeful than concerned.

Henry's eyes were darting and scanning the entire horizon now.

"But our cavalry's probably just nervous, Henry," Hawk replied, his voice reeking of disappointment that the fuss up north beyond the station might be all about nothing. Hawk knew that if it was Reb cavalry, it wouldn't be any trouble for *him* anyways. No trouble at all. Shooting a man on a horse was much greater sport than shooting at one just standing.

And besides, all this talk of a fight seemed all the better to Hawk…he didn't sign up to just do endless marches and half-starve. He'd volunteered to kill secessionist Rebs. Of course, only *he* knew why he wanted to do *that*. And he'd keep it that way too. That was a promise he'd made to himself long ago.

"Battalion! Attention!" Lieutenant Greene's voice boomed. Greene strode toward the front of the column, then turned and carefully watched his men. Lieutenant Green waited for just a moment and then yelled, "Keep your eyes forward, men! We're going into picket line beyond the station."

Greene paused and wiped his brow. The men watched, shifted nervously. The squad of Union cavalrymen had disappeared over the ridge toward the station, but the infantrymen could hear muffled shouts in that direction.

"Battalion!" Greene shouted, his sword unsheathed and pointing north. "Forwarrrrd! …March!"

With a clattering of tin cups and canteens and the trampling of brogans, the Indiana veterans quickly resumed the march toward the small village. Lieutenant Greene led with Company E, and behind them, Company B followed. The column zigzagged forward along the muddy wagon trail, then rounded a bend that brought the station in sight just ahead. After passing a few houses, they reached the torn-up railroad bed and then followed it toward the station.

Ahead, wagons and horse teams filled the street. Black teamsters, wet with sweat, worked laboriously loading the wagons and tending to horses. The cavalrymen they'd seen earlier, plus about ten more of them, were there too, barking out orders at the teamsters.

Closer, just ahead in the column, Lieutenant Greene stopped and pointed north. "This way, men!" he shouted, leading his Company E men off the railroad bed.

As Company E spread out into the fields to the north, Solomon and the thirty-one men of Company B continued forward. Lieutenant Colonel Dudley, still mounted, quickly rode up to Lieutenant Schlagle who was leading the Company B men. After a brief conversation, Schlagle turned to the men and shouted, "Company B! Halt!"

Stopping, Solomon cursed his blistered feet. His shoes, now worn with holes, were almost useless. Although the new socks had helped, they were wet now too. He'd seek out new brogans as soon as he could but also knew that not marching any more was the only true cure.

Dudley had dismounted and addressed the men. "We're going to the station and assembling near the buildings there," he said.

Footsore and tired, the men exchanged glances. They'd been to freight stations before. The crates looked heavy, and the wagons were still mostly empty. The rain wouldn't help either.

"Some of our cavalry are there," Dudley continued. "They need our help with their wagons. Keep your eyes on the horizon, men. And watch the buildings. There's Rebel raiders in the area."

Dudley paused when he felt a sprinkle of rain and then scanned the horizon. With a nod toward Lieutenant Schlagle, he said, "Lieutenant, let's get busy before it rains."

"Corporal Conley, Corporal Wasson," Schlagle shouted, "take your men over there and assist with those wagons at that freight house. Hustle…go!"

Lieutenant Schlagle paused as the two squads hurried off. Turning toward Sergeant Boller, Schlagle yelled, "Sergeant, go with the rest of the men over there…to the passenger house where those New Yorkers are. Give whatever assistance they ask for." Lieutenant Schlagle paused again, letting Boller take over.

"Williams…Grear!" Sergeant Boller shouted. "Take your squad to those wagons where those cavalrymen and their teamsters are fightin' with them boxes. Go!"

Not waiting for a response from Grear or the rest of the men in his squad, Boller turned toward Solomon. "Whitlow, take Schultz and Billy over to that building. Hawkins too. Help with them darky contrabands over there."

Hawk scoffed, watching Boller try to lead. "How 'bout next time, Sarge, when we go into bivouac, you don't volunteer us to set up out on the edge of camp near the damned train station."

"Just go, Hawkins," Boller shot back.

"We oughta be back there restin', all snug as bugs. Instead, we're out here loadin' wagons."

Boller turned away. He'd lost enough squabbles with Hawk lately.

"Come on, Hawk," Henry said, making peace and leading the squad toward the passenger station and the wagon teams.

Hawk started toward the wagons but glanced out beyond the fields to the north where the Company E men had set up their picket line. They were in the tree line's underbrush and spread out in two-man teams. "Jesus," Hawk said, wishing he were out *there* and not loading someone else's damned wagons.

Henry, out front, ignored him and quickened his step. He didn't like the way Boller talked, not one bit. But Hawk wasn't much better.

Herndon's modest passenger house was a one-story building with open doors facing the wooden platform where the tracks had been. The boardwalk in front of the building was bustling with activity. About a dozen blue-clad cavalrymen were moving about among the wagons and horse teams resting in the street next to the building.

Solomon also noticed several freed slaves…*contrabands*, he'd heard them called ever since the war began. They were helping the cavalrymen and looked up when the Indiana men approached. Other than a few cooks and laborers around the army, Solomon hadn't seen very many black men before. And never up close. Now, though, several of them were just in front of him, and he had to force himself from staring. One of the colored men was standing inside a wagon and, after placing a wooden crate inside, looked up and met Solomon's gaze.

Solomon nodded and tried smiling but wasn't sure if he did or not…at least not until he saw the colored man smile too. But it was only for a second. The man had already turned away to help one of his partners handing up another crate.

"Hurry up!" the cavalry lieutenant yelled, his fury directed toward the black men loading wagons. Another cavalryman nearby shouted at them too, his foreign-accented voice carrying a barrage of profanity and insults. Knowing they couldn't load the wagons any faster, the teamsters put their heads down and continued working.

"*Nicht nur da stehen, Privatsoldat,*" a German voice said from behind him.

Quickly turning, Solomon saw one of the cavalrymen from earlier. He wore a corporal's stripes on his sleeves, Solomon noticed. His bearded mustache was slicked and turned up in a way only a European's did, but his face was worn and his eyes bloodshot.

"*Folge mir,*" he said, waving for the Indiana men to follow. The cavalry corporal stepped up onto the boardwalk with a clattering of spurs, boots, and buckles and a clanging of his sword. Exchanging glances, Solomon and Henry followed him, with Hawk and Billy just behind them. Passing more wagons and horses, Solomon glanced at the cavalry corporal again. He hadn't noticed earlier but now saw bloodstains on the man's pants where his sword hung.

"What happened?" Solomon asked, pointing. "The blood...on your pants?"

When he glanced down, it was obvious he also hadn't noticed the bloodstain before, or at least hadn't paid attention to it. He looked away and didn't seem too concerned about it now either.

"*Nein, nicht meins,*" the cavalryman said casually and then grunted. "*Gester...yestday, a Rebel's. Maybe several. No matter... Pfffttt...*"

He looked angry now and pointed ahead where the last of the horse teams and wagons waited along with several more cavalrymen. "*Hier,*" he said before storming off in the other direction.

"Privates, over here," the New York lieutenant shouted as he approached the Indiana men. "Help us with a few of our wounded here. We're taking them inside. And, oh, yes...sorry 'bout Corporal Heine back there. He's not happy. He lost some friends in the fight...at Aldie."

The cavalry lieutenant paused, lowering his head. He'd lost a *lot* of men at Aldie. When he looked up, Solomon noticed his eyes had swelled wet with tears. The lieutenant quickly wiped his face with his handkerchief and, thinking of Corporal Heine again, said, "And a few days ago, three men from the corporal's squad…they were friends of his…they deserted."

"*Pffftt*…deserters," Sergeant Boller snarled, walking up and joining the conversation, interrupting the lieutenant.

"Yes, we've had several men desert," the lieutenant said. "Living on a horse isn't easy. Fighting atop one is even worse. But still, we are trying to find the deserters. Several, we believe, have ridden this way."

"Shoot them all," Boller said in a voice faking disgust.

"Funny thing for a shirker to say," Hawk said, but only loud enough for Billy, Henry, and Solomon to hear. Billy looked puzzled. Henry and Solomon didn't…they'd seen many times what their sergeant had done when a true fight came. At South Mountain, Boller hid in a barn, and he'd stayed back in the woods at Antietam. At Fredericksburg and Fitzhugh's Crossing, where he couldn't hide, he cowered like a puppy's first night away from its litter.

"We've got a few wounded over here," the lieutenant continued. "One of them, Private Campbell there, thought he could ride…and did, too, for a while. We've been taking them from the wagons and placing them inside."

"We'll help, sir," Henry said.

"Thank you," the lieutenant said. "We'll need more wagons to have these men taken to Alexandria or Washington. But right now, we need these wagons to take supplies and ammunition back toward Aldie and Middleburg, where the rest of the regiment is."

"These too?" Solomon asked, pointing toward the wagons around the side of the station.

"Yes, Private. And those over there too. Go ahead and jump in and help. I'll be with the other wagons out front. And… thank you," the lieutenant said before turning to leave.

The Indiana men quickly walked over to one of the wagons that still had a wounded man lying in it. He was the man the lieutenant had pointed to and called *Campbell*. He was shirtless, but a bloodstained bandage covered most of his upper torso.

"What's your name, soldier?" Solomon asked, stepping around the wagon and closer to the wounded man's head.

"Isaac…Isaac Campbell," he said.

"We're gonna get you outta this wagon and inside the building here."

"Thank God," the man said, grimacing. "I've been in the damned thing almost all morning. 'Bout killed me, too…rattlin' and bangin' through fields. I think the lieutenant's lost, to be honest. We ain't been on a road since leavin' the mountains. Just been bouncin' around back here. Ribs didn't hurt that bad 'til I got in the wagon. Should've stayed on the damned horse."

Solomon chuckled. It wasn't funny, but he knew that Isaac probably was…the man still had a sense of humor, even after he'd gotten himself wounded. Hearing Isaac made Solomon think of his own father. Despite Pa's toughness, he had a humorous side to him too and would have liked someone like Isaac. James and John would've too if they were here.

A crackle of thunder made them all look upward. The clouds to the west had darkened, and they could see rain not far away.

"Ready?" Solomon asked the wounded cavalryman.

"Jesus, yes. Get me out of here."

"Get his legs, Henry," Solomon said, reaching under the man's shoulders and carefully sliding him to the rear of the wagon.

Private Campbell was clutching his chest and in obvious pain. Solomon could tell that he wanted to scream. As Henry and Solomon picked him up to lay him on a litter, the man fought back tears.

"What happened?" Solomon asked, hoping to get his mind off the pain. Another clap of thunder and then raindrops kept Campbell from answering.

"Put 'em inside the station house," a voice said, this one also heavy with a German accent. It was another cavalryman who was also assisting one of his wounded comrades.

After looking over and nodding, Solomon and Henry leaned down and grabbed each end of Private Campbell's litter. "So, what *did* happen?" Solomon asked, lifting the stretcher and carrying Private Campbell toward the passenger station.

After a long pause and with a grimace, the soldier finally responded. "Yesterday...I got shot. Minie ball hit me in the chest. Heard it break ribs...never felt nothin' like it before."

Solomon felt a lump in his throat and exchanged glances with Henry. "Here," Solomon said, handing Isaac his canteen and not knowing what else to say.

"Thanks," he said, taking a drink. "Got whiskey?"

Henry and Solomon looked at each other and then toward Hawk over by the wooden crates. Catching their glances, Hawk didn't need an explanation. Hawk sprang forward and handed the man his flask he'd had inside his coat.

After a swig and another painful grimace, Isaac smiled and tried to lift his hand to return Hawk's flask.

"Keep it," Hawk said. "I can always go get more."

"Thanks," Isaac said, looking at Henry and Solomon. Their smiles told Isaac that Hawk definitely would go and get more...and that he'd enjoy doing it too.

"It happened just beyond a gap in the mountains," Isaac continued. "*Aldie*, I heard 'em call it. We rode through town towards the gap. That's where we ran into an entire brigade of Rebel cav...Jeb Stuart's men."

Henry and Solomon carried the man inside and carefully set him down next to the window beside one of his fellow wounded soldiers. A few civilians were there too and were already tending to the other soldiers in the station. This was the best place for them, they all knew.

"What unit you with?" Solomon asked.

"New York Cav…Fourth," he said. Proudly too, they noticed.

One of the other cavalrymen stepped over toward the Indiana men and extended his hand. "Thank you, soldiers."

"Our pleasure, sir," Henry responded. "We hope for the best for your men here, sir. And that they're able to return to your regiment soon."

"Thank you. It looks like we're going back today. Jeb Stuart's cavalry is in them hills, and General Lee's whole army is just beyond there, moving north. Hooker and Pleasonton want us probing those mountains looking for Lee's main body. So, it looks like there'll be a lot more fighting like yesterday's."

"Again, thank you, men," the cavalryman said, shaking the Indiana veterans' hands.

Solomon and Henry nodded at the soldiers before turning away and walking toward the door. As they stepped outside, they could see the last of the wounded being unloaded from the wagons and carried into the station. The clouds were even darker now, and the earlier sprinkles had turned to rain. After walking around the corner, they found the rest of the company gathered near the supply wagons.

"Let's go!" one of the cavalrymen shouted at the black teamsters now soaked with both sweat and rain. "Finish up with these crates here…before the roads are flooded in mud."

Sergeant Boller saw Solomon and Henry approaching and quickly lashed out. "Whitlow, Schultz, grab Billy and Hawkins from over there and help get these wagons loaded."

The cavalryman helping load the wagons wiped rain from his face and looked at Solomon. "Thanks," he said. "We've got a lot of supplies to take back over them hills. Apparently, the damned quartermaster in Washington ain't got a map and left this stuff here."

"Uhhh, yes sir," Solomon said, stepping forward and picking up a crate. Beside him, Henry and Billy had begun assisting too. Hawk, however, arms crossed and standing in the rain, just watched.

"Get to work, Hawkins!" Sergeant Boller shouted from underneath the building's awning.

"Come on out in the rain yourself, Sarge."

Boller, raging inside, sprang forward with fists out.

Hawk, grinning, kept his arms crossed but turned slightly to meet the sergeant's assault.

Pulling up just short of Hawk by only a few inches, Boller opened his mouth to yell, but no words came out, only a seething rage of inadvertent spit and snot.

Hawk met the sergeant's glare and said, "Get up there with the *darkies* yourself and load the damned wagon, Sarge. Of course, you won't do *that*, will ya? And only *you* and *I* know why."

Hawk's comment hit home.

Truth hurt.

Hawk, and Boller too, for that matter, both knew that Boller would never get in a wagon with a black man. Hawk had never known someone who hated another race as much as Boller did. Hawk had always been indifferent to black men, at least until learning about the awful things the sergeant and his gang had done before the war.

Grabbing Hawk's collar, Boller leaned in close and hissed.

Hawk still had his arms crossed and hadn't moved. But he wasn't grinning anymore either.

Billy stepped in first and then Solomon. Henry, along with the teamsters and some of the cavalrymen, looked on but didn't get involved. They'd all seen rumpuses before. Best to not get involved, they knew.

Hawk stood his ground for a while but finally backed away, even though he knew the *real* order of things. But not here in front of these other men watching. In their eyes, Hawk knew he was still just a private and Boller the sergeant.

But he wouldn't go help load wagons, though, not after the sergeant stood there out of the rain barking at him. Hell no, he wouldn't. He didn't mind helping black men; that wasn't it at all. Taking orders from Boller who thought he looked down on the rest of the world—that was the issue. Orders were orders, but not from someone like Boller. Not with the things he'd done.

That last thing he'd said to Boller, though…he already regretted that, like letting a man see your poker hand. No one but him had ever known about any of *that*, and now there'd be questions. For now, it'd be best to let that wait.

Hawk turned and spat…made a show of it too. Then he glanced at the men in the wagon and smiled. But he made sure the smile died before he looked at Boller one last time. Then, he spat once more, shook his head, and walked away.

"Why…why ain't yur…yur friend helpin' us, mister?" one of the men on the wagon nervously asked with a stutter. Henry glanced at Hawk and then toward the colored man. Henry could tell the man was strong, inside and out. But life had been hard on him, for sure. Even his arms and face showed scars. And although he wasn't in chains now, he still worked like it, just doing the work for someone else now. He felt sorry for the man, all of them. To Henry, it all felt so strange. Then suddenly, he realized he'd been staring. He looked away, felt sick.

"What's…what's wrong, mister?"

Henry didn't answer.

Solomon also noticed something wrong with Henry. "Henry, ya all right?" he asked.

"Yeah, yeah. Fine."

Henry turned and looked for Hawk. He had walked off somewhere. The sarge was gone too, probably back inside. Henry noticed the colored laborers had been watching him, concerned. He didn't want that. Henry shook his head, snapping himself out of his trance.

"Where you going next?" Henry asked the laborers, changing the subject.

"Uhh, we're going with the cavalry...with the wagons."

Henry and Solomon exchanged glances, then handed up another box.

"We're freedmen," the other one said proudly, believing it.

"Where are you men from?" Henry asked.

The two colored soldiers smiled and seemed surprised that white soldiers were talking to them in a way that showed genuine concern...and respect.

"We...we is from Maryland," the younger of the two teamsters said as they pulled the box to the front of the wagon. "We went to Washington when Mista' Lincoln wrote the Emancipation."

One of the cavalrymen nearby overheard him and turned with a scowl. "Get back to work!" he yelled before spewing a storm of profane expletives.

Henry, again, didn't understand the treatment the colored men were receiving. Wanting to help, he smiled and then stepped between the cavalryman and the black laborers. "We're from Indiana," Henry said.

The black men smiled. Apparently, they had heard of Indiana before.

"We're Quakers...both of us," Henry continued. "Some say we're fighting for your freedom. You know...to free the slaves."

"Underground...rail...road?"

Henry nodded and smiled. He felt proud, but it still didn't make up for the way the rest of the soldiers were treating them though.

The four men—two soldiers from Indiana and two freed slaves now serving with the army—worked in awkward silence for several minutes. While putting the last of the boxes on the wagon, the rest of the company, along with the teamsters and cavalrymen, finished up with their own wagons.

With rain coming down steadily, there was suddenly a rattle of gunshots from the distant tree line. Solomon quickly looked up.

"Henry!" Solomon shouted, pointing across the field.

Off in the distance, a dozen horsemen dressed in gray were wielding revolvers and carbines. Shrieking and howling, the riders spurred their horses along the edge of the trees.

"Rebel raiders!" Henry exclaimed. Then, thinking of the Company E pickets, he mumbled to himself, "Oh, no."

"There's not many of 'em, Henry," Sol said. "And they're riding the other direction."

They both watched as small clouds of gun smoke erupted from the Rebels' revolvers, harmless at this distance, especially wildly aimed from horseback. Hawk stared too. Right now, he wished he was out there with Company E, even though they were barely close enough to the Rebel raiders to get off a few improbable shots. But even their chances were gone now. With a flurry of shouts, the gray-clad horsemen had hurriedly ridden over the ridge, disappearing to the northeast. A few more sporadic gunshots were followed by the riders' fading yells as they rode farther away. Then it was quiet again, just thumping heartbeats.

"Mosby's Rangers…gotta be," Henry said.

"Could be, Private," the New York cavalry lieutenant said, having walked up upon hearing the distant shots. "But could've been anybody. There's a lotta Rebel cavalry around here...small bands of 'em like that."

"They were probably planning to raid the station," Henry said.

"Nah, not with all of you here," the lieutenant replied. "They're nothing more than Rebel bushwhackers with horses out makin' some noise."

The lieutenant turned and looked at his men. The wagons were almost loaded, and the wounded who couldn't fight were inside the building.

"Mount up, men!" the cavalry lieutenant yelled. "We're moving out in five!"

The Company B men watched as the small cavalry squad began assembling into a column with the wagon teams just behind them. The street was puddled in mud now, and the colored teamsters waiting in the wagons used their coats to shield themselves from the rain.

"We're going back to camp, men!" Lieutenant Schlagle shouted, having walked up from behind them. "And then, hopefully, we're staying in camp for a few days, especially with this rain."

Schlagle paused as they all watched the New York cavalry column begin to pull out. "We'll get some rest," Lieutenant Schlagle continued, "but eventually, we'll be doing some hard marching again, men. Even though General Lee stole a march on us, Hooker's got the inside track headin' north. There ain't no hurry yet. But there will be."

More of the Company B men had gathered now, and the pickets from Company E were returning from the tree line. Schlagle scanned the horizon for a few moments and waited for the men to assemble.

"Company B!" Schlagle shouted. "You're dismissed to the camp! Fall out!" The lieutenant then put his head down and turned toward the south, the direction they had marched from.

"We're done, Henry," Solomon said. "Let's go." Hawk and most of the rest of the company had already begun walking in the rain away from the station.

"Hang on, Sol," Henry said just prior to turning and jogging over to the wagon they'd helped load. Solomon watched him, not sure what he was doing. Then he could see Henry shake one of the black men's hands, thanking him. Then Henry went to another wagon and shook those workers' hands too. As Henry turned and jogged back toward the freight house, Solomon made eye contact with a few of the black men who smiled and tipped their hats. The men looked worn out and were soaked with rain. But now, after what Henry just did, they were smiling and didn't seem bothered by such small things as being overworked in bad weather.

"You ready, Sol?" Henry asked, returning from speaking with the colored men.

"Yeah, let's go," Solomon said, stepping out the door and into the rain. Then, they made their way down the boardwalk and turned onto the muddy road.

"That was nice, Henry…treating those black men like that. And seeing their smiles…that meant a lot."

"Me too. I don't think they've had a lot to smile about. They're *men*, Sol. Just like you and me."

"I know," Solomon said. They were both silent for several moments as they turned onto the path that led toward camp. Solomon noticed Henry seemed to have begun brooding over something. The rain was coming down steady now, a soaking downpour. Solomon knew that whatever was bothering Henry, though, was something else.

Finally, as they stepped over a small stream, Henry cleared his throat and said, "Mister Lincoln's army…"

But Henry didn't finish. Instead, he looked ahead toward their camp.

"Go on, Henry."

"Nah, forget it," Henry said. "But this war, Sol…it's not *about* what I thought it was. Not anymore."

Solomon glanced at him, saw teary eyes. He could tell Henry wanted to say more…a *lot* more. But he didn't. They walked in silence for a while, and then, approaching the camp, Solomon finally spoke up again but changed the subject.

"I don't think we're marching any more today, Henry. I think we've finally caught up to General Lee…and gotten between him and Washington."

Henry had his head down, didn't speak at first. Then he looked up at their tents just ahead.

"I hope so."

-7-

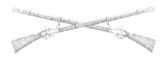

Near Herndon Station, Virginia
June 19, 1863, 1:30 p.m.

The previous afternoon's rain ended around midnight and brought a much-appreciated cooler morning. Other than yesterday's short march to Herndon Station and back, the men of the Nineteenth Indiana were allowed to remain in camp and rest until almost noon. After striking their tents, the Iron Brigade packed their knapsacks and haversacks, grabbed their muskets, and began assembling to await further orders. Solomon looked toward the road where the entire First Corps had gathered and was now forming into a long marching column.

"We were wrong, Henry," Solomon said, realizing they would indeed be marching again today.

Henry, with a dour look on his face, didn't respond. In fact, he hadn't spoken a word or smiled since the bugler sounded assembly thirty minutes ago.

"Attention, Company!" Lieutenant Schlagle shouted. He paused and waited while the two rows of men looked up and turned their focus toward him. "Shoulder Arms!"

All thirty-one men of Company B quickly raised their Springfield muskets and rested them against their right shoulders. The lieutenant had their full attention now. Walnut wood gunstocks and steel barrels glistened in the bright afternoon sun as Lieutenant Schlagle looked up and down the two rows of veterans, rows much shorter than they had been just a year ago. They were good men, he knew, and it was hard to think about so many of their friends who had fallen.

"Left face!" Schlagle shouted, shaking off thoughts of men long gone.

Tin cups and canteens clanged and rattled as the men refaced to the left. Schlagle paused, and the men waited. Up ahead, more officers gathered.

Solomon glanced to his left. Henry was next to him, and the frown on his face was even gloomier now than before. None of them wanted to march today, especially Henry. To *him*, marching meant they were another day closer to fighting. And fighting, he learned early on, was the one thing in the world he'd come to hate.

Earlier, Henry had said he actually slept well last night and didn't have his usual nightmares. He even came out of the tent with a smile after the bugler sounded reveille a little after dawn. But that all changed when word spread that the army would be on the move again.

In the row behind them, Hawk was also brooding. That wasn't like him, and Solomon knew he would have to ask him about it later. Hawk didn't go out foraging last night, probably hadn't even replaced his flask he'd given the wounded cavalryman either.

Billy was standing next to Hawk and, standing on the other side of him, was Billy's cousin Grear. At least Billy seemed to be in good spirits. Grear's squad had joined them last night, and Billy had played his harmonica until the fire had died.

"How's your feet, Sol?" Henry asked, finally breaking his silence.

"Uhhh, better. Maybe a little, anyways."

Solomon's voice wasn't convincing, and Henry decided to change the subject. "What's wrong with Hawk?" Henry whispered.

"Don't know," Solomon said. "Something yesterday maybe?"

But there was no time for Henry to answer. Colonel Williams had ridden up and was speaking with the company officers, and within a few seconds, the lieutenants and captains began shouting out orders.

"Forward! March!" Lieutenant Schlagle shouted, pointing toward the rest of the First Corps that had been assembling on the road up ahead. As Company B approached the long blue column, Solomon gazed ahead in wonder. The First Corps had over ten thousand men, all of them veterans. Despite witnessing hundreds of marches over the past two years, he still found the sights and sounds of the army on the march an amazing spectacle.

"Company, halt!" Lieutenant Schlagle shouted as they neared the road. "Column of fours, men!"

The men quickly took position in the waiting column, which was nearly a mile long. The men didn't have to wait long. Up ahead, the Iron Brigade soldiers heard commands to begin the march. The orders filtered back through the ranks, and with regimental and company officers loudly echoing the orders, the men finally stepped off.

With the blue column stretching out on the road, the Army of the Potomac's First Corps snaked its way forward through the farms and woodlots of Northern Virginia. The road paralleled the Alexandria, Loudon, and Hampshire Railroad which led northwest toward Guilford Station and beyond to Leesburg, Virginia.

Only a few miles into the march, Solomon couldn't help but think of his sore, blistered feet. He tried to hide his limp but couldn't. One of his worn-out brogans had a loose sole and flapped in the dirt as he walked. Glancing to his left, he noticed Henry watching him closely, concerned about Solomon's limp.

"Looks like the rain will hold off," Solomon said, changing the subject and looking up at the sky.

"Hopefully," Henry said, also looking up but then glancing down at Solomon's shoes. He wasn't sure, but he thought he saw blood. "We gotta get you new shoes, Sol. You're limping."

"I just hope we're not marching far today."

"I heard 'em say we're just going to the next town," Henry said. "*Guilford* is what I heard the lieutenant call it. And I think it's just ahead."

Sergeant Boller, who had been marching a little farther back, had approached and was now just behind Solomon's right shoulder. He had apparently eavesdropped on the end of Henry and Solomon's conversation and angrily said, "Don't slow anybody down today, Whitlow!"

"Yes sir, Sarge," Solomon responded, fighting back a grimace. "Just a couple of blisters, sir. I'll keep up."

"Well, you just keep movin', Private," Sergeant Boller sneered.

Hawk, marching two rows behind Solomon and only a few feet from the sergeant, couldn't hold back. "He never fell outta the march yet, Sarge, has he?"

Boller didn't know Hawk was so close and quickly turned. Slowing down and glaring at Hawk, he growled, "Just keep marchin', Hawkins...*Private* Hawkins."

Hawk noticed the sergeant's arrogant smirk but decided to look away and, instead, focused his eyes forward again. Hawk, seething inside, fought back words. He remembered what his father had taught him when he was a boy. *Rise above your rage,* he'd told him...many times too. Hawk had lost his father when he was young. But that lesson was learned over and over, recognizing your anger, holding it back, and *controlling* it. He'd thought of his father's words a lot. That little bit of time, just a few seconds, gave him time to channel his anger...and make it *useful* when necessary.

"All of you, just keep marching," Boller barked again.

Hawk knew that, sometimes, you have to hold back anger forever. This wouldn't be one of those times, though. For now, he decided he would push the sergeant. He knew it wouldn't take much. Hawk was sure the sarge hadn't learned many of the lessons *he* had.

"Oh, we're marchin', Sarge," Hawk said, waiting for Boller's response. Hawk was the one smirking now.

Sergeant Boller turned away from Solomon and put his face within a few inches of Hawk, the new target of his anger.

But before Boller had a chance to speak, Hawk said, "We're doing twenty miles a day some days, Sarge, ever since leaving the Rappahannock. And not *one* of us here fell outta line. Not even Sol with his worn-out brogans."

"You listen here, Hawkins!" the sergeant shouted. "You just keep standin' up for yur Quaker pals here, and you'll find yourself in a box."

Sergeant Boller was walking backwards now and facing Hawk, creating a spectacle. Several soldiers walking nearby distanced themselves from the sergeant as the column continued its march.

Not backing down, Hawk leaned in even closer and replied in a low voice that only Sergeant Boller could hear. "You lighten up on Solomon, Sarge. And on our squad. Or you'll be the one in a *box*. Now, move on."

"You're dead, Hawkins!" the sergeant shouted. His face had turned red and contorted into a seething rage.

"Sergeant, what's going on here?" It was Lieutenant Schlagle, who had noticed the disturbance from the other side of the column. The sergeant's expression softened, and slowly, he turned away from Hawk and looked toward the lieutenant.

"Nothing, Lieutenant," Boller said, trying to regain his composure. "These boys are just complainin' 'bout nothing…that's all."

Schlagle looked around at the men, taking stock of the situation. Satisfied there would be no more problems, he nodded and slowly turned away. Boller waited a few seconds before looking back toward Solomon and then at Hawk. He started to point his finger in Hawk's direction but decided to pull it back. Shaking his head angrily, he finally retreated and stepped to the side of the moving column.

"Good choice," Hawk said as the sergeant disappeared toward the rear behind several rows of soldiers.

"Dang, Hawk," Solomon said. "Thanks, but you didn't have to do that."

"That son of a bitch had it comin'," Billy said loud enough for the men around them to hear. Not all of them had liked Hawk, not even now. But *none* of them liked the sarge.

Solomon forced back a smile. But then the pain from his feet surged through him again. His limp was severe now, and he winced with every step.

"We're almost there, Sol," Henry said, noticing how much pain Solomon was in.

Up ahead and off to the right, a group of mounted officers had assembled and engaged in a discussion near a farmhouse. After several minutes of pointing at the surrounding fields, the officers turned and looked at the column. "Halt!" one of them shouted. "Fall out!"

"Thank God," Solomon said. When he stopped walking, he felt a wetness in his socks. Looking down, he saw why...fresh blood.

*****

A few hours later, around sunset, the Nineteenth Indiana was in its new bivouac for the night near Guilford Station. The men's spirits were high, despite the army's most recent defeats at

Chancellorsville last month and Fredericksburg in December. They had been moving north and northwest for the past week and were now just south of the Potomac River at the foot of the Blue Ridge Mountains. Somewhere over those mountains, they knew, was General Lee's army.

Word had also come down from officers higher up that the army would be remaining in camp for several days to resupply. The men looked forward to getting rest, and today's relatively short five-mile march from Herndon was a welcome change from the long, grueling, hot marches of the past week.

"Looks like some old salted pork…and these," Billy said, returning from the commissary wagon and holding two packages of hardtack crackers for all of them to see.

Hawk looked up and laughed. "There's always a farm not too far away. And you know they'll have loaded cupboards… and a henhouse full of eggs."

Hawk noticed Henry ignoring him, instead, sitting on a log and poking at the fire he and Solomon had built. "What you think, Henry?" Hawk asked, leaning over to Henry and giving him a friendly slap on the back.

Henry, still focused on the fire, continued to ignore him.

"Once it gets dark, Henry, let's go get us a meal we can cook up."

"No thanks," Henry finally said, dismissing Hawk's invitation and returning his attention to his efforts with the fire.

"How 'bout you, Sol?" Hawk asked.

Solomon chuckled and pointed at his feet now sockless and bandaged. "Not tonight, Hawk."

"Billy?"

Billy threw his hands up and shook his head *no*. "Go ahead by yourself, Hawk."

Henry looked up and, with a smile, said, "Yeah, Hawk. Go on. We won't stop ya."

"Bunch a weak sisters," Hawk said, laughing and then standing up. "I'm gonna at least go get some firewood. Come on, Henry. You comin' with me?"

Henry looked around the rest of the camp, then grinned at the squad around the fire. "Sure, Hawk," he said, standing up. "Guess we'll need a big fire for your breakfast."

"That's the spirit, Henry," Hawk said, turning and starting toward the woods.

Solomon, grinning, watched them leave and then looked around the camp. It was almost dark now, and all around them, men had gathered near small fires. Nearby, Grear's squad had a poker game going atop a cracker box. A little farther away, laughter erupted among the Company A men when someone lost a checkers game and tossed the board and pieces. Solomon looked up at the sky. There were stars out now, and he stared at the brightest one, a brilliant white planet high in the western sky.

"Venus," Billy said, noticing Solomon stargazing.

"You sure?"

"Yeah, learned it from all that city book-learnin', as you and Hawk call it."

Solomon laughed, then, still looking up at Venus, said, "Must be over Indiana."

"Yeah, maybe," Billy said. "You miss it?"

"Indiana?" Solomon asked.

Billy nodded and spat in the fire. "Yeah."

"I dunno," Solomon said. "This is where I'm supposed to be, ya know? Sure do miss Mother and Pa for sure. Sisters too."

"What 'bout James? ...and John?"

"Yeah, for sure. James will be back though. Hopefully soon. But he might be better off missing this *next* fight." He paused and thought of his brothers. Billy had grabbed his harmonica... *that* would make Hawk happy when he and Henry came back.

Hawk sure loved Billy's harmonica. Hawk had said it was the best gift he'd ever given anyone.

"James *will* be back soon," Billy said. He said it confidently too, Solomon noticed. Billy then blew a soft, high-pitched note that he let fade among the rest of the sounds of the camp.

"As for John, I'm not sure when I'll see him," Solomon said. He stared into the fire a few moments, then looked up at Billy. "What 'bout you, Billy? You miss home?"

"I wanna see my boy, Sol. She named him *Billy*, just like me."

"Li'l William Williams," Solomon said with a chuckle. "Hawk know you named him that?"

"Nah, he knows my wife had a boy though. Just not the name."

"Don't worry, I won't tell him," Solomon said, still laughing. "Hawk'll be calling you 'Big Billy Billy'."

Billy laughed, then said, "You're right…he will. But that's okay. I kinda like Hawk now."

"Yeah, I do too."

They sat in silence for a few moments, and then Billy brought his harmonica up to his lips again. After a couple of long, slow notes, he lowered the harmonica and said, "But yeah, Sol. I miss home."

Solomon nodded, agreeing. He did too.

"But volunteering was the right thing to do," Billy said. "Especially with Grear off fighting. And once the planting was done last spring, figured I'd do more good out here than back home. But going with Grear's ma and pa to Richmond to check the sick and dying list…that was worse than any fighting, for sure. And I sure miss poor Laura Rebecca. Glad I got a gal who writes. Some back home don't write. Wouldn't be able to handle that. Some of the boys here don't even know they got a new baby back home. I'm blessed for sure there, Sol."

Billy paused and blew a few more notes but then lowered his harmonica again. Looking around the camp, he said, "Didn't think the fighting would be like it was, though. Did you, Sol?"

"No, but when we got to camp and joined the brigade, I heard from the Second Wisconsin boys 'bout First Bull Run. Boys wet their pants there when the lead flew past for the first time. Seen a lot of men do it since too. The sound a bullet makes when—"

Solomon suddenly stopped, knowing it wouldn't do any good to talk about all that. He picked up another stick and jabbed at the fire. Seeing the embers brighten and rise into sparks, he looked up and watched them fade with the stars. Laughter broke out a few campfires away, and Billy raised his harmonica to his lips again. The tune he began playing was a soft, quiet hymn Solomon had heard in church many years ago.

Solomon stared up at the sky and slowly closed his eyes. Billy's tune reminded him of those early years of home. Feeling himself drifting off, he let himself go. He thought of his mother and father…and of his sisters. But then his thoughts turned back to James and his oldest brother John, both of whom he dearly missed.

He thought back to those days as a child in Kentucky. His mind filled with memories with his brothers in forests and pastures, and along creeks and rivers. The three brothers had spent many long, adventurous days together, often miles from their farm. Sometimes, it seemed like only yesterday.

The Georgia boy's harmonica hummed…softly, sadly. Then Solomon felt it fading further and further. He allowed it to fade even more, and then it was gone completely. Thinking back in time and away from the army camp and from the horrible war, he was dreaming now…of when they were young.

They were just teenagers then. It was a warm spring day. He was with John and James, together at the edge of the tree line. The three brothers were keeping watch over a large, grassy meadow when the four deer had walked out of the woods. When the deer stopped to graze in the tall grass, Solomon could remember feeling his heart race. Excited, he quickly raised his gun…

"Sshhhh…wait for the buck," James had said, reaching over and touching the top of Solomon's musket. Solomon had the white-spotted fawn in his gunsight but slowly lowered the barrel as his two older brothers calmed him down.

"Patience," he remembered John saying with a slight wink at his younger brother. Solomon was only thirteen then, but this was already going to be his fifth deer. Several miles from their farm, the three Whitlow brothers hadn't a care in the world except for those deer in that meadow. And of the buck that was sure to follow.

"Watch that tree line, Solomon," James had whispered. Even though only two years older at the time, James seemed like an adult to Solomon. And they both looked up to John even more. He seemed so wise and calm, especially here, at the critical point of the hunt. The two older brothers were watching Solomon closely, teaching.

"You gotta have nerves of steel," their father had told them years prior. Nathan Whitlow didn't go with them to hunt very often by then, normally staying home to tend to the family's horse farm. The Whitlow brothers loved growing up there in Barren County, Kentucky, along with their three younger sisters. It was only a few years later, however, that the political climate in Kentucky turned tumultuous and threatened to become violent. It was then that the Whitlow family made the long move north to Ohio, just across the state line from Richmond, Indiana.

"There he is," John whispered, pointing out the buck for his youngest brother. "*Steady, steady…*"

"Easy, Sol," James whispered. "Wait for him…*easy…*"

The three brothers watched silently as the buck strode out into the meadow, always eyeing the horizon for any danger to his small herd. Solomon felt his heart racing again as he tried to steady the musket's sights on the buck.

Only a few more yards, young Solomon thought. He remembered it like it was yesterday…the smells of the flowers and of the trees as they watched those deer in that meadow. He would never forget the excitement of the moment, steadying the musket on the log. Carefully aiming at the buck, he took a deep breath.

A sudden outburst of yelling woke Solomon from his dream. He wanted to cling to the dream as long as he could, but more shouts forced him to open his eyes. He turned toward the sounds. A brawl had broken out among the Company A men. Billy, still across the fire from him, had stood up and was watching too.

"What's happening over there?" Solomon asked.

"Company A…the boys from Anderson are at it again," Billy said. The corporals and sergeants finally took over, and apparently, things had begun calming down.

"Where's Henry?…And Hawk?" Solomon asked. Evidently, they had returned but were gone again… Solomon saw a fresh pile of firewood near the fire, but he didn't see Henry or Hawk.

"They dropped off the wood," Billy said with a chuckle. "You were asleep, and they heard the ruckus with the Madison County boys, so they went to see it. I saw 'em over by Grear a minute ago. I think Grear owed Hawk poker money again."

"Henry went?" That was odd, Solomon thought. It wasn't like Henry wanting to have anything to do with a fight.

"Probably wanted to keep Hawk outta trouble."

"Not likely," Solomon said, waking up a little more and coming back to the reality of army life and further away from his dreams of home.

"Here they come now," Billy said. He'd pulled his harmonica out again and was already blowing a tune as Hawk and Henry walked up.

"I'm beat," Henry said, plopping down on his blanket a few feet behind the logs they'd been sitting on earlier.

"The night's young, Henry," Hawk said, teasing and holding out a new flask he'd somehow acquired. After taking a swig, he said, "We ain't going anywhere tomorrow."

Solomon smiled, turned, and looked at Henry. He was already facedown and seemed to be asleep. Billy finished his tune and had gone to lie down too. It was just Hawk and Solomon at the fire now.

It was probably close to midnight, and most of the camp had settled down. Solomon stared into the fire and tried blocking out the sounds of the camp. But still, he heard sleepy groans and muffled voices of men still awake around the other campfires. It was a clear night, and most of the men hadn't taken the time to set up tents, instead, lying out in the open on blankets. Solomon watched the embers glow and occasionally turn to sparks that twisted and fluttered upward with the campfire's rising smoke. He'd always enjoyed watching sparks rise toward the distant stars during the summer.

"What you over there thinkin' 'bout, Sol?" Hawk asked.

Solomon looked across the fire at Hawk. He was sitting on a log and using his knife to whittle and sharpen the end of a stick.

"Ah, nothin'." There was a long pause, and they both watched the fire.

"Doesn't seem like nothin'," Hawk said, unconvinced.

"I was just thinking 'bout back home, when me was younger. Me and James…and John. …And the war, I guess."

"That'll make ya crazy fir sure, Sol."

"I know, probably already has. Some of the others, Hawk… they're a lot worse off than me, though. I mean, thinking about home 'n' all." Solomon lowered his voice and looked back at the blanket where Henry was sleeping.

Hawk watched Solomon carefully and stayed silent, knowing there was more.

"Just look at Henry over there," Solomon continued. "I'm afraid he's hit his limit with the army. I'm worried about what he's gonna do."

Hawk nodded, understood. He'd seen it too with Henry.

"Did you see him back at the station with the cavalry? When the shooting started out by the woods? We weren't even getting shot at then." Solomon glanced back again. Henry was still sound asleep, but still, Solomon lowered his voice even lower. Barely whispering now, Solomon said, "He was shakin' like a leaf. I'm 'fraid he's gonna desert, Hawk."

Hawk just stared into the fire as Solomon's comment sank in. They both knew that the only things Hawk hated worse than Rebels were deserters.

"He didn't say that, though, did he, Sol? Desert?"

"No, but he talks of home a lot. And of his sweetheart, Lillian. I don't want him to do nothin' stupid, Hawk. They're shootin' deserters. And they're gonna do a lot more of it too, with a big battle sure to be comin' up."

Hawk stayed silent for a moment. They both knew exactly what Solomon was talking about. It was only a week ago that Private John Woods was executed by a firing squad in front of the entire corps. Seeing Private Woods sitting on his own coffin and then being blasted backward—that was something that gave men nightmares.

"And the sarge ain't helpin' him none either," Solomon said.

"Boller...*pffftt*," Hawk scoffed. "He'll get his due."

"By the way, Hawk, that thing with Sarge today...you didn't have to do that. He don't bother me none."

"I'm not lettin' him beat any of us down anymore, Sol. He ain't no better than any of us. Just 'cause we lost a bunch of sergeants and corporals doesn't mean he deserves them chevrons on his sleeves."

"But he's the sergeant, Hawk. That's just the way it is."

"The hell it is," Hawk said, pulling out the flask from his jacket again. He took a long drink and then stared into the fire. Solomon watched him carefully. Hawk had always been good at hiding anger, good at hiding any emotions, really. But now, in the firelight, Solomon saw something in Hawk's eyes he hadn't seen before. At first, it was just a squint, maybe even a slight twitch. But then Solomon saw that his lip was moving too, an angry quiver.

Solomon wanted to ask him about yesterday at the station…about what Hawk had said to Boller. Solomon opened his mouth to ask but then stopped, knowing he shouldn't. Instead, he pointed at Hawk's flask and said, "You gonna be able to get more of that?"

Hawk glanced at the flask and smiled. "I always do, somehow." After taking another swig, Hawk held out the flask and offered Solomon a drink.

"Sure, why not," Solomon said as Hawk tossed the flask toward him. Solomon caught it, pulled off its cork, and took a long drink.

"Good, huh?"

"Yeah," Solomon said, tossing the flask back. The whiskey was strong. But felt good. "Thanks. I gotta give it to ya, Hawk. You have a knack for some things."

"Guess I do," Hawk said with a chuckle.

Solomon watched him closely again. Hawk was staring up at the sky and had a smile on his face. Apparently, for now, he'd dismissed thoughts of Boller and whatever else troubled him. Solomon smiled too, glad he hadn't asked about yesterday and the comments Hawk had made at the station about his and Boller's past.

Solomon looked up at the sky again too. The stars were bright now, and the camp had finally grown quiet.

Realizing again how tired he was, Solomon glanced back toward Hawk and said, "I'm beat."

Hawk, still staring upward, didn't respond.

"Guh' night, Hawk," Solomon said quietly. Then, being careful with his sore, bandaged feet, Solomon slowly stood up and stepped around the log toward his gum blanket.

After lying down, Solomon's thoughts quickly turned to his dream from earlier. With images of his childhood back home and of hunting with his brothers, he stared at the stars for a moment, then slowly closed his eyes.

Solomon wasn't asleep long, however, before hearing an angry voice. He opened his eyes and sat up on one elbow, looking toward the sound. The voice was Sergeant Boller's, arguing with some private. Solomon tried listening closer and thought he heard something or another about a dog.

"What's going on, Hawk?" Solomon asked.

"It's Boller again," Hawk said, looking toward Sergeant Boller's tent. Hawk, his angry look having returned, stood up and stoked at the fire. "He's over there peacockin' on a poor private."

Solomon looked through the darkness and caught just a glance of a soldier walking away from the sergeant's campsite. A dog was following close behind, he noticed. After the soldier and the dog disappeared into the shadows, Solomon lay back down and watched the embers from Hawk's fire float skyward.

"I'm goin' back to sleep, Hawk," Solomon said.

"Yeah, I reckon I will too in a while."

Solomon lay on his back and looked up. A few thin, high clouds had appeared just beyond the treetops off to the west. They were floating ever so slowly far above the camp.

"Hawk?" a voice asked.

Solomon barely heard it and thought he was dreaming. Then he heard the voice again, closer.

"Hawk?"

Solomon thought the voice was familiar. He opened his eyes and looked across the fire, which was burning bright again thanks to Hawk's most recent efforts. Solomon saw that Hawk had gotten up and turned away from the fire, staring into the darkness.

"Whose voice was that, Hawk?" Solomon asked. Hawk didn't respond but kept gazing into the darkness toward where they'd heard the voice.

From the shadows, the voice called again.

"Hawk? Is that you?"

Then the voice took the form of a dark shape approaching from the woods. It was a soldier…and a dog just behind him. Hawk sprang toward the voice with his arms outstretched to greet him.

Solomon stared in disbelief as he saw his brother James raise his arms and give Hawk a hug.

Looking past Hawk's shoulder, James saw Solomon getting up from the other side of the fire.

"Sol, is that you?" James asked, letting go of Hawk and walking toward his brother.

Solomon hadn't seen James in over six weeks and hadn't known whether he was even still alive. Stepping around the campfire, Solomon wiped tears from his eyes. Then, he cried out, "James!"

-8-

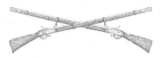

Six days later…

Potomac River
Near Edward's Ferry, Virginia
June 25, 1863, 2:00 p.m.

The afternoon sun, along with thousands of plodding boots, had created several inches of dust on the road. As the column crested the ridge, they could see a large valley and the Potomac River below.

"Look, Sol," James said.

Solomon looked across the river to where James was pointing. On the other side of the valley, a seemingly endless line of troops snaked its way northward, its massive dust cloud rising into the hills beyond.

"That column goes on forever," Solomon replied, his dry-mouthed voice unable to hide disappointment.

"Afraid we're going a long way today," James said, gazing at the column in the distant valley. Looking closer at the river below, he could see where the long column was crossing. The Eleventh Corps was on a bridge a half mile upstream, but the head of their own First Corps had just arrived at the river where their pontoons were still being assembled for their own bridge.

The column had bunched up again, and a few moments later, they all came to a halt.

Solomon, as he reached for his canteen, looked over at James and smiled. It really was good to have James back with them again. They'd all been worried, especially after receiving the letter from home that James hadn't been doing well. But that was several weeks ago, and now he seemed to be doing fine.

"How's your foot, James?" Solomon casually asked before splashing water on his dust-covered face.

"It's good, Sol. How 'bout you…your blisters?"

"I'm fine. I think they're finally gone." Solomon then waited for James to finish taking a drink from his canteen and then nodded toward the river. "The Potomac?"

"Yup," James replied, wiping water on his face and trying to get the dirt and dust away from his eyes.

"Amazing, huh?" Solomon asked.

"Yeah, but not quite the Ohio though, is it?"

Solomon started to answer but paused. It was many years ago when their whole family had stood at the edge of the Ohio River and waited to step onto the ferryboat. Crossing the river then was a day they would never forget. They were moving away from Kentucky then and trying to escape an inevitable conflict. Now though, apparently, James and Solomon were headed *toward* one.

"Gonna be in Maryland again, James," Solomon finally said.

Thinking of Maryland and the Antietam campaign of last year, James said, "Yeah. And I'm afraid the battle coming may be just as big, Sol."

Knowing James was probably right, Solomon didn't respond at first. It'd be best not to talk about that, nor the horrors of what happened in Maryland in 1862…at least not here and now. As he stowed his canteen and stared out at the army's column, he felt a chill he'd never felt before. Somewhere out ahead of them, a battle was inevitable. An unshakable fear came over him that, after crossing the river, life might never be the same.

"I think you're right," Solomon finally said.

Their section of the four-man-wide column started moving again, and no one spoke as they started down the slope. Following a curve in the road, they could see even more of the horizon ahead. Far on the other side of the river, rain clouds hung above distant hills, silhouetted against an even darker and more ominous sky beyond.

The dusty, thirsty column had slowed and now stopped again.

"Battalion! Halt!" a voice off to the side shouted. "Fall out, men!"

It was the order they had all hoped for, and they let out a collective sigh. They seemed to never know when they would get their next chance to rest and take their packs off...and possibly even make coffee.

"Thank God," James said, leaning on his rifle and slipping off his knapsack. For the past hour, his rifle had grown heavy against his shoulder, and the straps from his pack and cartridge box felt like they'd dug into his skin.

"Stay near the road!" an officer a little farther ahead shouted, seeing men scrambling off the road and looking for shade.

"This way," James said, pointing and leading the squad toward a clump of trees a few dozen yards away.

"Don't go far, Privates!" Sergeant Boller barked. "And be ready to march!"

James turned and met the sergeant's glare before turning toward the rest of the squad.

"Don't pay the sarge any mind, James," Henry said, trying to keep James's attention away from Boller. "He's been like that lately."

When James glanced at Sergeant Boller again, he noticed the sergeant had turned his stare toward Hawk. Boller's eyes seemed to be daring Hawk to venture too far away and not fall back into column when called.

"You hear me, Hawk?" Boller asked, prodding.

"Stayin' right here, Sarge," Hawk said in a voice that offered peace. Hawk knew he'd said too much to Boller several days ago, and there was no need to get the sergeant's guard up now.

Boller watched the squad closely, daring them into another response. Hawk noticed the sergeant had become arrogant with what little power he thought he had over them. It was probably because of Hawk's comment about what he'd done in Kentucky, Hawk thought. Or maybe it was a show for James since he'd just returned to the squad…showing them all that he still exerted control. After a few moments and seeing that even Hawk wasn't taking his bait for an argument, Boller turned away.

"James, where's that mangy mutt of yours, anyway?" Henry asked, changing the subject. He was referring to the dog that had followed James into camp several days ago and had hardly left the squad since.

"Dunno," James said, casually scanning the horizon. "I saw him a while ago…by that little creek where the other column turned off."

"That was at least a couple miles back," Henry said, his voice unable to hide his concern.

"He'll find us," James said dismissively.

"He hasn't missed one of our meals yet," Billy said. They all laughed knowing Billy was right… James's dog was always nearby when someone put their frying pan on a fire.

"The Wisconsin boys back there probably got him," Hawk chimed in. "They're hungry too, probably already got him over their fire."

James's look told Hawk that he had crossed another line. Hawk had grinned when he'd said it, but still, the dog had become one of them.

"He'll be back...just kidding," Hawk finally said, smiling.

James watched Hawk for a moment and noticed that he'd turned serious. He didn't have that mischievous, ornery look that he normally had, and James could tell that something was bothering him—despite having joked about their dog.

Deciding to change the conversation again, James asked, "Sol, still got all them coffee beans?"

"Yeah," Solomon responded, pulling out a small bag from his knapsack and tossing it in front of James. "Don't know how long we're gonna be here, though. You crush 'em... I gotta go to the woods."

The hint was all the squad needed, and they quickly stacked their muskets and began making a fire.

"We stopping long, ya think?" Henry asked, hopingly.

"We'll probably get called back onto the road right when we get that coffee fire started," Hawk quipped.

James, using the back of his bayonet to crush the coffee beans, looked toward the river. The engineers were still working, and the pontoons now stretched most of the way across.

"We'll be here at least a little while, Henry," Billy said, looking up from the fire where he was boiling water. After also glancing out toward the river, he said, "At least 'til they get that bridge finished."

"And with the Confederates all the way up in Pennsylvania," James said, "there's gonna be a lotta marchin' once them engineers *do* get done."

"How come?" Henry asked.

"Back when I was in Washington, I heard 'em say Hooker was supposed to...*stay between Lee's army and Washington and Baltimore*." James said the last part with emphasis, repeating exactly what his brother John had heard from another officer a week ago. "And now, we're following the Rebel Army north."

"How far away are they?" Henry asked.

"Not very far," James said. "Just on the other side of them mountains…right out there."

James glanced toward Hawk who wasn't paying attention. He seemed to still be brooding over something or another. That was rare for Hawk, he knew. James smiled in his direction and then said, "The Rebs are close. Hawk, you going out wanderin' around tonight the way you always do?"

"Ya'll will want breakfast, won't ya?" Hawk replied without looking up.

"Well," James said, "I'm worried you're just as likely to get caught by a Reb picket post as by an angry farmer."

Hawk didn't respond at first, but then he smiled and slowly looked up. Menacingly, he said, "All the better."

Henry, trying to not think of Rebel pickets, nor *anyone* in the Confederate Army for that matter, pointed at the pot of water. "It's boiling."

Solomon, closest to the fire, leaned down and poured some of the hot water into his own cup. Then he poured water into Henry's before handing the pot to Billy. The five-man squad sat in relative quiet as they mixed the water with their coffee beans. Drinking coffee and trying to relax, the squad fought off the sounds of the engineers' work down at the river.

"The coffee…it's good, huh?" Solomon asked.

They all nodded and smiled, but nobody answered until Henry finally raised his cup. Then, with a salute, he said, "This is for you, James. It sure is good to have ya back on the march with us."

"To James," they all said in chorus, raising their cups.

"Thanks, Henry." James knew that Henry was like a brother to him. They'd *all* been, really. And it really was good to be back on the march with all of them, despite sore feet and an aching back and shoulders.

A little farther down the slope closer to the river, voices echoed. The squad looked in that direction and saw men gathering on the road again. Farther ahead, several mounted staff officers had begun bringing the men to attention. As the officers made their way toward the middle of the column and the Nineteenth Indiana, the squad stood up and began gathering their packs.

"Kick that fire out, Whitlow!" shouted Sergeant Boller, stomping toward the squad.

"Lighten up, Sarge," James said, attempting a smile.

"Fall in!" Boller shouted again, this time angrily kicking at the squad's fire, tipping the coffee pot into the ashes and coals.

Seeing Henry reaching for the coffee pot, Boller screamed again, "And you, Private Schultz, leave it there!"

Henry paused and, considering his options, stared at Boller.

"Go get in line, Schultz!" Sergeant Boller yelled again.

The two soldiers' eyes were locked on each other, both not wanting to back down. But Henry knew he *had* to. Finally giving in, he took a step toward the road where the column was just beginning to reform.

"Easy there, Sarge," Hawk said, trying to de-escalate the argument. "He just wants his coffee pot back, is all."

James, seeing the sarge's attention on Henry and Hawk, quickly walked over and intervened again. "Here ya go, Henry," James said, kicking the coffee pot in Henry's direction.

Sergeant Boller, seeing James's defiant act out of the corner of his eye, turned toward James. His face reddened with rage, and he stepped forward.

"No disrespect, Sarge," James said. "Just getting our coffee pot."

"And I said to leave it there, Whitlow!" Boller screamed, still approaching, hands out and ready to pounce.

"Sergeant Boller!" A new voice behind them yelled. They all turned and saw Sergeant Major Blanchard approaching. Blanchard then yelled again, "Private Whitlow! Stand down!"

The no-nonsense sergeant major stormed forward and jumped between James and Boller. "Now's not the time, men!" he yelled, giving them both a shove.

Boller, stepping forward again, yelled out, "You're a shirker, Whitlow!"

They all knew how ridiculous *that* sounded coming from the sergeant. In every battle they'd been in, once the shooting started, Boller had never been anywhere near the front line. James, on the other hand, had been wounded twice in battles, both times up front and facing the enemy. But still, James was infuriated by Boller's comment.

"You, Boller!" James screamed. "*You* are the shirker! And every man here knows it!"

Sergeant Major Blanchard turned toward James and started to say something else, but Hawk, seeing how angry James was, knew he had to step in.

"It's okay, Sergeant Major," Hawk said, grabbing James's arm. "I got him."

James wrestled his arm free and angrily threw down his hat. "No one calls *me* a shirker, Boller!"

"You're alright, James," Hawk said, giving him a push away from Boller and Blanchard. "Come on."

Solomon and Billy had stepped in too and helped calm James down. Sergeant Major Blanchard watched and, after waiting for Boller and James to finally step away from each other, turned and walked away without a comment.

"This way, James," Solomon said calmingly, leading his brother forward with the rest of the squad. "Forget about the sarge."

James took a deep breath, grabbed his hat, and slowly placed it back on his head. It'd be best to just move on, he knew.

Today had already been rough enough, and the way things were going, it wasn't likely to get any better. As the squad approached the four-wide column on the road, they each took their places in line. They faced north, and the Potomac River was just ahead.

Still fuming over Boller, James felt Hawk in the row behind him lean in close. James turned toward him, and Hawk grabbed his arm.

"Don't worry, James," Hawk whispered, letting go of James's arm. "We'll get him."

"Attention! Battalion!" the lieutenant colonel yelled and then paused while the men adjusted packs and straps. With officers watching, the regiment now stood ramrod straight and waited.

"Shoulder arms!... Forward! March!"

The column stepped off again and began down the hill. The completed pontoon bridge was just ahead. General Meredith, along with his staff, had pulled off the side of the road and was waiting at the bridge. Sitting tall atop his large black charger, the Iron Brigade's commander smiled and nodded to the men as they approached the bridge.

"We're not turning back now, James," Solomon said to his brother while taking in the spectacular scene of the army crossing the river.

"Nope, not without a fight we're not."

Stepping onto the bridge, James looked at the men around him. There were smiles, proud smiles, and from somewhere, he could hear the words of the *Battle Hymn of the Republic.* The song gathered strength, and soon, all the men, including their squad, joined in and sang too. With the wooden planks screeching against the pontoon boats to which they were nailed, the bridge rocked in the water as the weight of the army marched across.

The men marched with purpose now, and they could all feel the army's strength. Thoughts of previous battles and the army's failures were far from their minds as they approached the Maryland shore.

"Hey, James, look!" It was Henry, pointing back up the slope behind them.

Running beside the column and toward the bridge was James's dog. Tongue out, panting, and with his tail wagging, he ran alongside the men until reaching the crowded bridge.

The men of Company B turned and began shouting.

"Here, boy!"

James smiled wide and yelled too. The whole company had embraced their new pet ever since he'd joined them.

"Come on!" Henry shouted, encouraging him down the hill and onto the bridge.

Several more men joined in and cheered too. Billy laughed and pointed when the dog jumped onto the planks and darted around men along the side of the bridge.

Hawk whistled in a way that only Hawk could, and more men laughed.

"Eyes forward, men!" shouted the sergeant, obviously perturbed by the men's attention to the company's new pet.

"We're still movin', Sarge," James quickly responded.

Sergeant Boller, still upset about the earlier encounter with James, stopped at the side of the column. He was waiting on the bridge as the men continued past.

"What ya doin', Sarge?" Grear Williams shouted from a few rows back. Boller ignored him and continued looking toward the rear.

"He's waiting for our dog," Solomon said.

The sergeant smirked.

"What's he gonna do?" James asked.

None of them were sure, but the sergeant was fixated on the dog as it sprinted closer. Recognizing his friends in the squad just ahead, the dog raced closer.

Boller's smirk reddened into an angry scowl.

Still at a full trot, their dog was only a few feet away, but Boller had stepped toward the edge of the bridge, putting himself directly in his path.

"Leave him alone, Sarge!" Hawk shouted.

"Sarge, no!" James yelled.

But it was too late. The sergeant's face was embroiled with rage as he jumped at the dog with a kick. The dog, in his attempt to evade the sergeant's boot, fought to balance himself along the bridge's beam.

Men yelled, but Boller wasn't done. He lunged at the dog again and, with another kick, sent him toppling over the edge. The dog yelped and then splashed into the water.

The men heard a desperate bark, and then the dog disappeared with the current underneath the bridge.

Hawk, full of rage, sprang at the sergeant.

"It's not worth it!" Billy shouted, jumping between Hawk and Boller.

"Billy's right, Hawk," James said, grabbing Hawk by the arm and holding him back. "He ain't worth it."

"You're a dead man, Boller! That's our dog! You're dead!"

Sergeant Boller, chest puffed out and arms crossed, laughed. Hawk's face was red with rage. Desperately wanting to get to Boller, he fought his squadmates to free himself.

Solomon and James both had him now and tried to calm him down. "It's okay, Hawk," James said. "We'll get our chance. Not here. Not now."

"I'm fine...lemme go!" Hawk shouted. "I'll get my chance at him. Lemme go."

"Let him go," James said softly, nodding at Solomon and Henry, who slowly released their grip on Hawk. "Come on, keep marchin', Hawk."

Hawk knew they were right—now wasn't the time, and slowly, he got back in line.

"Look!" Billy yelled from the right side of the column and pointing into the water.

"The dog! He's swimming!" another soldier shouted.

"Go, boy!"

The entire company looked on and cheered. James's dog had now drifted between two of the pontoons and was paddling desperately for the far shore.

"He's gonna make it, James!" Solomon said, excitedly clutching James's arm.

"He'd better," Hawk said, still irate. Then, under his breath, he muttered, "For the sarge's sake."

The Indiana men slowly resumed the march across the bridge but kept an eye on the dog. Sergeant Boller, who still hadn't moved from the same spot, glared at the squad. Other soldiers, also having witnessed the sergeant's behavior, stared at him loathingly as they passed.

James and his squadmates finally stepped off the bridge and onto the dirt path leading up to the road. Off to the right, James's dog had also made it across. The men watched as he waded through the water and up onto the shore. After shaking himself off, the wet dog trotted up the slope and disappeared into the weeds.

"I'm glad he made it," Billy said with a smile, slapping James on the back.

Hawk, on the other side of Billy, however, wasn't smiling. With a sneer, he said, "Boller…he's gonna get his due."

"Forget it, Hawk," James said. "It's okay."

Hawk didn't respond as they marched through the trampled weeds away from the river.

A few moments later, just to change the subject, Solomon exclaimed, "We're in Maryland, boys!"

"Maryland!" another man shouted, which led to another chorus of *John Brown's Body*. Zigzagging their way up the slope, the column turned onto another dirt road. Cresting a ridge, they could see miles of wide-open fields, occasionally dotted with enormous, red barns. The long blue column stretched as far as the eye could see, disappearing into the hills of the northern horizon.

James settled into a steady pace with the other men in the brigade. Up ahead, he could hear drums and fifes being played by the drummer boys near the front of the regiment. Several miles past the bridge, James had his head down looking at the dirt in front of him when he suddenly heard Lieutenant Schlagle's voice.

"Private Whitlow," Schlagle called from the side of the column.

James looked up. The lieutenant was on foot and holding his horse's reins walking beside him.

"Uhhh, yes sir," James said, realizing Schlagle was talking to him. Although the lieutenant's voice startled him, it didn't seem angry like it was before crossing the river several miles back. He was puzzled that the lieutenant was singling him out during the march.

"Come here, James," the lieutenant said, his voice pleasant. "Walk with me. Okay if I call you James?"

James quickened his step and moved to the side to join the lieutenant. "Yes sir, Lieutenant. Of course, sir."

James lowered his head slightly after answering and felt awkward walking with an officer in front of the other enlisted men. He suddenly thought of Sergeant Boller and their encounter at the bridge. He looked around but couldn't see him.

"James, how long have you been back with us now?" Lieutenant Schlagle asked. "A week?"

"Uhh, yes sir...about five days I think."

"How's your foot doing…from the wound at Fitzhugh Crossing?" Lieutenant Schlagle asked, watching James carefully and showing concern.

"I think fine, sir. This is really the first long march I've done on it since leaving Alexandria, sir." James and the lieutenant stepped to the side slightly to wait for a gap in the column so they could get around a large tree that had encroached on the road. As they rejoined the side of the column, a few sprinkles began to fall.

"I hope the rain holds off," the lieutenant said, looking up.

"Yes sir, us too."

"Anyway, James, I saw what happened on the bridge back there." He paused, waiting for James's response, which was only a slight nod. "You kept your cool, and I thank you for that. Sergeant Boller is a troubled man, as you know."

"Uhh, yes sir. He's *difficult*, sir," James replied, choosing his words carefully.

"I think he will be fine in the upcoming battle though, wouldn't you agree?"

"I'm not sure. I wouldn't want to speak unfavorably, sir. And I've been away for a while, sir." James paused, unsure where the lieutenant wanted to go with the conversation.

"James, I want you to watch over the squad closely for me…and even Sergeant Boller." James noticed the lieutenant was staring at him now as they walked.

"Sir?"

"Your squad has been missing a corporal since Fredericksburg, and it's important some of you seasoned veterans really keep an eye on things. And we're really glad to have you back, James. And God knows we're gonna need every man in the upcoming fight."

"Uhhh, yes sir. I'm afraid you're right."

James, feeling somewhat awkward, paused and looked around. Out of the corner of his eye, he caught a glimpse of the sergeant watching them from the opposite side of the column.

"And thank you, sir," James continued. "I'm glad to be back."

"This war, James…it's changed now that Lee's army is moving into the North. It's about more than just saving the Union or abolishing slavery now, ya see. They're invading *us*. And now we're defending *our* homes—at least the Pennsylvanians' homes. It's different now than fightin' back in Virginia. The Rebs were defending *their* homes then, but now we're defending *ours*."

"Yes sir. I think we're ready for a fight, sir."

"I understand your brother knows General Meredith up there?" the lieutenant asked, nodding toward the brigade's vanguard up ahead.

"Yes, sir. He met him at college…in Richmond. And my father knew him too. I remember Pa talkin' about Mister Meredith before we signed up. Henry and Hawk know him too. I think Hawk, in between orphan houses, might have even worked for him when Hawk was a kid…at General Meredith's farm back in Indiana."

Lieutenant Schlagle, apparently already knowing that story, smiled and said, "The general is a good man."

"Uh, yes sir, we think so too."

"I heard that Abe Lincoln calls him his only Quaker general in the Army."

"Uhhh…yes, sir," James said. "I've heard the President had said that."

"Well, he sure stands out on that horse, doesn't he?" the lieutenant asked with a laugh, looking ahead at Meredith. "*Long Sol*, they call him. Quite fitting I should say."

"Yes, it is."

"Your father…did he name your brother after him?" the lieutenant asked, speaking of Solomon.

"Oh, no. I don't think so, sir. We was born in Kentucky. Moved up to Richmond 'bout ten years ago. I don't think he would've heard of him then. Although everyone seemed to know Mr. Meredith around Richmond. He'd been the sheriff and US Marshall there. A congressman too, I think. How 'bout you, Lieutenant? What'd you do before the war?"

"I was a brickmaker," Schlagle responded with a laugh. "Never dreamed I'd be doing this."

"Me neither," James said with a fading smile as he thought about the last two years.

"What did *you* do before the war, James?"

"We were farmers…had a horse farm down in Kentucky, then moved up to Ohio…just east of Richmond, Indiana."

Lieutenant Schlagle nodded and smiled. "Horses? Ya think 'bout the cavalry?"

As James was about to answer, they heard a commotion farther up in the column. James could see the vanguard approaching a town where several civilians stood outside waving American flags.

"Excuse me, Private Whitlow," Lieutenant Schlagle said, turning serious. "I must attend to the company for a moment. But thank you for speaking with me, James." The lieutenant extended his hand and smiled.

"Thank you, Lieutenant, sir," James replied, shaking Schlagle's hand. After Lieutenant Schlagle turned and sped ahead, James returned to his place in the column. Out of the corner of his eye, he noticed Sergeant Boller's glowering stare. James ignored him and quickly turned away.

A steady drizzle was falling as the Nineteenth Indiana reached the outskirts of the town. Both sides of the street were filled with people. Women offered bread, water, and milk. And children, waving flags, cheered and sang.

"What town is this?" Solomon asked a young school-age girl at the side of the road.

"This is Poolesville, sir," she said, reaching out and offering him a cup of milk and a warm smile. "Poolesville, Maryland."

"Thank you," Solomon said after drinking the milk and handing back her cup. It was just before dark now as the army passed through the town. The brigade band played, and the soldiers sang, even after the tail end of the column was well beyond the town.

With the townspeople's waves and cheers far behind them now, the army continued to the north in a steady, cool rain. The dusty road had turned to mud, and the tired army plodded along in the dark. Finally, footsore and hungry, the Iron Brigade's tired soldiers trudged into camp near Barnesville, Maryland, eighteen miles from where they had started that day.

*****

A few hours later, approaching midnight, Private Hawkins kept a close eye on Sergeant Boller's lantern and watched for any movement in that direction. Most of the rest of the regiment had taken to their tents by now, and among their small squad, Hawk and James were the only ones still awake. Even James's dog had his eyes closed. He was lying just a few feet away from the men, and although asleep, his ears still perked up every time the fire crackled.

"Better stoke that log one more time, James," Hawk said.

"Yeah, sure. I'll get it," James replied. He then stood and poked at the log which sent a shower of sparks rising skyward.

Hawk used the chance to again look over at the sergeant's tent. The lantern was still hanging from the tree branch nearby, but he could see Sergeant Boller's shadow against the trees beyond the fire. The sergeant had been sitting just outside his tent and, for at least the past half hour, been talking with a lieutenant from one of the other companies. Finally, a few minutes ago, the lieutenant had gotten up and left. Now, Sergeant Boller was alone.

Hawk watched closely and could see the sergeant walk in front of the lantern. A small orange light flared up from the end of Boller's cigar as he leaned down close to his fire. As Boller reached for a pike at the fire's edge, his open coat exposed a pistol on his right hip.

"What you lookin' at, Hawk?"

James's voice startled him and made him realize he had been a little too obvious about watching Sergeant Boller's camp.

"Oh, nothin', James," Hawk said, quickly turning his attention toward the fire. Then, trying to change the subject, he looked up from the fire and toward the clouds above. "Looks like the rain's finally done."

But James, not letting it go, said, "You've been watchin' the sarge over there, Hawk." He let the comment hang in the air, hoping for a reply. None came, and James prodded. "He's been kinda rough on us all, huh?"

Hawk's face had curled into an angry scowl. His eyes were menacing and vengeful. After several seconds, he finally responded. "We'd all be better off if he *disappears.*"

The comment caught James by surprise. He immediately looked around at the nearby tents, nervously checking for any eavesdroppers. The camp was still quiet except for the restless groans and coughs of sleeping soldiers. Other than James and Hawk's campfire, Sergeant Boller's was one of only a few in the area still burning.

James stood up to pull his log closer to the fire and then sat back down. He nervously looked at the tents behind him again and then back at the fire. After carefully considering whether to say something about what Hawk had said, he finally whispered, "Uhhh, what do you mean, Hawk? About… *disappearing?*"

The orange glow of the flames and sparks illuminated an angry determination on Hawk's face. He stared into the fire for several seconds before finally turning toward James. "There's gonna be a huge battle in a few days, James," he said in a hushed voice. "A lot can happen in the smoke and chaos. We all know 'bout that. Many a good boy will die. And the sergeant...well, he'll probably die with 'em. That's all I'm sayin'."

"Don't do it, Hawk. He ain't worth it."

Hawk didn't respond at first, instead concentrating on the flames again. His face seemed to soften, almost as if a peace had settled over him. As he started to speak again, the slowness of his words showed James that he had chosen them carefully.

"Maybe the sarge will get better in the next few days, James. So, forget I'd said it. Okay?"

"Sure, Hawk." James meant it too. He wouldn't dare say anything to anyone. Hawk had been too good of a friend for the past two years to betray him like that.

James watched him carefully, looking for any sign of emotion. There was none. Hawk just stared into the fire. Even when the sergeant, a few dozen yards away, walked toward the edge of the woods with his lantern, Hawk didn't flinch or seem to even care.

Finally, James decided to speak again. It was something about Hawk that he and Solomon couldn't figure out.

"Sol said you knew something about Sergeant Boller... that he'd done something...in the past? Was it anything that had to do with you? Or the rest of us?"

James's question had caught Hawk off guard. Hawk smiled and opened his mouth to speak. He hesitated, though, and looked away. When he turned toward James again, his smile was gone and his look was serious. James could tell that Hawk wanted to answer him but knew that he shouldn't. It was something that had haunted Hawk for a while, James knew. Maybe it was even why he fought.

Over by Sergeant Boller's camp, a tin cup clanged. Hawk glanced that direction, scoffed, and then returned his stare into the fire.

"Why *did* you sign up to fight, Hawk?" James finally dared asking.

"It was a long time ago, the thing with Boller," Hawk said, breaking his silence without looking away from the fire. "But *why do I fight*, you ask? This is all I got, James. This war. Just this squad, really. You and Sol and Henry. And Billy too now, I guess…now that he's with us. But I don't really give a damn 'bout this war no more to tell the truth, though."

Hawk paused and spat in the fire.

James just watched, listening. He wondered about that last thing Hawk said because he still hated Rebels, that's for sure. And they had all wondered why.

"I was an orphan, ya know," Hawk continued. When he looked up across the fire, his eyes didn't show sadness like James had figured they would. But they showed anger…a deep, troubling anger too. "You guys are all I got. First thing I've ever had since I was a kid, really. The army…I guess it's where I belong. You all have families back home, and I'm happy for that. Couldn't ever fault a man for havin' something I don't. But not me. You all *are* my family, James."

James decided it was best to not say anything, but instead, he just sat on his log and stared into the fire. Hawk had never spoken about something so personal like this, and neither one of them spoke for several long minutes.

"You're our brother too, Hawk," James finally said. "All of us."

Hawk put his head down and nodded at the fire. James could tell that his comment had meant a lot.

James looked around the quiet camp, and his thoughts turned to the aches that engulfed his entire body. Seeing his dog lying sound asleep only a few feet away made James think of his own sleep.

"I think I'm gonna go lie down, Hawk."

Without looking up, Hawk responded, "Ya better. We're all gonna need some good rest, James. Tomorrow's settin' up to be another long march, I'm afraid."

"I think you're right."

"Hey, James..." Hawk said and then paused to clear his throat.

"Yeah?"

"Thanks for covering our backs today...with the sarge."

"You too, Hawk. We're all in this together."

"Yeah, we are."

"You have a good night."

"You too. G'night."

*****

For over an hour, Hawk stayed up and waited. It was well after midnight before the sergeant had finally gotten up again, retrieved his lantern, and walked into the woods to relieve himself.

Now, careful to not make a sound, Hawk stepped softly and quietly through the woods. Just ahead, he could see the glow of the sergeant's lantern only a few yards away. Hawk knew that beyond a few feet, Boller would be nearly blind with the lantern next to him in the deep, black woods.

Hawk had always known how to operate silently at night, but over the past two years, he'd nearly perfected those skills. Tonight, it would be critical. For Hawk, this should be much easier than what he'd done in Kentucky. *That* seemed like a lifetime ago. There were five of them *then*, but now it was just one man. But still, you had to be careful; there was no telling how a man would react or what he could do when his life was at stake.

He slowly crept closer and was now only a few feet from the sergeant's turned back. Although Boller had freed one hand by setting his lantern on the ground beside him, his other hand was occupied holding a lit cigar to his mouth.

Totally silent to this point, Hawk had his knife extended and was ready to close the last few feet. He looked around the woods one last time and listened carefully for any other threats. He took a deep breath. Then, in one fluid sweep, he flung his left hand around the sergeant's waist and removed the revolver while his right hand pressed the knife firmly against the sergeant's neck.

"*Don't moooove,*" Hawk hissed quietly, directly into the sergeant's ear, catching him totally by surprise. The lantern's glow illuminated a small line of blood forming just below the knife's blade. Sergeant Boller immediately knew any movement would mean a slow, painful death.

"You listenin', Sarge?"

Unable to nod with the knife against his throat, Boller mumbled something that sounded like "*yes.*"

"You get this, Sarge. And you don't forget it…"

Another faint "*yes.*"

"You leave our squad alone, Sarge."

"*Ummhuhh.*"

The sergeant squirmed, and the knife pressed tighter.

"If you say a word to James, Solomon, Henry, or Billy," Hawk hissed into his ear. "…If you say a word to any of us, yur dead. You got it?"

"I got it. But…I know what you did…*in Kentucky.*"

Hawk froze. Caught off guard by Boller's comment, he almost dropped the knife. Quickly, though, he composed himself and tightened his grip.

"You don't know anything," Hawk whispered.

Boller felt the knife being pressed even tighter against his throat now. The trickle of blood felt warm as it seeped down below his shirt. Careful not to move his neck, Boller took a deep breath before speaking again.

"You can't kill me, Hawk. What you did before the war down there…there's others that know too."

"I'll kill ya anyway," Hawk growled.

Boller squirmed, knowing he meant it.

Hawk looked around the woods and, putting his mouth right against Boller's ear, whispered, "And the general…he saw what you did on the bridge. Me and General Meredith go way back, Boller…back to when I was a kid. The lieutenant too. So don't even think 'bout mentioning any of this. You hear me?"

Hawk paused, letting what he'd said sink in.

Then, pressing the knife deeper, he said, "You leave our squad alone or you're dead, you got it?"

"*I…I…got it,*" the sergeant finally uttered.

"*Dead!*"

Hawk suddenly removed the knife and gave the sergeant a hard shove to the back of the neck. With Boller falling forward to the ground, Hawk quickly crept away in the dark and back toward the camp.

-9-

Five days later...

Near Marsh Creek
North of Pennsylvania-Maryland Border
July 1, 1863, Early Morning

For five days since crossing the Potomac River into Maryland, the Union Army, now commanded by General George Meade who had replaced General Hooker, had marched northward in pursuit of General Lee's army which was now spread out all through South Central Pennsylvania. The Confederates were as far north as the Susquehanna River and even threatening the state capital at Harrisburg.

The Union First Corps with over ten thousand men had taken the lead on the march and had completed over eighty miles during those five days, often on rain-soaked roads with mud several inches deep. The Iron Brigade, along with the rest of the Union First Corps, had crossed the Mason-Dixon Line into Pennsylvania on June 30th in a steady, drenching rain.

Although the rest of the brigade had gone into bivouac around Marsh Creek, the Nineteenth Indiana was sent two miles farther north up the road and assigned night picket duty. This made the Indiana soldiers the farthest north and the closest

124

to the Confederates of all the Union infantry units.

Company B scouted even farther ahead and, sometime before midnight, took up a position west of the Emmitsburg Road. With squads now split into two-man picket details, James and Solomon had chosen a spot against a stone wall about halfway between the road and a stone farmhouse and barn.

So far, the night had been quiet, and the only disturbance was several hours ago when, around midnight, they had seen a Union horseman hurriedly galloping up the road. Since then, however, the brothers had been passing the time trying to stay warm and as dry as possible in almost total silence. The rain shower had finally let up, but a light drizzle and fog still blanketed the area. Even cowered under their thick blue coats, the two brothers felt the cold and dampness through their clothes.

Suddenly, Solomon thought he had heard noises and quickly looked up.

James's dog Moses, lying a few yards away with his head on his paws, had heard the sounds too and was looking to the north.

Solomon listened carefully and then heard hoofbeats coming down the road.

Reaching over, Solomon gave his brother a shake on the arm.

"Pssst, James...horses," Solomon whispered to his brother. "Wake up, wake up."

Solomon looked toward the road. Billy and Grear, picketing closer to the road, had also heard the noises and were both standing up.

"They're coming from the north," Solomon said to James who was now rubbing his eyes and waking up.

Moses, ears fully erect, trotted out in front of the two brothers. He whimpered, then glanced back toward James and Solomon before returning his attention toward the horses. He could feel the tension too.

"Shhhh…easy, Moses," Solomon whispered, slowly raising his Springfield onto the fence rail. Glancing over at James, he saw that he was now wide awake and had raised his musket too.

"See anything yet?" James asked, staring through the darkness toward the sounds out on the road.

"Not yet, but they're coming this way," Solomon said, staring through his gunsight into the fog and mist. But having been on picket duty all night, his tired eyes strained to see.

Hooves pounded the road, closer now.

"There they are," Solomon whispered while keeping his rifle aimed on the target. James saw them too, and finally, they were both able to make out two horsemen riding at a fast gallop. They were coming from the direction of the town about five miles away and passing from north to south. As the horsemen rode closer to the two brothers' picket spot, the Whitlows fought the darkness to make out any of their features. The veterans had learned early on during the war that they could never be too careful about identifying friendly soldiers versus the enemy.

"What do you think?" Solomon whispered, his heart racing.

James stared and paused before answering. "They're ours… cavalry," he said, making out the yellow markings of the two riders' uniforms in the dark.

"Yeah, I see 'em now," Solomon whispered back. Taking a deep breath and lowering his rifle, he said, "They're definitely ours…cavalry."

Over on the Emmitsburg Road, several shouts pierced the night air as the riders approached the Nineteenth's pickets. Beyond Billy and Grear, several other small squads, mostly from Company K, were stationed at the road and had it blocked with fence posts. The riders, approaching the pickets, barked out commands to clear the road. The cavalrymen barely even slowed, and as they passed, they spurred their horses southward to a full gallop again.

"Those guys are in a hurry, James," Solomon said as the riders disappeared in the darkness.

"Yeah, probably cavalry couriers," James replied, now wide awake. "Some of Buford's men riding toward General Reynolds to bring up the infantry and get 'em headed toward that town."

Both brothers knew that the Union cavalry under General John Buford was in the area. They'd seen several of the cavalry's casualties down in Virginia and, for the past several days, had heard of more skirmishes in the mountains just to the west. As General Lee's army invaded deeper into Pennsylvania, it was the Union cavalry's job to follow, observe, and report on the Confederates. And now, General Reynolds's First Corps of infantry and the Nineteenth Indiana were only a few miles behind.

"That means we're gonna be movin' soon, James."

"Afraid so. Anything goin' on over by Hawk and Henry?" James asked, looking toward their squadmates near the barn.

"They're still there. I don't think they even heard the horses. I still see Henry's candle glowing though."

"It's probably Henry writing in that silly diary of his," James quipped.

"Maybe," Solomon laughed. "And one day, James, when this is all over, we'll all get together and read it. ...At a big reunion, years from now."

"If any of us make it out of this war alive, ya mean."

Solomon chuckled but knew his brother was probably right, especially considering the number of casualties the regiment had already suffered. Quickly changing the subject, Solomon said, "Tough night to get assigned picket duty."

"The rain hasn't helped us get any rest, that's for sure," James replied. "It'll be daylight in a few hours. And there's sure to be a lot of marchin' again tomorrow, Sol."

"That's not gonna help my feet none," Solomon said.

"They still okay?" James asked. "Since you got the new brogans back in Frederick a couple days ago?"

"Yeah, they're just a li'l sore, but they're fine. I'd rather be resting them, for sure."

"Well, the good thing is that we'll have less to march in the mornin' since we're already way out here."

"Yeah," Solomon said. "Guess if the army's still marchin' north, we'll be waiting on 'em here."

"Those two cavalrymen…," James said, then paused.

"Yeah?"

"They were ridin' with a purpose, weren't they?"

"Yeah, they weren't riding like that just to get to breakfast early," Solomon quipped. "And those civilians we saw yesterday fleein' the town sure were spooked."

"What ya gettin' at, Sol?"

"Well, we overheard that one lady say that the Rebels had come all the way up to the edge of the town around noon. Then they got chased away by General Buford's cavalry." Solomon paused while repositioning himself on his blanket against the fence. "I thought the Johnnies were up by Harrisburg… and York…not this close, way down here. We're barely into Pennsylvania, James."

James started to open his mouth to respond but stopped as if a revelation had just come over him. He looked over at Solomon, who had reached into his haversack and pulled out a hardtack cracker. After breaking it into two pieces, he ate half and tossed the rest to James's dog who had apparently dismissed the riders of a few minutes ago as not being a threat.

"You know he won't eat that, Sol," James said. "He only eats meat. Here, Moses…here, boy, eat this," he said, throwing a piece of dried pork toward the dog.

"That's why he's your dog, not mine, James," Solomon

said. "Why'd ya name him 'Moses' anyway?"

"Well, first off, Sol, he's not *my* dog. He's just followin' us a while, that's all."

"He's *yours* now," Solomon said, laughing and pointing at the dog quickly devouring the pork.

"Lieutenant Schlagle came up with the name. *Moses*, as in Moses parting the sea…leading us across the Potomac. Pretty smart, huh?"

James smiled and watched the dog lick his mouth and sniff the ground for crumbs before lying back down.

"That's a good idea, Moses," James said while adjusting his gum blanket and lying back down himself. He stared up at the night sky and the low, hanging clouds slowly drifting past. The drizzle had finally stopped, and the light of the moon and a few stars began to poke through from above.

"Ya know what, Sol?" James asked.

"Hmmm?"

"If the Rebs are near that town up ahead, and if Buford's cav are in the town…"

"Yeah?"

James stared up at the clouds and thought for a moment before continuing. "There's gonna be a fight today, Sol."

"I'm 'fraid so." Solomon's voice had a nervous edge to it. "We ain't been marchin' like this for nothin'."

"If we get into a big fight today, Sol, let's watch out for each other."

"We always do," Solomon said. "It's not like we haven't seen the elephant before."

"Ain't that the truth. This time feels different though, ya know?"

"Yeah, I know. I feel it too." Solomon paused while he stared out toward the road, then turned in the other direction toward the farm. He saw Henry in the candlelight and then thought about some of the comments Henry had been making during the past few days.

"Not a peep tonight from Hawk and Henry," James said, noticing Solomon looking in that direction.

"Ya know, James, Henry's been sayin' some strange things lately."

"Watcha mean?"

"He does a lotta prayin', ya know. A couple nights ago, when we was back near Frederick, he was prayin' and then started shakin' real bad. He sounded scared." Thinking about what a good friend Henry had been, Solomon hesitated and looked through the darkness toward Hawk and Henry. The glow of Henry's candle was still visible, and a few feet away, he could see that Hawk was also awake, kneeling down and apparently working with something on the ground.

"Anyway, James, I don't wanna say nothin' bad 'bout him. He's been a good soldier…and a great friend. But the war…it's been tough on him."

"The war's been tough on all of us, Sol," James said, still lying on his back and staring at the sky.

"But it's worse for him in a way," Solomon said. "Being a Quaker, this war is hell itself. Weren't even supposed to fight at all. Anyway, James…the day we did almost thirty miles up from Frederick…well, he was sayin' some scary stuff."

"Like what?"

"I dunno, James. I think I'm the only one that was supposed to hear it. But he was sayin' he couldn't do no more killin'…and that he *wouldn't* do no more killin'."

Solomon paused and noticed that, over by the barn, Henry's candle had gone dark.

"What'd he mean?" James asked. When Solomon didn't answer and just shook his head, James sat up and asked, "So what's he gonna do?"

"I'm not sure. At first it didn't mean much to me, but then the other night when he was prayin' again... I wasn't tryin' to eavesdrop on him or nothin', James. I swear, I wouldn't do that to a guy prayin', ya know? But he was getting all scared again and sweatin' and shakin' while he was talkin' to God."

Pondering what Solomon was saying, James said, "Go on. What was he sayin' exactly?"

Solomon looked toward Henry and Hawk's camp again. It was totally dark and quiet. "He was prayin' to God to give him the strength to get him home."

"We all do that, Sol. We all pray to get home."

"But then he said...*through the lines.*"

James's heart nearly stopped when Solomon said it.

"*Through the lines?*" James asked. "As in...*desert?*"

"I think that's what he meant, James. And then he said *tomorrow night.*"

James sat up straighter and looked over toward their squadmates' picket spot again. "That's *tonight*, Sol."

"Yeah, I know. But I just saw him over there a little while ago."

"There ain't nothin' we can do 'bout it now, Sol. But in the morning, we gotta talk to him. Desertion is death, Sol."

"*War* is death for him, James. I see what he's thinking. Sorry I brought it up. I don't like talkin' 'bout people, especially about their prayin' 'n' all."

James was still staring in the darkness, looking for any movement from Henry and Hawk. Brooding over Solomon's comments about Henry, he hesitated before finally speaking. "You should've told me earlier."

"I shouldn't have told you at all," Solomon shot right back.

"The good news is that Hawk wouldn't let him desert," James said. "Hell, he'd chase him down himself if he did."

"Yur probably right. Hawk hates deserters. You notice him smiling when they shot Private Woods?"

Over by the barn, there was movement again in their squadmates' camp. They both saw heads moving about and let out a collective sigh of relief...apparently, at least for now anyway, things with Henry were okay after all.

"Go on and go back to sleep, James."

"Nah, I'm wide awake now. It's your turn."

*****

It was a couple hours later when, off in the distance, the echo of a bugle startled Solomon awake.

"Dang mosquitos," he mumbled, flicking one away on his arm. Opening his eyes, he saw James a few yards away. James had a small fire going, and his tin cup full of water hung just above it.

"Good morning," James said, looking up from his fire.

"Mornin'," Solomon mumbled back. He turned and looked to the northeast where the first hint of gray light could be seen above the trees. Through the mist, he could barely hear a harmonica. Billy's, he assumed. Listening closely, he was able to pick up some of the notes.

"Sometimes, I wish he wouldn't play that song, James."

James scooted back from his fire and listened too. "*Home, Sweet Home?*" he asked.

"Yeah."

"Sometimes," James said, "I think it was the worst thing Hawk ever did...giving Billy that damned thing. And other times..."

James didn't finish his sentence but, instead, stood up and shook the dew and moisture from his coat. He liked Billy. Even though they'd all teased him at first when he'd joined the squad, he'd grown on them. It took Hawk the longest to come around and finally accept Billy. *Willy Willy*, Hawk had called him at first, making fun of his name. Hawk didn't like the bow tie he wore when they first met him either. And quoting Shakespeare didn't help, not to someone like Hawk.

But it didn't take Hawk long to realize that wearing a bow tie and being able to read classics learned at a formal school had nothing to do with whether someone was tough or not. Billy'd proven that, and not just with his lucky punch on Hawk's lip that day either, but also at Manassas, and South Mountain, and every battle since.

Looking toward Hawk and Henry, James saw they were busy doing something or another over there.

Solomon slowly stood up too and looked around. "Was that morning reveille I heard a little bit ago?" he asked.

"Yeah, I think so," James replied, nodding back toward where the rest of the brigade was bivouacked. "They must've got the army up early this morning."

"You mean everyone else who's not out here on picket duty? At least *they* were all able to get some sleep."

James chuckled but didn't respond, knowing it best to not dwell on it. "Coffee?" he asked.

"Sure."

"I've already got some beans crushed. Here, take these."

"Thanks," Solomon said, grabbing the small pan. After filling his own cup with water and setting it in the fire, he looked toward the barn. He smiled when he saw Henry and Hawk over there awake and fumbling with their knapsacks. "What are Hawk and Henry doing?"

"I dunno," James replied. "They've been up for a while. I see the other pickets stirring around too."

After looking away from Hawk and Henry and moving his blanket closer to the fire, Solomon sat back down and began mixing his coffee grains into his cup. "At least the rain stopped," he said, looking up into the gray, pre-dawn sky.

James didn't respond to Solomon's comment but, instead, also looked to the sky and smiled. He was glad the rain had stopped… marching in the rain was the worst. The two brothers then sat in silence for several minutes with their coffee until they heard the faint sound of another bugle call. Looking in the direction of camp where the bugle had sounded, they saw Lieutenant Schlagle approaching on foot.

"We're bringing in the pickets in a li'l while," the lieutenant said, scanning the horizon as he knelt down on one knee next to the fire. After removing his leather gloves and placing them on his trousers, he began rubbing his hands together over the fire.

"Coffee, Lieutenant?" Solomon asked.

"No thanks, Sol."

"How'd you do out here last night?" Schlagle asked.

"Fine, sir," Solomon responded.

"Any Rebs?"

"No, sir. Just a couple cavalry guys out on the road, is all," James said. "Pretty quiet night."

"Good…good. We're gonna form up over on the road in 'bout an hour. The whole First Corps is gonna be movin' up the road to the north. The Nineteenth will stay here 'til the rest of the brigade forms up back at the camp. We'll join 'em on the road…right over there. I'll send the sergeant major out here when it's time to form up."

"Thank you, sir."

The lieutenant gave each of them a quick slap on the back as he got up and rushed off to the next group of pickets.

A little over an hour later, just after dawn, the signal came to bring in the pickets. The gray dawn had given way to scattered rays of sunshine poking through the clouds. A bugle call rang out. And then another. A few minutes later, mess pans, canteens, tin cups, and the sounds of hundreds of men breaking camp echoed through the fields.

"Good morning, Sol!" It was Henry, walking a few steps ahead of Hawk and approaching from their picket spot near the barn. Both Henry and Hawk had already gathered up their gear and, as they walked up, were wearing their packs and had their muskets on their shoulders.

"Got any coffee made yet?" Hawk asked.

"Yep, help yourself," Solomon replied.

"Hawk, you go out 'n' get any good food last night?" James asked.

"Nah, it rained a little, so I just stayed wrapped up in my gum blanket all night," Hawk said with a deadpan, serious face.

"Really?" Solomon asked.

"What do you think, Sol?" Henry interrupted. His grin gave away the secret.

Hawk burst out laughing, then spun around and lifted the top of his knapsack, exposing the bloodstained, white feathers of a headless chicken.

"Chicken for lunch sound alright to everybody?" Hawk asked, still laughing. "I figure we'll all be eatin' real good on that first stop today. Ain't that right, Henry? Hell, boys, Henry here even helped me. He's startin' to fit right in with all this army life."

"Ya better close that flap 'fore the sarge comes around," Solomon said.

"Nah, the sergeant don't mess with us no more. He's alright. He's moved on to them Madison County boys in Company A to pick on."

"What's he doin' with Company A?" James asked. "He's just a sergeant. Shouldn't he stay in our company?"

"He's gotten all close with their captain. I heard he broke up a fight between a couple of Anderson boys. Their captain likes him now. Hell, I saw him hangin' out at Boller's fire a couple nights ago. The way I see it…it's all the better for us with him gone."

Several shouts out by the Emmitsburg Road interrupted the conversation. All four of the squadmates looked in that direction and saw Lieutenant Schlagle talking with several other officers. Dozens of the Nineteenth's men had gathered in the wheat field close to the road.

"Looks like we're gonna be movin' pretty soon," Solomon said.

"I think I hear drums now," James said, looking farther down the road to the south.

"Yep, guess we're marching."

After kicking out the fire, the squad hoisted their knapsacks onto their backs and slung their haversacks and cartridge boxes over their shoulders. The four Indiana men spent a few minutes adjusting their gear for the march before finally turning and facing the road.

"Ready?" James asked, picking up his rifle.

"Sure. Where's the party?" Hawk chimed in with a laugh.

"Let's go," James said, turning toward the road. As the squad walked along the fence, they could see that almost the entire regiment had gathered in a farmer's lane near the road. Off to the right and coming up the road from the south was the vanguard of the Second Brigade.

"Looks like General Cutler's gonna be leadin' the march this morning," James said, watching as several mounted officers confidently rode past. Just behind the officers, a team of drummer boys led the long column of infantry that marched steadily forward. The Indiana men looked on as General Cutler's brigade of Pennsylvanians and New Yorkers marched past on the muddy road. Behind General Cutler's infantry, several six-horse teams trudged past pulling black three-inch ordnance rifles and ammunition wagons.

"That's Captain Hall's battery," Solomon said over the noise of wagon wheels screeching and rumbling under the weight of iron cannons and fully loaded ammunition chests. "It's strange that they're going ahead of the rest of the infantry."

"Yeah, I agree," James said.

"Looks like we're gonna get a little break," Solomon said, noticing that the Nineteenth still hadn't been given any orders to fall in with the marching column.

"We'll get our chance," Hawk said. "Just lettin' Cutler's brigade muddy up the road a little more for us."

"Here comes our brigade now," Solomon said, pointing back to the south.

At the head of the next group of infantry, the Iron Brigade band—all members of the Sixth Wisconsin regiment—were leading the Second and Seventh Wisconsin regiments. The two fellow veteran Iron Brigade regiments filed past in columns of four as the Indiana men watched on. Next in line coming over the horizon was the Twenty-Fourth Michigan regiment.

Just as the vanguard of the large Michigan regiment approached, there was a flurry of activity and excitement from a group of arriving staff officers.

"There's General Meredith," James said as the Iron Brigade's commander approached and then reined in his horse, stopping just in front of the Twenty-Fourth Michigan.

"Colonel Morrow!" Meredith shouted. "Halt! Hold the Twenty-Fourth on the road!"

Then, turning to the Nineteenth Indiana's officers, General Meredith yelled, "Colonel Williams, get the Nineteenth on the road!"

"Yes, sir!" the regimental commander yelled back. The calls of bugles pierced the morning mist as the Nineteenth Indiana began forming on the road in columns of four. With rifles still loaded from the night's picket duty, the Nineteenth was on the road and ready to move.

"Attention, Company!" Lieutenant Schlagle shouted. He turned back to look over the men, then glanced at Colonel Williams. With a nod from the colonel, he paused, then bellowed out as loud as he could.

"Company, Forwarrrrrd…"

"…Marrrrch!"

And with that, the tired and dirty veterans began their march north. Other than the muddy roads, the remnants of the early morning showers were gone. With the sun just starting to break through the clouds, the Indiana men could feel the humidity as they settled into their march.

Suddenly, James heard a commotion behind him and quickly turned. Coming up the side of the column, a general on a black horse yelled, spurring his mount northward. Three other mounted officers trailed just behind him, racing to keep up.

"That's General Reynolds," Solomon said to James, seeing one of the riders carrying the blue-and-white First Corps headquarters' flag.

After watching General Reynolds and his staff race along the side of the column and disappear to the north, the men settled back into the march again. The sounds of the marching army dulled the voices of the men on the road. These were veterans now, weary but alert. Together for two long years, the battle-hardened survivors kept the chatter down. Today, they knew, they would need their energy.

Suddenly, they heard a low rumble off in the distance, and the men exchanged glances.

"Was that…artillery?" Solomon asked.

No one answered but, instead, just listened.

From beyond the horizon ahead, another rumble of artillery echoed across the fields. Lumps formed in the men's throats as they tightened up their formation and marched forward.

As the company crested a ridge near a peach orchard, they could see the rooftops, spires, and steeples of a town two miles ahead. Off to the left of the town, smoke was rising from beyond the treetops.

With bugle calls and yells from officers, the regiment was hurried forward. General Reynolds, at the front of the column just past a brick farmhouse, commanded a team of staff officers ordering the brigade's pioneers to tear down fences along the left side of the road.

Without even being told to do so, the brigade had picked up its pace to a trot. More officers commanded the men out into the field and toward the smoke. The sounds of cannons and gunfire were straight ahead.

The proud soldiers of the famed Iron Brigade were marching toward a battle again.

The town up ahead was Gettysburg.

-10-

Emmitsburg Road, South of Gettysburg
July 1, 1863, 9:30 a.m.

The sun was finally out...at least they wouldn't be fighting rain and mud today. But the air was thick with humidity...and tension too.

For the past several minutes, the men in the Nineteenth had begun to hear artillery in the distance to the north. Energized by the sound of cannons, the column picked up its pace. The men, breathing heavy, exchanged nervous glances.

Solomon, feeling a lump in his throat, looked over at James. Sweat dripped from underneath his hat and down onto his dirty face. James squinted and gritted his teeth as he trotted forward.

The artillery, although still far off, had become a steady rumble now.

"Too many cannons to be just cavalry," Solomon said, hearing another boom.

"Infantry...gotta be," James said. "Afraid we've found the whole Reb army, Sol."

Henry heard him too and shuddered.

"Yep, this is it," Hawk said from the next row back. "Gonna be a fight, boys."

Looking ahead, James could see the column had turned

off the road across from a brick farmhouse. At the front of the Nineteenth, Colonel Williams and Lieutenant Colonel Dudley urged the regiment forward.

"This way!" Dudley shouted from the side of the road, directing the regiment's vanguard toward an opening in a downed fence and out into a field.

Solomon glanced at Henry, just on the other side of James. Henry was staring straight ahead toward the sound of the distant cannons. His face had turned ghost white, and his eyes were wide with fear.

Billy had noticed too, and above all the clatter, he yelled, "You're alright, Henry. You're alright…keep going!"

Henry continued forward, but still his cheeks puffed in and out with each frantic breath. He shook so bad that he was almost crying. When another cannon boomed, closer this time, he flinched and made a sound. Barely audible, it came out as a nervous grunt signaling he was losing a battle against something inside. In the past, Henry had always fought when he was supposed to, but now he glanced from side to side as if scanning the horizon for other options.

Just ahead, Colonel Williams stood in his stirrups. "Quick time, men!" he shouted, pointing toward the northwest.

After crossing a ditch, the Indiana men jumped over the downed fence rails and rushed into a field of trampled wheat. The thunder of artillery was straight in front of them now. And closer too.

They'd be fighting for sure, they all knew.

The column bunched up and slowed as they approached a swale near another farm and orchard. "Drop your packs, men!" an unseen officer shouted. Another officer nearby repeated the command, and several of the men near him dropped their heavy knapsacks in the grass.

Hawk, remembering the dead chicken he'd put inside his

own pack a few hours ago, unstrapped his knapsack and laid it down. He looked at the knapsack and smiled, thinking of the poor fool who dared opening *that* up after several days in the hot sun.

Henry had dropped his pack too and, thinking of his diary, knelt down to retrieve it.

"You heard him!" Sergeant Boller yelled. "Leave it there! You're not gonna need any of that stuff where you're going!"

Henry ignored him and quickly pulled his diary from his knapsack and tucked it into his haversack still slung around his shoulder.

"Drop the haversack!" Boller sneered, approaching Henry and threatening to strike him with the butt of his rifle.

"It's his diary, Sarge," Hawk said, stepping between them.

Giving Hawk a shove, Boller yelled, "The hell with his Quaker fairy-tale book! He's leaving it."

Just as Hawk stepped forward to return the sergeant's shove, Colonel Williams's voice boomed from the front of the column.

"Attention! Battalion!" Williams shouted.

Heads turned, and Colonel Williams yelled again, "Forward! Double Quick!"

Hawk let the sergeant go. This wasn't the time for petty squabbles, and besides, Henry still had his haversack with his diary in it.

The Indiana men broke into a jog. Over a stone wall and through the orchard, the men rushed forward with their rifles at right shoulder shift. Solomon and James were near the front of the regiment and only a few strides behind the color guard who was carrying the battle flags still encased in their sheaths.

"Looks like you're gonna get yur chance to carry that flag today, Abe!" a soldier close by shouted.

Abraham Buckles, from Muncie, Indiana, was only fourteen

years old when he volunteered to fight with the Nineteenth's Company E. Although he had denied it, the men all knew that he'd lied about his age so he could enlist to fight. Abe had been severely wounded in the thigh at Bull Run a year ago, but still, he had begged to join the color guard when he returned to the regiment.

Now jogging alongside Color Sergeant Burlington "Burl" Cunningham, who was carrying the encased Stars and Stripes, Private Buckles looked over and smiled proudly. Being a color bearer during battle was a prestigious honor, but one that resulted in almost certain death. Hearing the battle raging in the distance, he knew that today he would get his chance.

"Yes, sir!" Private Buckles yelled, turning to answer and beaming with pride.

After passing a farmhouse and barn, the Nineteenth jogged through another field and then up a slope to a wooded ridge.

"Hurry up, men! Forward!" Colonel Williams shouted from his horse, riding toward the front of the regiment. "Close that gap on the Wisconsin men!"

After clambering over a low stone wall at the edge of the woods, the column hurriedly made its way along a wood line and out into another field. Ahead of the Nineteenth, the men of the Second and Seventh Wisconsin regiments crossed a road and into a wheat field between two ridges.

"Look, James!" Solomon shouted, approaching the road. About a half mile ahead on the western ridge, two cannon crews of Union horse artillery were feverishly working their guns. Beyond the guns, the treetops were filled with smoke, and artillery shells shrieked through the air.

"The cavalry's fallin' back," James said, pointing.

Quickening their pace even more, the Nineteenth Indiana men followed the Wisconsin regiments. A large, red brick building sat on the quiet ridge to the east, but to the west, the sounds of a raging battle and heavy smoke filled the air.

"Battalion, halt!"

James looked around at the other men near him. Sweat poured from their faces, and several were leaning over trying to catch their breath. Some even took a knee. A loud rattle of muskets off to the north made James look up. Across the pike where General Cutler's brigade had gone, the fighting had grown intense. A battery had unlimbered on both sides of the road and exchanged shells with Confederate artillery off in the distance to the west.

Mounted couriers and staffers frantically spurred horses between units.

"There's General Meredith," Billy said, pointing at their brigadier general who had ridden up and began shouting orders to his regimental commanders.

"And General Reynolds," James said, nodding toward the First Corps commander halting his horse in front of the Second Wisconsin troops. The Indiana men, still catching their breath, watched as the two Wisconsin regiments to their north shifted from column into battle line.

Closer, Captain Orr and Colonel Williams broke from a meeting in front of the Nineteenth, and Colonel Williams rode to the front. Standing high in his stirrups and with his sword unsheathed, Williams yelled above the roar of the cannons, "Attention! Battalion! On the left file!"

The men stood tall, faced forward, and then shifted to the left. They were now in a battle formation, two long lines facing the ridge to the west.

"Forward!" a Wisconsin officer shouted from off to the right. Then, the three hundred men of the Second Wisconsin began running up the gradual ridge and toward the woods. Seconds later, Colonel Robinson, riding in front of the Seventh Wisconsin, then yelled to his men, and the Seventh Wisconsin charged forward just behind the Second Wisconsin's left flank.

"Bayonets!" an unseen voice shouted from somewhere in the Indiana line. The command echoed all through the ranks. Obeying, the men pulled their bayonets from their scabbards and, with the clinking of steel, attached them to their muskets.

"We're going in next," Solomon said, his voice cracking just as a streaking shell exploded overhead.

Heads ducked, and men flinched.

James looked up and, through the smoke, could see that the Second Wisconsin had reached the woods at the top of the slope, and that the Seventh was going in just behind them. Hearing a new crackle of muskets from the trees, James felt his own heart racing and glanced toward Henry. Henry, praying, had his eyes closed and his forehead lowered against his fingertips. James noticed Henry was still shaking, and looking closer, James saw a tear had flowed down his cheek and mixed with sweat.

The Indiana veterans watched and waited…but only for a second.

"Ready, men!" Colonel Williams shouted between artillery blasts. He paused with his sword high in the air. Then, the Nineteenth's colonel abruptly lowered his sword and let out a yell.

"Double Quick! Forward!" Colonel Williams yelled, thrusting his sword toward the enemy.

Billy felt his heart race. Looking to his side, he saw Hawk lunging forward with his Springfield and bayonet out in front of him.

"Forward!" Hawk howled, repeating Colonel Williams's command as they broke into a run.

To the left of Hawk and running a half step behind, Solomon looked straight ahead.

A mounted staff officer had ridden around the left end of the line and spurred his horse to the front of the regiment. Passing the color guard, he looked back to Color Sergeant Cunningham and yelled, "Don't unfurl that flag yet, Burl!"

Cunningham, though, was anxious to let the Stars and Stripes fly. The regiment's national flag was new and had never flown in battle before. The old flag, bullet-ridden and tattered, had been sent back to Indiana several months ago. Hearing the battle raging beyond the ridge, Sergeant Cunningham couldn't wait any longer. As soon as the mounted officer passed, Sergeant Cunningham turned and shouted.

"Abe, pull the shuck!"

Without hesitation, the excited Corporal Buckles proudly pulled the chord, yanked the case off, and released the national colors. The new silk unfurled in the breeze and shone brightly in the morning sun.

"That a way, boys!" Hawk shouted, looking over toward the red, white, and blue flag flying high above the center of the battle line.

James glanced over too and proudly smiled. Somehow, seeing the flag made him forget how scared he really was…at least for now.

Ahead and to the right, the trees where the Wisconsin men had gone erupted with a storm of musketry, and just ahead, another shell exploded among the two Union cannons on the ridge.

"Protect that battery before it's forced to retire!" Colonel Williams shouted, pointing toward a two-cannon section of horse artillery near the crest of the ridge. The crews of the two Union cannons were engaged in a losing battle against several Confederate batteries, and a Rebel shell from the distant ridge had already crippled half of the left gun's crew.

Beyond the two cannons, the Indiana men heard a new sound. In the valley on the other side of the ridge came a howl-like roar.

"Hawk, what is that?" James asked, even though he'd heard that sound before and was afraid that was what it was again.

"Rebs," Hawk growled.

James glanced over at Hawk and saw that he'd quickened the pace and was now a half stride ahead of the line. Swiftly, though, the men around Hawk sped up too, and the front rank was aligned again and almost to the top of the ridge.

"The Rebel yell," Hawk hissed, hearing more howls and yells in the trees. He'd said it mockingly and in a voice venomous with hate.

James never did know why Hawk hated Rebels or their yell so much. They'd all wondered why, really. James remembered someone asking Hawk about it once, but he'd just bitterly stared into the fire. Now, hearing the Rebel yell beyond the ridge and knowing many men would die today, James realized they might never know.

"Look at that, James!" Solomon shouted as the Nineteenth crested the ridge and the Confederates came into view.

First, they saw the tops of large, red flags and then their long dirt-gray battle lines. The field was full of smoke, but still, the bright morning sun reflected off their muskets and bayonets as the Rebels came out of the wooded swale.

Seeing the end of the Rebel line directly in the Nineteenth's front, Hawk bellowed out a laugh and then yelled, "We're gonna hit 'em on their flank!"

Above the roar, an officer bellowed.

"*Forwarrrrrd!*"

Although the left half of the Rebel brigade was tangled with the Wisconsin men in the woods, the right end of the Confederate battle line was out in the open and only one hundred yards ahead of the Nineteenth Indiana.

"We got 'em!" Billy yelled, also seeing that the Nineteenth was headed toward the Rebel flank.

Sergeant Cunningham carried the Stars and Stripes high out in front of the line. He'd earned that honor at Antietam. Having picked the flag up there from its wounded bearer, he remembered the effect it had on the men as they had surged across the Hagerstown Pike and attacked a brigade of Georgians and then tried storming a Rebel battery near the Dunker Church.

Proudly waving the flag now, Cunningham felt its glory and the power it gave them all.

Men yelled and even cheered.

Young Abe Buckles looked up at the flag and, despite the fear, felt chills.

Running beside Buckles and Cunningham with the Stars and Stripes, Corporal Phipps lifted the giant blue regimental flag. The men were all just as proud of that flag with its gold embroidered eagle and "*19ᵗʰ Reg't Vols*" stitched below it. So many had died carrying those flags, and they'd all fought behind them.

But now, the Rebels saw them too. Their gray, howling battle line had come across the tree-lined creek and had been angling across the field toward the woods. Now, though, seeing the Indiana and Michigan regiments on their flank, the Rebels paused and tried to adjust to the new threat coming over the ridge.

"Forward, men!" Lieutenant Schlagle shouted, waving his sword above his head. The men were running even faster now. The rails of a busted-down fence where the cavalry had been fighting briefly broke their formation, but the regiment quickly reformed on the other side.

"Keep the line moving, boys!" a sergeant shouted from behind the line just as a shell screamed overhead and exploded behind them.

"Close up!"

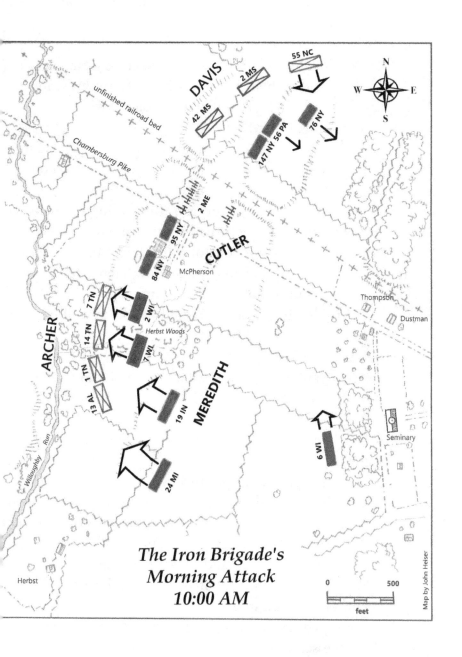

The Iron Brigade's
Morning Attack
10:00 AM

Map by John Heiser

More puffs of smoke came from the gray line ahead. Bullets screamed past.

"Steady!"

Henry fought for breath against swelling fear. "I don't know…," he said with a screech, unable to finish his sentence. He was so scared, his legs felt like they would buckle.

"Keep going, Henry!" Hawk shouted, seeing Henry waver.

Solomon noticed too. Leaning in and grabbing Henry's sleeve, he yelled, "You're doing fine, Henry! We got 'em out in the open!"

Henry wanted to turn and run. But feeling the men on each side of him, he knew he had no choice. He couldn't feel his legs and felt he'd lost control of his body, but somehow, he still ran. Momentum had them all now. Henry felt a shove from behind, and again, he cursed himself for ever enlisting to fight. He didn't know it would be like this. *Why, why, why…*

"Battalion! Halt!"

Seventy yards away now, another storm of lead balls whistled past.

"Fire! Fire!"

The Nineteenth's line erupted in fire and smoke and a deafening blast of muskets.

Off to the right, someone screamed.

Henry, hearing and feeling a thud against his back, looked down. Dust and smoke rose from two holes in his haversack where a minie ball had gone clear through. Still stricken with fear, he thought of his diary and tried to reach down.

"Henry, Henry!" James shouted, clutching Henry's arm and pulling him from his trance.

Henry tried looking ahead.

Invisible screams echoed from the smoke. Then, Henry saw a young, beardless boy wearing gray. The Rebel youth's wet and bloodshot eyes stared blankly up at the sky. And then the boy fell backward clutching his chest.

"*Forward!*"

Someone had Henry's other arm now, and he felt another push in the back. Henry looked down from the hell before them, and with quivering hands, he tried reloading.

Out of the corner of his eye and through the smoke, Henry saw the Stars and Stripes falling. He noticed the flag's staff had been splintered and at least a dozen bullet holes had been torn in its silk.

Suddenly, the flag fell to the grass. Sergeant Cunningham had been hit in the side and dropped to the ground atop it.

"Abe, throw down that musket and pick up that flag!" someone yelled. Private Buckles, though, already had it in the air before the man had even finished the sentence.

Colonel Williams's regiment had come onto the field from the perfect direction. The left half of the Alabama and Tennessee brigade was still tangled in the woods fighting the Wisconsin regiments. The right two regiments of General Archer's brigade, however, the Thirteenth Alabama and First Tennessee, had swung across the field to attack the Seventh Wisconsin, exposing the Rebels' right flank directly in front of the Nineteenth Indiana coming over the ridge.

"Reload! Reload!"

The command echoed all up and down the line. It wasn't necessary though; most of the Nineteenth's veterans had already pulled out another cartridge and stuffed it in their muzzle. It didn't take a colonel or even their own sergeant to tell them that, not with the enemy right in their front. Not to *these* men. Not anymore.

"Forward! Steady!"

The men, still in their rows, couldn't see through their own smoke. Still, though, they rushed forward and yelled.

Up ahead, they heard wounded cries from the Rebel line and then shouts from officers.

"*Fire! Fire!*"

Another crackle of muskets and flying lead whistled past.

"Steady, men!"

James looked forward and could see part of the Rebel line again. It was closer now, only forty yards away. Feeling Henry beside him, he glanced over and saw Henry's hands shaking and fumbling with his rammer.

"Keep going, Henry!"

"I don't know if I can do it, James!" Henry screamed.

Ahead, the red Rebel flags were still there, but many of the gray-clad men reeled in the grass. The Nineteenth's volley had hit them hard.

For some reason, James thought of his dog and looked behind him. He'd seen Moses back near the farm but hadn't seen him since.

While reaching for a percussion cap, James yelled, "Moses!" But he wasn't sure why…no dog would ever come anywhere near all that musket fire. Men said and did strange things while under fire, James knew.

"Hit 'em again!"

"Fire!"

From only a few feet away, a sudden scream pierced the air. James looked over and saw Andy Wood rolling on the ground with his uniform on fire. A ball had struck his cartridge box, exploding it and sending the Company C private airborne. Lieutenant Macy was on him within seconds, patting out flames.

"Go on!" Lieutenant Macy yelled to the line, commanding the men around him forward.

With Private Buckles and the national flag out front, the Nineteenth surged forward.

"Ready!" shouted Lieutenant Colonel Dudley from the left side of the line. "Fire! Fire!"

The Union line erupted in another explosion of flying lead and smoke.

The effects of the Yankee volley were devastating. Still moving forward and passing through their own musket smoke, the Indiana men could see dozens of wounded Confederates down in the grass.

The Rebel line was in shambles, not the perfect dress parade as it had been when the Nineteenth had first seen it. Most of the Alabamians had turned and ran, but still, several Rebels attempted to return fire. James saw one Rebel, a gray-bearded scarecrow of a man, place a cap on his musket's nipple and look directly at him.

The old soldier, his arm wrapped with a bloodstained bandage, grimaced and showed rotten teeth as he lowered his musket barrel in James's direction. The man pulled the trigger and vanished behind a white cloud of musket smoke. Knowing the bullet was coming his way, James quickly ducked and heard the screeching minie ball whistle past his left shoulder and thud into something behind him with a crunch.

James looked back at the sound and saw Private Joey Sykes spin backwards. Joey reached for his chest and tried yelling, but no sound came out.

"Joey!" his brother William screamed. Leaning down, William Sykes saw the lead ball had struck Joey's brass breast plate and knocked the wind out of him. Realizing his brother wasn't badly wounded, he quickly helped Joey back to his feet and rejoined the line.

Despite the chaos among the Rebels, puffs of smoke and showers of lead erupted from their muskets again. But still, the Nineteenth's battle line held strong and continued forward.

"They're running!" Billy shouted.

Hawk, not wasting time reaching for another bullet, surged ahead with his bayonet leading the way.

"Charge!" an officer shouted.

Ahead, most of the Rebels were fleeing toward the rear. One large group of Alabamians, about to be overrun, looked behind them for help and, seeing none, threw down their muskets and raised their hands.

The Nineteenth's men rushed forward and past the surrendering Rebels and now gave chase to the ones who ran. Hawk and James were in the lead now and sprinted down the slope toward the brush-lined stream and woods. With the large Twenty-Fourth Michigan coming up on the rear and left of the Nineteenth Indiana, the Confederates were in a desperate predicament.

James entered the underbrush with his rifle and bayonet leveled. Just on the other side of the creek, he could see a newly formed Rebel skirmish line crouching in the weeds and waiting for the Union battle line.

"Watch out, Sol!" James yelled over his shoulder.

"Get down!" someone else yelled.

The Alabama regiment lowered their muskets and let off a volley. Smoke and flying tree leaves filled the air. Despite the chaos, the Indiana men charged ahead.

James and Solomon broke out of the weeds at the creek bank and splashed into the shallow water. Hawk was a few feet ahead of them and lunged toward a Rebel in the creek who had just fired and was now reaching for another cartridge. Hawk didn't hesitate. Flipping his musket around, he swung the butt of his Springfield forward into the man's left eye and nose. The musket's wooden stock landed with a crunch, and blood gushed from the man's face. The Rebel staggered backwards and collapsed down in the rocks.

Seeing Hawk standing above him, the bloody-faced Rebel spewed curses and struggled in the water to get back to his feet.

"Stay down!" Hawk shouted. Then, when the man reached for Hawk's leg, Hawk lunged forward and drove his bayonet through his chest. Hawk didn't say another word...not even when he yanked out the bayonet and kicked the dead Rebel back down into the water.

Some of the Confederates still tried to fight, but most were retreating to the west. In addition to the Nineteenth driving the Rebels across the creek, the Twenty-Fourth Michigan slammed into their right flank and had them surrounded. By then, most of the Rebels who hadn't fled had dropped their muskets and thrown up their hands in surrender. Most of the Iron Brigade soldiers stopped just past the creek, but several of them were still giving chase in the fields beyond.

"Come back with that flag, Abe!" Lieutenant Colonel Dudley yelled, seeing their newest color bearer still running after the Confederates. It was only when young Abe saw he was alone in the field that he finally stopped and turned back toward the creek to rejoin the regiment.

Solomon grabbed two of the prisoners and gave them a shove toward the rear. James did the same with another Alabamian, then splashed through the creek to the other bank. He looked through the brush toward the west and saw hundreds of Confederates fleeing through fields and up toward another ridge beyond.

"You okay, Henry?" Solomon asked.

Henry, standing at the edge of the creek, had his hands on his knees and was trying to catch his breath. Hearing Solomon, he looked up and said, "I killed a man, Sol. For what? These are men too...just like us."

"I know, Henry."

"I can't keep fighting," Henry said.

"I know. None of us want to. Come on. Let's go." Solomon grabbed his Quaker friend by the arm and helped him through the creek. Together, they climbed the other bank and looked at the fields to the west.

"We got 'em runnin'," Solomon said, seeing the Confederates retreating up the distant ridge.

"Just keep on goin', Johnny Reb!" Billy Williams shouted with his rifle high in the air.

Hawk, watching the Rebels run, wished he'd killed more. Then, hearing shouts nearby, Hawk turned around and saw that Billy's cousin Grear had gotten in an argument with a Rebel lieutenant. The dispute was something or other about a sword. Hawk noticed the lieutenant had surrendered his pistol but still had his sword.

Striding over, Hawk looked the captured man in the eye and asked him who he was.

"Lieutenant Pond, Thirteenth Alabama," the Confederate officer proudly responded.

"Got a family?" Hawk asked.

The lieutenant glanced at Hawk quizzically then looked toward the others. Grear still had a hold of his arm and squeezed a little harder.

"Answer him!" Grear shouted.

"Uhh, yes. I do…they're back home in Selma."

Hawk stepped in close and reached for his knife. Without breaking eye contact, Hawk hissed, "Well, Lieutenant, hand over your sword or you'll never see 'em again."

The lieutenant didn't know what he'd done to anger this Yankee private. He smiled. But he definitely wouldn't surrender his sword to one of these two Yankees, not to mere *privates*, that's for sure.

Hawk, after pausing, watched the Confederate lieutenant smile. For a moment, Hawk was giving the man a chance, even if he was a Rebel. But then, the Rebel lieutenant's what-you-gonna-do smirk caused Hawk to snap. Hawk lunged forward and grabbed the lieutenant's neck. Even though the Rebel's arrogant smile was gone, Hawk sliced the lieutenant's belt with his knife and then yanked it free, dropping the belt, scabbard, and sword down on the rocks with a clang.

There was no time for the Alabama lieutenant to react. Hawk gave him a shove, and Grear quickly yanked his prisoner's arm and led him away…unsure if he did it to save the lieutenant's life from Hawk killing him or just to keep Hawk out of trouble.

Sergeant Boller, whom they all hadn't seen since going into battle formation, walked up and tried to figure out what had just happened. Seeing the officer's sword and scabbard lying on the rocks, his eyes widened, and he took a step toward it.

"Not a chance, Sarge," Hawk said.

Hawk glared, and Boller stopped.

Hawk then looked around at the men along the creek.

He knew that they'd all fought bravely this morning and also knew that quarreling over a captured sword wouldn't help anyone.

Hawk glanced at the sword and then at James who was now standing on the rocks right beside the sword. James had read his mind. Smiling, James reached down, grabbed the sword and scabbard, and threw it into the deepest part of the creek.

Hawk's glare let Boller know that *no one* would take that sword today.

There were officers there now too. Lieutenants Schlagle and Jones strode up, and so had Sergeant Major Blanchard. Colonel Williams was on his horse again and splashed through the creek toward them.

"Start breaking them extra muskets on the rocks," Williams shouted. "We don't want the Rebs getting 'em back and usin' 'em against us."

"Yes, sir," James chimed in, stepping forward and distancing himself from Boller who was still fuming over what he and Hawk had done with the captured sword.

"And stock up as much ammo as you can. Gonna be more graybacks coming in a while." After Colonel Williams said it, he looked to the west and stared. They all noticed his face had turned solemn.

"Yes, sir," several men replied.

Colonel Williams turned toward his regiment. He respected these men. Williams knew he'd gained their respect as well… long before here. They'd all done their duty this morning, but Williams also knew that they'd have to do much more.

Williams watched for a moment as several of the Nineteenth's men began gathering discarded muskets. Seeing the last of the prisoners being rounded up and sent to the rear, Colonel Williams abruptly yanked his horse's reins and turned away. Looking upstream toward where the Wisconsin regiments had fought, he remembered hearing someone had said that the Wisconsin boys had captured a Rebel general up that way…he wouldn't mind going and seeing *that*.

With the Confederates having withdrawn to the west, the Iron Brigade men reformed their skirmish line on the banks of Willoughby Run. The exhausted men sat down on boulders in and along the meandering creek's bank to catch their breath. While washing their hands and faces and filling their canteens, the veterans knew they had won an important fight.

"We made it," James said, slapping Henry on the leg.

"Yeah, most of us did anyway," Henry said, still shaking. "This war's hell, James."

James didn't respond at first. They both looked around the woods at the dozens of bodies strewn about in the weeds. Luckily, at least this time, most of them were Confederates.

"Sorry, Henry," James finally said. "We all know this ain't what we signed up for."

"I shot a guy I didn't have to, James. I squeezed the trigger just as he started turning away. But it was too late."

"I reckon he's good 'n' dead now," Hawk interrupted, looking up from splashing water on his face. "Ya did good, Henry."

Henry didn't answer but, instead, just stared at the water.

"Gonna be more fighting," James said. "A lot more Rebs to the west...out past them hills. We only fought one brigade. And General Lee doesn't come to a battle with just one brigade."

"Well, then, James," Hawk said, "we'll just have to kill more of 'em."

No one responded, but Hawk noticed Henry shaking his head.

"Ahh, come on, Henry. They're just Johnnies."

Henry still had his head down. His eyes were closed, but he finally looked up. "That could be us, Hawk."

Hawk grinned, and Henry angrily stood up.

Hawk then put his hands out and smiled even wider. He'd always enjoyed teasing Henry...even now.

"They're people too," Henry said, "just like us. Many a good boy just died here, Hawk. Some ma or pa somewhere is gonna find out their son is dead, Hawk. Or maybe their sweetheart will find out he's dead. Or maybe it's some little girl's daddy."

"They're just Rebs, Henry. They kill us or we kill them. And this time, we killed them."

"It ain't right."

"It's war, Henry."

Henry then looked down and stared into the water without speaking. He'd made a fist and shook his head. A few seconds later, he reached for his canteen and took a drink, and when he did, they could all see his hand was trembling.

Noticing Henry's anguish, James felt sympathy for him. "Ya did good, real good today, Henry," he said. "Fightin' is hard on all of us. We all just handle it different, that's all."

"I'm a Quaker, James. Not even supposed to be fightin' at all, ya know? And I killed two boys today. I gotta live with that."

"You killed two boys *so far* today, Henry," Hawk chimed in with a laugh. "And maybe you won't have to live with it for all that long anyways."

"Yeah, Hawk… well, maybe I won't kill another one either. How 'bout that?"

"Oh, you gonna talk 'bout *runnin'* again?" Hawk asked.

"Leave him alone, Hawk," James said, speaking up and defending his squadmate. Henry gave him a look and nod as if to say thanks but then turned away before speaking.

"Okay, James," Hawk said. He respected James…as a man and as a soldier. Always had. But Henry wasn't getting away with talking about deserting anymore. No way.

"This battle's not over, James," Hawk said. "Look at that tree line out there. There's more Johnnies in that woods now than there was in the whole battle a li'l while ago. We're gonna need *every* man. Every single one of us."

Hawk paused and looked at Henry.

It was Solomon who spoke up this time. Looking up from washing his face and hands in the creek, he said, "All we can do is be ready to fight again."

Hawk didn't let it go. Staring at Henry, he said, "And make sure no one's gonna turn and *run* on us and leave us hangin' out there alone."

Henry had pulled his diary from his pocket and stared back at Hawk.

"Two years, Hawk," Henry said. "Two years…"

"Two years *what*, Henry?" Hawk asked, glaring at Henry for an answer.

"Two years and I been beside ya fightin' the whole time. Two years of doin' my *duty* and killin'. Well, I've had it, Hawk."

"Henry's right, Hawk," Solomon said, defending his squadmate and friend of several years. "He's been there the whole time. Never turned and ran yet."

"I ain't sayin' I'm runnin' on nobody," Henry said. "But maybe this is the chance, up here in Pennsylvania during a battle. I'd be just another of the 'missing', ya know?"

"If you run, you let us all down," Hawk said. "A deserter's as bad as a Reb. Might as well shoot us yourself."

"Well, I *wanna* run, but I won't. Maybe I just won't shoot nobody though neither."

"Well, at least if yur out there takin' a ball, then that's one less for us," Hawk said. "So yeah, just go out there and be a target."

Seeing that Henry was busy with his diary and ignoring him now, Hawk pushed him a little harder. "What ya writin' 'bout in that stupid thing now? Ya writin' about how yur gonna run?"

"Let him be, Hawk," James said.

"I'm alright, James," Henry said with his hand in the air. "You don't have to defend me from Hawk. He's just sufferin' inside. He's got a hollow soul, ya know?"

Hawk scoffed and then spit out a wad of tobacco before responding. "Ain't gonna matter after we're all killed in the battle comin' up, is it?"

"The *soul*, Hawk. That's *all* that's gonna matter when this is over."

"Oh, how so?"

"You are a simple one, ain't ya, Hawk? It's a little late for a Bible lesson."

Hawk hesitated…a rare thing for him. He looked at Henry carefully and finally decided to change the subject.

"What *are* you writin' 'bout in that diary anyway?"

Henry put his pencil down and looked at Hawk. Then he looked at Billy and then at the Whitlow brothers. After leaning down to wash his hands in the water, he sat upright on the rock but still didn't speak.

"Well, what ya writin' about?" Solomon asked, jumping back into the conversation.

Henry looked down at the water and then back up again. When he turned to speak, they could see that his eyes were watering. He hesitated and wiped a tear across his dirty cheek before clearing his throat.

"It's about *us*."

-11-

Along Willoughby Run, Gettysburg
July 1, 1863, 12:30 p.m.

"James, look," Henry said, pointing.

James glanced up at Henry and noticed that for the first time today, he was smiling. Following Henry's finger, James saw Moses standing in the creek and lapping up water.

"Here, Moses!" James shouted with a giant grin, grateful that his dog had survived. After hearing James's voice, the dog's ears perked up and his head quickly turned. Seeing James, Moses jumped with a splash and ran toward him.

"Moses!" someone said with a laugh.

"He made it, James," Billy said. The men smiled and laughed as the dog approached, and some even cheered. The whole squad was there by then at the edge of the creek. Despite the carnage around them, James's dog had lifted their spirits. For the past week, he seemed to know just when to show up.

Suddenly, though, their mood quickly turned serious again as an artillery shell exploded in the treetops above and sent debris raining down around them. Even more alarming than the cannon shells flying overhead, however, was the increasing number of Rebel flags and lines of infantry forming on the distant ridge. Looking out across the fields to the west, the Company B men at the creek saw more Confederates gathering in the trees a half mile away. Although the morning infantry battle had ended an hour ago, the artillery duel between the two sides continued.

After watching the distant ridge for a few moments, James looked around at the men near the creek. Sergeant Boller was there too but had ignored the dog's return. James did notice, however, that the sergeant had also become nervous about the arrival of more enemy troops to the west.

"We can't hold this position if the Rebs attack here, Sarge," James said.

Boller knew James was right…their location was weak if they did have to try to defend it. But he wasn't going to let a *private* tell him that, especially someone from *that* squad. "Just fight where you're told, Private."

"This is suicide down in here, Sarge," Hawk interjected angrily. "You gotta say somethin' to the lieutenant. The Pennsylvanians over there on the left are gettin' shelled and already startin' to fall back."

James saw the sergeant's anger but sensed the panic in the men even more. Knowing the Nineteenth's position was untenable, James decided to risk facing the sergeant's wrath by speaking up again. "Once the brigade over there falls back beyond the ridge, Sarge, there's nothin' on our left flank but that open field. And when the Rebs attack, that field's gonna be full of thousands of Johnnies. Someone's gotta let Colonel Williams know."

"Quiet, Whitlow!" Sergeant Boller shouted back, trying unsuccessfully to hide his own angst about their vulnerable position.

"We're in a hole, Boller," Hawk said just as another shell landed on the ridge behind them. "We're sitting ducks out here. Look to the left, Sarge. Our flank's in the air."

Sergeant Boller, as well as several other soldiers nearby, anxiously looked at the open field to the south. Behind them,

Colonel Biddle's brigade of Pennsylvanians had already moved twice to escape Rebel artillery and were now being shelled again. Now, Biddle's brigade was moving back behind the ridge, leaving the Nineteenth Indiana's left flank even more exposed.

Boller didn't speak, but instead, turned and scanned the ridge to the west where a growing number of Confederates had assembled.

"I'm not lettin' us get slaughtered out here," Hawk said before angrily turning away and scrambling up the creek bank and into the woods.

After watching Hawk leave, Boller let out a nervous laugh. Then he looked at the rest of the squad and said, "Hawkins will get himself court-martialed all on his own. He won't need my help."

"They're right, Sarge," Solomon said. "We're dead if we stay out here unsupported in this low ground."

Boller began to respond but abruptly turned around upon hearing a horse splashing through the water.

"Here comes the colonel," James said.

Colonel Williams led his brown Morgan mare up the shallow creek and stopped just in front of Company B. Saluting no one in particular, he studied the squads of men before speaking.

"Gentlemen!" the colonel shouted, steadying his horse.

The men looked up, and someone said, "Guh' morning."

The comment brought a few quiet chuckles…it'd been a full day already and hadn't seemed like morning for several hours. Even the colonel grinned briefly before quickly turning serious again.

"General Reynolds is dead," Colonel Williams said.

As Williams paused, the men gulped and exchanged glances. Most of them had liked the First Corps general, and a few had even said John Reynolds should be the army's commander. According to camp rumors several days ago, President

Lincoln had actually offered him the job before George Meade, but Reynolds had turned him down.

"The Confederates are forming up to the west," Colonel Williams continued. "We must hold this position, men."

He paused and looked through the trees toward the distant ridge. James noticed the colonel's brow had furled while he scanned the horizon and then the Nineteenth's position along the creek. The colonel looked nervous…a rare thing for Sam Williams.

"Sir?" James said cautiously, deciding to speak up.

Williams turned and looked at James. "Yes…Private Whitlow?"

"Sir, no disrespect, sir. But this position is untenable against a large attack."

"I know, James. I know. I've already sent the sergeant major back to General Meredith and General Wadsworth."

Williams paused, and the men waited anxiously for more. They knew their lives were at stake after all.

"We are to hold these woods *at all hazards*." He paused. Those were words no soldier ever wanted to hear. Williams really was proud of these boys and knew he must say more. "And the general also said that if the Iron Brigade can't hold the position…*then no one can*."

Lieutenant Schlagle was there too and knew he should speak up. "Our left flank, sir. It's about to be in the air. Colonel Biddle's brigade on our left is pulling back behind the ridge, sir."

"Yes, Lieutenant. I know. We will have to hold here as long as we can. The rest of the army *will* be up." Williams paused again and looked to the south from where their division had come this morning. "And hopefully *soon*," he said… unintentionally.

"Yes sir, Colonel, sir," Schlagle said with a salute. "Then we *will* hold, sir."

Williams looked up and down their battle line which was just on the east side of the creek. While looking at the companies positioned upstream to the north, a solid shot cannon ball suddenly ripped through the treetops and slammed into a large branch overhead.

Colonel Williams, after fighting to steady his agitated horse, looked at their flag and then back to the men. "Boys, we must hold our colors on this line or die under them. This is an important fight. We must hold these woods until the rest of the army arrives. We must!"

The colonel paused as he looked down at his rugged veterans. "We fought well this morning, but we must fight even harder when they come at us again. And they will."

No one spoke, and the men exchanged nervous glances. Williams's mount neighed and spun around...even the horse seemed to know their predicament.

Colonel Williams yanked the reins to reface the men. Unsure what else to say, he shouted, "Good luck, men!" Then he quickly turned his horse toward the next company in line.

As the men watched their colonel ride away, several shells arced overhead in both directions. Solomon and James looked at each other and knew what that meant. The Confederates weren't going away.

"This ain't good, James," Solomon said.

"Nope."

A few minutes later, Hawk returned. He was sweating, and it was obvious he had been running. Catching his breath, he said, "That ridge out there...it's full of Rebs. And our line is staying here."

"We know," Billy said, his voice unable to hide disappointment. "Colonel Williams told us. He requested to move back to the ridge, but the generals said this is the line we must hold."

Hawk scoffed. "So sick of these fat, blue-bellied generals."

"We just gotta be ready to fight," James said, pulling his rammer out to clean his barrel again.

Hawk looked around. Now gazing at the field to their south, he shook his head in frustration. He spat and, thinking of their generals again, angrily said, "Every damned one of 'em."

"At least Williams and General Meredith care about us and tried to get our line moved," James said, defending their colonel and the Iron Brigade's general.

Hawk knew James was right, and besides, he liked those two officers too. Instead of trying to defend Colonel Williams and General Meredith, though, he just said, "We're gonna get destroyed here, James."

"Company B!" It was Lieutenant Schlagle running up from the rear. "Load and ready your weapons, men. And be ready to move!"

"Where we goin', Lieutenant?" Hawk asked.

"We've been assigned skirmish duty across the creek," he said, pointing west with his revolver which he began to load. "We'll be out in that wheat field. Between the orchard on this side of that farm and the small brook over there. We'll go in two-man teams, about two hundred yards out from the creek."

While stowing his rammer, James glanced at Henry. He'd begun to shake again, and his eyes scanned the horizon. Henry wasn't just looking toward the west where the rest of the men were looking but to the rear from where they had come.

"Sol," James whispered, nudging his brother and shooting a glimpse toward Henry.

"I know," Solomon said, still looking toward the west. "I noticed him earlier too. We gotta watch him."

Lieutenant Schlagle finished loading his revolver and returned it to its holster. "Keep your eyes open, men," he said. "Let's go."

Following the lieutenant's lead, the Company B men climbed up the bank of the creek and through the trees and brush on the other side. Trying to ignore the dead and wounded Confederates lying in the field, the men kept their eyes focused forward.

"Keep your head down, Sol," James whispered to his brother who was right beside him. James then glanced to his left. About a dozen yards away, Hawk was walking next to Henry.

Up ahead, a musket fired, and the men paused.

"Keep going," someone shouted. "Just a couple of Reb pickets."

Creeping forward again, James kept his eyes moving between the farm off in the distance to their left and the tree-lined ridge to the west.

"That's the ridge the Rebs retreated to," Solomon whispered to his older brother, pointing at the tree line six hundred yards away.

"Those trees are full of Rebs."

"There's a lot more of 'em now," James added. "And artillery too."

They both stopped, and while they scanned the ridge, they could hear gunners yelling out commands.

Suddenly, from closer than they had expected, a cannon on the ridge to the west boomed and sent a shell whistling through the air above them. Solomon and James both watched as the shell and its glowing fuse arced overhead and toward the Union cannons to the east.

After the shell disappeared beyond the trees, Solomon looked around the field again. "Where's Hawk and Henry going?" he asked. "They're awfully far off to the left."

"I dunno, maybe they're headin' to that orchard," James said, referring to the farm and orchard farther to the south.

As they watched their squadmates, they suddenly heard several musket blasts to the west. Turning that direction and seeing puffs of smoke coming from the weeds, James said, "Just keep your eyes forward for Reb skirmishers, Sol. Let's keep moving."

They had only gone a little farther in the trampled wheat when James snuck a glimpse toward Henry and Hawk again. The two squadmates appeared to be in an argument, and then James saw Hawk suddenly grab Henry by the arm. Henry was shouting, but another streaking artillery shell prevented James from making out Henry's words.

"What's going on over there, James?" Solomon whispered, also now watching the argument between Hawk and Henry. "Something's wrong."

James didn't respond but kept watching as Henry escaped Hawk's grip and scrambled several yards away. James observed them for several seconds until eventually seeing them move farther ahead together.

"I'm not sure, Sol," James finally said. "I couldn't hear what they were arguing about. They seem okay now, but we better keep an eye on 'em. Something's definitely not right."

"Henry's pretty mad 'bout something, James."

"So is Hawk. Come on. Let's keep moving."

As the two brothers continued forward, they kept their heads low and out of sight of enemy skirmishers. With James in the lead a few paces ahead, they used their long Springfield rifles and attached bayonets to slowly probe through the weeds. Looking to the right, James saw Billy and Grear had gone off farther to the right and stopped near a clump of bushes.

"We're about as far out as we should go, James," Solomon whispered.

James stopped and looked at the other Company B skirmishers. They had fanned out and were now covering a front several hundred yards wide. He then glanced back at the tree-lined creek behind them where the rest of the Nineteenth's battle line was deployed.

"The lieutenant said to only go about two hundred yards past the creek," Solomon whispered.

"I know," James whispered, nervously scanning the area. He could hear other voices and was worried their position was too exposed. Pointing toward a lower area just ahead, he said, "Let's get out to that depression. Come on."

Solomon nodded, and the two brothers crept forward again.

Around them, they could see several wounded and dead Confederate soldiers from the morning's fight. Most of the wounded were still lying where they had gone down, while others had crawled back to their own line on the ridge to the west.

Suddenly, they heard the crack of a musket near Billy and Grear. Quickly turning, they saw a puff of smoke and Grear dropping back down in the wheat to reload. Almost immediately, at least a dozen Rebel muskets returned fire.

"It's Grear," James whispered.

Grear's shot had apparently missed, and not only had it attracted several rounds of musket fire, but it had drawn taunts too. One Rebel even laughed.

"Ya blind, Billy Yank?" a North Carolina voice shouted, laughing.

A few of the Nineteenth's skirmishers shouted back. But when another muzzle blast echoed from Union skirmishers farther to the right, the no-man's-land they were in quickly turned serious again. That shot ended with a scream and a shower of whistling bullets.

"Let's go, Sol. A little farther."

Keeping their heads down, they crawled forward several more yards and then stopped.

"Stay down, Sol. There's Rebs down in the grass over there."

"James...look."

When James turned, he saw Solomon staring in the other direction. "What?" James asked, trying to see what his brother was looking at.

"It's Moses," Solomon said, pointing. James now saw him too. His tail was wagging, and he was sniffing at something in the grass.

"Let's go see what he's doing," James said.

Just as they began to move, they heard a weak voice.

"*Help me…water…please…*"

"It's a Reb, James."

"Be careful."

Moses's barking turned to a quiet whimper as they approached. Seeing the two Union men, the wounded gray-clad soldier desperately reached out with his bloody hand. He had been shot in the neck and shoulder and had fresh blood on him that covered the top half of his body. Solomon, horrified by the extent of the soldier's wounds, hesitated for a moment but then took a few steps closer and leaned down.

"Here, soldier," Solomon said, offering the man a drink from his canteen. Grateful, the wounded soldier poured water on his mouth and bloody face.

"God bless you," the wounded man mumbled, painfully handing back Solomon's canteen.

"What's your name, Private?" James asked.

"Virgil…Virgil Collester," he responded in a weak and cracking voice. "First Tennessee." He said the last part proudly, they both noticed, and even tried smiling. But the pain was too great, and he winced and then coughed up blood.

The two brothers looked at each other, not knowing what to do. Although the wounded man was suffering, they needed to watch for enemy skirmishers ahead. Solomon reached down to give the man another drink.

"He's in a lot of pain, James."

The wounded Rebel grabbed Solomon's arm. With his eyes wide open, he stared at Solomon pleadingly.

"I'm from Bristol. And I got a wife...and a boy." He was grimacing and holding the side of his neck which was still oozing blood.

He could barely get the next words out.

"My wife and boy...I ain't gonna make it."

His voice cracked, and then he painfully coughed. He tried to speak again, but the sounds came out as only a weak gurgle. Choking now, he reached up to the sky with his hand and grasped at air. Again, he wanted to speak. But he couldn't, and he dropped his hand with a sob.

"How can we help him?" Solomon asked.

James, noticing the man's eyes were closed, looked at Solomon and nodded. It was hopeless.

The wounded Tennessee soldier grunted and then spoke again. *"God, no! Please, no..."*

He wanted to say more, but his voice trailed off again. Not giving up, he wiped his face and tears with his bloody hand and sleeve. The man looked directly into Solomon's eyes. Every breath was a struggle now.

"What happened?" Solomon asked the man.

The Tennessee soldier mumbled something about a creek but then went silent. Solomon offered his canteen again, but the Rebel refused with barely even a nod. The man knew he was dying. Still, though, he opened his mouth to try to speak.

Solomon held the man's arm and placed his other hand on his chest. Solomon felt tears in his *own* eyes now.

The man's mouth stayed open, but no words came out. With eyes staring straight ahead, he exhaled one last time, and then he was still.

Solomon, eyes wet, looked up from the dead man whom he'd known for less than a minute. The scene around him was even more terrifying now. There had been too many bloody fields just like this one. Wounded and dead soldiers along with their equipment littered the field. Skirmishers' bullets screamed past, and shouts and musket blasts came from the ridge. And the worst was yet to come, Solomon knew.

Solomon glanced at James who gave him a nod and then turned away. Looking at the Tennessee soldier again, Solomon leaned down and gently closed the dead man's eyes. Even though it wasn't enough, he said a quick prayer for him. Then Solomon reached into his haversack, pulled out a handkerchief, and carefully covered the Tennessee man's face.

"Ready?" James asked.

Solomon didn't respond and then thought of James's dog. He didn't remember Moses running off, but now he was nowhere to be found. Solomon turned toward James again, who was now watching his brother carefully, apparently waiting for Solomon to be ready to go. Solomon took the hint and finally nodded. "Yeah. Let's go."

The two brothers took one last look at the man before slowly turning their heads.

"This way," James said, leading the way as they started crawling forward.

After only a few feet, however, Solomon stopped and felt himself trembling.

"Come on," James whispered, seeing that Solomon had fallen behind. Waving his arm signaling Solomon to follow, James said, "We gotta keep going, Sol. The rest of our skirmishers are just ahead."

Solomon hesitated but finally started forward again. Carefully avoiding being seen by the Confederates, they crawled another dozen yards before James looked back at Solomon.

"Let's stop here," James whispered.

Solomon halted and dropped his head below the grass.

They were in a small swale with a nearby stream. Off to the left and up a hill was the orchard that they had seen earlier.

"*Shhhhh*," James whispered, putting one hand on Solomon's arm. "Keep still."

"What is it?" Solomon asked in a hushed voice.

"There's Rebs…just past that clump of trees," James whispered, pointing. He then backed up and placed a percussion cap on his Springfield's nipple. "They're moving in on Hawk and Henry in the orchard."

Solomon finally saw them too and quickly reached for a cap. "Hawk and Henry don't know they're there, James."

"I know," James whispered, cocking his Springfield's hammer all the way back.

Solomon, seeing the two Rebels raise their rifles toward Henry and Hawk, frantically waved his arms trying to get his squadmates' attention. The enemy skirmishers were preparing to fire, and Solomon knew he had no other choice but to stand up and yell.

"Hawk, get down!"

At the same time, James quickly aimed at the closest Rebel and squeezed the trigger. His Springfield erupted with a blast, and his minie ball struck the Rebel's pants just above the knee, penetrating the skin and striking the bone.

"*Arghhh!*" the North Carolinian screamed out, dropping to the ground and reeling in pain.

Startled by his partner's scream, the other Rebel quickly turned away from Hawk and Henry and toward his new threat.

"Sol! Get down!" James yelled, seeing the Rebel taking aim in their direction.

James's warning was too late. Solomon was still standing and securing a cap on his Springfield's cone when the Rebel's musket erupted in a cloud of smoke, sending the minie ball whizzing past and ripping through the grass.

The Rebel skirmisher's bullet missed but jolted Solomon enough to send him to the ground. Solomon, quickly jumping back to his feet, raised his Springfield, cocked the hammer all the way back, and aimed. Without hesitating, he pulled the trigger and quickly dropped down in the weeds.

"Quick, Sol! Reload!" James shouted, just as two more bullets from other Confederate skirmishers screamed past and tore through the wheat behind them.

"Did we get 'em?"

"I dunno…maybe one of 'em, but we gotta get outta here."

"Hawk and Henry see 'em now too," Solomon said. "I think we just saved 'em."

"I think so too," James said, carefully raising his head to peer through the grass.

James then turned toward Solomon, and after waiting for him to finish reloading, said, "We gotta move. Ready?"

"Yeah, go."

"This way," James said, leading the way.

They were now crawling on their stomachs, and more bullets hissed overhead from both directions. The skirmishing had turned into a steady firefight between the Indiana men and Rebel pickets. Some of the shots were close, and the two brothers paused to scan their surroundings. Most of the Nineteenth's skirmishers were farther to the north, but Hawk and Henry were still several dozen yards to the south near the orchard.

"Why'd they go so far out here?" Solomon said.

"I don't know," James replied, listening to the continuous rattle of muskets. "There's a lot of fighting at that farm past those trees."

"The rest of Company B is off to the north, James."

"I know, I know." He paused, and they both scanned the area. "And it was Henry in the front when they moved out there."

"Something's wrong, James. Really wrong."

James knew Solomon was right, especially about Henry. "Let's stay here a minute and watch."

The two brothers lay in the grass for several minutes, listening to the fight at the farm on the other side of the orchard. Off to the west, the constant crackling of muskets between the pickets slowed to just sporadic gunfire.

"Hawk fired again," Solomon said, watching Hawk jump back behind an apple tree to reload.

"What's Henry doing, though?" James asked. "Let's go over there and bring 'em back in before they get themselves killed."

"Or captured," Solomon added. "Yeah, let's go. At least we'll see why they're way out there."

Crawling on their bellies, the two brothers carefully made their way to the south. With about forty yards of open field between themselves and the orchard, James and Solomon saw their squadmates under two apple trees. A few hundred yards beyond them, they could see Confederates running toward the barn.

Seeing James and Solomon, Hawk frantically waved them forward. "Come on!" he shouted, urging them to hurry.

"Ready to make a run for it, Sol?" James asked, nodding toward the orchard.

"After you. Let's go."

Staying low, they darted through the grass toward the trees. After reaching the orchard and dropping to the ground, they saw that Hawk was just ducking back behind the trunk of a tree after firing at enemy skirmishers to the west.

"What you doin' out here, Hawk?" Solomon asked.

"We're picking off Johnnies across that field," Hawk said.

"It's a no-man's-land out here."

"I know. But...believe it or not, it's Henry that got us all the way out here."

"What do you mean?"

"Henry started going this way, and I followed him," Hawk said.

James and Solomon looked at each other quizzically and then at Henry again. Henry's face was red, and he was soaked in sweat. He ignored them and, instead, just stared down his gunsight toward the fields to the west.

"What are you doing, Henry?" James asked.

"I dunno," Henry said, not looking up from his musket.

"Well, let's get back over to that field," Solomon said.

"Yeah, come on, Henry," James said.

Henry didn't move, his eyes now scanning between the fight at the farm and the Rebel skirmishers to the west.

"Henry, look at me," Solomon said.

Henry turned and looked at Solomon but didn't speak.

"You alright, Hen?" Solomon asked. They'd been friends forever, it seemed, but Solomon had never seen him like this.

"You guys, go on," Henry finally said. "I'll stay out here and slow 'em down when they attack."

"That's ridiculous," James interjected. "There's just one of you and hundreds of them. Come on."

"He wants to be out here," Hawk said. "I've tried bringing him back." Hawk had started to say more but was interrupted by a loud road of musketry at the barn.

"Looks like there's more Union men approaching that house and barn," James said, nodding at hundreds of blue-clad soldiers by the creek exchanging fire with the Confederates.

"There's been shots comin' from that house and barn all mornin'," Hawk said. "The Yanks are gonna finally try to fight 'em and get 'em out of there."

"Forget that barn, Hawk," Solomon said. "That's not our fight."

Hawk, though, still watched the growing fight around the farm. More Union men down near the creek had fired another volley toward the Rebels in the upstairs windows.

"Yanks are gonna take the house," Hawk said.

"Hawk, we can't stay here," James said.

More artillery shells arced overhead, and Solomon nervously looked to the west. Along the ridge, more red battle flags had appeared, and he could hear the faint sounds of bugles and drums.

"Look how many Rebs are forming out there along that wood line," Solomon said. "We gotta go."

"He's right, Hawk," James said, pointing at the ridge to the west. "There's thousands of 'em."

Solomon looked at Henry again. He was shaking. "Henry, let's get outta here!"

"Go ahead and go back," Henry said.

"No, Henry!" Solomon said desperately. "What are you doing? You're coming with us!"

The sounds of Rebel skirmishers' muskets closer to the orchard made all four of the Indiana men turn in that direction.

"Their pickets are movin' closer," Hawk said.

"Let's go, Henry!" James urged. "This is crazy. There's bullets everywhere."

"I'm not goin', James."

"Now, Henry, let's go! This is suicide."

"It's not suicide," Henry said. "I can't handle this war anymore. This is my chance."

"Chance at running? Here?" James shouted.

"Come on, let's go!" Solomon pleaded, grabbing Henry by the arm.

Henry yanked his arm free and yelled, "Leave me...go!"

Just as Henry said it, a bullet screamed past and shredded the tree's leaves right behind them before slamming into the trunk and splintering its bark. Henry didn't even flinch.

"Hawk, do something!" Solomon shouted.

"I've tried for a week, Sol. He's gonna run."

More musketry rattled from the field.

"We got no choice," James said. "We're gonna die out here. The rest of the company is off to the north, and the whole brigade is back behind the creek."

"James is right," Hawk said. "We gotta go now. We should be back over that way. You and Solomon, go back. I'll stay a minute and try to talk Henry out of it, but I'll be right behind you."

Behind them, another rifle volley from the Yankees at the creek echoed through the orchard. A scream from the barn was followed by dozens of shots from the Rebels.

"Don't do this, Henry!" Solomon begged. Henry didn't respond. Solomon watched Henry carefully and knew he had made up his mind. With the Rebels so close, the ordeal pleading with Henry to come back with them seemed like an eternity. Solomon knew that lives hung in the balance and that they had spent all the time they could.

Knowing they had to fall back and leave Henry to do whatever he was going to do, Solomon thought about all the battles in which Henry had overcome his fears and fought so bravely. Several times in camp and on the march, Henry had spoken of his beliefs against the war and the terror it brought him.

Yet Henry had always gone into battle and done his duty. Kneeling in the orchard with another major battle approaching, Solomon felt a deep sympathy for him that he had never experienced before.

"Henry," Solomon said, looking at him and waiting for Henry to turn in his direction. "If you make a run for it, you don't look back. You survive, and you make it. You hear me, Hen? You survive, Henry."

Henry nodded. Unable to hide his fear and guilt he felt inside, he looked at Solomon. He didn't want to let his squad down but didn't feel like he had a choice. He couldn't stand in a line and watch more men die. And he definitely wouldn't do any more killing either.

Solomon grabbed his arm again and looked in his eyes. "You get to them trees, Henry. Then you run to that creek way out there, and you follow it. You run and keep going, Henry."

Henry felt a lump in his throat. Solomon had always been a great friend, but Solomon's understanding of what he was about to do now meant more than anything. He took a deep breath and finally spoke. "Thanks, Sol."

Solomon felt tears forming and turned away.

More bullets whistled past and tore through trees and grass. A Confederate's voice could be heard not far away, apparently yelling to his comrades about the four Union men in the orchard.

Hawk looked away from the Confederates and back to his squad. "Sol, James, you have to go now," he said. "Go."

James knew they had no choice. "Come on, Sol," he said, slapping his brother on the arm and then darting low through the grass.

Just as Solomon turned to leave and follow his brother, Henry shouted, "Godspeed, Sol!"

Solomon quickly turned around and looked at Henry... for the last time, he knew.

Henry's expression had changed to a smile, and he appeared totally calm. This was the first time the squad had seen Henry calm and smiling in several days.

"And Godspeed to you, Henry!" Solomon shouted back. "Good luck."

As Solomon turned away, he noticed Henry was still smiling...crying too. But smiling.

The two brothers ran through the field toward the next squad of Company B skirmishers and dropped into the wheat.

James felt his heart racing when he looked back up toward the orchard. Solomon was watching too.

They saw Hawk try to grab Henry's arm again, but Henry had avoided Hawk's grasp.

"What's Hawk doing, James?"

"I dunno."

Hawk had his hand out now and seemed to be pleading.

Watching Hawk and Henry's conversation in the orchard made Solomon feel helpless. Glancing toward Billy and Grear, Solomon saw that more Rebel skirmishers had approached and forced them to fall back.

Looking back toward the orchard, they could see Hawk was still talking to Henry. Suddenly, though, Henry stood straight up and turned to the west as if to run.

"*Nooooo....!*" Solomon yelled from the wheat field, realizing what was happening.

Just as Henry had stood up, Hawk lunged forward toward him. But Hawk was too late. Henry had only taken one step before clouds of gun smoke erupted from the west followed by a burst of muskets.

A lead ball ripped through Henry's abdomen, and as it exited, the bullet opened up the side of his jacket in a pink mist.

The blast spun him around but somehow didn't knock him down.

Henry's mouth was wide open, and from eighty yards away, James and Solomon could still hear what he yelled.

"*Haaaaawwwwk....!*"

James and Solomon watched in horror.

Despite the pain, Henry reached into his haversack. He had his diary in his hand now and held it out for Hawk. Just as he started to toss it to Hawk, another bullet slammed into Henry's left shoulder, sending both arms awkwardly up into the air.

Henry looked as if he was frozen in place with his mouth wide open and his arms above his head. Henry's diary, as if in slow motion, seemed to float in midair before slowly drifting to the ground and landing halfway between Henry and Hawk. The blast of another musket echoed from the orchard.

It was much louder than the others, and the bullet found its mark.

It struck Henry in the back of the head and dropped him to the ground and out of sight.

-12-

West of Willoughby Run, Gettysburg
July 1, 1863, 2:45 p.m.

"*Henry!*" Solomon screamed out.

Both brothers, horrified, stared into the orchard but saw no movement where Henry had gone down. They saw Hawk crawling in Henry's direction, but he had now disappeared down in the grass too.

"What's Hawk doing?" James asked. The skirmish at the house and barn had spilled over into the orchard, and more Rebels were heading toward them.

"Hawk's gotta get outta there!" Solomon felt panicked. It was bad enough seeing his best friend killed, and now he was worried Hawk wouldn't escape either. "There's more Rebs heading toward the orchard, James."

Behind them, more shots rang out, and James quickly turned to see the other Company B skirmishers heavily engaged. The Confederates had advanced even closer. Billy and Grear Williams, the closest to the Whitlows, were reloading and firing as fast as they could. Lieutenants Schlagle and Jones were just to the north of them, as well as Corporals Crull and Conley. The entire company was in a no-man's-land and fighting for their lives.

"Hold, boys!" Lieutenant Schlagle shouted just before firing the last round from his revolver then dropping back down to reload.

James then looked further to the rear and saw Sergeant Boller. James had always known the sarge was a coward, and there he was again…back behind the rest of the men who were fighting out front. Boller was gazing forward, apparently having seen the entire episode at the orchard. The sergeant's face seethed in anger, but his expression changed to a sneer when he saw James looking at him.

"Sol, look at Boller."

The sergeant had always suspected Henry would desert one day, and now Boller had seen him stand up and begin to run away just before being shot. Even though James and Solomon had tried talking Henry out of deserting, they both knew that Sergeant Boller would accuse them otherwise. Without hearing the sergeant's actual words, the two brothers could easily recognize what he was thinking. *I've got you now,* he seemed to be saying, thinking about the four squadmates in the orchard.

Another storm of muskets echoed from closer to the orchard. The Whitlow brothers quickly turned and saw Hawk sprinting through the wheat field toward them. At least a dozen Rebels had stood up and fired at Hawk as he ran. Hawk had his rifle in one hand and Henry's diary in the other. The look of fear on Hawk's face was one that the Whitlows had never before seen on him.

Both brothers fired at the Rebels then quickly began reloading.

"We gotta move, James. Let's get outta this smoke."

"Come on!"

Without hesitating, James led the way toward the rest of the company skirmishers. Looking to the left, Solomon felt his heart jump when he saw the top of a Rebel flag appear from behind a crest in the field.

"I didn't know they were that close!" Solomon shouted as the rest of the battle flag and the first line of Rebel infantry came into view.

Hawk had made it through the wheat field and caught up to the Whitlows. They ran several more yards together then dove into a clump of untamed weeds.

"The whole Rebel Army is coming over that ridge!" Hawk shouted.

"Fire at those Rebs over there," James said. "They're right on top of our skirmishers."

"Hawk," Solomon said, "Boller saw the whole thing in the orchard!"

"So what?" Hawk said, still reloading.

"He's been waiting to get one of us, Hawk. He thinks Henry deserted."

"I'll take care of the sarge later," Hawk said, standing up and angrily pulling the trigger with a flurry of curses. Kneeling back down in the grass, he scanned the horizon to assess their position. They were still over a hundred yards from the rest of the Company B skirmishers, and the Rebel skirmishers had moved in closer.

"Let's fire one more volley and then get out of here," James said. "The rest of the company has fallen back toward the creek."

Solomon, having just reloaded, nodded.

Hawk finished ramming another minie ball down and placed a cap on the gun's nipple. "Ready," he said, already picking out a target.

The three Indiana men rose simultaneously and quickly fired. The Rebel skirmishers were mostly standing now and had become more brazen with their long infantry lines behind them. The squad dropped back down and covered their heads. Their volley had drawn a hailstorm of Rebel bullets that ripped through the weeds around them. They all took a deep breath, looked up at each other, and nodded.

This was their chance.

Without another word, James, Solomon, and Hawk turned and sprinted from their cover in the weeds and out into the open field. With bullets screaming past, they reached a clump of bushes near Billy and Grear who were both hunkered down in the weeds and reloading.

"We can't hold here!" Solomon yelled.

"*Ugggghhh!*"

Over to the right where the scream came from, they saw Lieutenant Schlagle falling backwards. A Rebel minie ball had just ripped through both of the lieutenant's thighs and sent him reeling to the ground in pain. Despite all the noise and chaos, they could all still hear his cries of agony even after he'd disappeared in the grass.

Further to the right, Sergeant Major Asa Blanchard was running between the Company B skirmishers.

"We're bringin' in the pickets!" Blanchard shouted, motioning with his arms for the skirmishers to fall back to their main battle line across the creek.

The Confederate line was within fifty yards now.

"Fall back!" Lieutenant Jones yelled from further to the right.

"Get one more shot off and then run!" James yelled.

With trembling hands as the Rebels approached, James, Solomon, and Hawk frantically reloaded their muskets. They could hear the drums and the Southerners' voices now and even felt the rumbling of thousands of bootsteps.

"Fire!" James shouted, standing up and squeezing his trigger.

Solomon peered through the grass and picked a target. Quickly standing and aiming, he pulled the trigger and then turned to run.

"Go! Fall back!" Hawk shouted. He hadn't fired yet but looked for a target that was the most immediate threat. "Get across the creek before it's too late!"

For several of the other Company B skirmishers, it *was* already too late. Johnny Markle, Bill Locke, Benjamin Duke, and several others hadn't seen the Confederates maneuver around to their rear. Now facing Rebel bayonets and muskets just inches away, they had no other choice but to throw up their hands and surrender.

Solomon felt his heart racing after seeing their comrades being captured. "Run, James!" he yelled. "Go!"

James was already in a full sprint when he heard the blast of Hawk's musket just behind them. Noticing the Whitlow brothers look back over their shoulders, Hawk shouted, "Run! They're right behind us!"

Solomon staggered but quickly regained his balance and kept on going. James was just ahead of him now and turned to look at his brother.

"Keep going, James! I'm right behind ya!"

All the skirmishers were in a do-or-die run for the creek. Men yelled and cursed. Stumbling over clumps of weeds, they sprinted toward the woods where the rest of the regiment's battle line was now arranged beyond the creek's far bank.

James saw the blue regimental flag and the national Stars and Stripes through the trees. They seemed so far away. *Oh, God, let me get there...*

Hearing angry shouts from the left, he looked over his shoulder. They were Southern voices, and more Company B men were being forced to surrender. Those men were his friends... friends he'd probably never see again. Being taken prisoner was a death sentence for many soldiers. James had known George Bunch and Jeff Kinder since he was a kid. Determined to not be captured himself, he ran even harder.

Suddenly, from just a few feet behind him, James heard a musket blast that sent smoke bursting right past his head. The lead ball missed by only a few inches and thudded in the ground just in front of him. He stumbled but desperately scrambled to his feet again and continued to scurry forward.

James was a few strides ahead of his brother as he approached the brush along the bank of the creek. Only a few yards from the tree line, they looked ahead and saw the entire brigade beyond the far bank.

With just a few more yards to the bushes, James dug deep inside for every bit of speed he could muster. The Rebels were just behind him when he heard their officers shout out a flurry of orders to their men. Sensing the attackers pause and raising their rifles, James's heart nearly stopped when a Rebel officer shouted out the next command.

"*Fire!*"

The entire Confederate battle line behind him erupted in a massive volley of muskets.

Whoosh! Thuuuddd!

Almost as soon as James heard the first muzzle blast, he felt the lead bullet smash into the back of his right leg.

As the hot, lead ball ripped through skin and muscle, James felt a pain worse than any he'd felt before. A fiery blast of agony rose from his leg and raced through his body. Already running at a full sprint, he lost his balance and went tumbling into the weeds just short of the creek.

"*Noooooo!*" Solomon screamed, seeing James go down just in front of him.

Landing on his rifle and haversack, James cried out in agony and struggled to roll onto his other side.

Solomon quickly stopped beside him and knelt down.

"We gotta keep going!" Solomon yelled, grabbing James's hand and trying to pull him up.

But James was too weak to stand and fell back down in the grass.

Reeling in pain, James reached down to the back of his thigh and felt his pants now soaked with blood. He knew the musket ball had penetrated deep. He opened his mouth to scream, but shock had taken him now, and all he could do was moan.

Sol's frightened face, white and ghostly, was right above him.

There were more screams…the Rebel yell. Muzzle blasts seemed just inches behind them now. He felt hot smoke, and bullets whistled past.

"Get up! Lemme help you up!" Solomon shouted, reaching under his brother's arm.

"I'm hit bad, Sol," James said, finally finding words.

"We gotta cross the creek now!"

Clinging his arm around Solomon's shoulder and neck, James fought with all his strength to finally get up to a crawling position. They crawled several feet forward together before losing their balance and stumbling among the weeds and rocks just short of the creek's bank.

Falling against the rocks, James screamed out in agony.

Solomon frantically wedged his shoulder under James's chest and, with all his strength, hoisted him onto his back. "Come on, James! I got you!"

Groaning, the two brothers lunged forward and into the shallow water.

"Just hang on to me!" Solomon pleaded. "We're gonna make it!"

Just ahead past the opposite bank, the entire Nineteenth Indiana regiment was formed in a battle line, waiting for the Confederates still rushing forward.

Struggling with the weight of his wounded brother on his back, Solomon fought to keep his balance in the shallow, rocky creek. He was nearly halfway across when his foot slipped on the rocks, sending both soldiers tumbling into the knee-deep water.

"Come on, Whitlow!" someone yelled from the other bank.

Solomon turned and looked over his shoulder at the Confederates who were coming through the brush behind them.

With several more of their fellow Indiana soldiers shouting out encouragement, Solomon struggled back to his feet.

"Keep going, James!" Solomon yelled. "Hang on! We gotta make it across!"

Splashing water, the two brothers struggled to get across any way they could. James's leg left a bloody, dark cloud in the water as he fought his way through the creek.

"Solomon!"

The voice was Hawk's. Hawk had already made it to the far bank but now ran back toward James and Solomon. Seeing James and Solomon struggling to cross the creek, Hawk threw his rifle and haversack into the grass and climbed down the bank.

"Get back in line, Hawkins!" an unseen officer yelled.

Seeing comrades in trouble, another man sprang forward to help out too.

"Hawkins!" an angry voice shouted.

Confederate bullets ripped through the air as Hawk stepped onto a large, flat rock and then splashed through the water.

"You can make it!" Hawk yelled as he lunged toward the brothers, both back down in the water again.

"Help me get him up, Hawk!" Solomon yelled above the sounds of guns now just a few yards behind them.

Hawk had already reached down for his squadmate and friend when Solomon yelled. Seeing the blood in the water from James's leg wound for the first time, Hawk immediately knew how desperate their situation was.

Then shouts echoed from the Union line.

"*Aim!*"

Hearing the command, James, Solomon, and Hawk ducked their heads and froze as hundreds of Union musket barrels were lowered and aimed at the Confederates across the creek.

"*Fire! Fire!*"

The Union line erupted in a storm of fire, smoke, and flying lead. Bullets screeched past, some hitting the water, rocks, and trees on the far bank. But most slammed into the front rank of Confederates, sending out a chorus of painful screams and howls.

"I'll get him, Sol! You go on!" Hawk shouted, ignoring the Confederates now at the creek bank just behind them.

"James, grab my arm!"

Hawk reached under James's arm, threw it over his own, and hoisted him over his back.

Solomon, meanwhile, had scampered through the creek on all fours to the other bank.

"Here!" Solomon shouted, turning around and extending his hand.

"Grab his hand!" Hawk shouted.

Using all his strength, Solomon helped Hawk and James across the rocks at the bank and up into the grass.

"*Uggghhh!*" James screeched in pain as he landed in the grass.

Solomon, just beside James, turned and looked back across the creek. The first volley by the Indiana soldiers had devastating effects on the front line of North Carolinians, but the gaps in the Confederate line were quickly filled.

"Let's get you back behind the line!" Solomon shouted, seeing the Rebels behind them preparing to fire another volley.

It was only a second later that the order to fire echoed down the line.

"*Fire!*"

The entire Rebel line suddenly erupted in another roar of muskets and a hailstorm of flying lead.

James couldn't move his leg at all and didn't dare look back. He felt himself start to fall, but Hawk and Solomon both had him now.

Ahead, he could see the red, white, and blue national flag and the blue regimental banner hanging just beside it. Burl Cunningham, jacketless with his side now wrapped in a blood-soaked bandage, had the Stars and Stripes, and young Abe Buckles stood next to him. Abe had a rifle again...the Nineteenth would need every musket they could get today. Between shots, Abe glanced up at the bullet-torn flag. He'd get his chance to hoist it again, he knew.

James felt weak and struggled to see through the smoke. Somehow, Grear and Billy had miraculously made it back from the skirmish line and were there in the line too.

James saw Colonel Williams, standing tall and leaning forward over the front rank of men. He had his Colt out and aimed at the North Carolinians in the creek. James had never known a braver officer than their colonel.

"Hold on, James!" Solomon yelled.

Fire erupted from muskets.

More men screamed, both behind them and ahead on the Nineteenth's battle line. Solomon and Hawk, still holding James from falling, reached the blue-clad battle line and dropped to the ground.

"Get him to the rear!" Hawk shouted. "Go!"

Solomon looked down at his brother and knew he had to make a quick decision. Part of him wanted to stay with the line and fight, but he also knew he had to save his brother.

"Come on, James!" Solomon yelled, leaning down and helping James to a crawling position.

James, trying to move, groaned and then cried out, "It hurts bad, Sol."

"I know, James. Keep going."

Together, they crawled several feet behind the battle line and collapsed in the trampled weeds. Solomon turned toward the Nineteenth's line, obscured in thick, dark smoke. The battle against the North Carolinians had raged into a storm. Solomon saw Colonel Williams shift men to the left where the Nineteenth was being hit the hardest. Lieutenant Jones and the few other Company B men still able to fight ran that direction and jumped back into the battle on the line's left flank.

Solomon looked at his brother. He'd lost a lot of blood and was grimacing in pain.

"Put pressure on it, James," Solomon said, pulling a hand-kerchief from his haversack and pressing it against James's thigh.

"*Uggghhh…*"

"Hang in there, James."

"It hurts, Sol."

"Help!" Solomon frantically screamed, looking up and not knowing what else to do.

Then he looked toward the back of the Indiana line. The men were making a stand and holding the North Carolinians at the creek. But Solomon had seen the length of the Rebel battle lines and knew the Nineteenth wouldn't be able to hold for long.

"James, you have to crawl to the rear."

James groaned.

"You have to, James. Go on."

The battle raged to an even louder roar, and Solomon turned. The national Stars and Stripes had gone down, and Solomon now knew what he had to do.

"Crawl that way, James," Solomon said, turning toward his brother and pointing up the slope and away from the fighting. "I'll send someone back for you."

Solomon grabbed James's arm and helped him get on all fours. With his arm around his brother, Solomon crawled with him at first, but then he stood up.

"Sol…"

"You're gonna make it, James."

"Sol, listen…you tell Ma and Pa I love 'em for me. You hear me, Sol?"

"You're gonna tell 'em yourself," Solomon said, turning away and hiding tears. He wiped his eyes and turned back to his brother.

Knowing neither of them had any time, Solomon firmly said, "Go on, James."

Then, with a determined look on his face, Solomon turned and ran toward the battle line.

Leaving his wounded brother behind was the hardest thing he had ever done.

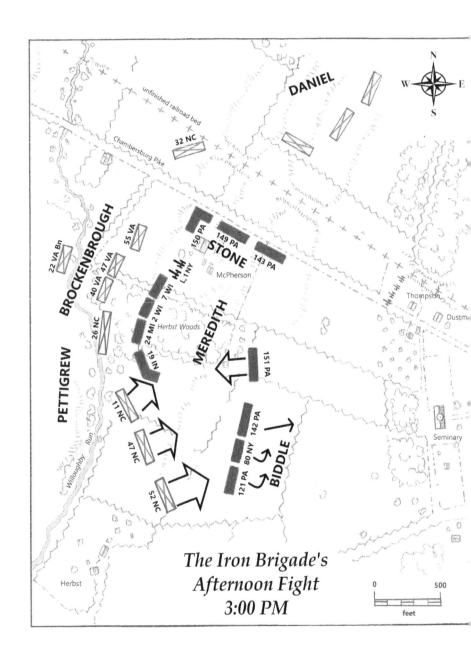

The Iron Brigade's
Afternoon Fight
3:00 PM

-13-

Herbst Woods, West of Gettysburg
July 1, 1863, 3:15 p.m.

Solomon knew he must return to fight with the rest of the regiment. Using his bloody hand, he put his black hat back on his sweaty head and sprinted toward the deafening roar of muskets.

Stepping up into a gap in the line next to Hawk, Solomon lowered his Springfield and stared in disbelief at the number of dead and wounded men lying in the weeds. The gunfire between the two lines was as intense as he had ever seen.

Rebels yelled like demons.

Men screamed and fell.

Solomon glanced at Hawk and wanted to say something about James. Solomon knew that Hawk had become one of their brothers too.

Thinking of James, Solomon turned and tried looking through the smoke behind him. He wanted to see James but knew it was impossible. Hawk caught his glance and forced a smile and nodded. That was as good as words, they both knew.

A shower of bullets whizzed past, and Solomon looked forward again.

"We gotta hold 'em back, Sol!" Hawk shouted, ramming another round down his barrel. "Fire, Sol!"

As Solomon reached for the flap on his cartridge box, he suddenly heard a screech that ended with a thud. He felt it too…a hard crunch to his left side. Quickly looking down, he saw his pants were wet, not just from the creek, but also from water now gushing from his canteen which had just been struck by a bullet.

Next to him, eighteen-year-old Johnny McKinney, a boy from Kokomo and now in the squad with Billy and Grear, threw up his arms and silently gasped. Solomon glanced over and saw that Johnny's eyes were wide and looked to the sky. A bullet had struck him in the chest, and he crumpled to the weeds.

Solomon looked away. Nothing seemed real.

"*Sol! Sol!*"

Hawk's voice sounded as though it was far away.

Through the smoke, Solomon stared toward the creek. Then, upon seeing the water flowing red with blood as it swirled around a dead North Carolinian, he felt a knot in his stomach and nearly vomited. Just upstream, more Confederates tried crossing the creek but were blasted backward, landing with splashes and yells.

Closer, he heard more deafening muskets and a piercing scream.

"*Sol!*"

To the right, there was even more blinding smoke, but then Solomon saw the national flag. Young Abe Buckles had it again and waved it wildly. Burl Cunningham, wounded for the second time today carrying that flag, was on the ground next to Abe and holding his leg gushing with blood.

"Sol!" Hawk shouted again, this time grabbing Solomon's arm to get his attention. "Fire, Sol!"

Solomon shook his head and blinked his eyes. He quickly picked a target—a blackened-faced, butternut-clad old man who had already raised his musket to shoot. Solomon hastily aimed and pulled the trigger. Fire and smoke erupted from his barrel, and the heavy lead bullet slammed into the North Carolinian's chest, sending his arms and musket flying wildly into the air. The old Rebel shrieked in agony, and his eyes locked onto Solomon's as he dropped to his knees. The sight made Solomon freeze, and they both stared at each other until the wounded man plunged all the way down and disappeared below the bank.

Reloading with trembling hands, Solomon finally looked away. He glanced at Abe Buckles and the Stars and Stripes again. Defiant, Abe yelled and angrily shook his fist at the gray-clad men who had marched from several states away to kill him and take his flag. And then another storm of bullets whirred in his direction, riddling the national flag with more holes and even splintering its wooden staff.

Solomon returned his rammer and again looked at the gray, yelling mass of Rebels to his front. Placing a cap, he cocked the hammer all the way back and aimed at a North Carolina boy in the creek. He fired again, but his bullet apparently missed. Through the smoke, Solomon saw his target still rushing forward and splashing toward the bank. Solomon's shot must have been bloodlustingly close though... the boy's one-man Rebel yell was now louder than all the others combined.

Solomon began to load again and, out of the corner of his eye, saw Billy falling with a scream that no one could hear. Solomon turned and stared in horror. Billy's pants around his groin were wet and black. When Billy reached down, fresh blood ran between his fingers. With his mouth still open in a soundless scream, he collapsed in the trampled weeds. Landing with a jolt, Billy looked over at his cousin just as Grear screamed and then fell too. Billy, gone-eyed now, stared as Grear clutched his own bloody leg and cried out in pain.

Solomon could feel the terror, and his whole body trembled. Forcing himself to look away from Billy and Grear, Solomon rammed black powder and another bullet down his Springfield's barrel.

"Pour it to 'em men!" Lieutenant Jones yelled, encouraging his men. Sword held high above his head with one hand, their red-haired lieutenant fired his revolver with the other.

More screaming Rebels climbed the creek's bank and advanced through the smoke.

"Hold 'em back!" Jones shouted again, firing off another round. Then, suddenly, he dropped his sword, and his hat flew off his head.

"Lieutenant!" a private called out, too late for his lieutenant to hear.

A Rebel minie ball had struck Lieutenant Jones above the eye, and he was dead before he hit the ground.

Quickly aiming, Solomon fired into the yelling mass of gray. Hawk spewed curses and threw down his powder-clogged musket. He leaned down and picked up another one lying among the dead and wounded, then quickly loaded it and fired.

Hawk was in a rage now. Reaching for another cartridge, he singled out another target before even tearing off the paper. With gritted teeth, he rammed the ball down, placed a cap, and aimed. Already knowing this shot would kill, he screamed out and pulled the trigger.

"Kill 'em, Sol!" Hawk shouted, already looking for another target and reloading.

Solomon fired another shot, but then, from off to the right, he heard Abe Buckles's voice scream out in pain. Abe had just been hit in the shoulder and now spun backwards. But his yelling didn't stop…only turned angrier…especially when he hit the weeds with the flag coming down atop him.

Next to Abe, Corporal Phipps somehow still stood and held the blue regimental banner high above their heads. A private from Company K grabbed the national flag, but he, too, was shot down before even getting a chance to hoist it.

Across the creek, the North Carolinians' line stretched to the south, disappearing beyond the foliage. More Rebel bullets flew through the trees and underbrush toward the Union line. Casualties from both sides mounted as the lead storm raged between the two sides. Dead and wounded Union soldiers lay in rows, and Company B was now only a small squad of survivors still standing and fighting.

Hands trembled and hearts raced.

Steady!

From somewhere in the smoke and weeds, a grown man cried out for his mother.

Piercing lead tore through flesh, and more men bled.

Bones splintered and cracked.

Solomon looked away from the horrifying scenes and, trying to focus, violently shook his head.

But then he heard bloodcurdling yells and saw red flags leading hundreds of screaming scarecrows clad in brown and gray. The field on the left was full of 'em now...but not in the straight, perfect lines as before. The creek and briars had broken those up. But still, on they came.

He lowered his Springfield and prepared to load. Looking at Hawk, he yelled, "We can't hold here!"

"I know, Sol!" Hawk shouted back. "I know! Keep firing!"

"Steady, men!" someone yelled.

Oh, God!

They fired and loaded as fast as they could. Glancing back while pulling another cartridge from his box, Solomon noticed Sergeant Boller hunkered down near a bush back behind the line.

"Hold that line!" the sergeant yelled up to the men in front of him. Just as he yelled it, a bullet whistled past and thudded into a tree. The sergeant then took another step back and frantically ducked even lower for cover.

"Boller ain't fightin', Hawk," Solomon said, pulling his rammer. But then, he wished he hadn't said it. Hawk had turned toward the sergeant and, seeing him cowering in the rear, redirected his fury.

"Boller!" Hawk shouted. "Load that musket and help us!"

Sergeant Boller looked at Hawk, then quickly turned away. Attempting to appear as though he was actually fighting, the sergeant yelled at another man farther down the line.

"Load faster!" Boller yelled, barely raising his head and still hiding behind the bush.

"That yellow belly ain't…"

Hawk then sprung toward the sergeant. Seeing Boller shirking behind the fighting line again brought him to a speechless rage. For months, the sergeant's mistreatment of the men in the company incensed them all, especially Hawk. But wearing that uniform, especially *that* hat, and not fighting…

"This ends right here!" Hawk shouted.

"Hawk, no!" Solomon pleaded, turning and seeing Hawk lunge toward the sergeant still cowering near the bushes.

"You coward, Boller!" Hawk snarled.

"What…" Sergeant Boller cried out, panicked. "What you doing, Hawk?"

It was too late for the sergeant. Hawk's rage had boiled over, and he grabbed Boller by the arm and yanked him up off the ground.

"Get up there and fight, you yellow-bellied coward!" Hawk yelled, pulling the sergeant up to the line.

"You're crazy, Hawkin—"

Boller tried to get the rest of Hawk's name out, but Hawk jabbed the butt of his musket into the sergeant's back. Boller screeched in pain and fell next to the rest of the Indiana men fighting on the front line.

"Load, you chicken-bastard!"

Another gust of bullets flew past, and the sergeant ducked again. Hawk didn't even flinch, instead, grabbed Boller's jacket and pulled him up. "Get up!" Hawk yelled. "You ever even fired a bullet at the enemy? See what a battle's like up here, Boller? Now…fight!"

The sergeant's hands shook as he loaded his Springfield, all the while staring at Hawk. Despite the gray battle line to his front with all their screams and muskets, Boller knew *they* weren't *his* greatest danger. Right now, Hawk seemed more likely to kill him than a Rebel did.

Still trembling, Boller turned and fired.

"There's too many of them, Hawk!" Solomon shouted.

"I know, Sol. Just kill as many as you can."

"There's more of 'em coming around our left!" Solomon shouted.

The survivors were now caught in a deadly crossfire from the Confederates in the woods at the creek and the hundreds of Rebels attacking through the field from the south. And they all knew it too. The Company B men were in a desperate fight to hold the regiment's left flank. Colonel Williams moved up and down the line and encouraged his men to hold.

"Lieutenant, the flag is down!" a private cried out.

Lieutenant Macy, nearby, shouted back, "Go and get it!"

"Go to hell!" the private yelled. "I won't do it!" He wasn't a coward though. At least he still stood on the line, firing his musket.

Crockett East, a freshly promoted second lieutenant from Company K, sprinted forward and hoisted the regiment's blue flag. He only had it in the air for a few seconds before he, too, was struck by bullets and fell to the ground.

Both flags were down now, and the roar of muskets had risen to a storm. Sergeant Major Blanchard, several yards away, saw the flags and turned to the nearest private behind him.

"Pick up that flag!" Blanchard shouted.

A private from Company E grabbed the national flag's staff but was quickly struck down as soon as he began to raise it. Despite the shower of lead, another private rushed over to pick up the flag. His chance for glory, though, ended with a Rebel bullet before he even reached it.

Seeing the Stars and Stripes still on the ground, Lieutenant Colonel Dudley quickly ran to the flag and hoisted it into the air himself.

"Rally, men!" Dudley shouted, reforming the men on either side of their flag.

He waved the flag back and forth…but only once and then screamed out in pain. Solomon was right beside him when the Rebel ball struck Dudley in the right leg. The bullet made a sickening sound when it hit the bone, breaking the lieutenant colonel's leg just below the knee.

Dudley, still clutching the flag's staff, cried out again and then dropped to the ground.

Seeing their lieutenant colonel on the ground, Sergeant Major Blanchard sprang forward. Despite the storm of muskets and flying lead, Blanchard knelt down and said, "Colonel, you shouldn't have done this."

Lieutenant Colonel Dudley, fighting off urges to scream out in pain, tried speaking but couldn't.

The sergeant major glanced down at Dudley's leg…and quickly wished he hadn't. It was gushing with blood where a splintered bone protruded. Blanchard then looked up at Dudley and, after swallowing a lump in his throat, said, "I shall never forgive myself for letting you touch that flag. That was my duty."

With gritted teeth, Dudley muttered, "Just get me to the rear, Sergeant Major."

"Yes…yes, sir," Blanchard said, then turned toward two privates and waved them forward.

As the two soldiers lifted their lieutenant colonel to carry him to the rear, Dudley grabbed Blanchard's arm. He glanced around at the fighting men, then up at Blanchard. "We're *all* doing our duty today, Sergeant Major."

Blanchard wiped away a tear and then said, "Colonel, now it is my turn to carry the flag."

-14-

Herbst Woods, West of Gettysburg
July 1, 1863, 3:30 p.m.

It had been several minutes since James had watched Solomon rush back toward the fighting line near the creek. After seeing his brother disappear in the smoke among the Nineteenth's men, James anxiously watched the battle for just a few moments, took a deep breath, and then struggled further toward the rear.

Crawling and dragging himself inch by inch, James reached a rise in the woods, and before starting down the other side, he turned around again. Through the trees and smoke, he could see part of the Nineteenth's line now. Their battle with the North Carolinians continued to rage. The American flag had been down, but now he saw someone lift it high above their heads and into another shower of smoke and lead.

Over on his right, the fight was just as intense. A Rebel battle flag fell but then rose again. The Confederate line surged ahead, and the roar of muskets rose to a fury. Michigan and Wisconsin men, firing volleys from just yards away, screamed and yelled. Their flags went down too, but for now, their thinning line held.

James saw more men fall, and those who could, crawled to the rear. Thinking of Solomon and the rest of the Nineteenth again, he looked toward their line one last time. It was ablaze with fire and smoke, and then he saw the Stars and Stripes disappear down into the smoke again. Several men screamed, and James saw even more wounded soldiers scurry behind the line.

Hearing their screams and seeing his regiment suffer brought an urge to return to the line and help. He sat up and even crawled a step in that direction, but a sudden rush of pain shot from his leg.

Looking down, he saw fresh blood. A muscle spasm shook his entire body, and he cried out in agony. The pain stole his breath, and his eyes blurred. Despite his efforts not to, he fell back down.

He still had his canteen somehow. He reached for it and, with a painful grimace, took a drink. The woods around him were full of dead and wounded men. Most of the dead were from the fight this morning, but now, even more bullet-stricken men limped and crawled to the rear any way they could.

James saw a Michigan man, blinded by blood from a head-shot, stumble and fall behind their line. Another wounded man near him cried out for help with his bloody, mangled leg dangling below the knee. James tried to look away from the two horribly wounded men but couldn't. With his eyes transfixed, he saw that the bloody-faced man had his arm around the crippled one now. One man could walk, and the other could see. And together, miraculously, the two Michiganders started toward the rear again.

Feeling more wet blood on his leg, James looked down at the handkerchief Solomon had hastily tied. Seeing it soaked with blood, James knew he had to stop the bleeding if he were to survive. But he also knew he had to keep moving. Even from this far behind the line, whistling lead balls pierced the air.

James looked up toward the Nineteenth's line again. Despite thickening smoke, he could see the field to their left was full of Rebels now, and some of the men on that flank had been forced to fall back. He knew the Nineteenth's fight had become desperate, and he wished he could return to fight and help. He also knew there was nothing he could do.

Again, he fought off the urge to turn back. Then, with the sounds of battle roaring behind him, he pulled his canteen strap back across his shoulder and resumed his agonizing crawl to the rear.

After just a few yards, the pain became too severe to go on. He felt so weak, he stopped against a tree to steady himself from falling prone. Even though he wanted to lie down, James knew he shouldn't. With the battle still so close behind him, lying down here would mean certain death.

Leaning against the tree, James surveyed his surroundings. A little further to the rear, the ground gradually dropped away. James lifted his head and saw a small trickle of water down in the wooded ravine.

I must get to that stream, he told himself.

Descending the slope was even more painful than going up. James could feel his rapid breathing becoming less effective as he worked to keep moving. His lungs burned, and his heart raced. Stopping to catch his breath, he suddenly heard an artillery shell ripping through the treetops above. James quickly dropped to the ground and covered his head just as the shell crashed halfway up a nearby tree. With branches and leaves raining down all around him, he hugged the ground and prayed.

He waited until the last branch fell, then slowly lifted his head. Despite bullets and shells shrieking above, he scrambled back to his knees and resumed his way toward the little creek.

Closer now, James paused when he saw a wounded Union soldier lying at the stream's edge. He'd seen dozens of dead or wounded men lying on the ground, but this man looked directly at James and lifted his hand.

"Over here," the man called out with a struggle, waving James toward him. "*Water...*"

James crawled toward the young soldier and leaned over him. The man grimaced while he forced his eyes to stay open.

"*Thirsty...,*" the wounded soldier said weakly.

The man's shirt was open, and James could see his bloody chest. The man was clutching his wounds with one hand and holding his Iron Brigade hat with the other. James noticed the hat's red circular badge with a brass number "2" and a "K" just above it. The man's Lorenz musket was lying underneath his arm, and his open cartridge box lay a few feet away.

James held his canteen to the man's mouth and, not sure what else to say, asked, "Wisconsin?"

The man nodded and drank a few drops before coughing.

"What's your name, soldier?" James asked.

The man grunted faintly and murmured something James couldn't understand.

James leaned in close and asked again, "What's your name?"

"Schu...Schuckart," he muttered. "Ernst Schuckart."

"Where you from?"

This time, there was no response at all. James looked at the wounded man carefully. His sack coat was open, uncovering a bloody shirt that had been ripped apart in the front. The torn shirt revealed missing flesh that exposed the soldier's wound now covered with dirt and mud from the man's own hands. His eyes were closed now, and his breathing was shallow.

James thought of his own wound and looked at his leg. It was still bleeding, and even the ends of the handkerchief's knot were soaked with blood now. Knowing he was losing a lot of blood, he looked around for something to tie around his leg.

Then he saw the wounded Wisconsin soldier's musket again and its attached leather sling. James reached over, grabbed the leather gun sling, and pulled it toward him. Using both hands, he unhooked the sling's buckle and pulled the leather strap loose from the musket.

James had never needed a tourniquet before but had seen many men who had. It would hurt, he knew. With a grimace, he pulled the leather strap under his leg a few inches above the wound and wrapped it around the front of his thigh.

He paused and took a deep breath. Then, gritting his teeth, he pulled the strap through the sling's buckle. He pulled the end as tight as he could and, with shaking hands, placed the buckle pin in its hole.

James had held it back as long as he could but now screamed out in pain. He felt light-headed but forced himself to focus.

The ridge to the front was full of smoke, and the battle had become louder. More men trickled back.

"*Run!*" an unseen voice shouted.

After glancing down at his tourniquet, James quickly looked away and toward the Wisconsin soldier next to him. Knowing they must move further to the rear, James said, "We gotta get out of here."

Seeing the man's eyes closed, James grabbed his shoulder and tried to shake him awake. The man didn't move.

James shook him again and, louder this time, said, "We gotta get to the rear. The battle's moving this way."

Still, the man didn't respond. Hearing the battle still roaring in front of him and seeing the Wisconsin man's gun, James realized that he might need that musket. James picked up the Lorenz, then crawled over and grabbed a handful of bullets from the man's discarded cartridge box and stuffed them in his pocket.

After checking the Wisconsin soldier again and seeing he was unconscious, James knew he would have to leave him behind. James then took another drink from his canteen, quickly refilled it in the muddy creek, and prepared himself to move. Then, just as he began crawling to the rear again, he saw a soldier run from the smoke and duck behind a tree. Unaware of James crouching down by the small stream, the man nervously looked around the woods and then suddenly darted toward another tree farther to the rear. James saw the man had blood on his jacket but appeared otherwise unwounded. A deserter for sure, James knew.

James turned away from the man and began to crawl again, but suddenly, a thought struck him.

The man…he looked familiar.

As soon as James turned his head to look again, he saw that the deserter was staring directly at him. Their eyes met, and James recognized him immediately.

Sergeant Boller!

Their eyes were locked for an awkward moment. James couldn't hold back and yelled above the muskets, "You coward, Boller!"

Without responding, the sergeant turned and sprinted to the rear.

"You'll be shot, Boller!" James shouted. "Coward!"

Thinking of Boller running away from battle enraged him, especially in these woods where so many good, brave men were now lying dead or wounded. James had always suspected the sergeant was a coward and probably shirked away from previous battles. Now, though, James knew for sure.

Just after the sergeant disappeared beyond a clump of trees, the musketry behind them rose to a roar. It was much closer now, and James quickly turned his head toward the Nineteenth's line.

"Oh, God," James said, seeing clusters of the Nineteenth's men now in a fighting retreat. They were just over the ridge, and James knew if he were to escape, he had to go now. With the Wisconsin man's Lorenz in one hand, James painfully crawled along the stream and then up the slope on the other side.

Dragging his leg and streaking blood, he dared looking back. Through the trees and smoke, he saw the Nineteenth's men trying to hold their ground. Beyond them, James caught glimpses of the attacking Confederates. And off to the left in the open fields, he watched in horror as hundreds of unopposed Rebels emerged beyond the Nineteenth's flank.

Despite the pain, James dragged himself farther from the fight.

Suddenly, from further to the rear, James heard a thundering of hooves and yells. Looking up, he saw a group of mounted officers come to a halt at another slight rise in the woods. General Meredith, mounted on his large black mare, led the group and barked out orders.

"If they fall back, reform our new line here!" General Meredith shouted to his staff. "We must hold these woods!"

James continued crawling to the rear but looked over his shoulder. He didn't know how far he'd gone, but through the smoke, he saw that the battle line had pulled back even further. They were within fifty yards of him now. The Nineteenth, with even fewer men than before, was attempting to make a desperate stand.

James was still looking back at the fight when, suddenly, he heard a loud blast near General Meredith and his staff. James quickly turned and saw a shell had exploded among the trees, showering the woods with hot metal and flames.

Staring in disbelief, James saw the general reel in his saddle and fall to the side. Meredith's forehead streaked with blood where shrapnel had struck. His giant horse had also been hit and raised up on its hind legs.

Neighing and groaning, the horse crashed to the ground and landed on top of the Iron Brigade's commander. The weight of the massive horse crushed the unconscious general's ribs and legs and pinned him to the ground. Yelling frantically, officers and staffers struggled to free their general from underneath his horse.

James watched in shock. He'd always respected Long Sol.

After pulling Meredith free, two of the staffers placed their general on a stretcher and rushed him toward the rear. One of the lieutenants spurred his own horse toward the Seventh Wisconsin. Their colonel would command the Iron Brigade now.

James glanced toward the battle again. Through the smoke, he could see that the fighting line had retreated even closer to him, and he knew he couldn't get away fast enough.

Above the sounds of muskets and yells, he heard Private Sinnex scream out. James and Solomon had both become good friends with the private from Pendleton, Indiana. Thomas Sinnex was a seventeen-year-old kid when he enlisted with Madison County's Company A. Thomas, dropping down to a knee and reloading, now had dead squadmates on both sides of him.

Beyond the Nineteenth, James could now see the Rebels too. A constant volley of musket fire roared from their line.

The Nineteenth's men seemed desperate, and it looked like only half of them remained.

Just above the Nineteenth's line, someone had raised the blue regimental flag again…but it quickly fell and disappeared among the smoke and men.

Another brave, young color bearer had just been killed, James knew. James crawled farther. The battle line wasn't far away from him now, and knowing he would need his musket, he reached into his pocket for one of the Wisconsin soldier's cartridges and began to reload.

James saw a mounted Union officer and his horse speed past him from the rear. The officer hurriedly spurred his horse toward the front, quickly dismounted, and ran toward Colonel Williams.

James heard more yells.

Rebels rushed forward.

James saw Tommy Sinnex had taken several steps back but quickly dropped to a knee, turned, and fired again.

Then, above the sounds of battle, James could hear their colonel's voice.

"*Fall back!*" Williams yelled, waving his sword high above his head and pointing toward the rear.

James knew the Nineteenth's men were in a desperate fight for their lives…and, as they fell back, were heading directly toward him.

-15-

Nineteenth Indiana's Battle Line
Herbst Woods, West of Gettysburg
July 1, 1863, Late Afternoon

Hawk, reloading, heard a bellowing voice and quickly looked up. A Rebel lieutenant was wildly waving his sword above his head and leading a group of yelling Rebels who were charging out ahead of their line. Hawk glanced over toward Solomon who had already placed a cap and raised his Springfield.

Solomon saw him too and aimed. He'd learned long ago that taking down an officer could stop an entire battle line. Hawk had taught all of them *that*...even well before Manassas. *Shoot their officers first*, Hawk had said. Even now, no one knew how Hawk had learned things like that.

Steady...

Just as Solomon was about to pull the trigger, the lieutenant passed behind the trunk of a large white oak. Solomon waited for the Rebel officer to reappear on the other side of the tree, then quickly adjusted his aim.

The Rebel lieutenant was now turned sideways toward his men and urging them forward. He swooped his sword downward and then angrily thrust it forward toward the Union line.

"*Forward! Forward!*"

"Kill him, Sol!"

Solomon squeezed the trigger. The Springfield let off a blast of smoke and fire that sent the lead minie ball spiraling toward its target. The one-ounce lead ball pierced the lieutenant's coat just above the left breast and then slammed into a rib before lodging in the muscle an inch below the left shoulder blade.

Solomon's bullet had broken and splintered the rib bone, and despite a newly ruptured lung, the Rebel lieutenant's scream pierced the air. The lieutenant's mouth stayed open as he crumpled sideways into another gray-clad soldier charging beside him. The two Rebels' legs tangled and sent both men to the ground. But still, dozens of Rebels rushed through the weeds directly toward the thinning Union line.

Lowering his rifle, Solomon reached into his cartridge box for another round and looked left and right along the Nineteenth's battle line. Both flags were down, and more men had fallen. Some tried carrying themselves to the rear and away from the hell of lead. Some couldn't even do that and lay where they fell. The luckiest of those died a swift, merciful death.

"Our line's beginning to waver!" Solomon shouted.

Hawk ignored him and fired another round.

Solomon had just finished stowing his rammer when, out of the corner of his eye, he saw Private Peter Foust's head jerk backwards. Foust then reached for his face and collapsed to the ground. The bullet had struck him in the jaw, and his face and hands were now covered in blood. Solomon froze and stared. Peter had a wife and daughter back home, Solomon knew… and a baby boy born just last year.

"Sol! Sol!"

Someone was yelling his name, but Solomon still stared as Private Foust finally stopped moving.

"Sol!"

The voice was Hawk's trying to pull Solomon's attention back to the fight. As Solomon forced himself to look away, he said a quick prayer for Private Foust…and for the son whom Foust would never get to see.

The North Carolina regiment was across the creek and just in front of them now. The greatest danger to the Nineteenth, however, was in the open field to their south where hundreds of Rebels were now angling directly toward the Nineteenth Indiana's left flank.

Solomon raised his Springfield toward the screaming mass of gray and fired. He knew his bullet must have hit something because, beside him, Hawk let out a whoop and even laughed.

Lowering his rifle to reload, Solomon glanced toward Hawk. Hawk's face had turned to a sneer, and then, as Hawk pulled his own Springfield up and aimed at the Rebels, he showed a bitterness they'd all seen before. Hawk sure hated Rebels. And still, two years into the war, no one knew why. There was something more to it, Solomon knew. Much more. Seeing Hawk now, Solomon decided he would ask him about it again…later…if they survived past today.

Hawk pulled the trigger. He also hit his target and laughed when he saw the Rebel drop into the weeds. Solomon didn't understand why anyone would laugh like that during a battle, but he'd seen Hawk do it before.

And now, as Hawk rammed another minie ball down the muzzle and stowed his rammer, he laughed again, all the while scanning the Rebels for his next target.

"Kill 'em, Sol!" Hawk yelled.

Glancing over, Solomon could see Hawk's devilish grin as he lowered his barrel and prepared to fire again. He was a madman now.

Solomon again raised his own musket toward the way-too-many Confederates. He pulled the hammer all the way back.

Then he took aim at a Rebel who had dropped down to one knee and had his rifle pointed directly at Solomon.

When Solomon saw the Rebel's musket erupt in fire and smoke, he knew he was too late. Just as Solomon pulled the trigger, he felt a bullet slice into his upper arm. He immediately looked down and saw blood had already begun to seep through his coat. Examining the damage closer, he saw that the ball had penetrated his coat and shirt just below the shoulder. With his other hand, he felt the wound and was relieved that the minie ball seemed to exit at the same place. *A flesh wound, is all.*

Quickly dismissing the minor wound, Solomon pulled a cartridge out of his pocket, rammed it down, and returned the ramrod to its channel. He looked through the smoke. Someone else had taken down the man whose bullet had grazed Solomon. Solomon quickly re-aimed at the mass of Rebels and fired.

"We can't hold any longer, Colonel!" one of the Nineteenth's men cried out.

"Close up, men!" Williams yelled. He desperately looked across the field to the left and prayed for help he knew wouldn't come.

"Refuse the line, men!" Colonel Williams shouted, pointing with his sword directing more men toward the regiment's left flank.

"*Steady!*" an officer from the middle of the line bellowed.

Off to the left, a mass of North Carolinians had stopped in the field and were preparing to fire another volley.

"Fire! Fire!" Williams frantically yelled just as a torrent of lead ripped through the air.

Hearts raced and hands trembled.

Men screamed.

Solomon focused on loading and didn't dare look up.

"Fall back!" Colonel Williams finally shouted, knowing to stay would lead to a useless loss of his men. "Reform in the woods to the rear!"

It was a matter of numbers, not courage. The North Carolina brigade was the largest in Lee's entire army. The Eleventh North Carolina regiment alone marched into battle with over 600 men, and the next regiment to the north, the giant Twenty-Sixth North Carolina, was now attacking with almost 850 men. With two more regiments to the south advancing rapidly across the creek and open fields beyond the Nineteenth's flank, the situation was bleak for the Indiana veterans.

Other officers repeated the order to retreat and reform along a new line in the woods.

"Run!" a man screamed, the voice fading with its terrified owner who had already run into the woods to the rear.

"Don't turn, Sol!" Hawk shouted, stepping backwards while reloading.

Solomon took another shot and then began quickly back-pedaling toward the rear.

"They won't see my back!" someone else yelled, taking a knee and firing.

Hawk looked at the Rebel line still advancing and quickly fired another shot. Not only was the left end of the Nineteenth's line being flanked, but now, the Rebel yell was just as loud off to the right.

"Keep moving back, Sol!" Hawk yelled, knowing the entire brigade was about to be overrun.

Along with the men around them, Solomon and Hawk continued to back up while firing and reloading. Now in the thicker woods, they heard the cries of their wounded comrades lying amongst the weeds.

"The regiment's reforming a line at the flag, Hawk," Solomon said, pointing to the rear where a makeshift color guard had again unfurled their flags.

"Let's go, Sol!" Hawk shouted, finally turning and breaking into a run. The few clusters of the Nineteenth's men nearby also quickly turned and hurried farther into the woods. In the middle of the Indiana men, Solomon saw that Sergeant Major Blanchard now held the national banner and had the flag's shuck wrapped around his waist.

"Rally, boys!" Blanchard screamed, waving the Stars and Stripes as more men joined the new battle line.

"*Solomon...*"

Solomon barely heard the voice between musket blasts and quickly turned to look who had said it.

"*Sol...over here,*" the weak voice said again, slightly louder this time.

Solomon peered through the smoke and trees where the voice was coming from...just on the other side of a small trickling stream.

And then Solomon saw who it was.

"*James! James!*" Solomon cried out, rushing toward his brother. Solomon sprinted across the stream and dropped to his knees.

James, lying on his back with his head propped against a fallen tree, was barely recognizable now. His face and hands were smeared with blood, sweat, and gunpowder, and his pant-leg was soaked in blood.

"You're doin' good, James! Real good!"

Solomon, not knowing what else to say, looked at his brother and smiled.

James tried smiling too and then mumbled something Solomon couldn't understand.

Solomon nervously glanced toward the smoke and the Rebel line. The Confederate assault had slowed down but was still moving toward them. "I thought you made it farther to the rear than this, James."

"How's the—" James began to ask but was interrupted by another volley of muskets.

Solomon offered his canteen and said, "Here…water."

James held up a hand, refusing Solomon's canteen. James still had his, Solomon noticed. And he had a musket too. Behind them, the sound of muskets roared. Solomon knew he had to do something quick. Solomon turned toward the line only a few dozen yards away.

"Let me help get you to our new battle line, James. This will be a no-man's-land here."

"Get me up…here," James said, reaching out with his arm while still clutching the musket with his other hand.

Solomon reached down and leaned in to wedge his own shoulder under James's arm. James groaned and then cried out in pain as Solomon helped him to his feet.

With one arm around the back of Solomon's neck and using his musket as a crutch, James weakly said, "Okay…go, Sol."

"I got ya," Solomon said, clinging to his brother and leading him toward the Nineteenth's battle line, now only a fraction of the size it had been earlier. Just ahead, Hawk was reloading and waving the two brothers toward him.

"Almost there," Solomon said.

James turned his head and, behind them, saw the Confederates advancing in their direction.

"Here you go, James," Solomon said, lowering James to the ground next to Hawk.

James quickly turned toward the Rebels and placed his musket on his raised knee.

"Here they come!"

"Rally, boys!" Blanchard yelled again, still waving the flag.

As the Indiana men in this new battle line reloaded and aimed, the Rebels let out a spine-chilling yell and charged through the smoke. Solomon loaded his Springfield and faced the sound. Surprised to see the Confederates already so close again, Solomon quickly raised his rifle.

"Take out that flag, Sol!" Hawk shouted. They all knew dropping the color bearer would slow their entire line. The flag and its bearer, along with the North Carolina regiment's colonel, were out ahead of the rest of the Rebel line.

The red and blue flag was so close that Solomon could see its thirteen white stars and even read the white *11ᵗʰ NC* printed on it, along with the names of battles the obviously proud regiment had apparently fought in—*Antietam, Frayser's Farm, Seven Pines, Malvern Hill…*

Solomon lowered his gunsight from the flag and down onto the color bearer's chest. He held his breath and squeezed the trigger. The effects were almost immediate. Hitting the North Carolinian in the shoulder, the bullet spun the young color bearer sideways. But, determined to not let go of that flag, he somehow still held its staff with one hand…even as he fell to the ground. The red battle flag seemed to hang in midair for a long moment until it also finally fell and landed atop its dying bearer.

"Take out that bastard colonel!" someone shouted.

James saw the colonel too and again raised his musket onto his knee. The colonel was the tallest Rebel James had ever seen, at least a foot taller than the color bearer who was now down in the weeds with their flag.

"Forward, men!" the Rebel colonel yelled wildly. The Confederate officer's European accent caught James by surprise. *Strange*, James thought, *an Englishman over here fighting with the Rebels*. Seeing his regiment's flag go down, the colonel reached down to pick it up and hoisted it high into the air.

"Shoot him, James!" Hawk yelled while throwing down his powder-clogged musket and wishing he could take down the Rebel colonel himself. Seeing the Rebels still advancing, Hawk then bellowed a stream of curses before leaning down and grabbing another musket from a fallen soldier.

"*Forward!*"

The Rebel colonel yelled again, urging his men forward and swinging the battle flag above his head. Silhouetted by the afternoon sun behind it, the flag gleamed a brighter red than James had ever seen. The flag itself took on a bloody and angry appearance as the Rebels rushed from behind it.

Despite the pain in his leg, James steadied his rifle on his knee and took aim. With the gunsight on the Rebel colonel's chest, James held his breath and squeezed the trigger. The bullet struck the Englishman-turned-Rebel in the arm holding the flag. The colonel's mouth was still open when the bullet hit, and his yell turned into a painful shriek. His arm and flag flew back over his head, but somehow, the Rebel colonel kept coming.

"I got him," Hawk said with a sneer, having finally finished loading the dead man's musket he'd taken. Hawk raised the Springfield toward the Rebel officer, cursed a storm of words no one could understand, and pulled the trigger.

Hawk's bullet hit his target in the hip, dropping the colonel into the grass with the battle flag falling atop him. With their battle flag down, the Confederates near their fallen colonel slowed their advance. But, within only a few seconds, the Rebel flag went back up, and with another unearthly howl, they surged forward again.

The Rebels had momentum now and charged ahead with a fury.

"Fire!" several of the Nineteenth officers shouted…the ones still alive, at least.

Solomon aimed again and fired. The target was a demon-screaming, blackened-face private wildly charging forward with his bayonet out front. Solomon's bullet struck the Rebel in the leg and silenced his scream. Somehow, though, he continued staggering forward and finally fell only a few feet to their front.

James's hands trembled as he loaded his musket and, with a struggle, finally balanced the rifle on his knee. The Confederates were just ahead of them now, and there was no way to stop them. Already weak and using all the strength and concentration he could muster, James aimed, took a deep breath, and pulled the trigger.

James didn't even look through the smoke to see whether the bullet hit his target or not, but instead, despite the pain, reached into his pocket and began reloading.

There was a constant roar of musket fire from the small squad of Indiana men gathered around their two flags. But still, the Confederates kept charging.

"We can't hold here any longer!" a private screamed.

Just as he said it, Asa Blanchard screamed out in pain. A lead ball had just struck the sergeant major in the groin and severed the artery. Seeing the blood spurt from his leg, Blanchard dropped to the ground, pulling the flag down with him.

Private Clifford rushed toward him and leaned down to help.

"Don't stop for me!" Blanchard yelled. "Don't let them take the flag. Tell my…"

The sergeant major tried to continue, but his voice was too weak. Then, when he saw another private take hold of the flag and begin to raise it again, Blanchard caught his breath and found the strength to continue.

"Tell my mother…that I never faltered."

Colonel Williams was there now too. The colonel looked around and quickly analyzed the regiment's predicament. With the Confederates almost on top of the Indiana men, they were about to be overrun. Sam Williams had no choice. He stood and, with a booming voice, shouted, "Fall back! Fall back! Reform beyond the woods!"

Private Clifford and Corporal Phipps from Company I quickly rushed to the rear with the flags. Phipps didn't get far before he too was shot down, sending the tattered and bullet-ridden Stars and Stripes to the ground for the eighth time on this horrific day.

Several more Union officers repeated their colonel's order, and the entire regiment was now in a full retreat toward the edge of the woods. Solomon dropped to a knee next to James.

"Go on, Sol," James told his younger brother.

"I'll carry you!" Solomon insisted as he started to put his arm under James's shoulder. "Come on!"

"No! Go!" James shouted.

Solomon looked at the Rebel line again. He was trembling and couldn't speak.

"We'll both die if you carry me, Sol. Save yourself."

Just a few yards in front of them, Hawk had clubbed a Rebel with the butt of his musket and was now turning to swing at another one.

"No, Hawk!" Solomon shouted, knowing Hawk's hand-to-hand fighting would prove suicidal.

Solomon yelled again, then leaned down to his brother. He placed his hand on James's shoulder but quickly turned away to hide his tears.

Another Rebel fell to the butt of Hawk's musket, but several more were closing in on him.

James, also seeing how close the Rebels were, grabbed his brother's coat sleeve and pulled him close. With sweat, dirt, and tears on his face, he looked directly into Solomon's eyes. After a painful grimace, he spoke. "Survive, Sol...and make it home. You make it home, Sol."

The angry, rushing Rebels were now only a few yards away. After swinging at and striking another Rebel, Hawk sprinted back toward the Whitlow brothers. The Confederates would be on top of them within seconds.

"Go, Sol!" James yelled. "I mean it! Go!"

"I can't…"

Solomon struggled for words.

"Now! Go!" James yelled again, looking up with tears in his eyes. James clutched Solomon's arm and shook it. He was desperately trying to save his brother's life.

Solomon looked at him again and desperately wanted to say something comforting. Unable to find the words, he got up and looked at his wounded brother. James turned away and began readying his rifle.

A shower of bullets whizzed past.

"Let's go, Sol!" It was Hawk this time.

Only a few yards behind them, there were howls and yells by the hundreds.

"Come on!"

Hawk urged Solomon again and grabbed his arm.

Solomon stood up, backed away from his brother, and then turned and broke into a sprint. Now sounding like thousands of screaming demons, the Rebels behind him kept rushing forward.

James watched as Solomon and Hawk turned and ran through the woods. Seriously wounded and likely to be captured, James knew this was probably the last time he would ever see his brother.

The Confederates behind him were almost atop him now, and James quickly turned around. Concentrating on steadying his rifle on his knee, he looked through the gunsight and aimed at the closest Rebel just to his front.

James pulled the trigger, and the gun let off a blast of smoke and lead. Not waiting to see the results of his shot, James immediately reached for another cartridge.

But it was too late.

The Rebel, a bearded and toothless brute of a man, lunged ahead with his bayonet. His rage had contorted his dirty face into an evil form. With fiery eyes, the Rebel let out a scream and pounced.

All James could do was lift up and raise his arms to try to deflect the blow. Down in the grass, he had almost no chance of escaping the steel blade's wrath. The Rebel grunted as he thrust the gun's bayonet.

The cold steel sliced through James's shirt and tore into the skin just below his right collarbone. James let out a bloodcurdling yell that echoed through the entire woodlot and beyond. The giant North Carolinian pulled the bloody bayonet back and looked at his victim with a remorseless stare.

Then, without speaking a word, he stepped over James and continued through the woods.

Feeling the blow, James fell back and stared up at the smoke and treetops above. The piercing pain lasted only a few seconds, then quickly gave way to shock.

James felt almost nothing now.

But the Rebels kept surging past…with their worn shoes, sometimes even barefoot, and their threadbare, gray uniforms. Their yells seemed to keep the entire mob moving, chasing the Yankees who had fled through the woods before them.

James felt himself drifting away. The sounds of the battle and of the soldiers racing past quickly faded. The artillery shells and the musket blasts now seemed so far away. As his surroundings grew distant, thoughts from another time filled his mind.

James thought of his family's farm, peaceful and quiet. His mother and father were there at the door, and his sisters were just inside running up from behind. He heard their gleeful voices shouting out.

Despite his wounds and weakness, James felt himself smiling.

"*James, James!*" one of his young sisters playfully screamed. He could hear the other girls cry out too from just behind his parents.

He tried walking closer. But, strangely, his legs didn't move. He was floating now.

Who else is there?

He tried to concentrate.

Solomon and John? No, couldn't be…they were much too old to be his brothers. Are they carrying me?

Then he focused on his father.

"Why are you crying, Father?" he asked. He extended his hand, but his father didn't see it.

He tried to speak again, but his voice made no sound.

His mother's face, so happy and full of joy, quickly turned to a look of fear and terror as he floated past.

His mother let out a loud shrill.

"Nooooo!"

James didn't understand the scream. He looked toward his mother as she threw her hands over her face. Tears flowed from her eyes and through her hands as she dropped to her knees.

"Sol, John…what's happening?"

They were now crying too.

James felt himself fading away once more, and then everything went quiet. The world was blurry, but he was lying in the woods again. He could see the battle raging all around him, but, eerily, there were still no sounds. The soldiers were running past, their mouths open and yelling…silently though.

Had the battle stopped?

But then, an artillery shell suddenly rocketed through the trees and exploded just a few yards away. But it seemed to be in slow motion…everything was moving slowly now.

And silent too.

James couldn't feel anything, only his breath and his beating heart. He forced his eyes to stay open and looked up at the sky. There was a blur all around him.

I'm so tired…so tired.

He drifted farther and farther from the battle and the woods. Blinking several times, he began to feel a calm overcome him, peaceful almost. He was floating again, so softly here just above the ground among the trees and the grass.

Fighting sleep, he forced himself to not let go.

But he couldn't control it anymore.

He tried staring at the tops of the trees, but they were blurry now too. Forcing his eyes to stay open, he took one last look.

And then, suddenly, he closed his eyes.

-16-

McPherson's Ridge, West of Gettysburg
July 1, 1863, Late Afternoon

Solomon knew he shouldn't look back. But when he heard the musket blast behind him, he quickly turned around. He saw a cloud of smoke from James's rifle and then saw James raise his arms in a hopeless effort to defend himself. The Rebels were upon him now, and one of them let out a bloodcurdling yell as he lunged at James.

Solomon stopped running and screamed.

"*James! No!*"

James swung his arms wildly, trying to block the attacker's bayonet.

Solomon yelled again, but there was nothing he could do as the Rebel thrust his bayonet downward.

"*No!*"

Solomon instinctively took a step toward his brother and the attacker. But then, James was gone, vanished among the smoke and the Rebel-yelling mass of butternut and gray.

Feeling helpless, Solomon froze. The Confederates surged past where James was lying and were now within a few paces of also overrunning Solomon.

Solomon had no choice and quickly turned to the rear once

more. He darted through the trees and raced up the ridge near the edge of the woods. Hawk was several dozen yards ahead of him, and the rest of their fleeing regiment was even farther ahead and already out of the woods.

"Come on, Sol!" Hawk yelled, looking over his shoulder.

Exiting the woods and jumping over a prone body in the wheat, Solomon nearly stumbled but regained his balance and continued to run. In the bright sun now, smoke, sweat, and tears stung his eyes. After wiping his face with his sleeve, he squinted through the smoke and saw the army reforming beyond the fields on the distant ridge.

He saw the cannons first. Their crews laboriously kept the guns firing at the Confederates behind him in the woods and against the Rebel artillery farther to the west. Out in front of the cannons and along an open grove of trees, the infantry was behind a barricade of downed fence rails, and several battle flags flew above the regiments in their new battle line.

"Hurry, Sol!" Hawk yelled, turning his head again.

Solomon gasped for air. The fervor of the battle and the anguish at leaving his wounded brother behind left him almost breathless. He wanted to stop but knew he couldn't.

"I must go on," he said to himself.

Solomon focused his eyes ahead. The Nineteenth's blue regimental banner was up again, and the national Stars and Stripes went up beside it. Then something caught his eye. Above the smoke, he could see the top of the red brick seminary building and its green and white cupola.

Solomon fixated on the building's cupola as he ran. Smoke obscured most of the building, but the dome-roofed gazebo atop it seemed to be suspended in midair. It looked so strange. Despite the booming cannons, the cupola seemed so still and quiet, almost as if a spirit inside it was looking down. Looming over the battle, it seemed to watch *too* closely, Solomon thought.

It appeared to be eternal…a timeless, reluctant witness above the roar, quietly gazing down and waiting to tell what happened here. Suddenly, the ground shook as a shell exploded in the trees behind him. He immediately thought of James, and still running, he turned his head toward the sound. While looking at the shell's destruction among the trees behind him, his foot landed crooked on a pile of trampled wheat, causing him to stumble and fall.

Solomon lifted himself up on one knee and then tried to stand, but his legs failed him, and he fell back down. Still gasping for air, he looked around. Several of the morning fight's victims still lay lifeless in the wheat. Dozens of wounded Union soldiers scrambled through the fields, seeking the refuge of their new battle line along the ridge. Behind him, the Rebels and their horrific yells had stopped.

Maybe I could go back, he thought to himself. A deep angst came over him. He knew he would always regret leaving his wounded brother lying back there in those woods.

Lying in the trampled grass, trying to catch his breath, Solomon knew he had only a few seconds to make a decision. This would be his only chance to save his brother.

Suddenly, the Union cannons up on the ridge bellowed again, firing toward the west. As the blasts faded, Solomon again heard Rebels in the woods behind him. They'd be charging out of the woods and over the ridge soon, he knew. He remembered from earlier that, behind the North Carolinians, there were more fresh lines of gray…a whole division probably.

Going back into the woods was probably suicide, but he didn't want to leave James behind to be captured either.

What do I do?

He heard more yells from the woods, closer now.

Then he heard another noise, a totally different noise, and quickly turned.

Was that…a bark?

Solomon heard it again. The sound *was* indeed a bark, and then he saw the dog.

"Moses!"

Solomon watched as he ran toward him. Ever since Moses entered camp with James two weeks ago down in Virginia, he rarely left the two brothers' sides. Occasionally on the march, he would run through the trees parallel to the regiment's route but would always return to the squad whenever the army halted. Today was different, however. Solomon hadn't seen him since they were on the other side of the creek on picket duty...so much had happened since then.

Although Moses now ran from the direction of the woods, he seemed to emerge from nowhere. The dog appeared agitated and continued barking as he approached.

Yes, it's me, Moses seemed to say.

"You made it, boy!" Solomon exclaimed, still crouching down in the trampled wheat. "You made it!"

Moses had stopped barking but let out a whine and then spun around in a circle.

Solomon watched him, more carefully now.

Much like their dog at home, Moses seemed to want to communicate with him but couldn't. He stared at Solomon and whined again.

"What is it, boy?"

Another cannon boomed from the ridge. Moses barked when Solomon looked toward the cannons nearly a quarter mile away. Solomon turned back toward Moses who nervously ran a circle around him. He barked again and then also looked up toward the smoky ridge and the Union guns.

"What ya sayin', boy?" Solomon asked, watching Moses closely.

Moses turned away and whimpered. *A plea,* Solomon thought. Tail wagging, he approached again. Solomon reached out his hand once more, but this time, the dog tugged on Solomon's sleeve…but only for a second before whirling away again.

Moses let out another yelp, a higher pitched, more urgent noise this time. Then Moses darted toward the cannons and stopped several yards away from Solomon. He looked at Solomon and barked.

So strange, Solomon thought. "What you telling me, boy?"

He whined and then barked again. To Solomon, the barks somehow sounded more confident…a command almost.

Solomon heard more yells behind him and then saw the Confederates had reappeared at the edge of the woods and were moving forward again.

Moses barked, and with his tail wagging excitedly, he ran a little farther toward the Union cannons and stopped again and turned.

"This way?" Solomon asked, pointing past the dog.

Moses barked.

Despite the chaos and the day's hell, Solomon smiled. Moses watched him for a moment, then ran toward the Union guns. Solomon pressed his hat down tight on his head, wiped his face, and, following the dog's lead, broke into a run toward the blue lines and the flags.

With the dog out ahead and slightly to Solomon's left, they raced through the field. The relative safety of the Union line was only a few hundred yards away. Moses barked again and slowed just enough to allow Solomon to catch up.

"Almost there, Moses!" Solomon shouted, pointing toward the Nineteenth's flag among lines of blue infantry up ahead. "This way, boy!"

Through the smoke, he could now see many of the Indiana men's faces as he sprinted toward them. Despite being one of the last to leave the woods, Solomon saw other men also just now reaching the barricade. Most were wounded and struggled over the stacked fence rails. Those who couldn't climb the barricade themselves were helped by the other survivors. Solomon knew that those men had also just retreated across the field and had only been behind the barricade for a few minutes.

The Nineteenth was much smaller now, and Solomon could see that both the national Stars and Stripes and the giant blue regimental flag were tattered and had been riddled with bullets. On both sides of the battle line, artillery crews sweated in the afternoon sun, furiously working their guns. All the while, Rebel cannon shells and solid balls from several directions landed among the Union gunners.

Still running next to Moses, Solomon looked toward the Nineteenth Indiana's line again. *Almost there.* Despite knowing he'd stayed in the woods too long, Solomon now realized he would make it back to the line alive.

"We made it, Moses," he said, feeling relief and glancing at James's dog and even allowing himself a smile.

Then, suddenly, something among the men caught his eye. Not far from the Indiana flags, a soldier had stood up and raised his musket. It seemed to be aimed in Solomon and Moses's direction. He looked closer and then stooped down when he saw the soldier was definitely aiming *at them.*

Solomon started to yell but was too late.

The man's rifle suddenly burst with flame and smoke.

The musket's booming rapport reached him a half second later. The dog let out a yelp and jumped as a bullet ripped through the wheat and thudded into the ground just beside him. Worried another shot would come from the Union line, Solomon zigzagged and screamed.

"*Nooooo!*" Solomon yelled as he reached for his hat and held it high over his head to identify himself as a Union soldier. He stared at the smoke cloud where the shot came from. The man was gone now.

"Don't shoot!" Solomon screamed, waving his Iron Brigade hat in the air. "I'm Union! Don't shoot!"

"Hold your fire!" one of the men peering over the barricade shouted, recognizing Solomon as one of their own.

Solomon and Moses sprinted forward. The barricade was only a few dozen yards away now.

"Come on, Whitlow!" a voice yelled between cannon blasts.

Moses reached the stacked rails first and quickly climbed through. Cheers for their dog went up from the men.

And then, just ahead, the man who had shot at Solomon and Moses reappeared from behind the barricade. As the smoke cleared, Solomon recognized the shooter's face… *Sergeant Boller.*

Solomon gritted his teeth in rage. He hadn't seen the sergeant since earlier in the fight near the creek when Hawk had caught him shirking back behind the line. But he had quickly gone missing again, probably having escaped to the rear while the rest of the men bravely fought.

Solomon felt his blood rising to an angry boil. Now only a few strides from the barricade, Solomon changed direction and ran directly toward the sergeant.

Raging inside, Solomon approached the rails and clambered over.

"Oh, Private Whitlow," Boller exclaimed ingenuously.

"You!" Solomon yelled as he leapt from the barricade and stormed forward.

"I thought you were dead," Boller said, "…along with your brother."

Solomon charged with his arms out and reached for the sergeant's neck. "You! I'll kill you, Boller!"

The sergeant blocked Solomon's hands with his musket, but Solomon surged forward again with an angry shove that sent both men to the ground. Ending up on top of the pile,

Solomon forced his knee into the sergeant's chest and reared back with his fist.

The sergeant's hands flailed wildly trying to block the blow, but Solomon's punch still firmly landed with a cracking noise on the side of Boller's jaw. Solomon reached back to strike him again.

"Solomon, let him go!" a corporal from Company A shouted, lunging forward and grabbing Solomon's arm.

Solomon was still in a rage and fought to free his arm to punch Boller again. "My brother...he ain't dead, Boller! James ain't dead!"

Solomon couldn't control his rage and struggled against the corporal's grasp. "You're a dead man, Boller!"

Luckily for Boller, and probably for Solomon too, the corporal was much bigger than Solomon and was able to restrain Solomon from getting free.

Despite the corporal having a hold of him, Solomon still kept his knee atop the sergeant, pinning him to the ground. Knowing it was hopeless to free himself, Boller wiped blood from his mouth with his free hand and then spat into the grass.

"He'll be dead soon enough, *Private*," Boller hissed, looking Solomon in the eyes. "There'll be the devil himself doing his work in them woods tonight."

Solomon seethed and angrily struggled to free his arms.

"Let him go, Private," the corporal yelled at Solomon. The corporal now had the help of another soldier, and together, they both held Solomon's arms.

Solomon was still in a wild rage, and when he tried to yank his arms free, they tightened their grips even more.

"Why'd you shoot at me, Boller?" Solomon yelled. "You 'fraid I'm gonna tell 'bout yur shirkin' back at the creek? You coward! I saw ya myself...back there hidin' behind the line!"

Solomon struggled again with his captors and felt his strength draining. "And now, everyone saw you shoot at me!"

Solomon slipped a hand free and started to take a swing at Boller again when he heard a new voice. It was Hawk, only a few feet away.

"Sol, let him go!" Hawk shouted, stepping forward and grabbing ahold of Solomon's free arm. Hawk then gave the other private holding Solomon a gentle shove and said, "Let him go, Private."

Solomon struggled for breath, and his rage had turned to exhaustion.

Now looking at the corporal, Hawk said, "Corporal, I got him. Let go."

The corporal eased his grip but still clung to Solomon's sleeve.

Hawk looked at the corporal again and, faking a smile, said, "He's alright, Corporal. He's upset, is all. He'll be okay. I'll take him."

The corporal, still feeling Solomon as a threat, didn't let go.

Hawk continued in a quieter voice, "You gotta understand, sir…his brother's out there wounded in them woods. And then the Sarge here tried to shoot him. You saw it. I got him now. We gonna be havin' more Rebs to fight in a few minutes."

Hawk looked at Solomon for approval.

"You alright, Sol?" Hawk asked.

"Okay, okay," Solomon said, finally lifting his knee from Boller's chest. "Lemme go. I'm done with him."

The corporal released his grip but watched Solomon closely. Solomon slowly began to get up and nodded to the corporal to let him know he wouldn't attack the sergeant again. But inside, he still felt his anger.

Sergeant Boller sat up in the grass and wiped more blood from his mouth.

Solomon looked at the sergeant again and pointed. "You're a murderer, Boller. You knew me and the dog weren't Johnnies, and you shot at us anyway! Luckily, you're a lousy shot...and a lousy soldier."

"Come on, Sol," Hawk said, pulling on Solomon's arm.

Solomon backed away a few steps but then turned back toward the sergeant. "You're a coward, Sarge! The whole line saw you shirkin' back at the creek, hidin' behind a bush...while we're spillin' our blood."

Boller looked for help, but the men only stared.

"Then you shot at me. A coward and a murderer!"

"Let's go, Sol," Hawk said, jumping between his squadmate and the sergeant again. He had Solomon's arm in a tight hold and stepped into him with all his weight to force him away.

But Solomon couldn't let it go. With his face covered in sweat and red with rage, he looked at the sergeant and yelled again. "Couldn't recognize the blue pants, Sarge? Or how 'bout the hat?"

Hawk gave Solomon another shove that sent him tumbling backwards. "Go, Sol!"

"Coward, Boller!"

Solomon could barely get out the words. His exhausted body and mind had hit their limits. With eyes now blinded in tears, he finally turned away.

"You're alright, Sol," Hawk said, putting his arm around him and leading him away. "Let's go."

With Hawk holding Solomon up, they walked down the battle line and then stopped among the rest of Company B's survivors. There were only five of them now...five out of the thirty-two brave men who went into the fight this morning.

Solomon threw himself on the ground, then dropped his rifle, cartridge box, and haversack in the trampled grass at his side. Solomon's lungs felt like they would burst. He tried taking a deep breath but then thought of James out there in the woods. A cannon boomed…and then another. Wanting it to all go away, he beat his fist into the ground.

"God! God! God!" he shouted, his heart still racing. Clutching a fistful of grass, he cried out again.

"God! Why?"

He stared at the ground. More officers yelled and cannons bellowed. Wounded men moaned. Solomon put his hands on his ears and closed his eyes, but he still couldn't block out the horrible sounds all around him.

Solomon wanted his mind to escape. He forced his eyelids closed even harder and gritted his teeth. Furiously shaking his head, he pressed his hands hard against his ears, but muffled sounds still came through. Wishing it was all just a nightmare, he slowly uncovered his ears and began to open his eyes. It was all still here…the yells, the cannons, soldiers wounded and dying.

He slowly sat up and looked around. A few dozen men off to the right of the Indiana men knelt behind the barricade. Most of them had bandages. A captain barked out orders.

With his back against the stacked fence rails, Solomon looked up at the sky. Another Rebel shell arced overhead. He watched the shell's orange flame streak eastward and disappear beyond the smoke and the trees. It was headed toward the large building behind the battle line. He listened for the explosion. Nothing. Another bad Confederate fuse, he assumed.

He looked through the smoke at the large brick building again. His eyes drifted upward toward its roof and the cupola above, still overseeing the battle. Something about it engrossed him and made him stare. There was movement inside it now. He looked closer and saw a group of officers, one of them looking through field glasses aimed toward the western horizon. Another was pointing toward the woods from which Solomon had come and where James still lay. The cupola watched on, silently.

"It's a *seminary*, they say," Hawk said, breaking Solomon's trance. Hawk was still beside him, kneeling on one knee.

"Huh?" Solomon asked, realizing his mind had drifted. Shock probably, he thought.

"Ain't that the damnedest thing?" Hawk asked.

"What?"

"That building you been starin' at...it's a preacher school. I heard 'em call it a *seminary*. Ironic, ain't it?"

Solomon shifted his gaze away from the building and looked at Hawk. Hawk's normal smirk wasn't there. Solomon saw something serious in him now, deeper.

Solomon stared at him for a minute before finally turning away and looking at the other survivors around them. The bloodied Iron Brigade was bunched together, facing the field and the edge of the woods from which they had just escaped. The Nineteenth Indiana regiment was reduced to not much more than a handful of squads now. He looked up and down the line. There wasn't a clean uniform in sight. All were covered with dirt, and most with blood. Many of the soldiers wore bandages now, and he guessed that, of the three hundred men in the regiment who had gone into battle this morning, there were now less than one hundred survivors.

Although the artillery crews still worked their guns, there was a lull in the fighting. But Solomon remembered the masses of Confederates to the west, in and beyond the woods.

"They're gonna be comin' at us again, Hawk," he said.

"I know."

"Here," Hawk said, tossing Solomon his canteen.

"Thanks."

After taking a drink, Solomon splashed water on his face and looked at Hawk. Hawk had set his barrel on the fence rail and was staring blankly down his gunsight aimed to the west. He looked worried now, almost remorseful, Solomon thought.

Hawk was still a fighter, for sure, but he didn't look invincible the way he always had.

Solomon reached out and handed the canteen back, laying it against Hawk's leg. Hawk didn't seem to notice and still stared down his rifle barrel toward the field through which they had just fled.

"Thanks, Hawk," Solomon finally said. It was more of a query than a thank you.

Hawk nodded but didn't respond as he slung the canteen's strap across his shoulder.

"We left most of our regiment in those woods, Hawk."

"I know," Hawk said, breaking his silence but not his blank stare. "I'm really sorry 'bout James."

This time, it was Solomon's turn to not respond.

Hawk licked his dry lips and lifted his finger from the musket's trigger to rub his eye. Solomon studied Hawk carefully as he put his hand back on his rifle. Hawk moved his mouth to speak, then paused.

A yell came from the woods to the west. One of Stewart's brass Napoleons across the pike bellowed. The gun section's lieutenant and one of the sergeants were excitedly pointing to the west—they were both watching the Confederate infantry reappearing at the top of the ridge.

Solomon peered over the top rail of the barricade. To the southwest, across the creek where they'd fought earlier, a house was burning and filled the sky there with black smoke. It wasn't far from the orchard where Henry had been shot a few hours ago. Solomon glanced at Hawk and saw that he was staring at the burning house.

"Hawk, that house…," Solomon said.

Hawk shook his head and put his hand up, gesturing Solomon to say no more. Solomon stayed quiet and quickly looked away. He'd seen that look on Hawk's face before…it was almost a year ago when their column had marched past a Virginia farm that had been set afire. Hawk hated Virginians, for sure.

All Rebels, for that matter. But something about that burning barn—even though it was a Southerner's—had upset Hawk in a way they hadn't seen before. And now, Hawk had that look again.

Then, Hawk began speaking in a low tone Solomon hadn't heard him use before.

"Finally, be strong in the Lord and in His mighty power," Hawk said, still staring beyond the advancing Rebel battle line at the smoke in the distance.

Solomon listened, speechless, as Hawk continued.

"Put on the full armor of God, so that you can take your stand against the devil's schemes… For our struggle is not against flesh and blood, but against the rulers, against the authorities, against the powers of this dark world, and against the spiritual forces of evil in the heavenly realms."

There were more yells from the woods, and a Napoleon thundered from off to their right…one of Stevens's guns, closer this time and on this side of the pike.

Hawk only paused for a second. "Therefore, put on the full armor of God, so that when the day of evil comes, you may be able to stand your ground and, after you have done everything, stand firm then. With the belt of truth buckled, take up the shield of faith, with which you can extinguish all the flaming arrows of the evil one…"

Suddenly, from off to their left, a cannon bellowed a thunderous roar and sent a storm of flame, smoke, and metal toward the Rebel lines. It was one of Cooper's three-inch ordnance rifles just to the south of the Nineteenth Indiana.

As the smoke drifted over their line, Solomon dropped his head for cover. Hawk, though, hadn't even flinched and kept his eye still squinting down the barrel. With his blank stare gone now, Hawk gritted his teeth, concentrating. Solomon thought he looked somehow more sinister and committed to the killing that he was ready to do.

After the cannon's roar faded to echoes, Hawk continued. "To take the helmet of salvation and the sword of the Spirit, which is the Word of God. And pray in the Spirit."

Hawk stopped, and Solomon didn't know what to say.

"Ephesians," Hawk said, taking his eye from his Springfield and looking at Solomon.

Hawk had tears on his face.

Solomon was stunned. For two years, he had never seen Hawk cry... nor even come close. And he certainly had never heard him say a Bible verse.

"Here they come!" a man screamed, his voice cracking as he yelled it.

"Oh, no!" another soldier cried out.

When the Confederate battle line emerged from the woods and into the sunlight, they let out the Rebel yell.

Solomon quickly looked forward again, and out across the field, he saw the Confederates emerging from the woods and stretching in both directions well beyond both flanks of their battered brigade.

There were thousands of them now.

"Load!"

Hands trembling with fear reached for cartridges and rammers.

"Ready, men!" an unseen voice shouted.

Oh, God.

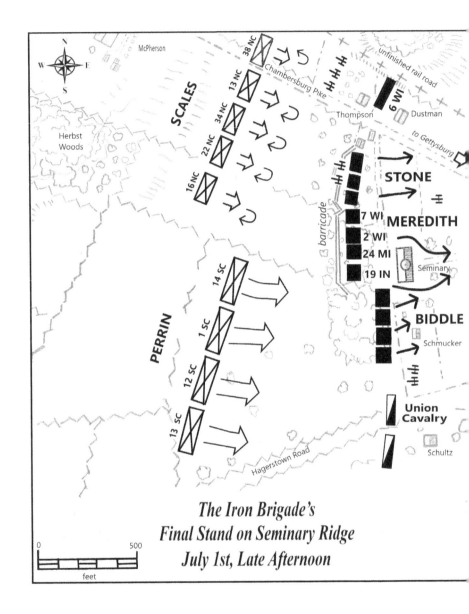

McPherson

SCALES

38 NC
13 NC
34 NC
22 NC
16 NC

Chambersburg Pike

unfinished rail road

6 WI

Thompson · Dustman

to Gettysburg

barricade

STONE

MEREDITH

7 WI
2 WI
24 MI
19 IN

Seminary

Herbst
Woods

PERRIN

14 SC
1 SC
12 SC
13 SC

BIDDLE

Schmucker

Union
Cavalry

Hagerstown Road

Schultz

The Iron Brigade's
Final Stand on Seminary Ridge
July 1st, Late Afternoon

0   500
feet

-17-

Behind the Barricade, Seminary Ridge
West of Gettysburg
July 1, 1863, Late Afternoon

Colonel Williams stood in his stirrups and yelled at the top of his lungs. "We must hold as long as there are men to hold the line!"

Nervous fingers caressed their triggers. A single shot rang out from the line.

"Hold your fire, men!" the colonel shouted. "Wait until they reach that fence!"

Solomon, crouching behind the barricade, thought of James. And of Billy and Grear. And of Henry and Lieutenant Schlagle out beyond the creek. There were so many more. He tried to block them out but could still see Dudley and Blanchard going down with their flags. His gut churned.

And now, there would be many more.

Soon, too.

Solomon peered above the top rail and stared out across the fields—the same fields the remnants of the battered Iron Brigade had just retreated through. Masses of butternut and gray emerged from the woods and crested the ridge. To Solomon's right, General Scales's fresh brigade of North Carolinians numbering over 1,400 men was already taking destructive fire from Union artillery. Behind and just to the south of Scales's brigade, Colonel Abner Perrin's South Carolina brigade marched across the ridge with over 1,800 men.

Solomon looked left and right at the Union men behind the barricade. Their infantry battle line was in the shape of a shallow semi-circle among an open grove of trees out in front of the seminary building. The Union line here was about three hundred yards in length...alarmingly shorter than the long Confederate battle lines approaching from the west.

The Union First Corps' survivors were intermixed now. Soldiers from Pennsylvania and New York had been hastily assembled with the Iron Brigade men from Wisconsin, Indiana, and Michigan. Up and down the line, artillery batteries had been placed between the regiments. Together, they would all have to make their final stand here.

A staff officer from the Seventh Wisconsin, yelling and encouraging the men, rode along the line flying the 142nd Pennsylvania flag. Any Union flag belonged to all the men now.

To the west, the Confederate battle lines were out in the open. As shells from at least twenty union cannons began exploding among the Rebels, their collective howl pierced the air again.

Solomon looked beyond the Rebel infantry and at the treetops where James was lying. While still staring at the distant woods, he said, "Hawk, we just left him out there."

"We had no choice, Sol. *All* of us would have been killed if we tried to carry him."

"It just doesn't seem right, ya know...leaving him lyin' out in them woods while I ran."

"He couldn't move, Sol," Hawk quickly said. "There's nothin' we could do. We 'bout got killed out there helpin' him the way it was."

"Do you think he's dead?"

Before Hawk could answer, a Confederate shell streaked past and exploded just behind them.

"Get down!" somebody screamed, a little too late as dirt and sod from the blast rained down among the men.

Solomon didn't move, however, and continued to gaze out at the woods and the massive lines of Confederates advancing across the fields. Cooper's guns bellowed again and covered the battle line in smoke.

"Keep your head down, Sol," Hawk said, thinking of not just the Rebels out front but also of the incoming Confederate shells from the distant ridges.

"Solomon," Hawk said, trying to get his attention again.

Solomon, unfazed by neither the cannons nor Hawk's voice, remained fixated on the trees where James was lying.

"Sol, snap out of it!" Hawk yelled, this time grabbing his arm and putting his face next to Solomon's.

Solomon finally turned away from the woods and looked at Hawk. "I talked him into volunteering, Hawk. It's my fault. John, James, and me...we all three signed up because I talked them into it."

"Listen, Sol. It doesn't matter now. Here, take these cartridges. You'll need 'em."

Solomon nodded at Hawk but didn't respond. After taking the cartridges, he looked away and thought about his brother again.

"It's war, Sol. And you gotta get yourself ready again if you're gonna survive."

Solomon knew Hawk was right. He blinked several times and then looked at the rest of the men along the Union battle line. Just to the right, he saw the Twenty-Fourth Michigan's national flag. It was torn in several places and stained red with blood. Beneath it, he saw the battered remnants of the Michigan regiment, most of them bloodied or bandaged.

"Good God," Solomon said, realizing that was the Twenty-Fourth Michigan's entire regiment. "Is that all the men the Twenty-Fourth has left?"

Hawk quickly glanced that direction, then turned back toward the west. "Their colonel went down just before he reached the barricade," Hawk said. "He was carrying their flag."

Solomon remembered him, the Michigan colonel. He had seen him just this morning, proudly mounted on his horse at the front of his regiment, where the Nineteenth had joined the road ahead of them on their way toward Gettysburg. That seemed like a lifetime ago now.

Despite all the chaos, Solomon thought of James again and looked through the smoke at the top of the distant trees. Solomon had hoped the Rebels would pull back after the previous assault, allowing him time to rescue his brother, but they had paused only long enough, however, to regroup for another attack. And now they came with an entire fresh division. The two long battle lines steadily advanced in nearly perfect formation toward the battered Union regiments.

"You loaded?" Hawk asked. "Store them cartridges...looks like you're gonna be using every last one of 'em."

"Yeah...thanks," Solomon said, looking down and filling his cartridge box and stuffing the rest of the cartridges in his pants pockets.

"There's a lot of Rebs out there, Hawk."

"Yep. And they're comin'."

"There's *too* many of 'em, Hawk."

"I know, Sol. I know."

Between cannon blasts, Solomon heard the Rebel yell. And then, from somewhere deep in their line and despite all the noise, he made out the steady beat of a marching drum.

Looking up, he saw reflections of sunlight gleaming from their musket barrels...

And from their bayonets.

"We won't be able to hold this line, Hawk," Solomon said.

Hawk didn't respond but, instead, looked at the Confederates ahead and to the right. They were still over two hundred yards from the Union infantry line but were already taking massive casualties from the Union artillery. Hawk then looked to the left. The Rebel line there was farther away but was larger and out-flanked the Union battle line by several hundred yards.

Turning around, Hawk scanned the horizon in all directions. While looking toward the rear, he said, "Sol, I don't think we'll even be able to hold the town behind us."

Nearby, an anxious Pennsylvanian fired his musket.

"Hold your fire!" an unseen Union officer angrily yelled. Now, they would need every shot to count, not just wild misses from several hundred yards away.

Solomon watched the Rebel battle flags flying several paces out front.

"That blue flag," Solomon said, pointing far to the left, "the one with the tree and moon…ain't that South Carolina?"

"Yeah, the bastards that started this war," Hawk angrily replied. Hawk then reached for a percussion cap and, after placing it on his Springfield's nipple, pulled the hammer all the way back.

"Don't do it, Hawk," Solomon urged.

But Hawk already had the rifle leveled on the fence rail and aimed toward the South Carolina color bearer three hundred yards away. Captain Orr, the only captain remaining in the entire regiment, must have also seen what Hawk was about to do and quickly stepped forward.

"Just wait, Hawkins," Orr said, kneeling down beside them. "Not yet. They're coming. We'll get our chance at 'em."

Hawk slowly took his eye from the gunsight, lifted his face from the gunstock, and took a deep breath. He was still thinking about that South Carolina flag though.

Captain Orr had just finished reloading his own revolver and looked out over the barricade. While surveying the Confederate line to the front, he glanced at Solomon. The captain then put his hand on Solomon's back and said, "Whitlow, when you get a chance, take care of that shoulder."

Solomon had forgotten about the minor wound from earlier and quickly looked down. It didn't hurt, but the stain of wet blood on his coat had grown larger.

"Thanks, Captain. I'll get it looked at when this is over."

Captain Orr looked at Solomon and, with a solemn face, said, "Sorry about your brother, Solomon. We'll get him back."

Without looking at the captain, Solomon nodded and quietly said, "Thank you, sir."

"He'll make it, Sol."

"*They're coming, boys!*" someone yelled.

The captain patted Solomon on the back and then, while still crouching, quickly moved to another cluster of soldiers up the line. "Make every shot count, men!" Captain Orr shouted. "Be ready!"

The men, fingers on their triggers, stared out at the Rebels who were now approaching a split-rail, worm fence. Solomon glanced over at Hawk and saw that he had that look again, quiet and focused on his gunsight.

Hawk didn't wait this time though. He pulled the trigger, and his gun erupted with a blast. Above the Rebel yell and artillery, they could hear a painful scream from the Rebel line, a victim of Hawk's musket. Hawk didn't hit the color bearer, though…the blue and white South Carolina flag was still flying. It was defiantly higher now, too. Hawk seethed, and without looking away from the Rebel line, he reached into his cartridge box, pulled out another round, and rammed it down the barrel.

"Hold your fire, Hawkins," Captain Orr shouted after looking back and seeing where the shot had come from. Hawk ignored him and glared at the Rebels as he stowed his rammer and readied another percussion cap.

"Hawk, don't fire," Solomon said. "You heard him. Wait for the order. If you do live through today, they'll put you on the wooden horse for a week. Or worse."

Hawk lowered the barrel on the rail again and pulled the hammer all the way back. Threats of discipline had never stopped him before.

"Wait," Solomon said, this time placing his hand on Hawk's shoulder.

Hawk, knowing Solomon was right, lifted the barrel off the rail and held his fire. He knew he'd get his chance soon enough.

Behind them, Colonel Williams rode past again. "Ready, men!" he shouted. Men lying prone rose to a kneel, and musket barrels went up onto the wooden rail.

A nervous musket fired from off to the right. A few more followed.

"Hold your fire!" Colonel Williams yelled from behind the line. He didn't blame whoever had the impatient trigger finger though... Williams wanted to shoot at the Rebels now too.

The Rebel battle line to the Nineteenth's right was about two hundred yards away, and the South Carolina brigade on the left wasn't far behind. Williams jumped from his horse and stepped up to the line. Moving between two Company K soldiers, he took his place up along the men at the barricade. They would need every man, he knew. Colonel Williams then pulled his revolver from its holster and spun the cylinder to check that it was loaded. With his Colt in one hand and his sword held high in the air with the other, Colonel Williams looked out at the North Carolinians.

"Ready, men!" the Nineteenth's colonel yelled. "Aim low!"

Another Union cannon boomed. A flash of fire, smoke, and dirt flew skyward from the Rebel line again, this time carrying a pink mist and an upside-down, legless man with it. The gruesome hole in the line was quickly filled, and the nightmarish Rebel yell rose again, closer and louder now.

Off to the right beyond Cooper's guns, the Union infantry line erupted with a volley of muskets. Scales's North Carolinians had been stubbornly advancing against exploding shells and canister from Union artillery, but now, they also faced a solid sheet of flame and lead from well-aimed rifles. Scales's brigade halted their charge and fired a volley, but now, with their momentum stalled, large gaps opened up in their lines.

Along the Nineteenth Indiana's barricade, bullets slammed into wood by the dozens, and hundreds more whistled past. Just a second later, Colonel Williams thrust his sword forward into the storm of Rebel lead.

"Fire! Fire! Fire!" Williams yelled.

The barricade erupted with muskets as the Nineteenth Indiana let out a deadly volley into Scales's North Carolinians.

Solomon stared through his gunsight and paused before firing. He saw that the Rebels had disappeared in the smoke. But just above, he could still see a lone, defiant Rebel flag. Lowering his barrel down into the smoke, he pulled the trigger. A bloodcurdling shriek pierced the air, and the flag hovered for a moment before disappearing into the smoke below.

Suddenly, closer, he heard a Union soldier cry out in agony. Solomon turned toward the sound and saw Robert Conley painfully staggering away from the barricade. Private Conley, who had been a fellow classmate at Earlham College, was one of Henry and Solomon's best friends. Conley's face was covered in blood, and he reeled backwards before letting out another painful screech.

Solomon stared in horror as his friend stumbled and fell to the grass.

"Sol!" Hawk shouted, grabbing Solomon's arm to pull his squadmate's attention back to the fight.

Solomon quickly looked away from Conley and began to reload. In front of them, Rebels staggered and fell.

"Take out their officers!" someone shouted.

Between clouds of smoke, Solomon could see that the Confederate brigade on the right had been completely stopped. Hundreds of their men were now lying lifeless in the field, and those who could, staggered toward the rear.

Another Rebel yell pierced the air, but this time from the South Carolina brigade on the left. Even after facing the Rebels for two years, Solomon could feel his blood curdle at their hellish sound. The Union gun crews had noticed too and turned their cannons toward the South Carolinians.

The Rebels had reached another fence and quickly climbed over. More well-aimed blasts ripped gaps in their lines that were quickly filled. Solomon finished reloading and lowered his Springfield toward the Rebels. He pulled the trigger and, without watching the effects of his shot, quickly began reloading.

For several minutes, the battered Iron Brigade continued firing and reloading. The sky was dark with smoke, but the Nineteenth's men could still see rows of dead South Carolinians in the field to their front. The Rebels wavered for a moment, but then, one of their officers on a horse rode out front and yelled. With his sword held high above his head, he was directing his men toward a gap in the Union line farther to the south.

"Shoot that bastard on the horse!" Hawk yelled as he rammed another cartridge down his barrel. "Kill that general... or colonel...or whatever-the-hell he thinks he is!"

"He's leading them around our flank!" someone shouted.

Solomon and Hawk could both see what was happening. The Union men at the barricade had completely stopped the Confederates to the right and were slowing the assault just to their front. But now, this brazen Rebel officer who had ridden ahead of his men, was leading one of his regiments toward a break in the Union line. Once through that hole, the South Carolinians would be around the Union flank and in their rear.

Solomon knew what he had to do. He turned slightly, raised his rifle, and aimed.

"*Forward! Forward!*" the Rebel colonel madly yelled, riding with his sword high in the air.

Solomon momentarily lost sight of his target in a cloud of smoke. He took a deep breath and concentrated to steady his barrel. Then he saw the sword again, and just below it, he saw the colonel's glove and then his sleeve still waving wildly above the smoke.

As the horse and rider reemerged, Solomon clenched the barrel tightly and squeezed the trigger. He peered through the smoke and immediately began reloading.

"*Forward!…into that gap!*"

The Rebel colonel's voice echoed through the smoke and told Solomon that his shot had missed.

"Take him down!" Captain Orr yelled after firing another round from his Colt.

The Rebel colonel continued to yell, riding crazily forward and now bringing two of his regiments with him.

It was Hawk's turn now. Steadying his rifle on the barricade, he aimed at the Confederate's chest. He held his breath and pulled the trigger.

Hawk's barrel erupted in smoke and fire, but the Rebel colonel's horse jolted just enough to cause Hawk's minie ball to miss wide to the right.

The crazed Rebel colonel galloped closer, hundreds of his men following at the double-quick. Solomon quickly took aim again and pulled the trigger. The lead ball missed the colonel but slammed into the Rebel officer's sword with a clang. When the bullet struck, the colonel let out a yell, and his horse rose up with a twist.

The South Carolina colonel spewed curses but, somehow, still clung to the sword that led all of his men. Regaining control of his horse, he and his mount were charging ahead again, bringing with them a screaming mass of gray.

"*Forward! Forward!*"

He looked even angrier now. Despite facing the most destructive storm of bullets they had seen during the entire war, the South Carolinians rushed forward. Now only a few dozen yards from the barricades, their Rebel yell was deafening. The Rebels fell by the hundreds and littered the field with butternut and gray. But still, on they came.

"They're breaking our line on the left!" a private yelled.

For now, though, the Nineteenth held. But they all knew this would be their final stand.

Many of the South Carolinians in front of them paused and fired a volley. The Indiana men ducked and covered their heads as the torrent of lead flew overhead, slammed into the barricade, and tore up sod out front.

Solomon heard a bullet whistle past and then slam into something with a thud and a whoosh. Hearing a scream, Solomon looked over and saw Corporal Wasson staggering backward. Blood poured from above his left eye, and as Corporal Wasson crumpled to the ground unconscious, Solomon turned away and raised his musket again.

Solomon looked to the left and saw the situation was desperate.

Although the Confederate attack against the barricade on the Union right had faltered, the South Carolinians to the south were slamming into Colonel Biddle's brigade on the Nineteenth's left. As Perrin's men swarmed forward, Biddle's brigade wavered and began fleeing to the rear.

"Biddle's men are falling back!" one of the Nineteenth's men on the left end of the line shouted.

Several Yankee units were rushed to fill gaps in the Union line, but still, the Rebels were overrunning the barricade and enveloping the Union left flank.

Solomon fired at the South Carolinians again, and as he lowered his musket to reload, he suddenly heard a flurry of voices from behind the line.

"Pull back! Retreat!" Colonel Williams shouted, mounted again. "Retreat through the town!"

Up and down the line, the men fired one last shot and quickly began to fall back.

"Let's go, Sol!" Hawk shouted.

Solomon froze, staring at the woods to the west. Another shout went out from the officers in the rear, but Solomon couldn't understand what they said…something about a hill… and a cemetery.

"Sol! Come on…"

"Retreat!" shouted Captain Orr. "This way, men! Fall back!"

Solomon took a step backward but then stopped and became transfixed on the woods again. An overwhelming guilt came over him, thinking of his brother and not being able to save him. But then, a loud roar of muskets startled him from his daze.

More Rebel lead screamed past. Hawk, desperate now, grabbed Solomon's arm. "Sol, don't be a fool!" he yelled. "Getting yourself killed won't save him. Let's go!"

Solomon, finally turning to the rear, saw that all around them, men had broken into a run. What had begun as an organized, orderly retreat was now a desperate sprint to the rear…a total rout. Men scrambled around the north end of the seminary building and then to the east. Beyond them, the pike was jammed with men, wagons, horses, and artillery, all fleeing toward the town.

"Run, Sol!"

Bullets ripped past. There were no thoughts of stopping to shoot back. To Solomon and the rest of the Nineteenth's men, simply escaping seemed almost hopeless now.

"This way!" someone shouted.

Solomon started in that direction, and then he heard the bark.

"Hawk, it's Moses," Solomon said, pointing toward the southwest corner of the seminary building. Most of the regiment's survivors were sprinting to the north end of the building, but a few, including Moses, were running around the south side.

"He's looking this way…at us," Hawk said. The south lawn of the seminary was full of Biddle's troops being chased by Colonel Perrin's Confederates, but the north side was jammed full of limbering Union batteries and a panicked army.

Moses let out another bark, a high-pitched yelp this time, and then ran in a tight circle before rounding the building and disappearing.

"Follow him!" Solomon shouted, pointing. "This way!"

Bullets whistled past as Solomon and Hawk sprinted around the corner of the building and into the grounds on the seminary's east side. Ahead were hundreds of Union soldiers fleeing to the east, but then, off to the right, Solomon saw a new threat. A mass of South Carolinians had stopped and assembled a firing line.

"Run, Hawk!" Solomon yelled, even though both were running at a full sprint trying get away from the musket volley they knew was coming.

"*Aim!*"

The Southerner's voice sent a chill down Solomon's spine, and he strained for every bit of speed he could.

"*Fire!*"

"Go! Go! Go!" Hawk screamed.

Hawk was just in front of Solomon when, suddenly, musket blasts erupted from the Rebel line. Bullets slammed into the right side of the fleeing mass of Yankees, and blue-clad men dropped by the dozens.

More bullets hissed past, and then Solomon heard the *whoosh*. He recognized the sound of the lead ball's impact but didn't know what it had hit.

Then he saw Hawk's legs buckle and Hawk awkwardly twist to the right. Hawk stumbled and started to fall but, somehow, stayed on his feet. He then screeched out in agony and looked to the sky. Solomon watched in horror as Hawk dropped his Springfield and reached for his gut.

"No!" Solomon yelled, seeing blood gushing through Hawk's jacket and shirt.

When Hawk turned around, Solomon saw his face contorted in shock. Hawk collapsed into the grass and gritted his teeth.

"I'm hit, Sol. Go on."

Solomon stopped and dropped down on a knee beside him.

"*Hawk...*" He tried to say more but couldn't find any words.

The wound was the most intense pain Hawk had ever felt. Quickly ripping away his blood-soaked coat, he looked down and saw dark blood gushing through his shirt. He clinched his stomach and let out another agonizing scream as blood ran between his fingers.

"Leave me, Sol," Hawk said. He paused and then, with a grunt, said, "It's okay, Sol. Go on."

"No, Hawk. I got you...I got you."

"It's bad, Sol," Hawk said weakly.

"You're gonna make it, Hawk," Solomon said, desperately looking around trying to figure out what to do.

"I'm going…" Hawk started to say. But the pain overtook him, and his voice trailed off.

"Keep pressure on it, Hawk. Don't let go."

More bullets whistled past, and yells went out from Perrin's South Carolinians. Solomon looked up from his wounded friend and saw Perrin's men weren't letting up. More fleeing Union men rushed past, retreating toward the town.

"Sol, go on," Hawk pleaded again, sitting up and grabbing Solomon's coat just below the collar. Too weak to hold on, he released his grip on Solomon's jacket and fell back down.

"No, Hawk," Solomon said, reaching down and placing his hand on Hawk's chest. "I'm not losing you too. Listen, we're getting out of here…together."

"Go."

"You're going with me, Hawk," Solomon said as he put his arm behind Hawk's shoulder and neck. Hawk clutched Solomon's jacket and fought back screams of pain.

"Here we go!" Solomon said with a groan, putting all his weight under Hawk and starting to lift. "Up!"

"*Awghhh!*"

With Solomon's help, Hawk ignored the pain and got to his feet. But when he let go of his stomach to keep his balance, more dark blood streamed from the wound.

"Hang on to me, Hawk," Solomon said, using all his strength to keep Hawk on his feet. Together, they turned toward the east. All around them, the entire Union First Corps ran, staggered, and crawled toward the town.

"I can't go anymore, Sol," Hawk said, feeling his legs giving way underneath him.

"I got you, Hawk," Solomon said, facing him and pulling him up again. "Hang on tight!"

Descending the gradual slope, Solomon struggled to keep his balance and still carry Hawk. A shot rang out behind them, and a Pennsylvania man running next to them suddenly tumbled and rolled. After a flopping of deadweight arms and legs, he came to rest on his side with his eyes staring lifelessly at the sky.

Ahead, Solomon saw that the pike was clogged by Union soldiers and horse teams pulling artillery and their ammunition wagons. Confederates giving chase from the north side of the pike fired into them as they tried to escape. A lone Federal battery remained unlimbered there, buying time for the rest of the army to flee.

"Keep going, Hawk!" Solomon yelled.

Hawk was almost totally limp now, and his legs were doing more dragging than running. Using all the strength he had, he clung to Solomon's back and forced himself to not drop to the ground.

The pain in Hawk's stomach was so bad, the world around him had blurred. Trying to focus, he forced his eyes open wider. He looked toward the pike and watched as a shell exploded among a horse team retreating with a cannon.

Everything seemed to be in slow motion as the mangled wreckage of horses and harnesses careened off the road and crashed. Confederates from near the railroad embankment peppered the teamsters with lead. The Union artillerists and wagon teamsters desperately tried to cut the bridle reins to untangle the wreckage from a broken fence. Leaving the cannon, dead horses, and several wounded cannoneers strewn along the pike, only a handful of men were able to escape.

"Solomon…," Hawk said.

Solomon glanced down at his squadmate's face covered with sweat, gunpowder, and mud. Hawk was looking straight ahead toward the town. With a pointing nod, he forced a smile and said, "Look, Sol…Moses."

Moses had reappeared and was running ahead of them on the dirt road that led to the Chambersburg Pike. But now, he cut to the right and leapt over a stone wall and away from the chaos on the pike.

"This way!" Solomon said, also turning off the dirt road and turning directly toward the town.

Approaching the low stone wall, Solomon paused. Hawk mumbled something about leaving him, but Solomon clung on tighter.

"I'll help you over, Hawk," Solomon said just as more bullets hissed past and crashed into the rocks.

"I don't think..."

Hawk tried to say more, but his voice trailed off.

"Yeah, you can, Hawk! Hang on!"

With all his weight being supported by Solomon now, Hawk felt himself drifting away. Solomon grunted as he hoisted Hawk onto the rock wall and then carried him over.

"Stay with me, buddy," Solomon said, now on the other side. He looked ahead to the town again, now a few hundred yards away.

"Come on, Hawk!" Solomon said. "We can make it to the town. It's just ahead, Hawk...not much farther!"

Hawk mumbled weakly and tried to look ahead. He'd lost his strength to hold his head up though, and he looked back down. He heard Solomon yelling but couldn't respond.

"Hawk! Keep going, Hawk!"

Feeling himself drifting even further, Hawk closed his eyes.

Struggling to keep his balance carrying Hawk, Solomon glanced back and saw a mass of Confederates firing into the rear and flanks of the fleeing Union men. With more Rebels emerging behind them, Solomon felt even more panicked to get to the safety of the Union lines beyond the town.

Solomon looked at Hawk again...and wished he hadn't. He was hanging his head weakly with his eyes closed. And for the first time, Solomon noticed blood had dripped from the corner of Hawk's mouth. Seeing him in this condition was terrifying.

To Solomon, Hawk had always seemed invincible, even in battles amidst storms of bullets. He was always up on the front line, steady and fearless…careless almost. It was what the men needed. But now it was Hawk who needed the assistance of a fellow soldier. *No way I'm leaving him behind…not after leaving James out in those woods.* Solomon knew that no one would ever be able to replace either of those two men.

"Stay up!" Solomon shouted, not knowing if Hawk was still even conscious. Clutching him even tighter to keep him from falling, Solomon said, "I got ya, Hawk. I got ya."

Solomon used a combination of carrying and dragging to keep them moving. Just ahead, there was a little grassy stream lined with rocks.

"We're almost there, Hawk," Solomon said, pausing at the edge to tighten his grip. Hearing Hawk groan, Solomon said, "We gotta get across this creek. The town's just ahead."

Solomon slid down the grassy bank and awkwardly placed his brogan onto a rock in the stream. Leaning down, he scooped up a handful of water and splashed it onto Hawk's face.

Feeling the cool water, Hawk mumbled something and opened his eyes.

"Ready…let's go," Solomon said with a grunt, lifting Hawk up again. Realizing he couldn't balance himself on the rocks while carrying Hawk, he splashed both feet into the stream and slogged across.

After climbing the grass embankment on all fours, he dragged Hawk up beside him. Leaning down, Solomon lifted Hawk up and turned toward the town again. The streets and alleys were packed with scrambling bluecoats. Up ahead, two Union cannons were blazing away, sending loud blasts echoing through the streets. Rebel cannons from the north and west continued firing shells into the town, shattering bricks and roofs that rained down on the retreating Yankees.

As Solomon and Hawk approached the first row of houses, groups of butternut-clad soldiers were filling the streets from the north, many capturing fleeing Federals along Chambersburg Street. To the right, a squad of South Carolinians had rushed ahead and blocked Middle Street, forcing the Federal troops to cut through yards, houses, and over fences to escape.

Solomon's only choice was to head for the less crowded alley to the right. Every soldier was now his own general, he knew. Right now, his goal was to survive and escape to the rear. Later, he would worry about rejoining what was left of his regiment which was now fleeing through the streets and toward the heights south of the town.

"They're everywhere!" Solomon exclaimed, seeing Rebels in every direction. Several bullets whistled past, thudding into fences and houses behind them. Unsure which way to go, he cut through a backyard where he'd seen Moses disappear earlier.

He glanced down at Hawk's face and heard him mumble something about a house. Solomon fought to keep his balance and turned behind a row of houses. As they reached a dirt alley and turned east, Solomon almost stumbled again but somehow stayed on his feet.

When Solomon looked up, he suddenly stopped in his tracks.

Just ahead, Rebels had formed a skirmish line at the next intersection. They had the north-south street blocked and were exchanging musket shots with the Federals trying to retreat to the south. Solomon watched in horror as Rebels captured Union men and took them as prisoners. It made him think of James, probably a prisoner now too.

Seeing the alley ahead blocked by Rebels, Solomon dropped to the ground and quickly surveyed his options.

"I'm not gonna let them capture you too, Hawk," Solomon said, looking around and seeing a gate into a fenced backyard.

Looking at the back of the two-story brick house, Solomon knew it was his only option.

"This way, Hawk," Solomon said, carrying him toward the gate. Collapsing just short of the gate, Solomon glanced back toward the Confederates up the alley. They hadn't seen them yet, but it was only a matter of time.

"Through here," Solomon said. "Let's get to this house."

Hawk was even weaker now and didn't respond.

Solomon picked Hawk up again and carried him through the gate and all the way to the door. After setting Hawk down at the step, Solomon grabbed the door's handle.

Finding the door barred from the inside, he wildly banged his fist on it.

"Let us in! We're Union soldiers!"

Solomon pounded on the door again and then looked down at Hawk.

"Please!" Solomon shouted, turning toward the door again. "Let us in!"

Finally hearing voices from inside the house, Solomon pleaded once more.

"My friend needs help…he's dying."

-18-

Two and a half years earlier...

Near Jericho Creek, Kentucky
January 1861

Elijah Hawkins watched closely as the horse-drawn carriage approached. It was on the dirt road just beyond the meadow and heading toward the town a mile away. Bundled up against the cold morning air, the three occupants of the carriage were quiet as it passed, the only noises being the squeaking of the wheels and the plodding of the horse's shoes against the road.

After they passed, Elijah waited several minutes before moving. It was important that no one in the small town knew where he rode in from or where his hiding place was. Making sure no one else was coming, he mounted his horse to make his way toward the church in town.

Elijah felt the cold wind against his face as he left the cover of the trees and guided his horse toward the road. Pulling his collar up over his neck, he tugged the reins to the right and gave the horse a gentle kick. With a slight neigh, Elijah's horse turned onto the dirt road. It was the same route he had taken when he was young, but it wasn't much more than a wagon trail back then.

Elijah Hawkins grew up here near Jericho Creek, but ten years ago, he had suddenly moved away to Richmond, Indiana, one hundred miles to the north. Until then, the small Kentucky town and the rolling wooded hills and fields surrounding it were all Elijah had ever known. Other than the past few days, he had never been back…and never wanted to either.

The road came to a small bridge spanning a narrow, wooded stream. Elijah still remembered it well. And despite his somber mood, now looking down at the stream's water made him smile. Some things seemed like forever ago, but the fun times and childhood memories he experienced in and around that little creek seemed like just yesterday.

It was near here that he had fished with his father and floated boats with his older sister. And on many hot summer afternoons, he had swum in the stream's cool water. After passing the creek, his smile faded as he thought about his family… and about the business he planned on doing here.

It was only a few minutes later that Elijah rode into the small town. Most of the congregation had already entered the church when Elijah casually rode up. Along with a few horses, several empty carriages waited outside. The church lot was mostly empty of people other than a family walking toward the entry steps and a group of four men talking near the carriages. These were the same four men Elijah had been watching for the past few days.

Keeping his distance and not wanting to be noticed, Elijah stopped across the road from the church and slowly dismounted. Remaining inconspicuous and waiting to be the last one to enter the church, he stood on the far side of his horse and fumbled with his saddlebag. He took his time tying the reins to a tree, all the while keeping his eyes and ears on the four men gathered outside. Elijah listened carefully but still only heard snippets of their conversation, something about a *shipment* and *wagons*.

Elijah saw the ropes move in the church's bell tower just as he heard the first bell ring. Then, as the bell stopped, he heard the word *tonight*. The men seemed to be in agreement about something, and after exchanging handshakes, they broke up their meeting and headed toward the church's entrance.

Elijah continued to watch closely as the last man entered the church and closed the door behind him. Elijah then quickly walked across the grass to the brick walkway and up the steps. Slightly lowering hat, he pulled the door open and quietly stepped inside. He took a seat in the back pew and kept his head down for several seconds before slowly raising his eyes to look around the small Baptist church's congregation.

A few seconds later, the preacher announced his presence with a loud *Good morning*. Elijah watched as the last few churchgoers still standing took their seats. A unanimous murmur of *Good-mornings* echoed through the building, and then a hush fell over the room before the preacher began the worship service.

After lowering his head slightly, Elijah removed his hat and laid it in his lap. Carefully scanning the congregation, he saw the four men he had been watching were scattered throughout the crowd. He noticed two of them were seated with their wives, one of whom had two small children. The thought of any of these men having children shocked Elijah, and he quickly looked away.

What am I doing here? he asked himself. He had repeated the same question several times over the past week since leaving Richmond. His job back in Indiana as a farmhand was the most recent of many. Elijah had worked at several different farms outside of Richmond, and before that, he had lived in various orphanage houses. After leaving Kentucky many years ago, he had quickly developed a hardened heart that led to a thick-skinned roughness. Even at his first orphanage as a young boy, he had learned that he had to be tough.

The preacher rambled.

Elijah thought of the long, cold journey from Indiana he had made this week. Surviving harsh weather and exhausting hours in the saddle, he finally had arrived near Jericho Creek four days ago. Luckily, he had found an abandoned wooden shed that he made his temporary home. Every time he had doubts about his willingness for revenge, his thoughts had always turned back to memories of his family and reinforced his quest for vengeance.

"The New Testament tells us God is a peaceful God," the preacher bellowed, interrupting Elijah's thoughts. "But I will tell you this, my flock…"

Elijah, realizing he had been staring, blinked several times and then looked at the preacher again. Today's sermon was much more peaceful than the rebel-rousing, political tirade that the same preacher angrily shouted at the tavern two nights ago. Defending states' rights, forming a militia, and secession were the themes then.

Glancing around the congregation again, Elijah saw that one of the four men he was watching had fallen asleep. Elijah had remembered the man as soon as he saw him three days ago walking from the tavern on Elijah's first night back in town. *Peterson* was the man's name, and Elijah remembered more than once being shocked by his father's uncustomary profanities when talking about him. And later, the image of Peterson's face emerging from the barn and silhouetted by the flames was etched into Elijah's memory forever.

That was the night that Elijah couldn't shake off what he had thought at first were just nightmares. But they weren't… when he woke and hurried to the window, he saw his father running from the house, and then his mother following behind trying to stop him. They had heard his sister's screams first, and then Elijah heard them. Even now, years later, remembering the sounds he heard that night still haunted him.

And then he had seen the four men emerge from the barn. By the time smoke and the first flames came from the barn's roof, his entire family was already dead. The men's bloody clothes, the knife, and the pistol were all clues of what they had done to his sister and parents. The *proof* came a few minutes later when they talked about their crimes while searching the house for him. He was only eight years old then, but he would never forget.

And now, ten years later, Elijah Hawkins would have his revenge.

He felt a rage boil inside as he watched the congregation and listened to the preacher. More animated now, his sermon had turned to politics.

And rebellion…and even a possible war.

"If the Northern states shall cast us into war and not grant us our independence," the preacher said. "Kentucky *shall* and *will* defend herself." Elijah watched the *flock* closely, especially the men he was here to "visit." A round of *hear hears* and *amens* echoed through the small sanctuary.

"A neighbor who injures his neighbor," the preacher continued, his voice rising, "shall be injured in the same way…*An eye for an eye!*"

Mumblings and murmurs from the crowd had turned into shouts of agreement. Peterson and the other three men Elijah had been watching were among the most vocal.

Elijah had heard enough. He placed his hat on his head and quietly slipped out the back of the church.

After mounting his horse and turning toward the road, he began his ride back to his hideout in the woods. He had prepared long enough and knew he would need his rest for tonight.

*****

That evening, after trying to sleep most of the day, Elijah finally left the small cabin sometime shortly after dark.

The clouds hid the moon and stars. Elijah welcomed the night's nearly total darkness. Although he didn't follow the men and their wagons an hour ago when they took the river road out of town, he knew where they were going. Elijah took a different route through the woods and dismounted several hundred yards away from where the men said they'd be. After leaving all his belongings with his horse, he slowly crept forward from tree to tree. The dock and the men were just ahead.

There were five of them now. They brought two empty wagons, each pulled by a two-horse team. The fifth man, whom Elijah hadn't seen before, had ridden at the head of the small convoy on his own horse.

As Elijah approached the light of the lanterns near the dock, he was careful to not make any noise. Hearing their voices now, he stopped behind a tree and carefully looked toward the men. They were at the ferry dock where the road ended, and they had parked their wagons with the backs of them facing the river.

"Which way they comin' from, Charles?" It was Peterson.

"Down river…that way."

After hearing the word '*they*', Elijah felt a knot in his stomach. Already outnumbered five to one, his odds would soon be even worse. He looked out at the dark river and then back at the men again. They seemed nervous, looking in the direction that Charles had pointed.

Who are they waiting for? Elijah wondered.

Elijah pulled his head back behind the tree and felt for one of his Colts. He had *borrowed* the two Navy Colt revolvers from his employer in Indiana last week. Loaded with six bullets each, both were tucked into his belt.

But if his plan was to succeed, he would have to work silently at first. He pulled out his handmade knife and slowly crept forward toward the next tree. Now only a dozen yards from the front wagon's horse team, he ducked into cover again and listened.

This is my chance, he told himself, slowly peering around the tree. He was ready to move in when a voice pierced the still night air.

"There it is, Charles."

Johnson's voice sent a chill down Elijah's spine. It was only yesterday in town that he had found out the man's name was *Johnson.*

The last time he had heard that voice was ten years ago. With his family already dead and the barn ablaze, Elijah had been hiding under the bed while Johnson was searching the house. He was so scared then; he didn't breathe the whole time Johnson was in his bedroom. Still thinking about that horrible night ten years ago, Elijah remembered Johnson's last words when he finally left the house. *There's nobody else here in the house.*

Elijah thought of those words now and smiled… Johnson was about to find out that he had been wrong.

Elijah looked toward the five men on the dock again and then at the blackness of the river where they were all staring. One of them, apparently signaling, waved a lantern back and forth.

"There it is," Johnson said, pointing for the other men…at something out on the river.

Elijah strained to see but still saw only darkness.

"Over here!" Johnson yelled in the direction of the river.

The man on the dock with the lantern anxiously waved it back and forth. Then Johnson yelled again, "Over here, Boller! Over here!"

"I see ya, Johnson," a voice from the river yelled back.

Elijah stared into the darkness past the men and finally saw the boat's lantern. With more people coming, Elijah's plan would have to wait. He had been cautiously anticipating this moment for ten years and knew it wasn't the time for brazen recklessness.

As the boat approached the dock, Elijah saw two men guiding it with long oars. Once it was within a few yards, one of the men onshore threw a rope and pulled it in.

As the boat came closer and within range of the torches, Elijah could see several Negroes crowded inside it. They were escaped slaves or free blacks being brought South into slavery, Elijah assumed.

"It's about time, Boller."

"It's into the damned current, ya know, Charles." The man's voice was gruff but didn't have the Kentucky drawl that the rest of the men had. *A Northerner,* Elijah thought.

"Help us get these darkies unloaded," the boatman said.

Still hidden in a low area of brush, Elijah looked on as the two men on the boat began shoving their prisoners forward toward the edge of the boat. As the slaves were led onto the dock and entered the light, Elijah could see there were eight of them. Their hands were tied at the wrists, and a long rope bound them all together. Elijah looked closer and could see the look of fear in their eyes as they were led toward the wagons.

"They is all yours, Charles," the man from the boat said as they approached the two waiting wagons. "We've still got a long way back."

"Yeah, go on. We got 'em. They ain't gonna be no trouble."

"None at all," one of the other men replied with a threatening sneer toward his newly acquired captives.

"Split 'em up, Peterson. Cut that rope behind the tall one there."

Elijah watched as the five men separated their prisoners and began putting them into the two wagons. He then looked closer toward the dock, waiting nervously for the boat and the two additional men with it to leave.

"Get in there!" Johnson yelled, jabbing a club into the first Negro captive. Elijah glanced toward the wagon and then back toward the boat. With the two oarsmen pushing off from the dock, the boat slowly began floating away into the darkness.

Elijah waited. *A little farther,* he thought anxiously. The front wagon was now full, and the men began loading the second one.

Downriver, the boat's lantern had finally disappeared into the darkness.

God, forgive me, Elijah said to himself.

He then took a deep breath and leapt from his cover. Quickly moving around the front horses, he snuck past the first wagon. Glancing into it, he saw that one of the Negro captives was staring at him. She looked to be about his own age, he guessed. Although her eyes were wide with fear, she remained speechless.

Just ahead, Johnson's back was to him and only a few feet away.

With his knife held wide in his right hand, Elijah sprang forward. He reached around and covered Johnson's mouth while he plunged the knife into his back. As Johnson dropped to the ground, Elijah went down with him, all the while holding his mouth and twisting the knife.

Elijah had just yanked the knife free when he heard a shout near the rear wagon.

"Johnson!" the man yelled, having just walked around the wagon and seeing his partner on the ground. Elijah released his hand from the dead man's mouth and pulled a Colt from his belt. He had it up and leveled at his new target before the man knew what was happening.

Elijah pulled the trigger and then heard the man scream. Looking through the smoke, he saw the man had fallen to one knee but was still able to pull a revolver from his holster. Seeing the revolver reminded Elijah of so many years ago. He was the same man with the gun hanging at his side, walking from his family's burning barn. Without looking away, Elijah gritted his teeth in anger and cocked the hammer back. He squeezed the trigger, and the bullet struck his target in the chest, sending him falling backward to the ground.

Quickly looking up, Elijah saw Peterson and one of the other men emerge from behind the rear wagon. They both had turned toward him but, being caught off guard, hesitated before pulling out their revolvers.

Elijah, still having the element of surprise, immediately dropped to the ground and fired first. The bullet struck Peterson in the shoulder and spun him backward with a painful groan.

The other man's revolver erupted in smoke and fire, but the bullet missed, harmlessly whistling past Elijah's ear. Elijah cocked the hammer back again, but the man was gone, having darted for cover behind the wagon.

Elijah looked toward Peterson. Despite the pain, he had turned toward Elijah and raised his revolver. Again, Elijah didn't hesitate. He quickly aimed at Peterson's head and fired. Striking him between the eyes, the bullet knocked his head backward, dropping him to the ground for the final time.

Elijah ran to the rear corner of the wagon and paused. He knew he had probably mortally wounded three of the men, but two of them remained. Knowing he no longer had the advantage of surprise, he had to think fast. In the wagon, the captives looked terrified and stared at him, pleading.

They can help me, Elijah suddenly realized. He knew that freeing them would not only give them a chance to escape, but would also cause a distraction allowing him to complete his vengeance. Waving the captives to the back of the wagon, he held out his knife.

"Here…come here," Elijah whispered. One of the prisoners realized what Elijah was saying and quickly crawled to the wagon's rear.

"Thank you, mister," the slave said, holding out his bound wrists.

As Elijah started to cut through the rope, he saw the shadow of one of the two remaining captors moving around the wagon toward him.

"Here, take it," Elijah whispered, leaving the knife with the captives and darting toward the front wagon and horses.

"*Help us!*" one of the captives pleaded as he scurried past.

"*Shhhhh,*" he whispered. "Cut the ropes…quick!"

Rounding the corner and hiding behind the front horses, Elijah looked toward the rear. The fifth man, Charles, whom Elijah hadn't seen until tonight, was standing back near the trees with a shotgun and facing the rear wagon.

The other man who had already shot at Elijah and escaped had returned to the rear of the wagon. "They're dead, Charles!" the man shouted upon seeing his partners on the ground.

"Get back over here, Jamison!" Charles shouted.

Jamison… Elijah remembered the name now. He also remembered the man's face at the barn ten years ago. And at the church…with this wife…*and two children.*

Elijah pulled the other Colt out from his belt and backed away slowly, slipping further into the darkness. His mind raced. The image of the man's son looking at his father was now burned into his mind. Elijah felt his hands trembling. Then he saw one of the captives moving behind the rear wagon.

"Get back in there!" Charles screamed, also seeing the Negro and stepping forward with the butt of his shotgun. The black man held his hands up defiantly as Charles approached, not to block the blow, but to fight back and buy time for the other captives to free themselves. Jamison slowly raised his pistol.

Elijah knew he must act fast.

"Stop! Stop!" Elijah yelled as he raced out into the open with both Colts aimed at the two men.

Charles lifted his shotgun and took aim, but Elijah fired his Colt before the man could get a shot off. The bullet struck Charles in the arm and knocked the shotgun to the ground.

"Drop it," Elijah said calmly, now staring at Jamison and aiming at his forehead. Jamison hesitated then slowly lowered his revolver. Off to Elijah's right, Charles was on the ground and reaching for his shotgun.

Elijah quickly shifted his aim to Charles and pulled the trigger. His shot was fast and accurate, striking Charles in the leg. His Colt was already cocked and ready again before Charles could even react to the pain.

"You're...you're crazy...," Charles started to say, falling with a contorted grimace. He clawed at the dirt and scrambled backward. Pointing at Elijah, he screamed, "Crazy...you're a crazy son of a bitch!"

Elijah, now focused on Jamison and the slaves, wasn't watching Charles anymore. But Charles's stream of profanities and painful groans continued as he tried to escape into the darkness. Elijah didn't focus on him though...it was the four men who murdered his family that he wanted.

"I said drop it!" Elijah shouted, walking toward Jamison with his Colt still aimed between his eyes.

The freed slave began to step in as if to strike his former captor, but Elijah quickly waved him away.

"I have kids…," Jamison pleaded, letting the revolver slide from his hand and slowly backing up.

"And *I* had a family," Elijah said, approaching and holding his aim on the man's forehead.

"But…my children," Jamison pleaded, eyes wide with fear and hands up in the air.

Elijah lunged forward and pressed the Colt into Jamison's forehead.

"You killed my parents!"

Jamison tried backing up, but Elijah pushed the revolver's barrel harder against his forehead. "And my sister!"

"I'm…I'm sorry," Jamison said, begging for his life. "There's not a day goes by I don't think about what we did." His legs trembled as he backpedaled.

"Not a day goes by for me either!" Elijah screamed, feeling himself raging. His finger, shaking, twirled around the trigger.

"I'm sorry…I shouldn't have gone out to that farm. Peterson…he put us all up to it. We was all drinkin'."

Elijah glared but didn't speak.

"Your sister…," Jamison continued, his voice cracking with fear. "Peterson wouldn't take no for an answer. I didn't touch her…I swear."

Elijah pulled the revolver back, but only for a second. That night his family was murdered had changed his life forever, and a lifetime of nightmares surged through his mind. Suddenly, Elijah slammed the butt of the Colt across Jamison's face.

Jamison let out a scream as he felt bones crush in his nose now flowing with blood. "I…I'm sorry," Jamison pleaded. "I didn't mean to hurt no one. We were stupid kids back then. I'm…"

Jamison was abruptly cut off when Elijah stuck the Colt's barrel in his mouth and pushed him backwards. Jamison's cries were muffled now, and he desperately shook his head. Feeling himself falling, he swung his arms wildly, all the while begging for mercy with his eyes.

Elijah shoved the Colt deeper and gave Jamison another push that sent him onto his back with a crunch. Still holding the barrel in Jamison's mouth, Elijah kept him pinned to the ground. Jamison's face shook with terror, and his eyes and hands begged for his life.

Elijah heard the rustle of weeds and branches past where Charles had been. He glanced over and saw that Charles, although wounded twice, was making an escape into the woods. Elijah quickly looked back down at Jamison whose eyes were wide with fear. Tears streamed from his eyes.

"You wanna live, Jamison?"

He couldn't speak, but his head's frantic shake gave the answer.

Yes…

Elijah looked up at the wagons and then back to Jamison. "Those slaves…"

Jamison was nodding in agreement before there even was one.

"Those slaves…," Elijah repeated. He was still thinking as he began to say it. Knowing he could use them as a distraction again, he said, "You're gonna untie the rest of them. And then you're gonna take all eight of them in one of them wagons… and you ride that way…*north.*"

Elijah paused. Jamison's eyes were still agreeing.

"You hear me?"

Another nod.

"You ride all night and all day tomorrow if you have to."

Elijah looked at the first prisoner he had untied and waved him over. "You listen to me," Elijah said.

"Uhhh, yes sir."

"Listen…this man is gonna drive you north. If he doesn't, then all eight of you…you kill him. That knife I gave ya is yours."

"Yes, sir."

"What's your name?" Elijah asked.

"Rocko, sir. My name's Rocko."

Elijah smiled briefly and looked away. He slowly removed the Colt from Jamison's mouth but still threatened him with his eyes.

"Rocko, there's a house…in Covington…just before the Ohio River. Not this river here…the big one…the Ohio."

Rocko nodded, understanding.

"You heard of the underground railroad?"

"Yes, mister. Yes, sir."

"It'll take you several days, maybe weeks, but you get to Covington, up on the Ohio River. Understand?"

Rocko nodded again and then repeated the town's name. "Yes, sir…Covington, sir."

"Use the North Star, travel at night. This man here, he'll get you to the Kentucky River. Cross it and follow it north. Then go east before the Ohio River and follow along the river until you get to Covington, Kentucky."

Elijah leaned in close to Rocko's ear before whispering the next part…something he wouldn't want someone like Jamison hearing. Elijah knew the house well. It was *his* first orphanage ten years ago, although he had stayed there only for a week before crossing the Ohio River.

"The Carneal House," Elijah whispered. "The Carneal House on the Ohio River where Licking River flows into it."

Elijah pulled away and looked him in the eyes. "Will you remember where I said?"

Rocko didn't speak, but his eyes and his nod said *yes*.

Elijah looked over at Jamison again. "Jamison, get moving. Ride all night. You get them to the Kentucky River and show 'em the way north."

"Yes, sir," Jamison responded. "Thank you…thank you, sir."

"If they don't make it to the Kentucky River, then you're dead. I'm giving you more of a chance than you gave *my* family. I'll kill you if these people don't make it. You hear me, Jamison?"

"Yes, sir."

Elijah watched him closely, making sure Jamison knew that Elijah meant what he said.

Jamison, shaking his head, repeated himself again. "Yes, sir. Yes, sir."

Then, with his eyes still threatening, Elijah said, "Then get going. Now, go!"

Jamison took a quick step backward, then turned toward the wagons. Elijah followed and then helped Rocko and Jamison gather the other seven Negroes into one wagon. After closing the back hatch, Jamison climbed up on the wagon's front seat and grabbed the reins as Rocko jumped up onto the seat beside him.

Elijah took another look into the wagon and saw the Negroes' eyes were wide with fear. Just in case Jamison gave Rocko any trouble, Elijah reached down to one of the men he'd killed and pulled a knife from the man's belt. Two of the slaves armed with knives would be much better than just one.

"Here," he said, offering the knife to the wagon's passengers. One of the slaves, the young woman who was the first to have spotted him earlier, immediately scooted to the rear and grabbed the knife. She then quickly returned to the front of the wagon and knelt down right behind Jamison. With the knife held close to Jamison's back, she glanced toward Elijah and smiled.

"Use those knives if you have to," Elijah said.

Jamison, who was now just as afraid of the woman as he was of Rocko, said, "They won't need 'em, sir. I promise."

"Ride all night, Jamison," Elijah said. "Or your family will never see you alive again."

"Yes…yes, sir."

"Go!"

Elijah watched as the wagon began to move. It rolled a few yards up the road before turning into the weeds to the north. He stood there and watched until the wagon disappeared into the darkness. Still catching his breath, Elijah waited and listened. Finally, after the sounds of hooves and wheels faded, he tucked his Colts back into his belt and turned toward the woods.

He walked slowly at first and then picked up his pace. Exhausted, Elijah reached his horse and took a deep breath. After untying the reins from the tree, he stepped into the stirrup and climbed onto the saddle. Then he yanked the reins, turned the horse, and quickly sped away.

He'd thought through this plan a hundred times and knew that there was still much that could go wrong. Without wasting any time, he headed east where he would cross the Cumberland River and then turn to the north toward Indiana. Elijah Hawkins knew he'd be in the saddle all night, and hopefully, by morning, he'd have at least a few rivers and streams between himself and the little town of Jericho Creek.

Lawmen in this part of the country worked fast. And vigilante bounty hunters seeking revenge for their dead friends worked even faster.

-19-

135 West Middle Street, Gettysburg
July 1, 1863, 5:00 p.m.

Using all his strength, Solomon banged on the door again.

"Please, let us in!" he yelled.

Looking back, he saw that the Rebel skirmishers were moving down the alley and rounding up prisoners. He could only see a few Union soldiers now. Most of the survivors had already been captured or had retreated through the town.

"Sol...," Hawk said barely above a muffle. "They're coming this..."

But his voice broke and then trailed off.

"I know, Hawk," Solomon said. "Stay down out of sight below the bushes."

When Hawk didn't respond, Solomon looked down and saw Hawk's head had dropped and his eyes had closed. Although Hawk was barely conscious and more trickling blood had emerged at the corner of his mouth, his hand was still pointing up the alley toward town. Solomon looked in that direction again and saw that the Rebels had begun moving toward them.

Solomon felt desperate now and unslung his rifle. Just as he turned to bang on the door with it, he heard a young boy's voice from inside along with women's voices and the sound of the door's wooden latch being moved. The door opened, and Solomon quickly lowered his gun.

Just inside was a boy of about nine years of age.

"Quick!" the boy urged, frantically waving them into the house.

"Hurry!" a woman's voice shouted. "Don't let anyone see you!"

Solomon quickly looked in and slid his rifle across the floor before turning back toward Hawk. "Come on, Hawk!" he said, reaching down and pulling him up the step. Solomon hauled him through the door which was promptly slammed behind them. After collapsing on the floor of the kitchen, Solomon tried to catch his breath.

Inside, two women were cowering on the other side of the room near a large corner stove. Just a few feet away, an open door exposed a flight of stairs leading to the cellar where the family had been hiding. The boy ran to the window facing the alley and looked out. Even at his age, he knew the seriousness of their situation and made no effort to hide his nervousness.

"Son," Solomon said to the boy to get his attention, "we need your help."

"Yes, sir."

"Stay down and don't be seen…but go look out the front windows and tell me what you see." The boy was gone before Solomon completed the sentence.

The women stared, shaking.

Solomon looked at them and pleadingly said, "My friend here…he needs help."

Not hesitating, both women quickly approached and dropped down next to Hawk.

"He's bleeding badly," one of them said. She reached for a cloth on the table and held it against Hawk's stomach. "Tabitha, hold this on here to stop the blood. I'll get water."

Solomon sat up and looked at the two women. "Thank you," he said.

"Mister," the boy said anxiously, having returned from the front of the house. "There's Rebs out there...everywhere."

"How many?"

"Hundreds of them, sir." His voice cracked, and then he continued. "They went down the street out front...Middle Street. They were runnin' that way, toward the center of town. And there's more coming. Chambersburg Street is already full of Rebels too."

"Thank you, son," Solomon said calmly. "What's your name?"

The boy was already at the back window again, scouting. While still watching the backyard and alley, he replied over his shoulder, "I'm Jacob...McLaughlin. That's my mother and my Aunt Tabitha there with your friend."

"Where's your father?"

"He's off fighting," the boy said proudly, even turning away from the window and looking at Solomon with a smile. "He's a soldier like you. Pennsylvania Reserves...the First PA Reserves."

Solomon sympathetically looked at the boy who was still at the window and again looking out in both directions. Seeing him made Solomon think of his own family back home. Although Solomon didn't have any children of his own—he was too young for that—he always worried about his mother and father with three of their sons away fighting in the war. His mind quickly turned to James, who probably wouldn't ever come home.

The boy's voice interrupted his thoughts. "Your friend... he's hurt bad, ain't he?"

Solomon nodded before answering. "Afraid so..."

"He got shot?" the boy asked, now looking at Solomon with a look of concern.

"Yeah, took a ball up near the seminary…back that way. Rebs had us surrounded. We was runnin' for the town."

Outside the window toward the alley, loud voices came closer. And then there were angry shouts. More prisoners being taken by Rebels, Solomon assumed.

"Jacob, get down!" his mother said nervously.

Solomon looked to the boy and waved him over. "Jacob, take me to the front of the house. I need your help."

Sprawled out on the floor and clinging to a table leg, Hawk watched as the boy sprang from the window and led Solomon toward the hallway, leaving Hawk alone in the kitchen with the two women. Hawk tried to push himself up to a sitting position, but an intense pain from his stomach surged through him. With a grunt, he collapsed back down.

Jacob's mother, seeing Hawk's pain, carried a pail of water over and knelt down beside him. "Here, water," she said, pulling the dipper from the bucket and bringing it to Hawk's mouth.

"Thanks," Hawk mumbled after taking a sip.

With the two women hovering over him, he forced a smile and took another drink. The water felt good against his lips and dry mouth but brought another fury of pain as it went down. More blood gurgled. But he forced a smile again as he waved the water scoop away.

Aunt Tabitha looked back down to Hawk's stomach and frowned. Seeing that the cloth was now soaked with blood, she reached for a new, clean bandage and then dabbed at the wound. Hawk let out a grunt when she pressed it against his stomach.

"What's your name, soldier?" she asked.

"My name is Elijah…Elijah Hawkins. But they've called me 'Hawk' ever since…"

His voice gave up on him again.

"*Hawk*…I like that name," the mother said. "You seem like a nice young man."

Despite the pain, Hawk smiled. He'd never been called a nice young man before. He tried to respond but, instead, coughed up blood.

"Where you from?" she asked, now clinging to his cold hand.

Hawk thought about what to say, and then he felt himself begin to fade. He felt cold, and his lips quivered.

"Hawk?"

A warm flash of his childhood took the chill away. He was at the stream not far from his home. "*Elijah, look!*" The voice was his sister's as she played with the small wooden boat that he and his father had built. It bobbled as it floated in the current between the rocks. A gust of wind caused the sun to dance on the water as it flashed through the autumn leaves above. All the while, his father's blurry reflection fluttered on the water's ripples.

"Kentucky," Hawk muttered out loud, somehow the voice finding its way through from the past…but only for a moment before fading again.

He was standing in the creek again, and the water felt cool as it circled his ankles and flowed past. He'd dreamed of the scene a hundred times since. It was fall…he'd always loved that time of year. A bird's whistle broke through the crickets, and high overhead, a blackbird crowed.

"But I ain't…"

Hawk began to speak aloud again, but a taste of blood interrupted. Trying to swallow led to another gurgle rising from his ravaged midsection. After a drink from the mother's dipper and a painful swallow, Hawk continued.

"I got no family down there anymore though. Been gone a long time."

"I'm sorry," the boy's mother said.

He was cold again.

And shaking.

And then there was another voice. He opened his eyes slowly. Everything was blurry at first, and then he saw Solomon leaning over him.

"Hang in there, Hawk," Solomon said.

Hawk's eyes darted around the room. They were all staring at him now…the two women, the boy, and Solomon.

"Sol…," Hawk tried to say more, but that was all that came out.

Solomon leaned in closer. "You're gonna be alright, Hawk."

The blood felt warm on his mouth, but then a single, subtle cough caused him to choke. Hawk swallowed hard, painfully, and then spoke again. "You can make it, Sol. Please…save yourself."

Solomon didn't respond and looked away when more voices and shouts came from outside. Hawk stared straight up at the ceiling, but the other four all stared at the window. Between the sporadic shots of muskets and echoes of distant cannons, they heard the Rebels in the back alley and at nearby houses.

"They're next door!" Aunt Tabitha frantically exclaimed.

It was Jacob's mother who went to the window this time and stared toward the neighbor's house. Now the voices were close enough to hear their Southern drawls and even some of their words.

Hawk's head also turned to the window when he heard the word *Yankees*. The way the Southerner said it reminded him of the rebellious men in the tavern and in the church two and a half years ago in Jericho Creek. Thinking of those men caused his mind to drift even more, this time to the horrible night his family was killed many years ago. For a moment, anger took over the pain from his wound. Then another voice next door startled him and made him look to the window again.

"You's all hidin' Yankees in there?" The voice was high-pitched and reckless.

Another yell from the neighbor's yard followed, a deeper, angrier, and less compromising voice.

"We's comin' in one way ur another!" the Southerner shouted.

"Jacob, Tabitha…go to the cellar!" Jacob's mother screamed hysterically, turning from the window. "They're comin' around the front!"

Hawk, still angry, turned to the boy. "Jacob, your father…" Hawk took a deep swallow so he could finish. "Does he have any guns in the house?"

Jacob looked at his mother and aunt who were at the cellar door.

"Come on!" his mother yelled, already two steps down.

But Jacob was gone, darting from the kitchen and heading for his father's guns.

"No, Jacob! No!" his mother yelled, but the voice trailed off as his Aunt Tabitha grabbed her arm and urged her down the steps.

"Go on, go to the cellar," Solomon shouted. He then rushed past the door and into the hallway to have another look from the front of the house.

Hawk opened his eyes when he heard the boy return and drop down beside him. "Here, mister," Jacob said, holding an old Colt Dragoon revolver.

"Thanks, Jacob," Hawk said, looking at the gun and forcing a smile.

The boy beamed proudly and didn't leave.

"But my eyes aren't too good right now," Hawk said. "Your pa teach ya how to load it?"

"Yes, sir," Jacob replied, already standing up and reaching for the powder flask and bag of lead balls he had set on the table.

"Listen, son," Hawk said with a grimace. "Soon as you get it loaded for me, you go to the cellar and don't leave."

"Yes, sir," Jacob said while he poured powder and then a ball into one of the cylinders. After ramming the charge down, Jacob quickly spun the cylinder and repeated the process.

Hawk smiled as the boy quickly loaded all six cylinders and then placed the percussion caps. For a boy that age, he was good with guns. Hawk knew that Jacob's father must've taught him the way Hawk's had.

"Here," the boy said, holding out the loaded revolver for Hawk.

"Thank you, son," Hawk said weakly while he took the Dragoon and placed it on his bandaged stomach. "Before you go, do something for me, okay?"

Jacob quickly looked toward the cellar stairs where a plea from his mother urged him to come.

"Yes, sir," he said. As Jacob responded, Hawk let out a groan while he struggled to reach into his coat pocket.

"Here, take…" Hawk's sentence was interrupted by a bloody and painful cough that engulfed him again. The boy stared while Hawk grimaced and pulled a small, brown leather book from his pocket.

"What is it?" Jacob asked.

"You'll know what to do with it," Hawk said, holding the book out with his bloody hand. "Take it, before it's too late."

Reaching out and taking it from Hawk's hand, Jacob studied the small book quizzically. After working to decipher the letters on the cover, Jacob looked up at Hawk again.

"Who's *Henry*?" he asked.

"Go to the cellar, son. With your mother and aunt."

Jacob stood up just as another Rebel shouted.

"*Open the door!*"

The Confederates were at *their* front door this time, not the neighbor's. Hawk sat up and leaned his back against the table leg.

"Jacob, you don't wanna be part of what's going to happen here," Hawk said. "Go. Quick."

Jacob was slowly backing away from Hawk when Solomon darted back into the kitchen from the front hallway.

"The street is full of Rebs out front," Solomon said. "Jacob, go to the cellar!"

Jacob turned slowly at first, then scurried toward the cellar door. As he started down the stairs, he could hear the shattering of the front door's wooden boards.

"Good luck, mister," Jacob said to Solomon from halfway down.

"Thank you, son. Now, go hide down there and don't come out."

The boy's eyes were wide with fear when Solomon closed the cellar door. Turning toward Hawk, Solomon raced over and knelt down beside him.

"What are you doing, Hawk?" he asked, looking at the old Colt Dragoon on his lap.

"*Open the door!*"

The Rebel's angry voice echoed through the house. It was accompanied by the banging of rifle butts and boot heels against the door.

"Don't do this, Hawk," Solomon pleaded, looking at Hawk's hand wrapped around the revolver.

"They're not taking me alive, Sol."

"The war will be over soon, Hawk. You'll be home in a few months." Solomon didn't believe his own words but wanted to try anything to keep Hawk from being killed by a Rebel bullet here in this house.

"I can't move from here, Sol. I'll buy you time. Save yourself."

Sol didn't know what to say.

"I'll take at least one of 'em with me, Sol."

The front door crashing against the wooden floor echoed into the kitchen. Solomon shook with fear. He was again forced with the agonizing decision of leaving a wounded comrade behind or facing certain capture or even death for himself. He felt selfish…but desperate too. The sounds of the Rebels in the hallway boomed closer. They were almost to the kitchen now.

"God bless you, Hawk! You're a good man."

"I'll know soon enough," Hawk said, now sitting upright with the revolver's hammer cocked and aimed toward the hallway.

"Go, Sol!"

Solomon took one last look at Hawk before opening the back door and lunging into the yard. The Southern-drawl shouts of the Confederates behind him could be heard as they rushed into the kitchen.

Then there was a pause before the distinct *ba-boom* of Hawk's Dragoon revolver. The shot from inside the house echoed into the yard and was followed by a scream. Solomon felt a desperate sickness deep inside knowing what would happen next. But going back in to help against at least a half dozen Rebels would be suicide.

At first, it was only one angry voice that yelled. Then several more. But the voices were quickly drowned out by the sounds of boots and banging chairs. Then a single musket blast came from the kitchen.

Horrified at what had just happened, Solomon held back a scream as he sprinted away from the house and toward the back gate.

-20-

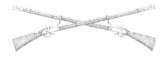

West Middle Street, Gettysburg
July 1, 1863, 6:15 p.m.

Hearing Confederates in nearly every direction, Solomon crouched down and stopped just short of the gate.

The alley was full of destruction. Shells arced overhead and slammed into buildings, and shattered bricks and debris filled the streets. The wounded and dead were lying among the devastation of the day's battle while General Lee's army redeployed in its newly conquered town.

"Take 'em back that way!" a Southern voice yelled.

Solomon quickly turned. Down the alley to the right, several captured Union soldiers were being corralled by a squad of Rebels. Beyond them, closer to the center of town, hundreds of Confederates filled the streets. Seeing more Rebels approaching to help with the prisoners, Solomon ducked his head back down and thought about what he saw.

The prisoners had looked terrified. Seeing them made Solomon think of the Company B skirmishers who'd been captured earlier across the creek. They were probably already being marched over the mountains to the west on their long journey that would eventually take them south. They'd all heard about Libby Prison in Richmond, Virginia, and every man in the Union Army prayed he wouldn't end up there. Solomon thought of James and wondered if he had been captured too… and whether he was even still alive.

A loud Southern voice, even closer, suddenly bellowed, "There's more of 'em two houses back."

"Tell the sergeant they're yours too!" a Rebel officer yelled. "March 'em up the street with the rest of 'em and out of town."

Solomon slowly lifted his head. Other than the prisoners, the only Union soldiers he saw were two dead men lying in a backyard across the alley. The rest of the Union Army had passed through at least an hour ago, and those who had escaped alive were well to the south of town by now.

Solomon then turned his head toward a sudden commotion farther down the alley. At the corner house at the next intersection, a gray-haired civilian was engaged in a heated argument with several Confederates.

"There's nobody in here!" the old man shouted from his doorway, waving his top hat wildly in protest. He was still yelling when two of the Rebels shoved him aside and forced their way through the door.

"Check every room!" one of them yelled.

"And the attic!" a deeper voice called out a second later.

Seeing the Confederates barge into the house made Solomon think of the house he had just come from. Turning around and looking at the back door, he thought of the two women and the boy hiding down in the cellar. He listened carefully. Barely, above the noise and chaos all around him, he could hear the Rebels' voices inside.

Solomon thought of Hawk just on the other side of that door and knew almost certainly that he was dead or dying. He remembered back to the day he had first met Hawk…before any of them had enlisted. He still went by *Elijah* then. Until now, that always seemed like a lifetime ago. Now, though, with

Hawk probably taking his last breaths, it suddenly felt like it was only yesterday.

Solomon remembered all of them there that day they had met Elijah…the entire mess squad…Henry, James, himself, along with several others who, now, were all long gone. Elijah was arguing with a loud-mouthed older man who was riling up a crowd outside the general store in Richmond, Indiana.

The man had been screaming for war. But after Elijah shouted it wouldn't be old men like him doing the fighting, the angry man focused all his rage on Elijah. Although at least fifteen years older, the man was a brute and looked almost twice Elijah's size. Nevertheless, Elijah didn't back down. The loud-mouthed man insisted the argument turn physical, and it was then that Solomon and the rest of the crowd quickly saw how tough Hawk was.

Hawk was quick. And had nerves as cold as ice too.

The bloodied man was still cursing and even angrier when several townspeople had finally separated them, although much too late to save the man's reputation from embarrassment. As the man was escorted away by his friends, Hawk coolly stared them all down. The thing Solomon remembered most, though, was his barely noticeable grin as the whole episode wound down. Hawk's grin was so quick and subtle, no one else in the crowd that day had seen it. Solomon, though, knew he'd remember it forever.

"Check the cellar!"

The loud voice from inside the house woke Solomon from his trance. He quickly turned and then heard more yells and boots against the floor inside. He stared but didn't dare move.

With his gun still loaded, he brought it up slightly and even thought of going back in. Immediately realizing that would be futile, he took a deep breath and lowered his musket. There was certainly nothing he could do for Hawk now. And the two women and boy would probably also be better off without his help. Hopefully, the Rebels would try to follow the rules of war and decency when among civilians…despite Hawk having shot at them while inside their house.

Solomon was still staring at the back door when it suddenly opened. Catching Solomon by surprise, a Rebel appeared in the doorway and immediately raised his musket.

Solomon quickly ducked and then dove to the ground.

"Stop!" the Rebel yelled.

Knowing he had no time to waste, Solomon desperately crawled through the gate and into the alley.

A musket erupted from the back door, and a bullet slammed into the wooden gate just after he passed through.

The Rebels down the alley toward the center of town also saw him and shouted. That was the direction he needed to go, but the streets that way were crowded with Confederates. With no other choice, Solomon quickly jumped to his feet and sprinted the opposite direction. More shots rang out, and he forced himself to not look back.

He was heading west, the direction he and Hawk had limped into town from. As he ran, a new storm of yells and muskets behind him echoed between the houses. Bullets whizzed past, and then the fence beside him burst with splintering wood as it was riddled with lead.

Solomon put his head down and angled to the left. Sprinting toward the fence, he reached for its top rail and started to climb over.

Suddenly, a bullet slammed into the wooden plank with a whack, missing his hand by only inches. Losing his balance, he fell back to the ground. Even more Rebels appeared in the alley now.

"Surrender, ya fool!" one of them shouted.

Another shot rang out, and then another. Solomon stumbled once more, struggled back to his feet, and finally leapt across. Regaining his balance on the other side, he looked for his path of escape. The last row of houses was just ahead. Running as hard as he could, he turned the corner and ducked into a patch of bushes along the side of a house.

Staying low, he crawled along the thick underbrush against the house but quickly stopped when he heard more yells up ahead. Just in front of him, Middle Street was jammed full of gray-clad soldiers marching toward the center of town. Behind him in the alley, his pursuers' shouts finally faded.

Not sure where to go, he lay flat on the ground and caught his breath. It was almost sunset, and the shadows had grown long. Peeking through the bush, he looked toward Middle Street again where the column of Rebels was pouring into town. They were only a few yards away, and the alley behind him was again swarming with Rebels too. The bushes along the side of the house offered him some concealment, but it was only a matter of time before they found him.

While he tried to decide what to do, a sudden pounding of hooves approached and stopped on the other side of the bushes. Solomon cowered lower against the house as the horse neighed and pranced in place.

"General Ramseur, sir," an officer from the column called out.

As the officer approached the horse and rider, Solomon, only a few feet away, remained still and forced himself to not look up.

"Form the brigade along the street here," the general commanded from atop his horse.

"Yes, sir!" the officer responded before hurrying back toward the column and shouting out the general's orders.

The general's horse spun in place but didn't leave. The horse sounded agitated, and its neighs and fidgeting hooves were so close that Solomon could feel the ground moving. Seconds felt like hours, and Solomon held his breath.

Just as Solomon thought the general and horse would depart, another thundering of hooves from up the street brought a second rider. The horseman barked frantic shouts that Solomon couldn't understand. All he could make out was something about prisoners and then a general named *Rodes*.

"General Lee is there too," the horseman said, speaking more clearly this time. General Ramseur immediately sounded angry, and Solomon could hear him adjust himself in his saddle before yelling out at his horse.

"*Heeyawww!*"

The other officer shouted at his own mount too, and finally, after the sound of snapping reins and kicking spurs, the horses galloped off with their riders.

Solomon exhaled and, finally daring himself to move, glanced toward the street. He saw more Rebels filing past. Most looked ragged and lean…and mean too, like prowling wolves.

Praying he wouldn't be seen, Solomon closed his eyes.

Survive…make it home, Sol. James's words rang in his ears. James had told him that only a few hours ago, but it now seemed like an eternity. James thought he was dying then, and all he wanted was for Solomon to make it home. That meant more to James than his own survival.

Solomon kept his head down as the Rebels continued past. Canteens and tin cups clanged above the chorus of Southern voices. Trodden feet and shoes thumped the dirt street by the hundreds.

…Make it home, Sol. Their mother and father deserved it. So did their sisters, even though life after the war would never be the same, especially if James were never to come home. He knew he must survive…for James and for his mother and father. Live through this battle, and maybe, just maybe, he would see his family again.

Solomon slowly opened his eyes. When he looked up, his heart jumped. A Rebel had spotted him and was gazing directly at him, speechless, as if uncertain of what he saw. Both soldiers, astonished, stared at each other silently, but then, the Rebel suddenly opened his mouth to yell. He paused for just a moment while his arm went up and pointed at Solomon. Then his Southern voice pierced the air.

"*There! Yankee!*"

When their comrade screamed out, the other Confederates stopped and turned. Seeing Solomon, they quickly lowered their rifles and aimed. Solomon knew he had no choice. He sprang to his feet and dashed back toward the alley.

"*Stop!*"

Out in the open again amongst the Rebels in the alley, he lowered his head and sprinted. Darting to the left, Solomon cut through the corner yard and headed for the north-south street ahead.

Yells went up from the Rebels again. A sole musket blasted from behind him. And then more followed. With bullets whistling past, Solomon sprinted up the street.

Suddenly, a bullet ripped through his coat and slammed into his Springfield's barrel, sending a shock through his arm that sent him and his musket tumbling to the dirt. His hand was still shaking from the sting of the blast when he reached to retrieve his gun. Seeing the rifle was badly mangled and now useless, he threw it back down and scrambled to his feet.

"Shoot him!" one of the Rebels yelled, angrier this time.

Solomon quickly glanced over his shoulder. Several of the Rebels had pursued him around the corner and now took aim again. With no time to pick up his hat and haversack, he sprinted for his life. Behind him, muskets erupted, and bullets whooshed past and missed by only inches.

Approaching Middle Street again, he saw the street was full of Rebels. Picking a gap where the street was thinly guarded, he sprinted through the intersection. The Rebels yelled and raised their muskets. Praying the bullets would miss, Solomon zig-zagged and sped toward the row of houses just ahead.

Muskets crackled, and the air whistled with flying lead. Bullets thudded and flew up dirt.

Solomon turned off the road, passed a house, and ran down another alley. Finally, after passing several houses, the yells and muskets behind him began to fade. He quickly climbed a fence and ducked behind a small woodshed against a house. After collapsing to the ground, he caught his breath and nervously scanned the horizon.

Knowing the small woodshed and house concealed him from the enemy troops in the alley behind him, he took a deep breath and leaned back against the house. He then looked around and thought about his escape.

To his right, he saw a large empty yard and the backs of several buildings along the next east-west street. Against the rear of these buildings were several empty carriages and wagons, as well as stacks of wheels, metal rods, springs, and wooden boards. In addition to the carriage and wagonmaker's shop, several other buildings and houses were arrayed on the streets to the east and south. Then he noticed open fields just beyond the next street. Realizing the Union lines were likely off in the distance beyond those fields, he felt a twinge of hope.

It was getting darker by the minute, and the darkness, he knew, would be his friend when it was time to make his final escape. Off in the distance, artillery rumbled. They were off to the south…Union cannons, he assumed.

Yes…

He remembered seeing them flee in that direction hours ago, and that was also where he would go to rejoin his regiment.

Closer, however, Confederates were moving along the road just in front of him, heading east toward the center of town. It was an entire brigade, he figured. Behind him, he heard the Rebels around Middle Street reorganizing their defensive lines. In nearly every direction, he could hear distant rifle fire and artillery, as well as the fainter noises of wagons, horses, and men. He slumped down lower against the home's stone wall and took another deep breath. Hopefully, after this group of Rebels marched past to the east, the street would be clear and he could make it to the open fields.

He might just make it yet, he told himself.

Then, just a few feet away, a sudden commotion startled him. Solomon quickly looked over and saw the house's side door being opened. Shrinking back into the corner even further, he stared as a terrified black family emerged from the doorway.

Two adults and three children rushed away from the door and along the side of the house in the opposite direction. A young girl, however, bundled with a hooded shawl and carrying a worn-out baby doll, had turned around and saw Solomon leaning against the house. She let out a startled shriek that caused her father to look back too. The father, appearing just as scared as his daughter, quickly pulled her close.

"It's okay," Solomon whispered, slowly raising his hands.

The father stopped and studied Solomon closely. After recognizing Solomon's blood-covered, Union-blue uniform pants, the man's look of fear gave way to an expression of sympathy and appreciation. He took a step toward Solomon and reached into his coat pocket.

"No, go on," Solomon said with a wave, trying to urge the girl's father away. Solomon had been worried about himself being detected by Confederates, but now he was even more nervous for this black family trying to make *their* escape.

As Solomon cowered even further back into his corner between the woodshed and the house, he waved the family away again. But instead of leaving, the father took another step toward him. Watching the man cautiously, Solomon wondered what he was doing.

As the man approached, he extended his hand holding a half loaf of bread. Just behind him, the family appeared terrified and nervously looked on.

"Bread?" the man asked.

"No, thank you," Solomon whispered, waving the bread away.

The father insisted with a nod and shook the bread. Solomon didn't want to take the family's food but also didn't want to delay their escape…nor cause a scene exposing his own hiding place.

The two men stared at each other. Knowing the man was risking his family's escape by stopping to offer him food, Solomon reached out for the bread. After tearing a piece away, Solomon quietly said, "Thank you, sir."

The man didn't respond but nodded and stepped back. He put his arm around his daughter again and, along with the rest of his family, finally turned away and crept along the side of the house.

Solomon watched as the family approached the corner. The father halted them again and stared out into the street. Although the rest of the family was looking beyond the house and nervously planning their escape, Solomon saw the little girl still staring at him.

Solomon smiled.

The girl opened her mouth to speak, but suddenly, her father pulled her by the arm. The family hurried along the side of the house, and as they stopped at the corner, the girl turned toward Solomon with a smile and spoke.

Solomon barely heard what she said.

"Th-th-thank you, mistuh."

Then the family was gone, having disappeared around the corner.

Leaning back, Solomon put his head against the house. He quickly ate half the bread and slipped the rest into his pocket.

He didn't have his haversack anymore; in fact, he didn't carry much of anything. His rifle had been destroyed and discarded, and even his hat, the tall black hat that identified his proud brigade, had been left abandoned in the street. What he knew he needed the most, though, was his canteen and water.

Shrinking back deeper into his corner, Solomon knew he couldn't stay here. Eventually, the yard would be full of Rebels as General Lee's army completely occupied the town. On the street to the south, Solomon saw more Confederates marching by the carriage house.

Remaining hidden, Solomon watched them march toward the center of town. After the last of the Rebels filed past the carriage maker's buildings, that part of the street was empty again.

James's words came to him again.

Survive…make it home, Sol. Make it home.

He looked out at the vacant yard, took a deep breath, and rose to his weary feet. Now was his chance to make a run for it. With a spring forward, he put his head down and ran as fast as he ever had, first through the yard and then to a stack of wagon wheels at the rear of the building. He then dropped to the ground, quickly crawled along the wagon wheels, and then took cover between two carriages.

Telling himself he was almost to the open fields, he caught his breath and looked around. Across the street in the upstairs window, something moved and caught his eye. He stared, but whatever had moved was gone. Hearing footsteps approach, he leaned back into his hiding place and listened. Inhaling quietly, Solomon didn't move as a lone, gray-clad soldier approached to within a few feet and then, luckily for Solomon, continued jogging past.

Solomon exhaled slowly but still didn't move. Just as he was ready to get up and resume his escape, the figure in the upstairs window reappeared. She was a middle-aged woman whose eyes darted nervously. When their eyes met, she gave

Solomon a quick but hesitant nod. It was obvious to Solomon that she had been watching him…and watching the streets and fields. She then looked away and up the street to the west. Solomon watched closely as her expression turned from concerned to almost panicked.

She quickly looked back to Solomon and mouthed something he couldn't understand. Her eyes darted back and forth between Solomon and the road to the west. Solomon, hearing noises up the street, looked in that direction too.

"Go! Go!" she shouted. This time, Solomon could hear the words. He glanced up at the window again and could see her frantically pointing across the street toward the fields to the south.

Solomon looked to the west again. The noises in that direction were Rebels…hundreds of them all heading straight for him. He nodded and mouthed a *thank-you* to the woman as he sprang to his feet.

"Run!" the woman yelled from the upstairs window, pointing even more urgently this time. "That way! Hurry! Go!"

Suddenly, a deep voice bellowed from up the street.

"*Stop! Yankee, stop!*"

Solomon turned his head toward the voice and saw a butternut-clad Rebel pointing at him. Several more Confederates saw him too and shouted. Suddenly, the entire mass was in pursuit.

Solomon sprinted toward the west side of the building and then around the corner and across the street. After jumping a fence and landing with a tumble in a waist-high wheat field, he got back to his feet and fled to the south. Shots rang out from the fence behind him. With bullets whistling past, he ducked his head and zigzagged through the wheat.

Seconds later, he approached a post and rail fence. Despite the growing darkness, he didn't dare stand up to climb over and expose himself to the Rebels behind him. Dropping down to his knees, he clambered through the bottom rails and crawled through to the other side.

Suddenly, a bullet whooshed past and thudded into the ground only an inch from his hand.

"Stop!" another Southern voice yelled but from much farther away this time.

Solomon stayed low in the wheat and continued crawling as fast as he could. "Keep going," he told himself, hoping the next Rebel bullet wouldn't find its mark.

Finally, from behind him, he could now hear only a few distant, sporadic shots. Still crawling, he slowed his pace but continued away from the town. As the last of the Rebel muskets faded, he stopped and took a deep breath.

Totally exhausted, he rolled onto his side. The fading sun had finally dropped below the horizon, and the nearly full moon was just beginning to crest over a long ridge to the east.

Only a few distant cannons interrupted the still night air, but they were sporadic and sounded less desperate than before. The day's battle seemed to finally run out of steam. Welcoming the darkness, Solomon realized he might actually make it out alive. For just a second, he even allowed himself a smile.

Solomon spent several minutes hunkered down in the field before finally looking up and scanning his surroundings. The Rebels were several hundred yards behind him now. Farther to the south, he saw a large barn and house surrounded by an orchard. The farm's long, dirt lane stretched back toward the town behind him.

He stared through the darkness toward the barn where he thought he saw movement. Then he saw it again. At the back of the barn and in the nearby orchard, he could barely make out the silhouettes of men. The dirt lane leading toward the barn, however, seemed totally vacant.

After finally having caught his breath, he told himself he must keep moving. Cautiously, he lifted his head. Slowly creeping through the grass again, he approached the dirt lane and looked down it in both directions. Seeing no one, he quickly rose up and sprinted across.

Suddenly, a bullet whistled past and slammed into the dirt. As he dove into the grass on the other side of the lane, he heard the echoes from the carbine's shot that barely missed him. It had come from the ridge ahead.

Forced to crawl on his stomach again, he felt his heart race. The echoes of the gunshot had faded, but he knew there could be more. Safely hidden in the wheat again, he stopped and lay flat.

He waited and listened. After several moments and hearing no more shots, he raised his head.

Off in the distance ahead, Solomon could see the silhouettes of horsemen. Most were dismounted, although he could also see a few of the men atop their horses. The horsemen seemed to be in a thin skirmish line with a fence-lined road running a few hundred yards behind them.

Farther to the south, he saw a barn and house along the road. He remembered that was where they had turned off the road earlier after marching up from Emmitsburg. That seemed so long ago to him, yet that march was only this morning. This was the longest day of his life.

Beyond the horsemen and the road, he could see the orange glow of hundreds of campfires along the ridge. He crawled forward a few paces and examined the horsemen more closely. Along with their moonlit silhouettes, he could also make out what appeared to be the shape of a cavalry guidon flag. Unable to identify the flag, he inched closer through the wheat.

Not knowing if these were Confederates or Union troops, Solomon slowly raised his head to examine the flag. A slight breeze twisted the flag ever so slightly. Barely visible in the dim light of the moon, he could make out its faint red and white stripes.

It was a Union cavalry flag.

Union!

His heart surged with joy.

"I'm Union!" he shouted. "Don't shoot!"

Solomon raised his arms and then stood up. "I'm a Union soldier!"

Walking slowly with his arms raised and repeating his pleas for them to not shoot, he approached a group of four cavalrymen.

"*Halt there!*"

The cavalryman's heavy New York accent pierced the quiet air. With several carbines aimed at Solomon, one of the men approached and roughly grabbed him by the arm.

"No one gets through the skirmish line here," one of the horsemen shouted. "General Buford's orders. I heard him myself."

"I'm Union," Solomon said again.

The cavalryman turned to one of his men and said, "Hackett, go get the major and bring him over here. Go."

"What regiment you with, Son?" one of the cavalrymen asked, still mounted on his horse. He was a sergeant, Solomon noticed, and glared down at him skeptically.

"Indiana… Nineteenth," Solomon replied. The men exchanged surprised glances.

"I'm trying to rejoin my unit, sir…what's left of 'em anyway. We ran through town, sir. A bunch of us…we got cut off. Please, sir, can I have some water?"

Solomon's tired weight made the man struggle to help hold him up. With a nod from the sergeant, another trooper stepped up and handed him a canteen.

"What you doin' way over here?" the sergeant asked.

Before Solomon could answer, two riders galloped toward them and slowed their horses. The lead cavalryman, an officer, brought his horse to a halt among the other soldiers and quickly dismounted. Solomon noticed his uniform was covered in dirt and that his boots and pants made a cloud of dust when he landed. His sword, dangling from his belt, clanged against his boot as he approached.

"Who do we have here, Sergeant?" he barked, looking at Solomon suspiciously.

"Says he's trying to get back to his unit, Major. Says he got caught up in the town during the retreat."

Stopping a few feet in front of Solomon, the officer removed his riding gauntlets and stared scornfully. "Where's your regiment, soldier?"

"I don't know, sir," Solomon replied. Solomon then nodded up toward the campfires on the ridge a few hundred yards away. "I hope they're up on that ridge, sir."

"What unit you with?"

"Nineteenth Indiana, sir."

"Your accent sounds like a Southerner." The major paused and, still looking at Solomon doubtfully, asked, "How can I trust you're not a Rebel?"

"I grew up in Kentucky, sir. Moved to Ohio when I was a teenager…just across the state line from Indiana. Me and my brother signed up with the Nineteenth when the war started, sir. General Meredith was our first colonel."

"Go on."

"Never lost my accent, I guess, sir."

Only partially convinced and overly cautious, the major didn't respond and waited for Solomon to continue.

"We were fighting out northwest of town…all day." As he spoke, he felt his captor's grasp on his arm begin to ease up. Between gulps of water, Solomon continued. "We were surrounded in town… I was helping a squadmate who'd just been shot. I was carrying him, sir. We got cut off and had to hide in a house."

The major, who had been watching Solomon suspiciously, remained silent as he listened to the Iron Brigade soldier speak. His skeptical expression slowly changed to a look of compassion and admiration. He exchanged glances with his other cavalrymen and then nodded for Solomon to continue.

"I tried to stay with my regiment, sir. We was shot up bad. I couldn't…"

Solomon's voice trailed off as he thought about all the dead and wounded from his regiment. He paused and then said, "I'm trying to find the Nineteenth Indiana now, sir…what's left of us anyway."

The major nodded at the cavalryman holding Solomon, signaling him to release his captive. Approaching Solomon slowly and placing his left hand on his shoulder, he extended his right hand and offered to shake Solomon's hand.

"I'm Major Beardsley, Sixth New York Cavalry."

Shaking the major's hand, Solomon responded, "Private Whitlow, sir…Solomon Whitlow. Thank you, sir."

"Help this soldier to the rear, Sergeant. And get him something to eat."

"Yes, sir," the sergeant quickly replied. Then, turning toward Solomon, the sergeant waved his hand, indicating for Solomon to follow. "This way, Private."

Solomon and the New York sergeant turned and walked slowly toward the rear. They stepped over a downed section of fence, crossed the Emmitsburg Road, and started the long walk up the gradual slope of the ridge. Reaching a low stone wall, they stepped over the rocks and walked between campfires. After passing clusters of tents and men, they approached a large tent with several flags flying out front.

"Stay here, Private."

The sergeant then walked toward the open side of the tent and exchanged words with a staff officer before disappearing inside.

The glow of several lanterns illuminated the grass outside the tent's opening. Just inside, Solomon could see several officers poring over a map stretched across a table. He listened carefully and heard the cavalry sergeant speaking with an officer at the map table. After a short exchange, Solomon heard one of the officers exclaim, "Iron Brigade...the Nineteenth? My God...yes. Where is he?"

Then suddenly, Solomon saw a haggard-looking, middle-aged officer with a tightly groomed mustache and curly hair stride out of the tent.

"He's here, sir," the sergeant said, pointing at Solomon. "Right over here."

The officer was slightly heavyset and was wearing a long, faded-blue, general's coat unbuttoned halfway down. He turned and saw Solomon standing a few feet away. The general wasn't wearing a sash or a sword belt, and the only insignia indicating his rank were stars on his shoulder boards. He approached the weary private before him and examined him closely. He nodded in admiration at the Iron Brigade veteran and slowly extended his hand.

"I'm General Doubleday. Proud to meet you, soldier."

"Thank you, sir. I'm...I'm Private Whitlow." Up close in the dull light, Solomon could now fully recognize the general's fatigue. His bloodshot and baggy eyes drooped as he looked down at Solomon.

"The Iron Brigade fought bravely today, Private."

"We've all had a very tough day, General...sir," Solomon replied, adding the *sir* almost too late as an afterthought because of his own fatigue.

General Doubleday nodded slowly. He then forced a grin, but the light from the lantern at the front of the tent showed the reflection of tears welling up in his eyes.

Doubleday hesitated before speaking again.

"Many a good soldier still lies out in those woods and in those fields."

Solomon glanced away for just a moment, then turned toward the general again.

"I know, sir. I know."

-21-

Herbst Woods, West of Gettysburg
July 1, 11:00 p.m.

"S*hhhhh*…they're coming."

Despite the pain from his wounds, James forced himself to remain still and quiet. Staring through the darkness, he could now see the Rebels' silhouettes as they approached the woods.

"They're looking for water," Will whispered. "There's at least ten of 'em."

James lowered his head deeper into the weeds along the little stream and looked at Will. Will was breathing hard too and stared at the approaching Rebels.

"We…we should move," James replied in a low voice, gritting his teeth and fighting off painful groans. He felt his heart pounding as though it was going to jump out of his chest.

"No…just stay down," Will whispered, softly placing his hand on James's back.

"*Shhhh…*"

The Rebels were in the woods now and headed toward the trickling stream. With the Confederates only a few yards away, James put his hand on his mouth to hide his own breathing.

"Jimmy," one of the Southerners suddenly called out, his voice even closer than James expected. "The stream is over here…this way."

James then heard a clattering of canteens hitting the ground as the Rebels stopped at the stream's bank. Unaware of the two wounded Union men hiding nearby, the Rebels continued their chatter as they knelt down and began scooping up water.

James dared a peek in their direction. Will was right… there were about a dozen of them.

Will leaned in close and whispered in James's ear. "They can't see us. But stay still."

Without moving, James and Will watched the Rebels fill their canteens and splash water on their hands and faces. Several of them stood up again, and canteens clanged as they pulled the leather straps over their shoulders.

"Where's them dead Yanks Eddie was talkin' 'bout back in camp?" one of them asked.

"Up in the woods…over here, this way."

Seeing the Rebel point up the slope in the opposite direction, James slowly exhaled.

"Let's see if they got anything on 'em," a gruff-voiced Rebel said before turning and starting up the rise.

"Not me," a tired Southern voice replied.

"Me neither…I've had me enough for one day," another one said, also standing and beginning to walk toward the field from where they'd come. "Ya'll can pick over the Yanks' corpses yourselves. I'm headin' back to camp."

Will and James waited quietly, knowing that making any sounds now would result in a long journey to a Confederate prison camp. Praying all the Rebels would leave, James watched as several more turned away from the stream and exited the woods. The three Southerners looking for dead Yankees had also begun walking through the woods in the other direction.

As the Rebels disappeared in the darkness, James began to breathe easier again, but suddenly, he heard approaching footsteps along the edge of the little stream. Without moving, James peeked through the weeds. One of the Rebels had separated from the group and was walking directly toward them. He was only a few paces away, and James held his breath again.

The Rebel was probing the ground with the point of the bayonet attached to his musket. He weaved his way around a bush along the creek's bank and then came closer again. The man was so close now that James could almost reach out and grab his ankle.

James put his head down as low as he could and felt Will's hand pressing against his back.

The Rebel stopped.

James could smell the man's sweat and body odor and could even hear him breathing.

Will's hand pressed harder, and neither of them dared moving.

Suddenly, a voice from up the ridge pierced the air.

"*Over here, Carter!*"

James heard the Rebel beside him suddenly move and turn toward the voice.

"Ya find 'em?" the Rebel next to James shouted back.

The voice was so close, James nearly jumped. He could now even smell the Rebel's whiskey breath.

"Yep," a voice from the group replied. "Got about four dead Yanks right here together."

James and Will waited. The Rebel standing above them stayed where he was, just a few feet away. James could then hear the soldier moving his feet and turning around.

Thoughts raced through James's head. *Oh, God, please don't let him see us.*

The Rebel seemed to be examining the darkness again, and his bayonet blindly poked at weeds and rocks.

James and Will didn't move while time stood still.

The voice from up the wooded slope called out again.

"Carter, come on. They're up here."

"What you doing down there?" a different voice called out.

The Rebel still didn't move but, instead, scoffed and spat in the weeds.

Why isn't he moving?

Then, after several long seconds, he finally turned away and walked off toward the rest of the group.

After the Rebel disappeared in the darkness, James let out the breath he'd been holding. He quietly thanked God and then looked over at Will. Will also exhaled and now looked to the sky.

Neither of them spoke, and the two wounded Iron Brigade soldiers lay next to the little stream for several minutes. With the Rebels finally gone, James felt the pain from his wounds again. He knew they were serious. He'd lost a lot of blood from his leg, and the bayonet wound to his shoulder and chest made his breathing painful and difficult.

Seeing James weak and wincing in pain, Will said, "We gotta get you to a doc."

"It's just Rebs here now…and I don't…"

Pain surged through him, and his voice trailed off. Feeling as though he would pass out, he closed his eyes.

"Even if it's a Reb doc, James. We gotta get you help."

"It hurts, Will…hurts…"

James's voice faded again.

"Here…drink some water," Will said, raising his canteen up to James's mouth. With a grimace, James drank a gulp of water and then leaned back again.

"Thanks…"

Up on the pike beyond the fields, the rumble and squeaking of wagon wheels disturbed the night air as the Rebel Army moved supplies and artillery closer to town. James and Will could also make out the distant sounds of an officer's voice and a moan from a wounded soldier. The Rebels who'd earlier found the Yankee corpses had been making a lot of noise, but they had apparently become bored with their find and were now leaving the woods toward their camp.

James heard more Southern voices from deeper in the woods and quickly looked in that direction.

"We can't stay here," Will said, also hearing the voices.

"I…I can't move," James uttered weakly.

"The Rebs are gonna be combing these woods all night, James. And you're not gonna make it if you don't get help."

James felt even weaker, and the thought of crawling anywhere caused him to close his eyes again.

"James, listen to me…"

James looked up. Will was hovering just above him.

"There's a farm past the edge of the woods right over there," Will whispered, pointing up the little stream toward the north end of the woods. Beyond the trees and ridge, he could see campfires and the top of a barn and house. Earlier, Will had seen several other small outbuildings there too and remembered wounded men lying around the barn. After the fighting here in the woods, many of Will's own captured Michigan comrades had been led away toward that farm.

Glancing down at James, Will asked, "You see the farm over there?"

James lifted his head to look, but pain surged through him again. A grunt and a nod were all he could do to respond.

"If we get you there, you can get help."

Forcing himself up onto his elbow, James risked even more agony with a look through the trees toward the farm.

"Yeah, I think I see it," James said. When he glanced back at Will, he noticed him grimacing while taking a drink from his canteen. James thought about the Michigan soldier he barely even knew.

James waited for Will to lower his canteen and then asked, "What 'bout you, Will?"

Will raised his foot up so James could see his bloody pant leg and sock. His ankle and shoeless foot were covered in blood and dirt.

"I took a ball in the ankle," Will said. "I don't think it broke a bone, but it's still bleedin'. This up here on my head is just a scratch."

James glanced at the bloodstained bandage loosely tied around Will's head.

"What happened?" James asked, sitting up slightly.

Will's face wrinkled into a frown. He thought of the afternoon's horrible fight and of all those Michigan boys. He felt a chill and shuddered.

All those boys…maimed or even killed. Many were up at that farm now, he knew.

"Our line was 'bout twenty yards away from the Rebs," Will said. "We were holdin', but the Johnnies just kept coming. We held for 'bout thirty minutes 'til our line finally broke."

Will paused and swallowed a lump in his throat.

"That's when the ball hit me in the ankle," Will continued, looking at James again. "I went to the ground, and by the time I tried to get back up, the Rebs were already on us. All I could do was just lay there. I stayed down in the weeds until it got dark. The Rebs took a lot of prisoners…"

Will suddenly stopped. He didn't want to think about that again. Changing the subject, he asked, "Your leg…what happened to it?"

"Shot in the back of the leg…across the creek. Our company got sent out as skirmishers. We'd just got ordered back when the Rebs came. My brother and I…we were almost back to this side of the creek when the ball struck my leg. We made it across…barely."

James paused. It was a struggle to speak, even at a whisper. Finally continuing, he said, "Got away as far as I could, then the regiment fell back farther in the woods. Just up there."

Will stared at him and waited for him to continue.

"Then I couldn't get out of the way of a Rebel bayonet," James said, pointing at his shoulder. For some reason, he laughed at his own words and quickly wished he hadn't. Pain surged through him, and nearly choking, he coughed up blood.

Will watched as James struggled to compose himself and catch his breath. When James didn't speak again, Will said, "Let's get you to the edge of the woods…so you can get help in the morning."

James nodded, knowing the Michigan man was right. He'd have to stop the bleeding. He also knew that staying in these woods beyond morning was certain death. Being taken prisoner with the other wounded Union men at the farm was his only chance to survive. James took in a deep breath and gathered enough strength to speak again.

"What *you* gonna do?" James asked.

"I'm gonna help you get close to that barn and a doctor," Will whispered.

"Then what?"

"I'm making a run for the town…while it's still dark."

"Don't let me hold you back," James told him. "Go ahead and go now."

"Tell you what, James…if I help you get to that tree line over there, do you think you can move in the morning? At least a little bit…just across that field to the farm?"

"I…I think so."

"There's a fence…at the edge of the trees. From there, it won't be far to them doctors at the farm. Then, come morning, you crawl that direction and scream out for help. You're a tough one, James. You're gonna make it."

James realized that he had to get out of these woods and get the help of a doctor…even if it was a Rebel doctor.

"You ready?" Will asked.

"Yeah."

Will leaned down and pried his back and shoulder underneath James's outstretched arm. Struggling because of his wounded ankle, Will lifted and helped James up to his feet. As they began to move, James let out a grunt.

"Take it slow, James," Will whispered, fighting to hold him up. The two wounded men took a few steps along the stream, but then a sharp pain shot up from James's leg.

"*Ughhhh!*" James groaned, stumbling and pulling Will down with him.

Will looked at James and saw him gritting his teeth in pain.

"I'm okay," James murmured, holding out his arm and allowing Will to help him up again. "Let's keep going."

They plodded forward again, pushing their way through a large summer sweet bush that was growing out of the stream's bank.

"I know it hurts, James. Go slow…take it easy."

Just past the bush, Will looked to the left and suddenly stopped.

"James, wait," he said, looking across the stream where a soldier was lying partway up the rise. The prone man's back was to them, and he was still wearing his knapsack.

"Psssst," Will said in the man's direction. The soldier didn't move.

"Is he alive?"

"Dunno. Hang on, James. I'll check." Will then let go of James and stepped across the ditch. After limping toward the motionless soldier, Will knelt down beside him.

James watched closely but also scanned the woods for any signs of Rebels nearby. When he saw Will look at the soldier's face and then pull his canteen away from him, James knew the man was dead.

Will didn't waste any time near the soldier and quickly scurried back down toward the stream next to James.

"One of ours?"

"Yeah, Second Wisconsin. His hat was next to him. I saw the '2' on it. They were on our right and lost a lot of good boys today."

"We all did," James responded.

Will looked toward James and knew he was right. The woods were full of their dead now…boys from Wisconsin, Michigan, and Indiana. Neither man spoke, but finally, after a long pause, Will said, "Here…take my canteen. I'll use this one."

"Thanks," James whispered, grabbing ahold of Will's canteen and pulling its strap over his shoulder.

"Let's keep going."

The two wounded men hobbled a few more steps along the trickling stream before coming to a large fallen tree that was lying across it and blocking their path. Will held up his other hand, signaling James to stop. They both scanned the area.

"Shhhh…," Will whispered, pointing toward a campfire in the nearby field where several Confederate soldiers were gathered. Although the enemy soldiers were facing the fire, James and Will knew making any loud noises would result in almost certain capture.

"We'll go this way…around the tree," Will said in a hushed voice. He was pointing across the little stream and up the small rise in the woods. Using the fallen tree for balance, the two wounded men quietly stepped into the muddy water and onto the opposite bank. Will was still supporting James, who was now completely relying on the Michigan man to hold him up. Together, they clambered up the small wooded ridge and paused at the top.

"I have to stop," James whispered. He was grimacing in excruciating pain again. His breath was rapid and shallow.

"Alright. We'll rest."

Noises filled the woods and the field to the north.

"Just stay low," Will whispered.

They were only a few paces from the edge of the woods. Looking between the trees and weeds, they could now see the entire barn, house, and outbuildings. Small, low-burning campfires with clusters of men around them were scattered all around the farm. Listening closely, they could hear the steady murmur of Southern voices beyond the fence line.

"There's hundreds of 'em," James whispered, looking at the soldiers lying near the house and barn and also lying in the field closer to the woods.

"Those are wounded men," Will whispered. Off to the right, James and Will could see several white tents, but most of the men were lying in the open night air. Along with the steady murmur of the giant Confederate bivouac, the woods and fields smelled of campfires.

Occasionally, other men carrying torches or small lanterns would move between the soldiers lying on the ground. Along the ridge to the east, hundreds of campfires and thousands of men silhouetted the night sky. The Chambersburg Pike to the north still bustled with horses and dozens of wagon teams that thudded, bounced, and squealed through the darkness.

"Looks like General Lee's whole army has moved up," James whispered, speaking of the ominous hum in the night air from the sounds all around them.

"Yeah, and more still coming."

Will's voice sounded uneasy. Unable to hide his fear of being captured, he peered between the trees and studied the fields beyond. Enemy soldiers were everywhere. Even more unsettling, though, was seeing the horrible day's casualties now strewn about in the trampled grass. Lying under the dim light of the moon and stars, their lifeless bodies gave the field a ghastly eeriness.

Looking toward James again, Will said, "In the morning, can you make it to that barn?"

"I can make it…I think," James responded hesitantly. He knew it was his only choice.

Noticing Will looking back through the woods behind them, James asked, "How 'bout you? You going back that way…towards the town?"

"Yeah, but first, let's get you to that fence."

James nodded, and the Michigan soldier helped him back to his feet again. Together, they turned toward the split-rail worm fence at the edge of the woods. After crawling through the weeds, they stopped at the fence and dropped to the ground. Will turned and started to pry the bottom rail away from the posts holding it up.

"Help me get this off, James," he whispered. "So you can crawl under it in the morning."

James tried helping but was too weak. Will, though, quietly dislodged the bottom fence rail and dropped it into the tall grass. Now, there was just enough room for a man to crawl under.

"You got about four or five hours 'til daylight," Will said. "Then you gotta get up near that barn, James."

James took a deep breath and thought of having to make his way across the field. He finally nodded and looked at Will. "You make it to town, ya hear? …You make it."

"I will, James. And when I get back to the brigade, I'll let 'em know you're out here."

"I have a brother…in the Nineteenth. His name is Solomon."

"Solomon?"

"Yeah…," James replied, "…Solomon Whitlow."

"I'll find him, James. I'll tell him."

"Thank you, Will."

Will extended his dirty, bloody hand. "Good luck, James." Propping himself up on his elbow, James shook the Michigan soldier's hand.

Then, releasing Will's hand, James forced a smile and said, "Go on."

As Will turned to leave, James leaned back against the fence post. He watched as the Michigan soldier scampered away with a limp and then disappeared into the dark woods.

James knew he owed his life to that man. Now alone and frightened for his life, James turned and stared through the fence rails toward the farm. Thinking about what tomorrow's daylight would bring, he leaned back and tried closing his eyes.

The pain and sounds didn't go away though, and he looked up at the sky. The stars were out, and he tilted his head to the west. He saw Venus, and it made him think of home.

Feeling tears, he wiped his face and let out a sigh.

It would be a long night, he knew.

And he also knew…that it might well be his last.

-22-

Culp's Hill, Gettysburg
July 2, 1863, Mid-Morning

A Napoleon startled him awake. Solomon started to open his eyes to look toward the blast, but the sting of the bright sun forced them closed. Rolling onto his side, he felt the sweat that was trapped between him and the wet grass. The air was already muggier than yesterday.

He braced for another cannon shot, but none came.

Squinting as he looked up, Solomon slowly opened his eyes again. Although he was lying among tall trees, the sun still found its way through.

Trying to bring his mind back to life, he moaned when he felt the aches all over his body. Solomon knew he must have slept a long time, judging from the sun high overhead. Glancing over toward the knoll from where the cannon fired, he saw its smoke lingering in the calm morning air.

A shirtless gunner pulled the sponge end of a rammer from a nearby bucket and carried it toward the cannon. Solomon stared as the sponge dripped water all the way to the hot gun's barrel. Even from this distance, Solomon could see the steam as the gunner inserted the wet sponge rod into the Napoleon's brass muzzle. The entire crew worked the gun slowly, deliberately.

The knoll and the hill beyond were full of guns, but none of the others fired. Instead, the cannoneers rested in the grass and behind the dirt lunettes they had built. The previous blast was a ranging shot, Solomon assumed. He looked through the trees out toward the rolling plain below to where the cannon's shell exploded. Although it was an empty field, several of the cannons up on the hill were aimed in that direction...a sure sign the gunners believed an attack would come from there. *But later, much later,* Solomon hoped as he lowered his head back down in the grass.

This was the first morning he could remember that the rest of his mess squad wasn't in camp with him. He was by himself now. Hawk and Henry were gone...and so was Billy. And James.

Solomon shook his head, and his weary mind quickly drifted to yesterday.

He hoped it was all a bad dream, but as he looked around, he knew it was real.

Lying in the grass with the rest of the regiment's survivors scattered around the hill, Solomon thought about where he was and how he had gotten here. Although remembering his encounter with the cavalrymen well past dark and being led to General Doubleday's tent last night, he couldn't recall how he had rejoined the brigade here on this hill. A cavalryman had escorted him through throngs of resting soldiers, but that was all he could remember.

Voices a little farther down the slope made him look up again. Just below him and through the trees, he noticed several soldiers with shovels.

"Keep digging!" someone shouted. It was a voice he'd heard before.

Solomon looked closer. It was Sergeant Boller. Suddenly, Solomon's mind filled with images and sounds from yesterday's heavy fighting at the creek. That was where Hawk had yelled at Boller, Solomon remembered. Hawk's words jumped into Solomon's mind as though it had happened only a few minutes ago. *Get up here and fight with the rest of us!*

The regiment had been standing shoulder to shoulder, fighting and trying to hold off the Rebels then. Solomon remembered the skirmish line at the creek and turning to look for the sergeant in the rear. But Boller had already skedaddled by then and, later, showed even more cowardice at the barricade in front of the seminary.

Seeing the sergeant now angered Solomon, but he decided to ignore him as much as he could.

"Get down here and get to diggin', Whitlow!" someone yelled.

Solomon sensed movement at the breastworks and realized he had been staring. Looking toward the voice, Solomon saw Sergeant Boller had taken a step away from the men digging and was now looking up the hill directly at him.

Solomon looked away and tried to stand up. His aching body faltered, however, and he had to painfully regain his balance. Boller yelled something else, but Solomon blocked him out and turned the other direction. He wouldn't let the sergeant get to him ever again, he told himself...not after the hell they had all experienced yesterday.

His sore legs finally cooperated, and he stood all the way up. He noticed more soldiers now, most of them behind freshly made breastworks about fifty yards down the hill. Along the top of the dirt and rock earthworks, the men had placed branches and logs, making it a formidable wall. After taking an enormous number of casualties yesterday fighting out in the open, the survivors here on this hill wanted to have an advantage if they were attacked today.

Looking to the left, Solomon saw the Twenty-Fourth Michigan's flag hanging limp among a group of its men. Solomon then turned the other direction and saw a Wisconsin flag jammed in the breastworks up toward the higher part of the hill to the right. Between the trees just below him, the Nineteenth's bullet-riddled blue flag hung against its splintered staff.

Solomon saw several of his regiment's men there. With their packs and muskets stacked and leaning against the breastworks, several of the survivors dug while others rested. With sore legs, Solomon slowly and wearingly started walking toward what was left of his regiment.

"Whitlow," a voice from behind him called out.

Solomon quickly turned and saw an officer striding down the hill after him. "Sir? Captain Orr?"

"Your shoulder…it's covered in blood."

Solomon saluted the captain and then glanced at his sleeve. He had forgotten about the flesh wound that he received at the creek early in yesterday afternoon's fighting. He now saw that dirt had mixed with the dried blood.

"Uhhh, it's nothing, Captain," he replied. "It's not bleeding anymore, sir."

"Well, get that looked at and bandaged up today anyway."

"Yes, sir."

"I'm just coming from brigade headquarters. Walk with me down to the skirmish line, Solomon."

They took only a few steps before Captain Orr turned to Solomon again. "Or should I call you *King*?"

The word stunned Solomon, and he stopped.

"*King*, sir?"

"Your name. It's *King*, isn't it?"

For over two years, Solomon hadn't heard the first name that his parents had given him. "Uhhh, yes sir."

"We were just checking the roster…of our survivors."

The captain suddenly paused. Thinking of yesterday had scourged his face into a wrinkled gloom.

"Captain?"

The captain, forcing himself from frowning, smiled and took a deep breath before speaking again. "Your name is listed as King...King Whitlow. I didn't know which of you was King. I only knew the two of you as James and Solomon."

"Yes sir, that's me," Solomon said. "They call me 'Sol', sir."

Solomon quickly realized that until now the captain hadn't known which of the Whitlow brothers was missing and who had survived. There were several brothers and cousins in the regiment, Solomon knew. Today would be a difficult day for the survivors.

"Sorry...I'm sorry about your brother, Sol."

Solomon didn't respond and looked away.

"Come on, Sol," the captain said, putting his hand on Solomon's back. "Keep walking with me. I need to speak with the colonel."

After moving between trees and arriving at the breastworks, Captain Orr turned toward Solomon once again and shook his hand. "Good to see you back, Sol," he said before turning and surveying the battered regiment.

Orr looked at the men closely, sadly...seemingly searching for names no longer there. Then he turned, put his head down, and walked away. Solomon noticed he was wiping away tears as he headed toward Colonel Williams who was farther up the hill.

After a few moments, Solomon turned and also scanned the regiment's survivors. There were about sixty remaining, he guessed. They looked ragged and tired. In the past twenty-four hours, all of them had lost squadmates, friends, and even relatives.

"Here, help us dig, Sol," a private from Company A said, holding a shovel out for Solomon to grab. The soldier had a slight smile as he handed it to Solomon. Both knew it was a favor. Digging would help Solomon get his mind off of yesterday…and hopefully away from thinking of all their dead and missing comrades.

For several minutes, Solomon shoveled dirt and placed it on the works, all the while listening to the men around him talk in hushed tones. Despite all the aches, the digging felt good. He looked up and leaned against his shovel, gathering his breath. Seeing the survivors as they were now, Solomon knew the decimated regiment would never be the same. Feeling his eyes beginning to water, he quickly looked back down and rammed the shovel deep into the dirt.

His eyes wouldn't focus, but still, he pulled up a load of dirt and threw it on the works. He tried to let his mind wander and forget about yesterday. He couldn't, though, and worked the shovel even harder. With tears on his cheeks, he finally gave up and thought of his brother and friends that he had lost.

He dug. And sweated.

Finally, after several minutes of hard digging, his mind drifted away.

Suddenly, a clattering of canteens landing in the dirt brought Solomon's mind back to the earthworks. Covered in dirt and sweat, he looked up.

"Go get water, Whitlow," Sergeant Boller said. "Take Private Sinnex with you." The sergeant pushed one of the canteens toward him with his boot and pointed down the hill.

Private Sinnex, the Company A soldier who had been digging next to Solomon, stood up straight and laid his shovel against the earthworks. Solomon and the rest of the squad had gotten to know Thomas well over the past two years. He had shared several books and newspapers with the Company B men and often spent long evenings sharing stories around the campfires.

Although Company A was on the opposite end of the line from Company B at the morning fight near the creek, they had fought side by side with them during the worst part of the afternoon battle in the woods. Solomon remembered looking over toward Thomas before they were forced to fall back. All around him, soldiers had fallen. Like Solomon, Private Sinnex was the only soldier in his squad to make it out of yesterday's battle without being killed or seriously wounded.

Thomas nervously looked to the north where the sergeant had pointed and then back at Solomon and Boller. "That way?" he asked.

"Yeah, fill them canteens and bring 'em back," Boller barked. "There's a spring that comes out of the middle of that other hill over there. Down below us it forms into a stream before it goes into the big creek to the east."

Off in the distance down the hill, a musket popped. And then another. Thomas stared and then swallowed a lump, speechless.

"Ya better grab a rifle from that stack, Whitlow," Boller said. "There's plenty now."

Solomon noticed that Boller's words didn't show even the slightest hint of remorse for the rifles' previous owners. Solomon didn't respond but laid his shovel down and grabbed a handful of canteen straps and reached for one of the Springfields.

Thomas pleadingly looked at Solomon who had picked up a cartridge box along with more canteens and was now slinging them around his shoulder.

"But…," Private Sinnex started to say. But his voice failed him and cracked with fear. After a pause, he cleared his throat and said, "Them fields is thick with Johnnies all over the place down there, Sarge."

Before Boller could respond, Solomon stepped between them and tossed several canteens toward Private Sinnex. "Carry these, Thomas," Solomon said, looking at Thomas to avoid making eye contact with the sergeant.

Thomas looked at Boller and cleared his throat to speak again, but Solomon cut him off before he could argue further.

"Grab your musket," Solomon said.

With a jangling of canteens, Solomon helped Thomas with the leather straps. After a few moments, Thomas finally had his half of the canteens and his Springfield slung over his shoulder.

"Come on," Solomon said, stepping up onto the breast-works. "Don't waste any more precious breath on Boller. He ain't worth it."

With Private Sinnex in tow, Solomon clambered down the other side of the works and started down the hill. They had only walked a few yards before the sounds of the Union shovels behind them began to fade.

Then Solomon felt Thomas tug on his sleeve.

"*Shhhh...,*" Thomas whispered. "Stop."

Quickly halting behind a thick oak tree, they both crouched down in the weeds. Thomas was staring through the trees and across the field toward a small wooded knoll.

"What is it?" Solomon whispered.

"There's voices over there to the left. Rebs have been out here all morning, Sol. They've been placing pickets out by that knoll... and along the creek over there," he said, nodding to the right.

Standing motionless, they listened. Behind them, they could still barely hear the faint clinks of spades striking dirt and rocks. Further to the rear, an occasional voice or musket shot would mix with the distant sounds of horses and wagons.

"Let's avoid that knoll, Sol," Thomas whispered, wishing he could have avoided leaving the safety of the earthworks and not had to have come down this hill at all.

"I agree," Solomon whispered. Then, pointing to the right, he said, "This way."

With Thomas taking the lead, they started off down the hill again. Quieter now, they stepped softly on the grass, avoiding fallen branches and twigs. Solomon held his left arm tight around the canteen straps, trying to keep them from clanging.

Farther from the Union line on the hill behind them, they were now at the lower edge of the trees. Just ahead, there was an open meadow of tall grass that ended at another thicket about forty yards to their front.

Suddenly, Thomas stopped, and his hand quickly went up, signaling Solomon to halt again. Solomon stared as Thomas slowly and carefully unslung his Springfield. Thomas lowered the barrel partway and then froze.

Solomon could hear his own breathing now. The stillness had an eerie quietness to it. Unslinging his own rifle, Solomon stared as Thomas lowered his musket and looked down the gunsight toward the thicket. Solomon felt the perspiration on his forehead dripping down and beading on his brow. As the sweat entered his eyes, he forced himself to stand perfectly still. He stared ahead, but the sweat stung. Slowly raising his arm, he wiped his face with his sleeve. His canteens barely whispered. Then stillness again, even quieter now.

Whooosh!!

The grass in front of them exploded with movement. Thomas suddenly fell to the ground with the clanging of canteens. Solomon quickly dropped to a knee as well and aimed his Springfield ahead…just in time to see the rabbit hop from the weeds and lunge into the thicket and disappear.

Solomon stared. When Thomas finally turned around, their eyes met. They both laughed. It was the first time Solomon remembered laughing in days. Embarrassed, Thomas turned back around and signaled them forward again.

Out in the grass now, they headed toward the underbrush along the creek. More faint voices echoed from the knoll, causing both men to crouch even lower.

"Keep going, Sol," Thomas whispered. "Almost there. I hear the stream."

They entered the thicket slowly, pushing away branches as they squeezed their way through the brush. After a few steps, Solomon also heard the trickling water and then came to the stream's grassy bank. The creek was only a few feet wide, but the water was clear as it meandered gently over its rocky bed.

Solomon didn't hesitate and knelt down to the edge. With both hands, he scooped the cool water onto his face. Its taste was refreshing, and he reached down for more. Thomas had unslung his canteens onto the bank and was also using both hands to quench his thirst.

For several seconds, they both drank from the little stream. Solomon looked to the right where the water trickled its way into the woods. Then a reflection in the water caught his eye, and he quickly lifted his head.

His heart jumped as his mind realized what he saw. On the other bank and only a few paces away, a young soldier dressed in gray was kneeling down with his canteen in the water. By instinct, Solomon reached for his rifle. But only for a second. When their eyes met, the Rebel didn't move. He had been watching them, Solomon quickly realized.

Then Solomon heard a click behind him. Quickly glancing back, he saw that Thomas had cocked his Springfield and begun to raise its barrel.

"No," Solomon whispered, reaching out for Thomas's rifle and giving it a slight downward push.

Solomon looked toward the young Rebel again. The boy couldn't be over fifteen years old, Solomon knew. His face, wet from the stream's water, gleamed, but his eyes were wide. Although he had his musket with him, its leather sling still hung across his shoulder with the gun resting harmlessly against his back. He didn't move, but instead, he just stared.

His woven wool trousers had many tears, some patched with multiple colors. Other rips showed the boy's dirty skin beneath his clothes. The grime-covered pants were tucked into filthy cotton socks that hung loose over the top of his worn brogans. The shoes, covered in dry mud, had many holes that even exposed his toes. Still floating in the shallow stream, the wood on his canteen looked thin and worn. And the red color of his blanket roll that hung around his butternut jacket had been faded by the sun into a dull, grayish pink.

The boy moved his hand slightly, dipping the canteen's spout into the water. All the while, however, he kept his eyes locked on the two Union soldiers nearby on the opposite bank. With a wet finger, he pushed his dark-colored felt slouch hat a little further back on his head, exposing even more of his face. He looked more sorrowful than scared.

Unintentionally, Solomon stared. He could tell by the boy's eyes that he had already seen much horror in his short life. The boy was a fighter for sure, though. Solomon could tell that too. But right now, the boy seemed more desperate than hardened.

A blast and a puff of smoke from the weeds off in the distance to the west made Solomon and Thomas flinch and turn in that direction. Several musket pops followed, and Solomon watched before looking back at the young Rebel across the creek. The boy seemed to ignore the gunshots and hadn't looked away. Hearing the musketry made the boy's eyes seem to open slightly wider, however. But still, he stared at his two new counterparts with whom he now shared his stream. He dipped his canteen into the water a little deeper, and air bubbles surfaced. Solomon glanced away slowly and reached for one of his own canteens.

More puffs of smoke rose from the pickets. Solomon also ignored them this time. He looked at Thomas, who had also grabbed a canteen and begun filling it in the stream.

A picket's musket boomed again, a little closer this time. The three soldiers exchanged glances, and all their expressions seemed to say the same thing...

It's not our fight...not this time at least.

As Solomon filled more of the canteens, he looked over at the boy again. He was washing his face and slowly began to stand. He stared as Solomon and Thomas filled the last of their canteens and slung the straps across their shoulders.

Off in the distance, another squabble between the pickets had bloomed into a storm. This time, the young Rebel glanced in that direction. When he turned toward Solomon and Thomas again, he looked a little more dangerous.

And then he brought his hand to the brim of his slouch hat and gave the slightest nod. The three soldiers stared at one another for only a brief moment before the Rebel slowly took a step backward and then turned away.

Solomon watched closely as the Rebel ducked and disappeared through the underbrush in the direction of his regiment.

For several seconds, Solomon watched the brush where the Rebel had gone before finally turning toward Thomas. "Ready to go?"

"Yeah, you lead this time," Thomas said with a smirk, thinking of the encounter with the rabbit.

Solomon chuckled and, without speaking, started toward the rear. After quickly crossing the small grassy meadow and starting up the hill, he thought of the young Rebel again. He wondered where he was from and whether he had brothers too. He hoped he wouldn't see him again...at least not with rifles in their hands, pointed across a bloody, smoky battlefield.

Seeing the boy made Solomon think of Henry...and why Henry had stopped wanting to fight.

Right now, Solomon felt the same way.

For some reason, he pictured the young Rebel's face again. Thinking of the boy, Solomon thought about the other boys he'd shot and killed.

He'd heard many times to not do that. He should have listened.

He's just another boy like us.

Shooting someone would be even harder now.

-23-

Woods near McPherson's Farm,
West of Gettysburg
July 2, 1863, Morning

Their buzzing had become part of the dreams. Still asleep, James twitched and flicked. But his efforts were useless, only interrupting their incessant attacks until he was still again.

He cursed them…mosquitoes and God only knows how many other bugs. Slowly, though, they were stirring him back to life.

The cycle went on like that until he finally woke, but the light was blinding and added to the delirium. Trying to block the pain from his wounds, he closed his eyes. His mind wandered, and finally, he withdrew back into his fitful, troubled sleep.

The dreams returned too, even more real this time.

"James…James…reach!"

James tried lifting his arm, but it wouldn't move.

"Grab my hand, James!"

Solomon was on the creek bank, and his face was contorted into a panic as he yelled. James stared and saw that his brother's mouth was open, still screaming, but now, no words came.

Other men were screaming and yelling too, but no sounds came from them either. Still, though, he could feel the chaos all around him…bullets ripped through the stream's water and slammed into rocks.

Confused, James reached out his hand again. Hawk had him now, but they were on all fours. They were up on the bank and in the weeds. A dead Rebel from the morning fight was there too. James looked away. The flags…the men…they were just ahead.

"Hang on!" someone yelled.

James saw Solomon next to him, crawling too. He was pointing backward toward the Rebel line.

"Go!"

Good men fell…silently though.

What's happening?

Suddenly, it was calm and quiet again; the battle had stopped. The men were all gone, and time seemed to stand still. But somewhere, a steady melody echoed from a distant fife.

Then, behind him, he heard another voice. James turned. The voice sounded like Henry, and they were out where the last of the pickets had been left behind and captured.

"Henry?" James felt himself call out.

But now it was his own voice that failed him. He stared and then saw the company pickets appear from the wheat.

But he remembered they had all been captured. He didn't understand.

They were all there…Privates Bunch, Lock, Markle, and others. "This way," they seemed to be saying, waving him toward them.

And then he saw Lieutenant Schlagle's face, the rest of him down in the wheat. Schlagle's arm suddenly rose high above his head and signaled, a begging gesture. And then the lieutenant stood… A miracle, James knew. It was just a few minutes ago that the bullet had struck both his thighs. But the dark blood on Schlagle's pants was suddenly gone, and his pants mysteriously returned to their light-blue color as though the wound was never there.

"Help us, James!" the lieutenant shouted with a painful screech that faded into a dying plea among musketry and yells. But Schlagle's face somehow turned to a smile, and James felt himself shudder.

James stared, unbelieving.

Where am I?

The horror of it all…

Then, even more suddenly than they had appeared, the lieutenant and all the Company B pickets faded into darkness.

James felt a shudder as he woke.

It was all a dream.

But was it?

Fighting the urge to stay in the safety of his sleep, he slowly opened his eyes. He looked out, but the morning sun stung. Blinking several times, he squinted as his eyes tried to adjust.

Beyond the treetops above the eastern horizon, the sun illuminated the gray and purple clouds. Their pink edges gave them a Godly brilliance and drew him in. With a grunt, he raised up and stared. The sky seemed more beautiful than he had ever remembered. Then something caught his eye through the trees, and then it was gone. He tried to focus, but the pain surged again and blurred his vision.

The trees…

He concentrated, but their shapes were chaotic. His mind wandered, but still, he remembered. Beyond that wooded ridge was the large, red brick building they had seen yesterday as they ran across the fields. That was just prior to going into battle—a battle like no other fight he had ever seen. It was glorious, he remembered.

Oh, so glorious…

They had run across those fields with their flags flying, officers pointing and yelling, and men screaming. Through the field and into the woods, the brigade advanced like it never had before. Then it became so horrible. The excitement had turned to fear as the regiment's battle line charged and threw back the Confederates. He thought of the fight in the afternoon. It was the worst they'd seen in the entire war.

He shuddered. In an attempt to oust those memories, he shook his head and tried sitting up.

He then remembered the flask Will had left for him and quickly reached for it. Raising it to his lips and tasting the whiskey, he thought back to the first time Hawk had told the squad how important liquor was to fighting. None of them believed him at first…at least not until the day following Antietam when they were walking among the wounded.

"Water…"

"Whiskey…"

Almost every wounded man on that battlefield had begged for both.

After another chug, he gently tipped the flask toward the sky. "To you, Hawk," he said to himself, thinking of his friend he didn't know was even still alive or not. He thought of his other squadmates too and then slowly lowered his chin and closed his eyes. He was weak and began drifting off again.

Suddenly, though, he heard a thundering of hooves and voices that startled him from his slumber.

Horsemen…

James quickly opened his eyes and saw a group of gray-clad riders approaching along the fence line. Dropping deep down into the grass, he pulled himself into a bush growing beneath the fence. With the horses only a few strides away and riding quickly toward him, James forced himself even lower.

Even in the tall grass, the horses' hooves pounded and shook the ground. With shouts and yells, the Rebel riders punished their mounts. Riding crops snapped, and the horses neighed in protest. But still, they raced down the slope and leaped the stream.

Holding his breath until they were past, James watched the riders clamber up the ridge and disappear to the east. Then, as he tried sitting up, James felt a torturous pain erupt from his shoulder. Looking down, he saw most of the blood had dried into a crusty black mess. He knew the bleeding should have stopped by now, but near his collarbone, he felt wet blood. After painfully repositioning himself and finally sitting up, he reached for the flask and took another gulp.

Telling himself he must get help, he turned toward the farm. With a grunt and dragging his leg, he crawled from underneath the bush and looked past the house. Sitting along the ridge and perpendicular to the Chambersburg Pike, the large, white wooden barn had a stone foundation with five open doors along its eastern side.

Suddenly, from inside the barn, a scream pierced the morning air. James listened closely and heard the scream again.

"*God, no!*" a suffering voice cried out. "*Please stop! Nooooo!*"

The man's pleas were so horrific that even some of the Rebel guards glanced in the direction of the barn. The screams finally stopped, and James scanned the area again. All around the house and barn, the grounds were full of wounded soldiers lying out in the open. The hot sun would play hell on them later today, he knew.

From somewhere on the farm, a fife played. James realized it was the fife from his dreams. He looked around for the boy who was playing it, but before he found him, the sound faded away. Then, he heard a steady, low voice.

Looking toward the voice, James saw a chaplain leaning over a wounded soldier near the farmhouse. The chaplain was holding a Bible in one hand and had placed his other hand on the wounded man's chest. The chaplain spoke softly and then looked toward the sky. James had seen it many times before…a soldier being read his last rites.

James, still looking toward the farm, then saw a man emerge from one of the barn's lower doors. Seeing the man was wearing a shirt soaked with sweat and a white apron covered in blood, James could tell that the man was a surgeon. James watched closely and then saw him toss something onto a pile a few feet away.

What was that? James wondered.

Staying motionless, James stared as the man wiped his brow and looked up at the sky. He seemed to be praying, and after a few moments, the surgeon looked down and shook his head. Even from this far away, it was obvious that the surgeon was dreading going back into that barn. Finally, however, the man wiped his hands on his bloody apron and dutifully stepped back inside.

James carefully slid a few feet closer and, with his head just barely above the grass, examined the grounds around the farm. He saw hundreds of helpless soldiers who were suffering from wounds and shifting about in agony. Their moans and pleas for help reached all the way across the field to his hiding spot near the woods.

So far, he had only seen one surgeon. James again looked toward where the surgeon had been standing. Now seeing a wet sheen atop the pile that reflected in the morning sun, he winced as he realized what it was—a bloody mound of discarded, amputated limbs.

James quickly looked away, and as he leaned back against the fence, he heard another voice, weak and barely audible from across the field.

"Water...please...water..."

Then another man's scream came from the barn. The surgeon's break was over, James knew. Slowly, and with a shivering terror, James slipped back down into the grass and thought about his own situation.

What do I do?

The nearest enemy soldiers were at least fifty yards away, and thus far, he had avoided being seen. He thought of his wounded leg and whether he could even move. Below his knee, his leg was numb, and combined with the dried mud and blood on his pants, his leg had turned into a gruesome dead weight. Any movement would be a slow and painful crawl.

Another sharp pain from his shoulder caused him to let out a groan. Looking at his shoulder, James saw that more blood had seeped through the bandage. Although the pain was unbearable, he knew it would be much worse if he ended up in that barn with the surgeon. His stomach churned again, and he closed his eyes and lowered his head.

A sense of loneliness and then fear came over him, and he began to shake.

God…please, God.

He clinched his fists to make the shaking stop, but it wouldn't. Feeling tears forming, he looked up at the sky.

Please, God, make it all go away…

Still shaking, helplessness took over.

Then, from somewhere, the fife played again, and James looked across the field.

"*Water…*," another voice from up near the barn cried out.

This time, though, James looked away from the farm. He'd seen enough up there. Instead, he thought of his own dry and parched mouth and reached for his canteen. It was nearly empty, and after drinking the last of the water from it, he thought of the little stream where he and the Michigan soldier had filled their canteens.

Where was it?

Using his good elbow, he propped himself up and scanned the area. He looked to where the grassy swale fell away toward the woods and then became the little stream. That was where the water trickled under the fence and disappeared among the brush and trees.

After taking one last look toward the farm and all the wounded soldiers, he made up his mind. *No,* he decided. *I won't go to the barn and lie in misery with the other wounded men, captured and thirsty, hoping for unlikely mercy from enemy captors.*

He also knew that to stop the bleeding, he would have to get help. Then he thought of the town. It could be his only chance to not be captured. Maybe in town, he hoped, there might be people other than Confederates who could help him.

The town… It was still far away, but he remembered being able to see it from the ridge near the edge of the woods. That ridge wasn't far, he knew.

Maybe crawl to that ridge and see…

But first, he needed water. He scanned the area for enemy soldiers and then looked toward the stream. He took a deep breath, then, clinging to the fence rail, he began painfully scooting down the slope. Every inch was a struggle. But knowing he had to go on, he reached the little stream and collapsed beside it.

After quickly scooping the water into his mouth, James filled his canteen. Then, telling himself he must keep moving and despite the excruciating pain in his leg, James adjusted the tourniquet the best he could and trudged into the stream.

With the field to the north full of Rebel soldiers, James followed the stream deeper into the woods and clambered up the other bank. Dragging his bad leg, he painfully crawled his way through the woods and up the slope.

Stopping next to a large oak tree to rest, James suddenly heard noises toward the middle of the woods. James didn't move and concentrated on the sounds. With his body and face tucked low in the weeds and mostly concealed by the tree, he carefully looked forward.

At first, he couldn't see anything, only heard the clinks of shovels hitting dirt, rocks, and roots. Then he heard Southern voices not far away, and he dared looking closer.

When he first saw what was happening, he felt a lump in his throat. Several men were digging, and he could see fresh piles of dirt along the side of a trench.

It was a burial pit, he knew.

Nearby, James saw a row of at least a dozen dead bodies lying side by side.

Suddenly, a voice cried out from the far side of the trench. *"One…two…"*

James quickly looked.

Two Rebel soldiers who had been dragging a corpse had the body by its hands and feet. They both grunted, and on *'three'*, they heaved the dead man into the trench.

"Let's go, Piney," one of the Rebels said, wiping his hands on his pants. "We got us about ten more of 'em."

Looking at the two Rebels' clothes caked in dried blood and dirt, James could tell they'd probably already buried at least that many. James quickly pulled his head back behind the tree and slipped backward away from the trench.

Keep moving, he told himself.

He crept a little farther, but the pain in his leg and shoulder forced him to stop. Dropping to the ground, he rolled onto his back, exhausted and shaking in agony.

After spending several minutes catching his breath, he turned onto his side. Ahead, he could see the sunlight shining in the open fields, and off in the distance, he saw the large red brick seminary building and its green and white cupola dominating the next ridge.

Sensing hope, James thought about his chances of making it to the town. He scanned the fields closer to him and saw dozens of Union soldiers lying still in the grass, probably just where they had been shot down a day ago. From a distance, he examined the bodies carefully, looking for any sign of life. The field looked to him like a harvest of death with the bodies in the trampled wheat staring lifelessly up at the summer sky.

My God, this war is horrible.

He continued to stare. A constant flurry of activity farther out in the field distracted him, but suddenly, out of the corner of his eye, he caught a glimpse of something move among the soldiers lying nearby.

James stared and waited.

Yes, there it was again…

A few yards beyond the trees, James saw a prone soldier with his arm in the air as if signaling for help. The man was lying near a damaged and abandoned artillery caisson wagon. It had collapsed on one side with a shattered wheel and axle, and the area around it was littered with debris.

Then James heard the soldier's voice, followed by a muffled groan. James stared at the man, and after several seconds, he heard his voice again.

"*Water…*"

James looked away from the wounded soldier for a second to examine the area. Although the pike and ridge closer to town were busy with Confederates, the only enemy soldiers near the wounded man was a squad of horsemen that had just ridden past. James inched his way to the edge of the trees and paused. Behind him in the woods, he could still hear the burial teams working, but out to his front, all was quiet in the field of fallen Union soldiers.

When the wounded man groaned again, James could sense his suffering. James stared and saw the man's fist open and close as if begging the agony to stop. Trying to forget his own pain, James felt mercy for the wounded soldier and quickly decided he must crawl out there. He felt a duty to help the man…even if only to let him know he wasn't alone.

James slowly crept forward. The man lifted his arm slightly above the trodden grass...another pleading gesture. James crawled a little closer and then heard the man groan again. Now a few feet away from the wounded soldier, James stopped and pulled his canteen strap from over his shoulder.

"Here...water," James said, extending his hand and the canteen toward the wounded man. The man's dust-covered coat had a blue circular patch over the left breast and had corporal's stripes on the sleeve. James looked closer and saw the man's bearded face was almost completely indistinguishable. Several flies hovered near his right eye, cheek, and temple where flesh had been torn away and now mixed with blood and dirt. James felt queasy but continued to look at the man whose neck, shirt, and arms were covered in blood.

The man didn't respond, and James scooted even closer. He noticed the corporal's hat had a brass letter 'H' on the front. In his hand, he was clinging to a small brass picture frame with an ambrotype photo of a woman. With a tear on his cheek, the man slowly opened one eye and looked at James.

"Here," James said, offering the canteen again. The soldier reached out slowly and grabbed it, then pulled it toward his mouth and took a drink. The man tried speaking, but he was too weak.

"Shhhh...just drink the water, Corporal."

"Th-thank you, sir," the man said with a tremble. After another drink, he let go of the canteen and grabbed James's hand. The man mumbled something about God and then about home.

"Just stay still," James said, looking around the field for enemy troops.

"God...God bless you," the man managed to say while still clutching James's hand.

"Where you from?" James asked.

"A couple days walk…"

The wounded corporal's voice trailed off mid-sentence, and he shuddered in pain. He looked directly at James and, finding strength to continue, said, "It's only a couple days from here…Strausstown."

"We'll get you home, soldier," James said.

"Berks County, Strausstown," he told James, distinctly repeating the town's name as a man would to a postmaster for an important letter. James could tell by the way he said it that he didn't think he'd ever make it back to there alive.

James nervously scanned the horizon for Rebels nearby, then looked at the man again. Nodding toward the photo in the corporal's hand, he asked, "Who's that?… In the picture?"

The man started to smile, but it hurt too much. He grimaced and then weakly said, "Elizabeth…my wife."

James could see the man was holding back tears.

"Home…it ain't far. I want to go home. We've got two kids. Elizabeth…my wife…my poor wife…she's expecting another child." The wounded corporal's eyes were wet with tears. He still had a hold of James's hand, and James could feel it trembling. The man was sobbing now.

James watched a group of horsemen that had turned off the pike and were cutting across the field toward them. After a few moments, however, they turned away and began heading toward the seminary building on the next ridge.

"What's your name?" James asked, glancing back toward the wounded corporal again.

The man didn't answer at first. Instead, grimacing, he released James's hand and picked up the canteen. He took another drink, even longer this time. The water dripped down his face, and he groaned when it flowed onto his wounded neck.

Forcing himself to speak, the man gritted his teeth and said, "Schaeffer…John Schaeffer." He paused. Then, weakly and with a cracking voice, he said, "I'm in the 151st...151st PA. Not much...not much left of us now though."

Looking around the field at all the bodies, James knew he was probably right. The man had closed his eyes, and James saw that he had grown weaker and was now even struggling to breathe. James could tell he was suffering...not only from his wounds, but also from thinking of his pregnant wife and kids he'd probably never see again.

The corporal tried to speak again but painfully coughed instead.

"It's okay, Corporal. Just rest."

James looked around the field at the dead and wounded. Then, assuming he was talking to himself, he said, "We gotta get help, or we're gonna die out here."

Corporal Schaeffer apparently heard him, however, and said, "I...I know."

The two wounded soldiers lay in silence for several minutes. James nervously watched the horizon and thought about his options. Up along the ridge near the pike, James saw a flurry of activity where horses and soldiers were gathered. Squinting, James could see flags flying outside a large tent across the pike from a stone house. Several mounted horsemen hurriedly galloped to and from the area around the tent. James knew the place was important. Even from this far away, he could see gray uniforms with shiny brass and dangling scabbards.

Peering closer at the seminary building, James could see men and several teams of stretcher bearers carrying wounded soldiers up the steps and disappearing through the front door. The area close to the building was crowded with soldiers, horses, and wagons. Beyond the seminary, the skyline was dotted by church spires, buildings, and houses. Seeing all the Confederates along the next ridge and on the pike made James realize what a dangerous place this was.

James then looked at the wounded Pennsylvania corporal and saw that he was asleep or had finally fallen unconscious.

"John," James whispered, shaking his arm to get his attention.

The corporal didn't wake but mumbled something James couldn't understand.

"We need to move back into those trees," James said, this time grabbing ahold of the man's jacket and shaking it to try to stir him awake.

Although the 151st Pennsylvania soldier's eyes opened for just a second and his mouth slightly moved, he still appeared nearly unconscious. Knowing the man was unable to crawl and he was too weak himself to help him move, James realized he would have to leave him. James glanced toward the edge of the woods about twenty feet away.

Just as he began to crawl back to the trees, James suddenly heard horses and wagon wheels to the north. They were on the other side of the crippled ammunition wagon and coming from the direction of the pike. James peered around the abandoned caisson and saw several mounted riders and a wagon being pulled by two horses. They were headed directly toward him, and his chance to get to the woods was gone.

"John, stay down," James whispered, sliding back behind the caisson and lying down alongside the corporal. The wagon team, escorted by three other horsemen dressed in artillery uniforms, was now bounding across the field and heading toward the abandoned ammunition wagon next to them. James kept his face down and could hear the Rebels' voices as the wagon approached.

"Shhhh...," James whispered just before the teamsters brought the two-horse team and wagon to a rattling halt.

"Check that chest!" one of the riders shouted.

James froze as he heard the other horses galloping to a stop and boots hitting the ground. He slowly opened one eye and dared a peek. The Rebels were now at the caisson only a few yards away.

"The captain wants every Yankee limber and caisson checked!" shouted a gruff Southern voice. "Levi and Josiah, take that wheel off!"

James put his face down and didn't move. Over by the Confederates' wagon, there was a clattering of metal and wood. More soldiers approached.

Suddenly, from much closer than James expected, a loud, snarling voice bellowed, "Sarge, this dead Yankee's still got shoes."

James didn't breathe and could feel the man stop beside him and start to lean down. James's heart nearly burst out of his chest when the Rebel put one hand on his leg and the other on his shoe.

"One of the brogans is all bloody," the Rebel said. Then, with a chuckle, he said, "But it'll clean up."

He was so close James could smell his breath.

"Check his pockets too," a voice called out from near the wagon.

"You don't gotta tell Jimmy to do *that!*" one of the other Confederates near the wagon yelled with a laugh.

The Rebel closest to James was just above him now, and James could feel him reaching down. He grabbed James's ankle and yanked on James's shoe with a twist. Pain surged through James's leg, and he suddenly lurched sideways and screamed.

The Rebel jumped back in shock.

"This one's still alive, Sarge!"

James rolled onto his side and faced the Rebels and, despite being weak and in pain, put his hands out ready to defend himself.

Two of the Confederates from the other side of the wagon arrived and pointed their bayonets directly at him. A third Rebel approached the wounded corporal.

"Grab him and put him in the wagon," a deep-voiced Rebel said, pointing at James.

James didn't move but saw the Rebel near Corporal Schaeffer lean down and reach for his pockets.

"Leave him alone!" James yelled.

The two Confederates nearest to James closed in with bayonets only inches away. James scooted farther back, but the two Rebels stepped in and grabbed James's wounded arm. James tried to lunge at the Rebel and, with his free hand, weakly swung at his captor.

Even though James was wounded and weak, he had surprised his captor, causing him to lose his grip on James's arm. The other Rebel, however, jumped forward and placed the point of his bayonet on James's chest.

"*Don't...move, Yankee,*" he said with a long, slow drawl. "Ya don't wanna do nothin' stupid now, do ya?"

With the bayonet pressing against his chest, James knew the fight was over and any resistance would be futile. For added measure, the first Rebel had James's arm again and placed the tip of his bayonet against James's neck.

James's energy had drained, and fresh blood gushed from his shoulder. Behind him, he heard the Pennsylvania corporal futilely fighting for his life. James looked over and saw the Rebel on top of the corporal with a knee against his chest.

"Please, please...leave him alone," James said. "Can't you see he's almost dead!"

The Rebel knew James was right and climbed off the wounded corporal. He took a step back and looked at the corporal and then at James. The Rebel captor, apparently realizing how defenseless the two wounded Union men actually were, smiled at James and put his hands in the air.

"Didn't mean nothin' by it, Billy Yank. But the way you swung at Jimmy over there, I figured you was both up fir a fight."

"Where you want him, Sarge?" the Rebel holding James asked.

"Put 'em both in the wagon," the sergeant said, angrily spitting out a wad of tobacco. Then, in a merciless voice, he said, "I heard a bunch of screamin' Yankees over by that barn. Take 'em over there."

As the captors were loading James and the Pennsylvania corporal into the wagon, a Confederate horseman approached from the south. The rider was wearing an officer's insignia and halted his horse just in front of them. Motioning toward the wagon, he asked, "Where you taking them prisoners, Sergeant?"

"Up to that farm, sir."

"General Rodes wants all the wounded Yankees in this field taken to that red building," he said, pointing at the seminary.

"Yes, sir," the sergeant replied.

The mounted officer, a lieutenant colonel, waited for the sergeant to act on his orders before riding off toward the stone house along the pike.

"Levi and Jimmy, take the wagon and haul these prisoners over to that building," the sergeant ordered.

"Yes sir, Sergeant," one of the Rebels responded, slamming the wagon's back latch closed. James was reeling in pain on the wooden floor next to Corporal Schaeffer as the Rebel teamsters jumped on the front of the wagon. With shouts and a tug of the reins, the horses quickly stepped forward, jerking the wagon with a clatter. The wagon turned to the east and started toward the seminary a quarter mile away.

The wooden planks of the wagon's floor banged against its metal frame as the wagon bounced through the field. By the time the wagon finally rattled to a halt in front of the seminary building, James's pain was so bad that he nearly fell into shock. Barely able to lift his head above the wagon's side boards, he saw hundreds of wounded soldiers from both armies lying under shade trees on the building's southwest side.

Sliding his leg forward and propping himself up against the wagon's side, James saw that his bleeding leg had left a streak of fresh blood on the wooden planks. The corporal was still lying longways in the wagon with his head down and motionless as the two wagon drivers walked around the sides.

"Out ya go, Yanks," one of the Rebels said as he unlatched the wagon's back gate.

Fighting off pain, James pushed himself toward the back of the wagon. Placing his hand on Corporal Schaeffer's back, James gave him a shake. But still, he didn't move. James shook the Pennsylvania corporal again and was relieved that he at least heard a groan.

"I don't think he's gonna make it," the other Rebel said, pausing at the back corner of the wagon. James noticed the Rebel's anger had changed to sympathy. He held out his hand and reached for James's arm, not as much as an enemy commanding his captor, but more as one soldier helping another.

"Here," the Rebel said, placing his shoulder under James's arm and helping him out of the wagon.

"Thanks," James replied, clinging to his captor's arm to help him stand. James then turned toward the wounded corporal still lying in the wagon. The other two Rebels were there now too, and as they reached down to pull the wounded man from the wagon, James said, "Hang in there, Corporal."

James then sadly turned away and, with his captor's assistance, staggered toward the seminary's front steps. His arm was completely around the Rebel's shoulders when they reached the bottom step and started up. Halfway up the steps, James's pain became unbearable. He began to fall, but the Rebel held him up.

James turned his head and looked to the west. With the four-story, red brick building towering behind him, he looked out over the vast fields and the woods where he'd fought. Far out on the horizon, he could see two long lines of Confederate troops marching to the south. Closer to him, the carnage of dead Union soldiers was spread across the field.

Near the pike, a Confederate burial detail was hard at work. They were throwing dirt on a line of bodies already in a mass grave, while at the other end of the line, more of their dead comrades were being dragged up to the trench's edge. James felt his eyes water as he thought about all the death suffered by both sides.

James noticed the Rebel next to him was also looking out across the fields. James quickly looked away and turned toward the flags and the large tents in the orchard that he had seen earlier. Just across the pike was the stone house. Next to one of the tents, a group of officers was poring over a map stretched across a table.

At the center of the group, James could see a tall, gray-bearded general. James looked on as the man looked up from the map and pointed to the south.

Something about that general fascinated James and caused him to stare.

"Don't ya know who that is?" the Rebel next to him asked.

Before James could answer, James's captor proudly answered his own question. "That's General Lee."

James stared but didn't respond.

"We'd all die for that man," the Rebel said.

The tone of his voice said he'd meant it too.

"Come on…let's get you inside."

-24-

Culp's Hill, Gettysburg
July 2, 1863, 7:30 p.m.

Solomon felt a hand on his arm and then heard a voice.

"How's the blisters, Sol?"

Realizing he had dozed off leaning against the breastworks, Solomon quickly opened his eyes and lifted his head. The men had been hunkered down behind the dirt, stone, and log wall for most of the past several hours. Although there was no Rebel attack directly in their front right now and the cannonade near them had ended almost an hour ago, the battle had been raging on the south end of the Union line since late afternoon. Raising his head further, he heard a new crackling of musketry in the woods off to the right. They knew the Confederates had been moving around the hill, and now, the attack must be happening there too.

The voice next to him was Henry Marsh, one of the Nineteenth Indiana's hospital stewards and assistant surgeons. Marsh was out of breath and soaked with sweat. Noticing dried blood on the front of the assistant surgeon's jacket, Solomon stared at it before looking up and meeting Marsh's gaze.

"Sir?" Solomon asked.

"I'm glad you made it back and you're okay," Marsh said.

"Thanks."

"I was asking about your feet…the blisters. They were giving you the devil the past few weeks."

Solomon realized he hadn't thought about the blisters since yesterday morning's march before the battle. "Oh, they're okay, Doc. Forgot all 'bout 'em with the fightin' 'n' all."

"Good. Lemme take a look at that shoulder though, Sol."

"Uhhhh, sure," Solomon said, pulling his shirt away and exposing dried blood near where the bullet had glanced through his skin.

"Captain Orr told me 'bout it. He said he knew you wouldn't get it looked at," Marsh said with a grin.

"But it ain't bleedin' or nothin'—"

Solomon was interrupted and both men quickly ducked when a Union cannon boomed from behind them near the cemetery.

"They been shootin' over our heads all day it seems," Solomon said, sitting up again after the blast's echoes faded into the valley below.

"Hold still, Sol. Lemme wash that off and get a bandage on it. You should be fine, but we gotta keep the gangrene out of it."

Solomon looked around at the men behind the earthworks while Marsh set his canteen on the ground and reached into his pack for a bandage. The Nineteenth's survivors looked anxious, several of them pointing toward the fields to the north from where a bugle sounded.

"I just came from the hospital down the pike a couple miles," Marsh said. He paused and, with a furrowed brow, shook his head. "Never seen anything like it, Sol. There's a lot of our wounded boys back there."

Solomon listened and thought of the wounded men in the Nineteenth. But then, suddenly, as Marsh splashed water on Solomon's shoulder and pressed a cloth on the open wound,

Solomon had to force himself to not cry out in pain.

"Sorry, Sol."

"Where's the hospital?" Solomon asked with gritted teeth, trying to block out his pain.

"That way...down the pike," Marsh said, nodding to the south. "It's about a mile past the big creek."

"The creek that runs just below us at the bottom of the hill?"

"Yeah, the Baltimore Pike behind us crosses it about a mile south of here," Marsh said as he began wrapping a bandage around Solomon's shoulder. "Go a little farther, and the hospital is on the right...maybe two or three miles from here. *White Church* or *White Run Church* or something like that, I think they call it." Marsh paused while he tied the ends of the bandage and slipped Solomon's shirt back over his shoulder.

"All of our wounded going there?" Solomon asked, thinking of James...just in case there was a miracle and he was still alive.

"Some of 'em...at least the ones that made it back to our lines. But most of the seriously wounded are in the town...or still lying out in the fields and woods on the other side of it. Out that way." Marsh nodded to the northwest and then paused.

Solomon lowered his head.

Marsh picked up on what Solomon was thinking. "Your brother James...I saw him."

Solomon quickly looked up. "When?"

"Yesterday...I was behind the line in the woods."

Marsh paused, and Solomon nodded, urging him to continue.

"The regiment was up closer to the creek. The Rebels were attacking, and the brigade was falling back. I saw him briefly. He was crawling. He looked weak, Sol."

"Go on, Doc," Solomon said.

"He already had a tourniquet around his leg. He must've

done it himself. But then the Rebels…"

Marsh stopped suddenly and looked at the ground.

"It's okay…then what?"

"There was nothing I could do, Sol. The Rebs were already on us, and I was helping some wounded to the rear."

"I know, Doc. You did all you could."

"I'm sorry that I—"

"Doc, thank you," Solomon said, cutting Marsh off. "I think he was shot again…or bayonetted…" Solomon paused and swallowed a lump in his throat before continuing. "I couldn't see…the smoke…the Johnnies stormed over the whole line. I haven't seen James since."

"I've said a lot of prayers for our men today, Sol. I'll say one more for James."

"Thank you. And thanks for the bandage too," Solomon said, looking down at his shoulder and nodding approvingly at the assistant surgeon's work.

"Hang in there, Sol. I gotta keep moving. I have a few more of our men to look at here…then head back to the hospital." Marsh gave Solomon a pat on the back and stood up to leave just as more rifles crackled from the wooded hill to the right.

"Good luck, sir." But the assistant surgeon was gone, already having scurried along the earthworks and stopping next to a soldier with a bloodied hand.

The musketry in the trees to the right had now risen into a steady storm and was accompanied with the yells of battle…and not just a few taunting skirmishers trading shots either. This was a full-scale attack. Solomon looked to the right and the higher part of the wooded hill. Behind him, mounted couriers and officers raced back and forth, yelling frantically. Then several of the regiments to the right of the Nineteenth Indiana, including the Sixth Wisconsin, were pulled away from their trenches and rushed toward the loudest area of fighting beyond the hill's summit.

The surgeons would be busy again tonight, Solomon knew. Then a new noise caught his attention to the north. It was another bugle that sounded from beyond the meadows below. This time, however, the bugle was louder and followed by yells. Looking out in the dying light, Solomon squinted and saw long lines of Rebels had appeared over the ridge several hundred yards away. The Confederates were coming for the key point of the entire Union line—Cemetery Hill.

The Union cannons in the cemetery and the knoll behind the Indiana men roared to life. They had been mostly silent for the past hour after driving the Confederate artillery from an angled ridge to the northeast, but now they were firing again. Solomon looked at the artillery behind him just as one of the Fifth Maine Battery's Napoleons erupted in fire and smoke. He ducked and covered his head. Still, though, he felt the cannon blast's heat and even its discharged debris.

Carefully raising his head again, Solomon looked to the west. With just a sliver of pink light on the horizon, the smoke-filled hill took on a dark and eerie appearance. The town cemetery's brick gatehouse was just barely visible through the smoke above the gunners. Another cannon bellowed from the cemetery and ominously illuminated the gatehouse in a fiery orange glow.

"They're coming!" Captain Orr suddenly shouted above the roar of the cannons behind them.

Solomon turned and adjusted his eyes to the darkness of the smoky pastures below. The Rebels had advanced and disappeared into a low field, but now their red battle flags and long lines reappeared and crested another ridge.

"They're headed directly toward us!" Sergeant Boller exclaimed.

Solomon and the men around him ignored the sergeant's comment. They all knew that Boller was already looking for a reason to retreat to the rear. Besides, the North Carolinians had wheeled to the right and weren't heading toward the Iron Brigade's position now but, instead, advancing toward Cemetery Hill. The Confederates' left flank, however, was now exposed to the Maine battery's cannons on the knoll and the Iron Brigade muskets on the wooded hill.

Although still several hundred yards away from the Rebel battle line, Solomon lowered his barrel onto the top log of the breastworks. Looking down the gunsight, he saw the Rebels had stopped to redress their lines at a rock wall. They only stopped for a few moments, however, before climbing the wall, advancing, and sending Union skirmishers fleeing backward.

Through the dark smoke below, Solomon took aim at the Rebel line the best he could and cocked his hammer all the way back. He squeezed the trigger, and his Springfield fired with a boom. Without trying to see the effects of his shot, he quickly looked down and reached for another cartridge. After all the killing he had done yesterday, he didn't care to see whether his minie ball had hit an individual target or not. Even at this distance, he didn't think he could handle watching more men die…not from *his* rifle.

"Make every shot count, boys!" Sergeant Boller screamed. Solomon noticed the sergeant seemed a little braver now that the Rebels had turned and were charging somewhere else. Boller bellowed out a laugh and then yelled again. "Kill every bastard one of 'em!"

Blocking out the sergeant's voice, Solomon steadied his gun on the log again and aimed. From this far away, and with the smoke and darkness obscuring his vision, it was nearly impossible to pick out a specific target. The North Carolina and Louisiana brigades continued their advance, and an ominous loud shriek came from the fields…the Rebel yell. Their howl echoed through the valley and up the steep slope of the wooded hill.

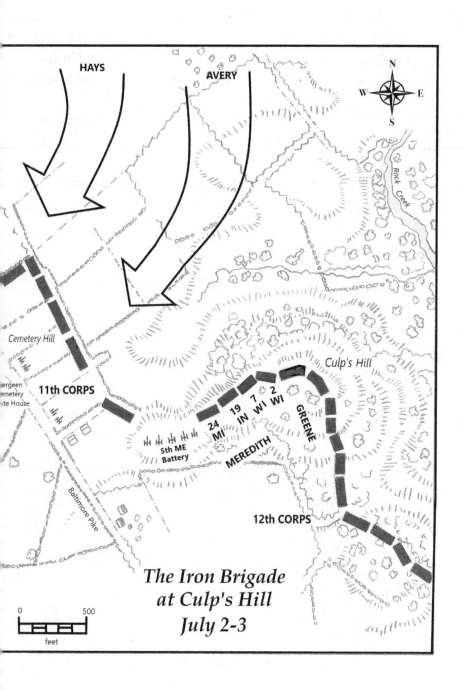

HAYS

AVERY

N
W   E
S

Rock Creek

Cemetery Hill

ergeen
emetery
te House

11th CORPS

Culp's Hill

24 MI   19 IN   7 WI   2 WI

GREENE

5th ME Battery

MEREDITH

Baltimore Pike

12th CORPS

The Iron Brigade
at Culp's Hill
July 2-3

0   500
feet

MICHAEL EISENHUT

Solomon, having long ago learned to hate that noise, pulled the trigger. Reaching for the flap on his cartridge box for another round, something strange behind him caught his eye. It was up on the knoll near the cannons. He looked again and stared.

A sole rifleman had raised his gun…*in their direction*. But he was wearing a *Union* uniform. *That makes no sense*, Solomon thought.

Then he saw fire and smoke erupt from the man's muzzle. Half a second later, Solomon heard the gun's rapport and then a shriek from one of the men on the line near him.

"*What…*"

"*Uggghhh!*"

The bloodcurdling yell was from Sergeant Boller.

Solomon looked over and saw Boller had turned pale and was writhing in pain. Not knowing what had happened, Boller reached for the wound. Blood gushed from his neck and flowed through his fingers and down onto his coat.

The gunman had shot him square in the back of the neck. Sergeant Boller tried screaming again, but his voice was hollow and only a shrill cry.

Solomon watched the wounded sergeant for only a second before quickly looking to the rear in the direction of the gunman. Although the smoke of the rifle blast still hung in front of the man, Solomon could see part of his face. The man's eyes were staring straight ahead at the sergeant and the results of his shot. Even through the darkness, the shooter's partially concealed face looked…*strangely familiar*.

Who is that?

Although almost ghostlike, the shooter's face had the appearance of…*John?*

Solomon couldn't tell and strained to see.

His brother he hadn't seen in two years?

No, it couldn't be. He's back in Washington, James had told him. Then the figure was gone.

But how? He was just there!

Solomon looked all around where the shooter had been only a moment ago. Sergeant Boller let out another bone-chilling yell, but Solomon didn't look. Instead, Solomon focused on the area where he had seen the shooter. Then one of Stevens's cannons erupted with a blast that covered the knoll with a cloud of smoke. Solomon kept staring but only saw smoke.

"Who *was* that back there?" Solomon asked, turning to Private Sinnex who was right beside him.

"Who?" Sinnex asked, obviously having not seen the gunman.

Solomon thought about the shooter again...*the ghost.*

He seemed familiar, but only eerily so. *James? No, definitely not. He was wounded too severely and would still be lying out in the woods.*

Solomon stared in wonder at the smoke on the knoll.

The shooter looked a little like...*Hawk? Couldn't be.*

The cannon's smoke began to clear but revealed nothing. Artillerists were scrambling to load the next gun, running right past where the gunman had been.

The neigh of a horse made Solomon look further up the hill and closer to the pike. Through the darkness, he could barely see a mounted rider. Watching closely, Solomon saw the horseman spurring his horse and quickly riding away in the other direction.

Solomon wasn't sure but thought the man was wearing a cavalry uniform. That is strange, he thought. *It couldn't be...a cavalryman? Not here.*

Solomon strained his eyes to get another glimpse of the shooter who was now riding away in the darkness. Suddenly, another flaming orange blast of a cannon illuminated the area.

Through the smoke, Solomon saw the rider again. *Yes, yes…he did indeed have a yellow cavalryman's stripe on his pant leg.*

Solomon continued to stare as the suspicious rider spurred his horse onto the Baltimore Pike and disappeared into the smoke and darkness.

Thinking of Sergeant Boller again, Solomon glanced toward where he had gone down. Boller was now clutching his neck with his blood-soaked hand and trying to scream while his body shook with pain. The sergeant made an awful shrieking sound, a tortuous pitch Solomon had never heard before.

Boller's other hand was in the air, an apparent attempt to signal for help. His efforts were useless, however, and his arm was suspended in midair as if painfully caught from something above. Then he cried out again, and his hand fell to the ground beside him as a spasm took over his entire body.

Looking away from the sergeant, Solomon stared back up at the knoll behind him. Boller had a lot of enemies, that was for sure…so many that Solomon knew he probably never would find out who had actually shot him. The rider was gone now, and all that Solomon saw were the artillerists doing their deadly work against the Rebels.

"Keep firing, Sol," a private next to Solomon said.

Solomon turned toward the valley below. After grabbing another cartridge, he realized his hand was shaking. Still though, he stuffed the round into the muzzle and reached for his rammer. Glancing over toward the sergeant, Solomon saw that Boller was now lying motionless in the dirt and apparently dead.

Wondering what he had just witnessed, Solomon turned and gazed out toward the Rebel battle line. Suddenly, the ground thundered, and the sky illuminated orange as all six of the Fifth Maine Battery's Napoleons fired almost simultaneously. Solomon felt the concussions reverberate through the breastworks. Debris rained down, and Solomon ducked. When he looked up, he saw the devastating effect the battery had on the advancing Confederate battle line. The regiment on the left end of their attack was being annihilated and was forced to find cover in a low area near a spring. The rest of the North Carolina brigade and the Louisianans on their right, however, continued to advance.

Despite the shells, case shot, and canister, the Rebels continued toward Cemetery Hill. Along a dirt lane at the base of the hill, Federal regiments fired from behind a rock wall. They fired several volleys and even fought hand to hand to try to hold back the Confederates. With overwhelming numbers, however, the Rebels stormed over the wall and forced the Federals to retreat up the hill.

"They're going to take the cannons!" Private Thomas Sinnex shouted. Well past nightfall now, the Nineteenth's men peered above the breastworks and strained to see the two Rebel brigades below attacking up the east side of Cemetery Hill.

"Keep firing, men!" Captain Orr shouted.

Solomon raised his Springfield again and fired at the Confederates who were now rushing up the hill toward the Union cannons.

At the top of the hill, Union officers shouted and ordered more regiments across the pike and into the fight. Suddenly, a cloud of fire and smoke erupted from a cannon atop the hill, and a deadly blast of cannister ripped another hole in the Rebel line. But still, the Rebels stormed forward toward the guns.

The Union artillerists used rammers and pikes and even threw rocks to fight back, but the Rebel onslaught was too much. Solomon, straining his eyes to see, saw a Rebel flag being waved from atop a captured Union cannon. It briefly disappeared into the smoke below, but another Confederate soldier quickly climbed on top of the gun and was waving the flag again.

The Nineteenth's survivors nervously gazed through the dark smoke. More cannons were captured, and the Rebels had taken the east side of the hill. Suddenly, though, a chorus of loud yells came from the cemetery, and a dark mass of troops stormed over the hill. The throng of men flowed around the cemetery's brick gatehouse and through its arched entrance. Through the smoke, Solomon could see that the Rebels had paused their attack, seemingly unsure if the new mass of soldiers was the enemy…or the friendly Confederate units they'd been expecting to arrive from the other side of the cemetery.

"They're Union!" Thomas shouted excitedly.

Solomon, still unsure, strained to see as the dark silhouettes rushed forward across the pike. When orange flashes of light erupted from muskets at the front of the column, Solomon immediately realized Thomas was right.

The few unsure moments that the Confederates had waited were deadly. After a pause, and realizing that the newly arrived regiments weren't their own friendly units, the Rebels finally returned fire at the oncoming muzzle flashes. The dark hill continued to erupt in musket fire in one of the most horrific night fights of the entire Civil War.

The Confederates had a hold of the east part of Cemetery Hill for a short time, but eventually, the outnumbered and unsupported Rebel brigades were overrun. Hundreds of Rebel hands went up surrendering, and the rest of the Confederates that could escape did so, fleeing back down the hill in the darkness.

The Indiana men watched on, but the field became even darker as the cannon blasts and muzzle flashes became more sporadic. Solomon took a step away from the rock wall and leaned back against a tall oak. After letting his back slowly slide down the tree, he dropped into a sitting position and looked up at the night sky. Smoke clouds drifted past, and slowly their edges became brighter until giving way to a clear hole. Finally, he saw the bright moon above.

A blast from behind the breastworks caused Solomon to lower his eyes and look at the men again. A nervous private in Company E had just shot his Springfield and was frantically reloading.

"Hold your fire," a calm voice said from farther down the line.

Solomon noticed Sergeant Boller's lifeless body lying right where he had fallen.

It was strange, Solomon thought, seeing Boller lying there dead. Still, though, the rest of the men ignored the dead sergeant and looked out at the fields below. Waiting for another attack, the men were anxious...until finally, they realized no attack would come.

Solomon looked up, and the night sky drew him in again. With his gaze wandering between the stars high above, his eyes had drifted to the western sky. And then he thought of home. It was below those stars in that direction, he knew. It seemed so far away.

"Don't think of home," Hawk had told them at a campfire early in the war. Solomon remembered Henry arguing, saying he had to. "It only makes it worse," Hawk had quickly shot back.

Thinking of home only makes it worse...

Solomon had repeated Hawk's words to himself many times. But tonight, Solomon allowed his mind to stray. He thought of home and the farm. And of James and John...and their sisters. And Pa, and Ma...she was always smiling.

Oh, how I miss them.

And then his mind wandered to his friends in the army. *They were almost all gone now. Henry and Hawk and Billy... all killed just yesterday. And so many more. And James... Where are you, James?*

His gaze dropped down to the western horizon and the distant mountains now silhouetted against the starry sky beyond. Staring blankly, he felt a tear and wiped his eyes.

How am I still alive? So many have died...so, so many.

Then he thought of James again, lying in those woods. With his eyes full of tears, he wiped them again and tried focusing on the church spires and steeples in the town...and then further...beyond the town and the treetops to the northwest.

I'll come for you, James...and, hopefully, I'll get you home.

Closing his eyes, he thought of the rest of his family again. And of home. And then he remembered James's last words.

Survive, Sol. Make it home.

-25-

Final day of the battle...

Culp's Hill, Gettysburg
July 3, 1863, Early Afternoon

In addition to the Rebel attack against Cemetery Hill, last night's fight off to the right and to the rear of the Iron Brigade had ended long after dark. The battle had resumed before sunrise this morning, however, preventing the Nineteenth's survivors from getting much rest. The fighting on Culp's Hill this morning was even more intense than it had been on July 2nd. Although the Nineteenth Indiana wasn't involved in that part of the fighting, the heavy musketry forced them to remain huddled in their breastworks while the battle raged just beyond their right flank.

Finally, around eleven in the morning, the loud storm of musketry had fizzled, and the area around the Nineteenth's earthworks was fairly quiet. With the fighting on Culp's Hill having subsided, the Indiana men finally had the chance to relax and had even built fires for coffee.

Solomon heard a harmonica from farther up the hill and immediately smiled. It made him think of Billy. He knew it wasn't Billy's though. After being struck in the groin two days ago out in those woods, Billy was dead even before the Nineteenth's line had been forced to fall back from their first position near the creek.

Trying to block out the other sounds of the battlefield around him, Solomon focused on the harmonica. A Wisconsin soldier was playing it, and although Solomon didn't recognize the tune, it had a slow, sad rhythm to it. Fitting, Solomon knew. The Wisconsin men had also suffered heavily two days ago. Listening to the music, he stared out at the fields below and allowed his mind to drift.

The harmonica reminded Solomon of nights in camp. He wished he could have those moments back now…Billy playing the harmonica while they all told stories…mostly of home, far away from the life of the army. He could still picture Henry across the campfire, drawing and writing in his diary. Hawk would tease Henry about his diary, but in a strange way, it was Hawk's way of showing he cared about it…even more than the rest of them did.

When it was just Solomon and James, they would talk about home, both the farm in Ohio and their childhood back in Kentucky. Already, Solomon missed those nights around the campfire.

Solomon closed his eyes and let the daydream pull him in, but off in the distance, a sole musket broke the calm. Solomon thought of the war again but then forced himself to think of peace—a peace they hadn't experienced for what seemed like a lifetime ago.

They all hoped for peace now. Hopefully, this would be the battle to end the war. He knew the battle's outcome hadn't been determined yet, and they all knew General Lee would be attacking again. He remembered Hawk having said, "General Lee hasn't left a battlefield to the enemy yet."

That comment had started an argument when Billy had quickly reminded Hawk of Antietam. Hawk, never wasting a chance to show his disdain for the Union high command, had quickly replied, "Lee only left two days later 'cause McClellan wouldn't attack him there again. Antietam was just one of the Union's many squandered opportunities, Billy."

"Coffee, Sol?" Thomas asked, interrupting Solomon's thoughts.

"Uhhh...yeah, sure," Solomon said, looking over toward Thomas who was tending to a boiling pot of coffee. The men had built the campfire on the backside of a giant boulder at a bend in the breastworks. As Solomon scooted closer, Thomas poured some of the coffee into a tin cup and handed it to him.

"Here ya go, Sol. Keep the cup."

"Yeah, mine is gone," Solomon said, reaching for the tin cup and then taking a sip. "Thanks."

Despite the heat and humidity, the coffee tasted good, and Solomon noticed the cobwebs from his daydreams quickly working themselves away.

"I got some hardtack too," Thomas said, reaching into his haversack and pulling out a bundle of dry crackers.

"Sure...thanks." After setting his Springfield against the boulder and taking the hardtack, Solomon untied the string around the package and pulled away the paper. Purposely not looking at the bland crackers, he grabbed one of them and put it in his mouth.

"These things sure ain't gotten any better, have they?" Solomon quipped after crunching into the hardtack.

"No," Thomas laughed. "And there's no foraging around here either. That's all we're gonna get for a while."

Foraging...

The word made Solomon think of Hawk and all the times Hawk had returned to camp with dried ham, eggs, or even a whole chicken. Then Solomon thought of the time that he had joined Hawk on one of Hawk's many after-dark raids. *Never again,* Solomon had said. After being chased by a farmer, shot at by a Rebel patrol, and waiting for their chance to sneak past the provost guards, they had finally made it back into camp just prior to sunrise. During the next day's march, they carried those two chickens under their frock coats for fifteen miles. Solomon smiled and then inadvertently laughed out loud.

"What's so funny, Sol?" Thomas asked.

"Ahhh, nothing. Just thinking about a friend." Solomon then looked over at Thomas and saw that he was also smiling, apparently thinking of some of the men in his own squad. But as Thomas stared out to the area beyond the town, Solomon noticed that Thomas's brow had furrowed and his face had turned serious. Yesterday, Thomas had said that he was also the only survivor in *his* entire squad.

Thomas and Solomon sat and quietly looked over the breastworks for several minutes. Solomon heard the Wisconsin soldier's harmonica again, its lamenting tune floating softly and slowly across the now peaceful hillside. Thomas finally cleared his throat and spoke again. "We both lost some good friends out there."

Nodding in agreement, Solomon opened his mouth to respond, but the harmonica's notes seemed to have a delicate hold on him. It was even sadder now, and Solomon didn't want it to end. Somehow, the tune was comforting, and Solomon continued staring into the fire. As the smoke slowly rose against the boulder's side and faded into the warm, muggy air, Solomon and Thomas thought of their former squads…and of home.

A crackle of musketry beyond the wooded hill interrupted the two soldiers' thoughts, and Solomon turned his head in that direction. The gunfire quickly died down, but behind them, Solomon noticed Colonel Williams talking to an officer whom he hadn't remembered seeing before.

"Who's that?" Solomon asked.

"Probably still a few nervous pickets out there," Thomas responded.

"No, no, not the musket fire...the officer talking to Colonel Williams," Solomon responded, nodding toward their colonel and the other officer.

"Oh...I'm not sure. I saw him walk over from the Twenty-Fourth Michigan a li'l while ago...a lieutenant, I think."

Solomon took a final gulp of his coffee, and as he threw out the last of it from the bottom of the cup, he noticed Colonel Williams was looking in his direction. The colonel then pointed directly at him and nodded. Then, a moment later, the Michigan officer also turned and met Solomon's gaze. *Strange,* Solomon thought.

"What do you think they're talkin' about, Sol?" Thomas asked.

Solomon didn't respond but, instead, focused on the Michigan man talking with the Nineteenth's colonel. Still wondering what their conversation was about, Solomon watched as the two officers shook hands just before the Michigan man turned away.

"He's coming this way, towards us," Thomas said.

"I know," Solomon said, watching the Michigan officer walk down the hill toward them. "I wonder why."

Solomon noticed he was wearing the insignia shoulder bars of a first lieutenant. He was limping, and his scabbard clanged against the top of his left boot as he approached. His long uniform coat was buttoned, although it was torn and dirty. There were bloodstains on the front of his coat that made the red First Corps badge barely visible above his left breast. The lieutenant looked haggard and tired but still stood tall and proud as he stopped just in front of Solomon.

Solomon and Thomas both quickly stood and faced the lieutenant.

"Sir."

"Private Whitlow?" the lieutenant asked. Unable to hide the effects of the first day's battle, the Michigan officer adjusted his stance and winced as he spoke.

"Yes, sir."

"I'm Lieutenant Norton with the Twenty-Fourth Michigan." After shaking Thomas's hand and then Solomon's, he asked, "Are you Solomon?"

"Yes, sir, they call me 'Sol.'"

"I've gotten permission from Colonel Williams for you to walk with me to our lines. There's someone there you should speak with."

"Uh, sure. Yes sir," Solomon said. "But…"

"The Nineteenth won't need you here for a little while."

"Sir?"

"I don't think the Rebs will be attacking *here* soon. They're pretty fought out in this area of the field. I'll have you back here shortly anyway. Ready?"

"Yes, sir," Solomon responded while grabbing his Springfield leaning against the boulder.

Lieutenant Norton noticed that Solomon had shot a quick glance at Thomas who was listening in. "He'll be right back, Private," the lieutenant said, looking at Thomas before turning and starting toward the Twenty-Fourth Michigan's line.

"What's this about, Lieutenant?" Solomon asked, hurrying forward to catch up.

"Edwin…call me Edwin. There's so few of us left now. I think we should probably all get to know one another well. Hell, the entire Twenty-Fourth is commanded by a captain now."

Noticing the lieutenant had dodged the question, Solomon changed the subject and said, "I heard you say you didn't think the Rebs would attack *here*. Why's that, sir?"

"Well, the Rebs threw everything at us they could for over seven hours this morning…all against the right end of our line. They gained very little." Approaching an open area, the Michigan lieutenant paused, crouched down, and looked at Solomon. "Stay low," he said, turning and pointing toward the town about a half mile away.

"Sir?"

"Reb sharpshooters have been firing at us from upstairs windows and some of the rooftops. See that gold dome on that bell tower and the steeple to the left?" he asked, pointing at the top of a church in the distance.

"Yes, sir," Solomon responded while keeping his head down.

"There's a Reb sharpshooter up in the top of that building right now. We're hoping one of our batteries up in the cemetery lands a shell in there on him. Just keep your head down. Come on."

Still limping, Lieutenant Norton started forward again with Solomon right beside him. As they approached the Twenty-Fourth Michigan's men and stopped behind their line, Solomon was surprised how few of them were left. Numbering nearly five hundred on the morning of July 1st, Solomon guessed there were fewer than one hundred survivors remaining. They looked tired and worn out, and their tattered regimental flag hung limp from its damaged staff jammed into the earthworks.

"Anyway, it's been quiet all day in the *middle* of the Union line…south of the cemetery," the lieutenant said, pointing back to the southwest. "But across from there…that's where General Lee has amassed his line of artillery over two miles long…across from ours. And there are reports of infantry forming in the woods behind them."

As the lieutenant paused, Solomon looked up toward the cemetery behind them and saw dozens of Union cannons that had been amassed on the hill. Beyond the cemetery, Solomon could tell that the line of artillery extended along the ridge and far to the south.

"This way…," Lieutenant Norton continued, leading Solomon down the short slope toward a group of soldiers behind the breastworks. "Let me introduce you to somebody."

After following the Twenty-Fourth Michigan lieutenant, Solomon caught himself staring at the battered regiment's survivors. He quickly looked away and toward the fields to the north. Rebel camps filled the ridges in the distance. And off to the left, the slope up to Cemetery Hill was strewn with dead bodies, broken artillery pieces, disabled wagons, and dead horses, all still lying where they were shot down during last night's fighting. Although the fight there took place in almost total darkness, the hot sun now fully exposed the horrors of the attack.

"Solomon," the lieutenant said, bringing Solomon's attention back to the Michigan men in front of him. "This is Private Kudish."

The soldier was standing on one foot and using his musket as a crutch. He had a blood-soaked bandage around his head, and his left foot—muddy and shoeless—dangled from his ankle wrapped in dirty linens.

"I'm Will," the wounded Michigan private said, awkwardly balancing himself while reaching out to shake Solomon's hand.

"Solomon, Sol Whitlow," Solomon replied slowly, not knowing what this meeting was about.

Will's handshake was firm and strong.

"As you can see here, Sol," the lieutenant interjected, "Private Kudish has been wounded…twice. We sent him to the hospital down the pike, but he insisted that he be allowed to return to the regiment. So, here he is."

The lieutenant paused and glanced at Will with a smile. Solomon could tell that he was proud to boast of the wounded private's courage to return to the line and possibly face more fighting. After a few moments, the lieutenant turned and began looking at the other Michigan survivors behind the earthworks. And continued smiling too, Solomon noticed.

"What happened?" Solomon asked, nodding at Will's wounds.

"The first day near the creek, I took a Rebel ball in the ankle. And then in the woods a little later, a shell. Well...I reckon it knocked me unconscious for a bit." Will stopped and glanced at the lieutenant and then stared at Solomon. Will swallowed hard and then looked away.

"Then what?" Solomon asked, still not sure where his story was going.

Will, as though asking for approval, looked at the lieutenant.

"Go on," the lieutenant said. "Tell him."

"I was trapped out in them woods beyond the town... behind the Rebel lines. It was well after dark." He paused for a moment, glancing at the ground before looking up again. His eyes were now bloodshot and moist. "That's where I saw James, your brother."

Solomon, in disbelief, began to ask how he knew it was James, but Will quickly interrupted him.

"I knew he was in the Nineteenth Indiana...and he told me he had a brother named Solomon."

Solomon, unable to grasp what Will was telling him, fought for words. "Is he alive? How...how is he?"

As Will began to answer, a cannon boomed from somewhere in the distance to the southwest, followed by a whistling shell that exploded in the far side of the cemetery. When a second cannon fired and its shell exploded even closer, Solomon, along with all the Michigan men, ducked for cover.

"Signal shots," Lieutenant Norton said, looking up as the blasts faded to echoes.

Solomon looked at Will again. "Is James alive?"

"Yes, I think so. But he's not in good shape. His leg is hurt bad. There's a tourniquet on it, and someone wrapped it up… but it was still bleeding."

Hearing his brother's grave condition, Solomon dropped his head and closed his eyes.

"His shoulder was hurt bad too," Will continued. "Your brother…he told me he'd been stabbed by a bayonet."

Solomon shuddered and then felt the lieutenant's hand pat him on the back. Finding no words, the three men sat in silence for several seconds before Solomon gathered himself and looked up at the Michigan private.

"Where is he?" Solomon asked.

"When I left him, well after dark, he was along the north edge of the woods…along a fence."

Suddenly, off to the west, several cannons boomed at once. The lieutenant nervously rose to his feet and looked toward the cemetery. Then, turning toward Solomon again, he said, "I hope you find your brother, Private."

"Thank you, sir."

"I must go," Lieutenant Norton said before stepping away and moving toward another cluster of men farther down the line.

There was now a steady roar of cannons coming from beyond the cemetery. Now lying flat on the ground, Solomon pulled himself closer to Will. Above the explosion of shells, Solomon raised his voice and asked, "Could James move? Where was he gonna go?"

"I don't know…" The cannons were so loud that Will was nearly screaming. "We crawled together to the fence. It wasn't far from where I found him…in the woods. I had to help him…"

Will paused as the Union cannons in the cemetery roared to life, returning fire against the Confederate artillery.

"The fence…from there we could see a barn and house."

Solomon tried to ignore the barrage of artillery and grabbed Will's arm. "Keep going," Solomon said. "Which barn? Where is it?"

"It's up along the pike...the road the Rebs came into town from on the first day. I gave him water there."

Suddenly, a shell exploded behind them, and both men ducked their heads for cover. After debris rained down through clouds of smoke and dirt, Will shouted, "Your brother...he couldn't move any farther, Sol. He had to rest."

"Go on," Solomon urged, pressing for more information.

There was a pause in the blasts of Union artillery, and Will continued, "In the morning, James was going to...try to crawl to that barn...to get help."

"Is that where he is now?" Solomon asked.

"I don't know. That farm had a lot of wounded lying around. I know a lot of our wounded also went to the big building west of town...the *seminary*, I heard some people call it. When I told him that I was going to make a run for the town, he told me to go on. But first, he told me about you."

Solomon put his head down and thought about what Will had told him. Closing his eyes, Solomon could picture James suffering and lying out there against that fence.

"Thank you, Will," Solomon said. "I'm glad you made it back alive."

"Thanks, but I wish...that I could've done more for him."

"It's okay, Will. Thanks for what you did. When this battle's over...which might be soon from the sounds of all them guns...I'll go out there and look for him."

"I hope you find him, Sol."

"Thanks."

Solomon then gave Will's arm a squeeze and held it for several seconds. Finally letting go, he said, "I gotta get back to my regiment, Will."

"James is a good man…a brave man too."

"Thank you," Solomon said before nodding and quickly turning away. He then crawled behind the rest of the Michigan men and paused next to a boulder at the end of their line.

Suddenly, just as Solomon was about to run across the short span of trampled weeds between the Michigan's right flank and the Nineteenth Indiana, Solomon heard a streaking artillery shell that slammed into the ground just in front of him. He quickly covered his head and face as the shell exploded with a roar.

With dirt clods and chunks of grass raining down, he peered ahead. A cloud of black smoke was still rising out of the shell's crater as Solomon got to his feet and sprinted toward the Nineteenth's earthworks.

After zigzagging between the trees, Solomon dove behind the wall right next to Thomas. Solomon looked around and saw that all the Indiana men were hunkered down.

Solomon lay flat on his stomach but turned his head and looked toward the cemetery. Through eye-burning, choking smoke, Solomon saw the Union artillerists returning the Rebels' cannon fire. Gunners frantically sponged their barrels and rammed home shells. Officers, lowering their field glasses, pointed and crazily barked out orders.

Lanyards were pulled, and cannons bellowed a thunderous fury of hell.

"Stay down!" Thomas shouted.

But the artillery battle drew Solomon in, and he found he couldn't look away. A solid wall of smoke now filled the sky beyond the ridge. Closer, clouds of black smoke rose from cannons and bursting shells.

Suddenly, a Rebel shell exploded among a group of officers just behind the Nineteenth Indiana's line. Solomon watched in horror. As the smoke cleared, all the officers got to their feet again, except one. The wounded man was Lieutenant Macy who was now crawling away from the blast with his head and face covered in blood. Seconds later, a stretcher team, braving the open air still exploding with shells and solid shot, ran toward the lieutenant. As they picked up Macy and began taking him to the rear, Solomon remembered that during the Nineteenth's retreat on the battle's first day, Lieutenant Macy had heroically picked up the flag in the woods and carried it away.

Up on the pike behind them, teamsters yanked horses' reins, hurrying ammunition wagons to the guns on the ridge. As officers and couriers frantically spurred their horses and barked out orders, chaos seized the battlefield.

Still looking toward the Baltimore Pike, Solomon saw a flaming shell screaming through the smoke. The shell slammed into the back of the horse team and exploded, igniting the limber wagon's ammunition case.

The ammunition inside the chest detonated, and the blast launched the limber wagon and part of the horse team skyward. The air thundered, and the ground shook. Solomon, still looking toward the explosion, saw smoking horse carcasses and shredded pieces of harness, collar, and reins. The wagon's teamster, having been hurled from the blast, was mangled and burned. Crawling from the wreckage, he screamed in pain.

Solomon felt himself shudder, and his stomach turned. He had had enough and put his head on the ground. Already, the artillery barrage had lasted over an hour and was the largest cannon duel he could remember during the entire war. Union cannons continued blasting, and the Confederate shells kept streaking closer.

All around, the sky thundered, and the earth shook.

And shook.

And shook.

He kept his head down and his hands over his ears. And, wishing it would all stop, he closed his eyes and prayed.

Then, with the ground still shaking, he forced himself asleep.

-26-

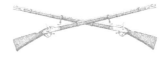

Two days later…

Culp's Hill
July 5, 1863, Mid-Morning

It'd been four long days since Solomon had been forced to leave his brother out in those woods. Yesterday, the Nineteenth's survivors had thought they would get their chance to retrieve their dead and wounded, but after joining several other units on a rainy foray into town, they were ordered back to their breastworks below Culp's Hill. Finally, today, Solomon knew he might get his opportunity to go and find James.

The battle had ended two days ago, and General Lee was now retreating away from Gettysburg. The ninety-minute artillery duel on the afternoon of July 3rd was one of the largest of the war and could be heard from over one hundred miles away, even as far as Washington and Philadelphia. Then, around three o'clock, Confederate infantry charged across one mile of open fields between Seminary Ridge and the heavily defended Union position along Cemetery Ridge.

Approximately thirteen thousand Rebel soldiers began the assault, and their battle line was nearly a mile and a half wide. Facing devastating fire from Union artillery, however, only half of them reached the Emmitsburg Road partway across the field.

After climbing the two post and rail fences on each side of the road, they then charged directly into musket fire from Union soldiers waiting behind a stone wall. By the time the Confederates reached the Union battle line, their ranks had been decimated, and only a few hundred of them made it across the wall. After intense hand-to-hand fighting, Union reinforcements surrounded the Rebels on three sides, repulsing the charge and ending one of the largest infantry assaults of the war.

The next morning, Independence Day, General Lee had pulled all his forces away from the Culp's Hill area and formed a new defensive line beyond the western edge of Gettysburg. By dawn of July 5th, the defeated Confederate Army had vacated Gettysburg and was on its grueling journey toward Maryland and the Potomac River. Trying to escape back to Virginia, the Rebel wagon train of wounded was over seventeen miles long. As Lee's retreating army slogged its way across South Mountain on muddy roads, they were forced to fend off rainstorms and probing attacks by Union cavalry.

For the Nineteenth Indiana men behind their muddy earthworks, July 5th had dawned partly sunny, although another line of rain clouds covered the mountains to the west. Solomon had already finished packing his knapsack and was just tightening the bag's straps when Captain Orr approached.

"Form up, men!" Captain Orr shouted. "We're moving out in five minutes."

At this point, they didn't need any more instructions than that. They knew where they were going and what they would have to do.

Since the major fighting ended two days ago, Solomon and the rest of the Nineteenth's survivors had plenty of time to ponder what had become of their comrades who had been wounded or left behind on the first day's battlefield. They were all happy to hear the captain's order that they would soon be heading in that direction.

Solomon stomped out the last of the campfire's smoldering embers and grabbed his Springfield which he'd leaned against a boulder. Slinging the rifle over his bandaged shoulder with a wince, he leaned forward to adjust the leather strap. Before picking up his new black Hardee hat lying on the breastworks, he paused. The quartermaster staff sergeant had just given it to him yesterday, replacing his old hat he'd lost during his escape through town on July 1st. Solomon suddenly realized he'd had that old hat the entire war. He then looked around at the men around him, and seeing them all still wearing the old-style black hats that had helped make the Iron Brigade famous, he put on the hat and smiled. With his knapsack, canteen, and loaded Springfield secured over his shoulders, he stood up straight and looked ahead.

"Gonna rain again today, Sol," Thomas said, nodding toward the west. Towering clouds had been moving in since early morning and now blanketed the battlefield in a thickening overcast.

"Yep, gonna get wet again today," Solomon replied, pushing his new Hardee hat further down on his head.

As the Nineteenth's survivors began to assemble, Solomon looked beyond the valley and town to the northwest. The mountains were obscured in clouds, and rain was beginning to fall on the distant trees. He knew that was where James and the rest of the Nineteenth's men were lying.

"I just wanna get out there," Solomon said.

"Yeah. Me too."

Thomas had squadmates to claim too, Solomon knew. They all did. Hopefully, some of them were still alive.

"Attention!" a sergeant shouted.

386

Solomon turned and saw Colonel Williams had ridden up and stopped in front of the Nineteenth's men. Williams was eyeing his men closely and then opened his mouth to speak. His voice failed him, however, and he suddenly lowered his head.

The gaze from the battered Nineteenth's survivors had apparently taken ahold of their thirty-two-year-old colonel. After a long pause, Williams pushed up the brim of his hat and looked at the men again.

He looked haggard and showed a deep sadness on his face. The last time he had addressed the entire regiment was on the morning of the battle's first day. There were 308 officers and men then. Now, four days later, he commanded only ninety-five. His eyes watered, and he cleared his throat.

"We have won a great battle, men," the colonel said. Knowing the men were anxious to move out, he glanced up toward the pike. A Twelfth Corps battery was still moving along it, but they would soon be past. Williams knew he only had a few moments before the Nineteenth would begin their march.

Solomon looked down from the colonel's face and noticed the horse he was mounted on. There was something different about the large, tan stallion. It wasn't the colonel's usual mount, yet it still looked familiar. The battle had been hard on horses, Solomon knew. Looking at the colonel's mount again, Solomon realized whose horse Colonel Williams was riding. It belonged to Lieutenant Colonel Dudley who had been gravely wounded and was now missing.

Dudley was the original captain of Company B. Solomon, James, and the rest of the company had become close with Dudley, even after he moved up the ranks to become the regiment's lieutenant colonel. Company B, the Richmond Greys, started with one hundred men in 1861. Now, there were only five of them left.

Thinking of their wounded lieutenant colonel and the rest of the regiment's casualties, Solomon lowered his own head and closed his eyes. He was now even more eager than before to start the march to the first day's battlefield.

"But at a great cost," Williams continued, looking at the men and pointing in the direction where the Nineteenth suffered so horrendously. "The cost will be felt in hundreds of homes, factories, and farms back in Indiana...not only now, but for generations. Although we'll be forever saddened by the price that the Nineteenth has paid on this field, we should always remember that those lives and limbs were not lost in vain."

Williams paused and saw that most of the men had their heads down, thinking of their friends and fellow soldiers. He looked toward the town...and then toward the fields and woods beyond. Raindrops had begun falling, but the men stood silent and waited for him to continue.

"Without those men's sacrifices—all of our sacrifices—the army would not have gained this victory here. The war's not over, men. Right now, Lee is moving his army over those hills back toward Maryland and the Potomac. We'll be chasing them soon...very soon. But today, we must tend to our own army and men."

As their colonel paused again, Solomon looked at the regiment's survivors. Their faces showed that the colonel's words had sunk in. They were anxious and ready to move but also knew that today would be a difficult day for the Nineteenth Indiana.

Williams climbed down from Dudley's horse and grabbed the reins. He'd walk with the rank and file today. After glancing up at the pike and seeing that the last of the wagons had passed, he cleared his throat.

"Let's go get our boys!" Colonel Williams shouted before turning away and pulling the horse's reins in the direction of the Baltimore Pike.

"Huzzah!" someone yelled.

Another man echoed the cheer. And then another...a subtle tribute to the brave men they'd lost. Then, in a steady rain, the loosely formed column of hardened veterans started through the grass and mud. The pike, a few hundred yards ahead, led toward Cemetery Hill and then bent to the right before descending toward town.

Then, only a few minutes into their march, Solomon noticed Thomas pointing down the hill and across a field to the right. Down the slope, a cluster of lifeless bodies were lying among the bushes near a spring.

"Sol," Thomas said, staring and pointing.

"I see 'em, Thomas," Solomon said, quickly looking away.

Glancing over at Thomas, Solomon saw that Thomas's hand was shaking and that his mouth was open but speechless. Solomon's eyes followed Thomas's finger and out toward the bodies again. A legless corpse stared out at its own outstretched hand that clutched a small brass frame. A photo of his parents...or his sweetheart back home, Solomon assumed.

Only a few feet away, another dead and bloated man's stiffened arms reached for the sky as if grasping the raindrops themselves. His gray unbuttoned shell jacket exposed stains of blackened blood on his chest where a Union minie ball had found its mark.

"Keep marching, Thomas," Solomon said. "Don't look at 'em."

Thomas had lowered his pointing finger but, mortified, still stared at the bodies.

Solomon put his hand on Thomas's forearm, trying to make him look away from the death scene near the spring. Instead, Thomas's gaze caused Solomon to turn toward the corpses again.

Solomon hadn't seen it at first, but now he saw what had taken ahold of Thomas. The skull's eyes were open, staring. Although the blood had dried, the rain mixed with it and caused it to flow again. Solomon tried to look away but, also like Thomas, he couldn't. The Rebel's corpse, a victim of a Yankee shell, was lying several feet away from the head. Blood, diluted by rain, flowed from the corpse and into a puddle.

Solomon stopped and closed his eyes. It was too late, though. It was an image he knew he'd never be able to forget. Feeling nauseated, Solomon blinked several times and looked up at the sky. He let the raindrops pelt his face as the column trudged past.

"Ya alright, Whitlow?" a voice asked.

"Yeah, fine," Solomon replied, looking up at the soldier who had stopped beside him. It was Joey Sykes, a private from Greens Fork, Indiana, and a member of Grear's squad. Solomon remembered that on July 1st, Joey was almost captured while on skirmish duty and barely made it back across the creek to the battle line…just in time to be standing between Grear and Billy when they were both shot down.

"Come on, let's keep going, Sol."

"Thanks, Joey," Solomon said, wiping his face and trying to shake the scene from his head. They would see a lot more dead bodies today, he knew. Following Private Sykes' lead, Solomon and Thomas started forward again and rejoined the column.

Now walking near the Baltimore Pike, the Indiana men worked their way between the scattered debris of artillery batteries and dirt lunettes where the cannoneers had fought on July 2nd and 3rd. The town's cemetery gatehouse was on their left, and as they passed it, Solomon noticed it was severely damaged. Bricks were missing where Confederate artillery shells and minie balls had struck it, and most of the windows' glass panes had been shattered.

The Nineteenth Indiana's rough-hewn column of veterans continued their march past the town cemetery and down the hill on the other side. Just before the road made a slight turn to the right toward town, Colonel Williams led the men off the pike to the northwest and into a trampled wheat field.

The Indiana men were stunned at the battle's devastation. For nearly a mile, the column passed through fields strewn with unburied bodies, horse carcasses, and abandoned uniform accoutrements. The fences had been destroyed, and nearly every structure they passed was riddled with bullets and shells.

Solomon, forcing himself to not stare at the death and destruction, looked straight ahead. The homes of the western outskirts of Gettysburg were just ahead of them now, and Solomon could see the red brick seminary building on the distant ridge. Solomon knew that somewhere past that building were the woods where most of the regiment had fallen…and where he had last seen James.

"We're almost there, Sol," Thomas said, walking alongside him again.

"I know, Thomas." And then, thinking of James, he said, "Afraid it's gonna be tough when we get out there."

"There's hope, Sol."

"I know." Solomon knew that they both had a lot of comrades they hoped to rescue, but he also knew that James's wounds were severe.

The wind had picked up, and they were now walking in a downpour. Trying to ignore the rain, Solomon looked at the buildings and homes on the edge of town. Suddenly, he was reminded of Hawk and felt a lump in his throat.

The house…

His heart surged.

Down the street past the intersection, he recognized the home where he had been forced to leave Hawk. Solomon stopped and stared.

"What is it, Sol?" Thomas asked.

Not answering and unsure what to do, Solomon desperately looked around the other men in the regiment. The house wasn't far. Although Solomon was hopeful that James was still alive, he also wanted to find out what had happened to Hawk and the family inside the home. For the past two years, Hawk had become another brother to the Whitlows.

"I want to go to that house, Thomas. One of my squad is in there."

Before Thomas could respond, Solomon saw Captain Orr approaching and quickly waved him over.

"Private Whitlow?" the captain asked.

"Captain," Solomon said, pointing toward the house along Middle Street. "Private Hawkins was in that house, sir. He was gravely wounded, and I'm afraid he's dead, sir. I'd like to go there."

Captain Orr didn't hesitate. "Take Private Sinnex with you and go do what you must. If Hawkins needs medical assistance, see that he gets it."

"Thank you, sir."

"Meet up with the regiment when you're done. The rest of us will be heading toward the seminary building and then out to those woods. And I'm afraid we'll be out there quite a while."

"Yes, sir."

Solomon and Thomas both saluted the captain and then quickly turned toward town. Almost as soon as the two Indiana privates left the column and began walking through the trampled oats, they came across a Union burial party digging two long trenches in the mud. Seeing the line of rain-drenched corpses lying alongside the mass grave made Solomon think of his own comrades who would also have to be buried today.

"We're gonna see enough of that kind of work today, Sol," Thomas said.

"Yeah, I know. Thanks for joining me, Thomas. I know we *both* have a lot of friends out in those woods."

"There's hope, Sol. We'll get out there, and hopefully, your brother's alive."

"Thanks."

"The house is just ahead. Let's find Hawk."

As they rounded the corner toward the row of houses, they saw the enormous toll that the three-day battle had on the small town. Along with the remnants of battle left behind by the two battered armies, pieces of the town itself were lying in the streets. An awful stench of human waste, dead horses, and decomposing flesh filled the air. Now walking on Middle Street, Solomon and Thomas stepped through the mud and around shattered bricks, broken glass, and pieces of rooftops that had been blasted away.

Now approaching the house, they saw a dark red cloth hung above the doorway, identifying the home as a makeshift hospital. The door was open, and Solomon stepped inside.

Inside and just to the left, two gravely wounded Union soldiers were lying on the front parlor's floor. Both men's eyes were closed, and they seemed to be unconscious.

Solomon waved Thomas forward, and as they headed down the hallway, they heard several voices coming from the kitchen. Stepping around the corner, Solomon saw the two women, both kneeling over a wounded Union soldier lying on the floor. Another wounded man wearing Confederate gray pants sat on the floor with his back against the wall.

Realizing that none of the four people in the kitchen had noticed them at first, Solomon made a subtle cough and knocked on the wooden entryway. One of the women— Solomon remembered she was the boy's mother—glanced up at him and then looked back to the man she was tending. At first, she didn't recognize Solomon who had been in her house four days prior. Suddenly, though, her face changed, and she quickly rose and walked toward him. They stared awkwardly at each other for a moment before she finally spoke.

"You survived," she said, her voice unable to hide surprise.

"Yes, ma'am. And I'm much obliged to you and your sister. And to your son. Thanks for allowing us inside your home that day."

Solomon and Thomas looked around the kitchen again and focused on the two wounded soldiers on the floor. Both were conscious but in obvious pain. The Rebel soldier was in grave condition with his head tilted sideways, and his chest and arm were wrapped in blood-soaked bandages.

The Union man's wounds, however, appeared to be less severe. Although his leg was bandaged and he appeared unable to stand, he had sat up and was now watching them carefully. Solomon noticed the soldier's hat beside him. Atop it, he saw a blue corps badge in the shape of a Maltese Cross. He was part of the Pennsylvania Reserves of the Union Fifth Corps, Solomon knew.

"You were lucky, I'd guess," the boy's mother said, bringing Solomon's attention back to the two women.

"Yes, ma'am. Lucky, for sure. Your name is…?"

"Anna," she quickly said. "Anna McLaughlin. This is Tabitha, my sister."

"I'm Solomon," he said. "And this is Thomas."

"Ma'am," Thomas said, politely bowing his head.

"Where's your boy?" Solomon asked.

She hesitated, and her face sank into a frown. Looking at the wounded Union soldier on the floor, she said, "Jacob is out trying to find help…for his father."

Solomon suddenly remembered the boy had said his father was a soldier and then realized the wounded Union man sitting against the wall must be him. The man grunted and attempted a smile that came out as only a grimace. He nodded painfully at the two soldiers standing in his kitchen and then closed his eyes.

"We were going to take him up to his bed," the boy's mother said, nodding toward her wounded husband. "But we need to get him help…at a real hospital. Some men from his regiment dropped him off here last evening. They said he was shot twice…in the horrible fighting a few miles south of town, in a wheat field. They said he wanted to come home."

"Your son…where is he?"

"He's out trying to find bandages, linens, food, anything he can…and a better place for his father and for these other wounded men here."

"His name is…Jacob?"

"Yes. He's nine years old. His dog followed him. That dog follows him everywhere now."

"His dog?" Solomon asked. "I don't remember a dog here four days ago."

"Showed up at the end of the first day of fighting," Anna said. "It was soon after you'd escaped, right after your…"

But she suddenly paused, and silence fell over the room for several seconds. Finally, the boy's aunt spoke up.

"Your friend…you're here to come and get him?"

Solomon nodded. He tried to answer, but no words came out. He knew that not seeing Hawk in the house was almost a sure sign that he was dead.

"Yes, ma'am," Thomas said, answering for Solomon. "Where is he?"

Solomon noticed the two women exchanging nervous glances. The boy's mother then turned away and knelt down to her wounded husband again.

"Anna?"

The boy's mother hesitated before answering her sister. Then, over her shoulder and without turning away from her husband, she said, "Show them."

"This way," Aunt Tabitha quickly said, leading the two Union soldiers to the rear door. Solomon knew it was the same door he'd carried Hawk through four days ago when they had first entered the house. He paused and stared at it and, for at least the dozenth time, questioned himself whether he'd done the right thing bringing Hawk here.

As the three of them stepped out into the rain, Solomon noticed two muddy mounds in the backyard. Ignoring the mud and raindrops, Solomon removed his hat and walked toward the two recently dug graves.

"Which one is he?" Solomon asked, staring at the two mounds of mud.

"That one," Aunt Tabitha answered, pointing. "The one on the left…that's your friend."

Solomon knelt down. "Who's this over here?"

"A Reb," she said. "We buried him too. Now we're not sure why."

Solomon didn't respond, and as she turned to go back inside, he gently placed his hand in the mud on Hawk's grave. He shook his head in sorrow. After two years of fighting, this wasn't the way Solomon thought it would end for Hawk…in a house in a small Pennsylvania town.

Hawk was one of the toughest and bravest men he'd ever known. They'd all thought for sure he would be killed while storming a hill or a stone wall with thousands of screaming Rebels behind it. Hawk had always made the other men around him better soldiers themselves. Solomon knew it was soldiers like Hawk who had given the Iron Brigade the reputation it had.

"There was never anyone like him, Thomas. I feel like I've known him my whole life."

"He was brave, for sure, Sol."

For some reason, Thomas's comment suddenly made Solomon think of Hawk during their battle at South Mountain a year ago. With dry canteens, the brigade was exhausted and had been marching up the mountain toward Turner's Gap. They heard an intense fight up ahead, and prior to reaching the summit, the Nineteenth was ordered into battle line and sent off the road to the left. In nearly total darkness, they all knew it was horrible ground for an attack.

Advancing uphill through trees and boulders, they were commanded to charge a stone wall. Unseen bullets slammed into rocks and trees. Men screamed, and the entire regiment had been stopped. Company G, in addition to several men from Company B, had been sent to the left to flank the Georgians and dislodge them from the stone wall.

Hawk, Solomon, James, and Henry had been pinned down at a giant boulder. Bullets flew thicker than hail and peppered the front of the rock. Company G had been stopped too. Then, all by himself and without being told, Hawk darted forward and disappeared in the darkness. They all thought he had surely been killed, but then they saw Hawk's silhouette up on a boulder ahead of them, waving his musket and urging them all forward.

"Forward! Forward!" Hawk yelled, an order normally only shouted by an officer. Suddenly, a bullet had struck Hawk's knapsack and spun him off the rock. He quickly climbed back up, fired through the darkness into the stone wall ahead, and then waved the men behind him forward again. It looked like suicide, and at first, only James advanced. After briefly hesitating, Solomon and Henry followed…and then several more, and finally, the entire company.

The Nineteenth Indiana suffered fifty-three casualties at South Mountain, and the brigade lost over three hundred. Later that night, General McClellan told "Fighting Joe" Hooker that Gibbon's brigade fought like they were made of iron.

Three days later, they had proven it again at Antietam.

"We should make a cross," Thomas said.

Solomon looked up and nodded.

Thomas had known Hawk too…they all had. But Thomas also knew how close Solomon and Hawk had been.

They were like brothers. A squad would become a family, and Thomas's squad had been the same way. And now, *they* were all gone too.

"I'll get some wood for the cross," Thomas said. Noticing Solomon was staring down at Hawk's grave again and didn't seem to hear him, Thomas quietly turned around and headed toward the house.

Solomon stood and looked at the scene around him. The quiet backyard and subtle raindrops were such a contrast to the fighting they had done for the past year. Solomon, letting the rain trickle down his face, closed his eyes and thought of what had happened here to his squad. Henry was dead, for sure. So was Billy. James was probably dead too. Even if he weren't, he certainly wouldn't be in any condition to fight anymore. Hopefully, he'd find him soon.

Feeling Thomas behind him again, Solomon turned around. Thomas was holding two pieces of wood from a busted ammunition box.

"Thanks, Thomas," Solomon said, watching Thomas kneel down and jam one of the boards into the mud.

Thomas straightened the piece of wood and then nailed the other board to it, making a cross. After standing up, Thomas glanced at the other grave beside Hawk's and asked, "What about him?"

"Nah…but do what you want," Solomon said.

Solomon then pulled his bayonet from its sheath. Firmly holding the wet piece of wood, Solomon jabbed the point of his bayonet into the cross and began carving out an 'H'. It made him think of all those hours together for the past two years… hours spent whittling sticks and telling stories next to camp-fires. Finishing the 'H' and beginning the 'A', he held back tears and looked down at the wood shavings lying in the mud. After completing '*H-A-W-K*', Solomon stood up.

"He'd like that," Thomas said.

"Yeah…I think so too. I wish I could do more for him."

"He's at peace now, Sol."

Solomon stared at the grave. He knew no words would be worthy of the brotherhood they'd felt. It was raining even harder now, and Solomon glanced at Thomas.

"Thanks, Thomas." Solomon knew that Thomas would also see his own squadmates' graves today. "Let's go."

Thomas, not wanting to hurry Solomon, allowed Solomon to lead the way. Re-entering the house, Solomon looked around the kitchen.

The two women were still there. They were both kneeling over Anna's wounded husband who was apparently in even more pain than before. Solomon glanced at the wounded Confederate soldier, and after seeing that he had fallen asleep, he looked again at the two women.

"Ma'am?" Solomon asked.

When the mother looked up, she had tears in her eyes.

"Thank you…for burying our friend."

Aunt Tabitha, who had still been kneeling over her sister's husband, also looked at Solomon. Both women stared, but neither spoke. Although the battle had just ended two days ago, their expressions showed that what happened here at their home would affect them for the rest of their lives.

"That's the least we could do," the mother finally said.

"And thank you, both of you," Solomon said, "for allowing us inside several days ago. And to your son Jacob for helping. I was hoping to see him…before we leave town."

"He's asked about you," the boy's mother said. "He was worried 'bout whether you…survived."

"Please tell him that I did. And that we said *thank you*."

"I will," Jacob's mother said.

"What's your last name, soldier?" Aunt Tabitha asked.

"Whitlow...Solomon Whitlow. And this here is Thomas...
Thomas Sinnex."

"And your friend we buried out back?"

"His name was Hawk."

Just then, a painful groan from one of the wounded soldiers on the floor caused both women to look away. Solomon
reached for his hat and, looking at Thomas, made a subtle nod
toward the hallway. Knowing they were both anxious to find
the rest of their comrades, Thomas led the two Indiana soldiers
toward the front door. They stepped out onto Middle Street
and glanced both directions before Solomon turned to the west
and pointed.

"This way," he said.

Walking west past the edge of town and through the fields,
neither Solomon nor Thomas spoke. Both stared straight ahead
and tried to block out the stench and vestiges of the battle that
lay in every direction. The brick seminary was just ahead of
them, and they could tell it had now been made into a giant
hospital, inside and out.

They continued to the seminary's grounds, and up ahead,
they could see what was left of the barricade and the field they
had retreated across. And beyond that, they could see the woods.

"This is gonna be tough," Thomas said, looking past the
ridge toward the woods where the Nineteenth had horribly lost
so many of their good men.

"I know," Solomon replied.

He also knew that today could end up being one of the
hardest days of his life.

-27-

Twenty-two years later...

Along Willoughby Run
Herbst Woods, West of Gettysburg
October 28, 1885

Thirty-one-year-old Jacob McLaughlin smiled as he watched his son wading and playing in the creek. Jacob found it funny the way a six-year-old boy was never bothered by cold water. Jacob was the same way when he was his son's age and used to play here in the same creek too.

That was long ago, even before the Springs Hotel was built on the other side of the creek and before the road and bridge were here. He used to find bullets in the water and even found a buckle once that had the letters '*CS*' on it.

Glancing up past the monument toward the road, Jacob saw his father and Aunt Tabitha sitting in their carriage. Physically, Jacob's father didn't get along well anymore. He'd been shot on the second day at the Battle of Gettysburg, and although initially hopeful that they could save his leg, the doctors had finally been forced to amputate it a week later. Until recently, his father had always done well with crutches. But now, at age sixty-four, having only one leg was taking its toll on him. Even though his father was staying in the carriage with Aunt Tabitha for now, Jacob knew that once the other old soldiers began arriving, he'd be right there with them sharing war stories.

Jacob's mother had passed away just a few months after the battle. The doctor had said she died of typhoid fever. Jacob was only nine years old then, and after her death, his aunt had raised him…along with his father whenever he was home. He wasn't there much, though.

As a veteran of the First Pennsylvania Reserves and having lost a leg fighting in the famous Wheatfield, his father seemed like a local hero…and didn't mind talking about it either. He would spend long hours in local taverns telling stories about the war, especially the fight here in Gettysburg. Jacob had been out to the Wheatfield dozens of times while his father talked and pointed out what had happened there. Jacob always loved hearing the stories…not just from his father, but from strangers too. But now, it seemed that he had heard them all.

As Jacob stood at the creek's bank and watched more people gather near the monument, he thought about his mother and all the things she had done for the soldiers during and after the battle. She'd cared for and tended to men from both sides. At one time, at least a dozen wounded soldiers were in their home on Middle Street. His mother, Aunt Tabitha, and Jacob did what they could for the men, but many were hopeless and died in their home. For several weeks, moans and cries had filled their house.

The experiences of July 1863 had been burned into his memory forever. Jacob could still remember the soldier from Brooklyn, New York. He was wearing red, baggy pants…like the *Zouaves*, Jacob had learned later. Jacob's son still had his red-and-black Kepi hat with a brass '*14*' and the letter *D* on its front. The man's name was George and was only twenty years old. He had been shot in the hip while fighting out near the unfinished railroad cut and, several days later, carried into town. Jacob was holding George's hand when he died.

The soldiers Jacob remembered the most though were the two soldiers from Indiana. On July 1st, the battle had been raging since early morning to the northwest of town. Late in the afternoon, the two Union soldiers were banging on their home's back door and demanding to be let in. One soldier, the taller one, had carried his wounded comrade all the way from near the seminary building. When Jacob let the two Indiana men inside, they were covered with the wounded soldier's blood.

Much later, when Rebel soldiers had banged on the *front* door and forced themselves inside, Jacob quickly went with his aunt and mother to the cellar. Even now, he could still remember the musket blasts and echoes as if they were only yesterday. He had nightmares for several weeks about what happened between the Rebels in his house and the wounded Union soldier. The sounds of men screaming, muskets, and bullets hitting flesh and bone were horrifying.

When he had come upstairs a few minutes later, the Union soldier named *Hawk* and a Rebel soldier were both dead on the floor. That evening, he had helped his mother and Aunt Tabitha bury the two soldiers in their backyard. The other Indiana soldier who was in the house had escaped out the back door just prior to all the shooting. Jacob remembered that the soldier's name was Solomon—a name Jacob promised himself he'd never forget.

Jacob never blamed Solomon for leaving; he had no choice. As soon as he'd darted into the backyard, at least eight Confederates entered the front door and stormed into the kitchen. After that, there would have been no chance any Union soldier was getting out alive without being captured.

Four days later, July 5th, two soldiers from the Nineteenth Indiana had come back through town and stopped at their house. His mother had told him one of them was Solomon and had asked where Jacob was. Every day since then, Jacob had regretted that he wasn't home when the Indiana soldiers had returned.

"Daddy, look!" Jacob's son exclaimed from the creek.

Jacob quickly turned around and, not knowing how long he'd been reminiscing, saw his son holding up a crawfish.

"That's a big one," Jacob shouted back.

His son was wearing a Kepi hat and had the old cartridge box Jacob had given him a year ago. Jacob and his son had come out to the monument around noon and had been waiting all afternoon. The veterans from the Nineteenth Indiana who had survived would be here, Jacob knew. And that was why Jacob came. He'd been waiting a long time for this moment. Hopefully, he'd get to see the soldier who was in his house that day over twenty-two years ago. Jacob knew it was a long shot though. He didn't know if the soldier had even lived through the rest of the war. Even if he had, that was a lifetime ago, he knew.

Earlier this morning, Jacob had taken his son out to the Twentieth Indiana monument dedication ceremony too. It was a cold horseback ride out the Emmitsburg Road, past the Peach Orchard, and through the Wheatfield to where the Twentieth Indiana monument was located. His son didn't complain though; he had never turned down a chance to ride on a horse. Jacob knew it would be worth the trip if the soldier he'd met in the house was there. Although the soldier was in the Nineteenth, Jacob also knew that the Nineteenth was merged into the Twentieth Indiana a year after Gettysburg. Unfortunately, Jacob hadn't recognized anyone who could have been Solomon, and they rode back into town for lunch before heading out to the Herbst family's woodlot.

Jacob glanced back up toward the Nineteenth's monument. It was still covered with a black cloth, but soon, at three o'clock, the monument dedication would take place, and they would remove the veil.

A few more people had arrived and were now standing near the monument. The men were attired in expensive dark suits and top hats, and the women all wore long dresses. This was an important occasion for those who could come.

After glancing down to the creek and seeing that his son was still okay playing in the water, Jacob looked back toward town. Springs Avenue was busier than usual for a Saturday morning, and he could see more carriages arriving from the direction of the seminary.

Jacob, feeling nervous, reached into his coat pocket again and made sure that what he'd been holding onto all these years was still there. Noticing his palms had become sweaty, he pulled his hand out of his pocket, removed his hat, and took a deep breath.

He was no less anxious, though...he'd waited over twenty-two years for this day.

Turning toward his son again still wading in the creek, Jacob realized he'd made the right decision to let him come. At first, he didn't think it'd be best for a six-year-old boy to come out here with all these old soldiers talking about war and the battle they'd fought here...and about all their comrades now long gone.

His son had insisted on coming though.

Jacob was glad he did.

After all, he was named after one of the soldiers from the Nineteenth Indiana.

*****

Solomon immediately recognized the seminary building just ahead. Although the trees around it had grown up, it looked almost the same as it had in 1863. Riding in the carriage with his wife, he felt a chill as he passed through the western outskirts of Gettysburg. His wife's hand squeezed a little tighter, and he forced a smile.

But still, he felt a tear forming and wiped his eye. For three weeks since leaving Oregon, he'd promised himself he wouldn't cry when he finally returned to the battlefield of 1863. His wife Clara had been right…he'd already broken the promise, and they weren't even there yet.

Ever since Solomon had mustered out of the army in 1864, he'd tried repeatedly to escape the memories of the war. He'd even moved his family away from Indiana a few years later to avoid the reunions and seemingly endless social gatherings where the conversations always evolved into war stories. Trying to get away from the war and start a new life, Solomon had moved as far away as Texas, California, and eventually, even Oregon. He wanted to be as far away as possible from the battlefields and horrors of the war. One place he always knew he must return to, though, was Gettysburg.

As they approached the seminary, Solomon thought back to the last time he'd passed by here. It was then that he had learned that his brother James had died from his wounds. One of the hospital stewards had later told him James was up on the seminary building's second floor when he had died. Solomon never did learn how or why he ended up there.

By the time Solomon walked past on July 5th, they had already buried James in the open grove of trees on the seminary's southwest side. Colonel Williams himself had come and told Solomon about his brother. The colonel had even walked with him in the rain to show Solomon where James was buried.

Initially, they'd spelled the name wrong on the wooden headboard. At least Solomon was able to get them to fix that before they moved James's body to the Soldiers' National Cemetery a few months later. Yesterday, that was the first place Solomon and his wife visited after arriving in town.

It had taken Solomon several minutes before finding James's grave there. It was an amazing place, his wife had remarked. She was right...it was absolutely beautiful. Up on the hill overlooking the town, you could see forever in almost every direction. Yesterday, while wandering the cemetery, Solomon finally realized that was probably why the Union had made Cemetery Hill their stronghold on July 1, 1863.

The enormous monument in the middle of the cemetery made Solomon feel proud to have fought here. He had spent several hours in the cemetery yesterday, mostly standing over James's grave in the Indiana section where eighty-seven other men from Indiana were buried. While there, an elderly local gentleman had pointed out the exact spot where President Lincoln had given the Gettysburg Address in November of 1863, four and a half months after the battle.

As the carriage crested the ridge and passed the seminary building, Solomon looked out ahead. The open field where they'd retreated was just in front of them, and other than the road and trolley line leading from the seminary, the field looked entirely unchanged. The woodlot was up ahead, and Solomon felt his heart quicken.

"The woods...," Solomon started to say, lifting his hand and pointing for his wife.

"What is it, Sol?" Clara asked.

Solomon stared but couldn't speak. They were at the southeast corner of the woods where so many in the brigade had lost their lives. Even though it was autumn now and most of the leaves had turned and begun to fall, the woods looked unchanged. The battle seemed like it was an entire lifetime ago, but still, he could tell exactly where everything had happened. Even from the road, he could see the spot where he had last seen James and also where the Nineteenth had made its final stand at the back of the woods.

He had hoped it would all be different, even unrecognizable. But, instead, there it was…just as it had been then.

Neither of them spoke as the horse and carriage followed the road along the south edge of the woods and gradually descended toward the low ground near the creek. After stopping near a group of people, Solomon stepped down from the carriage and then turned to help his wife down.

"Solomon…and Mrs. Whitlow," a voice called out.

Solomon quickly turned around and saw Lieutenant Colonel Dudley approaching. He was on crutches and only had one leg of course. The Rebel bullet that struck him while holding the flag in the woods had cost him the other leg a few days later.

"Lieutenant Colonel, sir," Solomon said, reaching out and shaking his long-time friend's hand. He and Dudley had remained close friends after the war…so much so that Dudley was even in Solomon's wedding with his first wife Maria in 1867.

"And this is…?" Dudley asked, smiling and nodding toward Solomon's second wife.

"This is Clara. Clara, this is William Dudley."

"I've heard much about you, Colonel," Solomon's wife said. "It's a pleasure."

"The pleasure's all mine, Clara," Dudley responded. "You're every bit the beautiful young lady I've heard about."

"Thank you, sir."

"I understand you've helped Solomon raise an amazing young lady…Maime," Dudley said, speaking of Solomon's daughter. "How old is she now?"

"She's sixteen," Clara said. "We'd invited her along, but it's a long trip all the way from Oregon for a girl that age."

"Indeed," Dudley responded. Thinking of Solomon's first wife, Dudley started to say something else but quickly caught himself. Maria had died in 1872 in western Missouri while the Whitlow family was en route to their new home in Texas. Dudley had known Maria since she was a child and was still in contact with her father, the infamous Reverend David Nation who had moved from Muncie, Indiana, to Kansas several years after the war.

"Travel can be difficult, for sure," Solomon interjected, sensing what his former lieutenant colonel was thinking.

"Yes, it can," Dudley said. "I'm pleased to see so many here."

"Looks to be a good turnout, Colonel. I even see *Private* Buckles over there," Solomon said, jokingly emphasizing Abe Buckles's rank prior to becoming somewhat of a legend. After heroically carrying the Nineteenth's flag on July 1st across McPherson Ridge and again in Herbst Woods, Abe had acted even more admirably a year later at the Battle of the Wilderness. For his actions leading a brave charge there, he earned the Congressional Medal of Honor.

"It's great to see Abe," Dudley said with a wide smile and nodding toward a group of people near the monument.

"Yes, it is."

As Solomon and Clara watched the crowd gather, Solomon noticed a man near the creek who seemed to be watching him. The man was in his thirties, and there were two elderly people standing with him. They were both probably in their sixties, and the man, who was missing a leg, was leaning on a pair of crutches.

When Solomon smiled and waved, he noticed the younger man tilted his head slightly and stared even closer. The man hesitated, touched the sleeve of the elderly woman beside him, and then waved back.

"Excuse me, Colonel," Solomon said, turning back toward Dudley and then reaching for his wife's hand. "I need to step away for a moment."

Gently leading his wife down the slope toward the creek, Solomon noticed the three people were all still watching them. A young boy who had been playing in the creek had climbed up the rocky bank and was now standing beside the three adults. The boy was wearing a blue Union Kepi hat and holding a stick he'd been using as an imaginary musket. Solomon hadn't noticed at first, but now he saw the boy had an old, worn-out cartridge box strapped around his shoulder.

"Good afternoon," Solomon said as they approached.

"Good afternoon," the younger man replied.

"You Yankees or *Rebs*?" the boy asked with a fake frown while raising his stick as if to shoot.

Solomon and Clara both raised their hands in a mock surrender and smiled.

"Yankees," Solomon said loudly. "I swear…we're Yankees."

"What's *your* name, soldier?" Solomon's wife asked the little boy.

"My name's *Hawk*. See, it says it right here."

Solomon froze when the boy reached for the old, worn cartridge box and showed them the letters scratched into the leather. Solomon stared at the cartridge box, and time stood still.

It couldn't be.

But then he realized there was no other explanation. That was Hawk's cartridge box. He remembered the night Hawk had scratched his name into it. They were in camp near the Rappahannock River in early June of 1863, just a few days before they had begun their march toward Gettysburg.

"Your name's really…*Hawk*?" Solomon finally asked, swallowing a lump in his throat and then looking at the boy's father.

"Yep. Tell 'em, Daddy."

Solomon's reaction had told Jacob that his instinct was right. This really was Solomon, the Indiana soldier who had escaped from his house that horrible day twenty-two years ago. Jacob slowly smiled. He'd waited a long time for this.

"You tell him, Hawk," Jacob said proudly, turning and looking at his son again.

"My mother and father...they named me after a soldier that was shot in our kitchen...during the battle."

The boy was smiling, proudly, and it was obvious he'd told this story before.

"This was his cartridge box. His name was *Hawk, too.*"

Clara had her arm around Solomon now. She knew the story too. Glancing at Solomon and seeing him fighting back tears, she decided to speak for him.

She knelt down and, in a friendly voice, asked the boy, "Do you know who this man here is?"

Little Hawk shook his head.

"This was that soldier's friend...Hawk's friend...the one who died in your house. His name is Solomon. He was in the house too."

"You're Solomon?"

"Yes, young man. Hawk was my friend."

"You want his cartridge box?"

Solomon laughed, wiped away tears, and said, "Oh, no. You keep it... Your name is on it. That's yours."

Clara, Jacob, Tabitha, and the boy's grandfather all chuckled too.

Looking at Jacob again, Solomon turned serious and said, "Well, I guess most of us have met. Except...this is my wife Clara."

After everyone introduced themselves, Solomon looked at the old man again. He knew that he was the wounded soldier from the First Pennsylvania Reserves who was lying on the floor that day. Looking closer, Solomon could see the sadness in the old soldier's eyes. Solomon wanted to ask about the man's wife but knew he shouldn't.

Jacob, knowing what Solomon was thinking, said, "Mother passed away a few months later…typhoid. The town went through some hard times after the battle."

"I'm sorry," Solomon said.

"It's okay. Thank you."

"We've got a good family," the old man said, finally speaking up. "But we couldn't have done it without Tabitha…especially helping raise Jacob and now helping with little Hawk."

"I understand *that*," Solomon said, looking at his wife with a smile.

"My grandpa was a soldier too," the boy said proudly. "Weren't you, Grandpa?"

The boy's grandfather smiled and said, "Yes, I was."

"He was in the *First PA Reserves*," the boy said, emphasizing the regiment's name just the way his father had said it twenty-two years ago. "He fought in the *Wheatfield*," the boy continued, trying his hardest to stress the word's importance. "It's near *Devil's Den*. Wanna go there? I'll show you."

"I'd like that," Solomon said with a smile.

Jacob was the one who had turned serious now. He studied Solomon carefully for several seconds and then reached into his coat.

"I have something for you. Your friend had it with him in his jacket…when he was shot."

Solomon watched as Jacob carefully pulled a small book from inside his coat. At first, Solomon had no idea what it was.

"It's a diary," Jacob said, handing it to Solomon. "It belongs to a soldier named Henry…Henry Schultz."

Solomon, for at least the third time today, was speechless. Until now, he had totally forgotten about Henry's diary. Henry had been his best friend, and Solomon thought about him often. Somehow, though, he hadn't thought about what had become of Henry's diary. But now, as if it had happened only yesterday, he could picture Henry tossing his diary to Hawk up in the corner of that orchard…just before Henry was killed.

The front of the diary was covered with a black stain. It was Hawk's blood, Solomon realized. Carefully opening it up to the front page, Solomon saw only two words, both written with large letters in Henry's handwriting…

My Pards

Pards…Henry used that word a lot. Friends, pals, brothers—it meant *all* of that to him.

"Th-thank you," Solomon managed to say, his voice cracking. Looking through the diary, Solomon saw the book was nearly full, written in small print, and even had dozens of detailed drawings.

"You keep it," Jacob said as Solomon thumbed through pages. "It's something I think *you* should have…and eventually pass on to future generations. There's a lot in there. I've read it several times. This soldier named Henry…I would've liked to have known him."

"He was a great person, for sure," Solomon said. Flipping through the diary's pages again, he saw all their names—Billy, James, Solomon, and Hawk. Even the officers' names were there. There were many other names too, including the ones from the early part of the war.

So long ago.

He saw that Henry had written about the marches, campfires, and even described the battles. Then Solomon saw that the diary ended at Gettysburg. Thinking of everything that happened on that horrible day in 1863, he looked up at Jacob. "Henry was killed that day, you know?"

"I figured that. We even looked for his grave. But he must've been one of the many *Unknowns*."

"So many of those," Solomon said, thinking back to the day the survivors had arrived in the woods to claim their dead.

It was four days after their fight here and had been raining since the previous day. Solomon had nightmares about the gruesome scenes they had all seen. Still, though, the men tried to identify as many of the fallen as they could. Solomon remembered taking two other soldiers with him across the creek and searching for Henry's body. That was where they had found Lieutenant Schlagle still alive, but they never did find Henry or any of the other Company B skirmishers over there. Most had been captured, they knew. Henry, though, was almost certainly dead before he'd even hit the ground.

Thinking back to July 5, 1863, Solomon suddenly remembered, when they had visited the house on Middle Street, that Aunt Tabitha had mentioned Jacob and his dog. "Jacob, what happened to your dog?" Solomon quickly asked.

"My dog? Max?" Jacob asked, smiling, then turning toward his aunt.

"I told them about him," Aunt Tabitha said. "That day they came by after the battle…I told them you'd gone to town with your new dog."

"You named him *Max*?" Solomon asked.

"Yeah. He showed up the night you escaped…right after your friend died. Max was my best friend…especially after my mother died. He went everywhere with me…saved my life, really."

Solomon grinned. There was no doubt… *Moses…it had to be him.* Solomon thought about Moses and how much the regiment's dog had meant to the squad and, apparently, to Jacob too.

A gust of cool wind rustled the trees, and falling leaves settled on the grass. Solomon then heard laughter up near the monument and quickly turned. A photographer was setting up a camera, and more of the veterans had gathered. Apparently, the ceremony was about to begin.

"Better come on over, Sol!" Grear Williams shouted from near the monument.

"Thanks, Grear. Be right there."

Turning toward Jacob and his family again, Solomon said, "Thank you."

"It was our pleasure, Solomon…and Clara," Jacob replied, bowing slightly and shaking both their hands.

Solomon looked at Jacob's father and Aunt Tabitha. He knew he'd always remember those moments in their home. No words could ever show how much Solomon appreciated what the family had done for him. Wanting to say so much more and feeling himself tearing up, Solomon looked toward the creek.

Little Hawk was wading in the water again, spearing at crawfish with his stick he was using as a make-believe musket and bayonet. He was standing in the same place where Solomon and Hawk had helped James cross the creek.

"Hawk," Solomon shouted toward the boy.

"Yes, mister?"

Solomon, with his arm around his wife's waist, smiled when the boy turned around and looked at them. Seeing little Hawk standing there with that stick, cartridge box, and Kepi hat was a scene he knew he'd never forget.

"You take care of that cartridge box of yours," Solomon said. Then, after turning toward the McLaughlin family one last time, Solomon nodded with a smile and led his wife toward the monument.

"Those are wonderful people," Clara said after they'd turned away.

"Yes, they are. I'll be grateful forever."

Solomon noticed that Grear was standing only a few paces from where he and his cousin Billy were both shot on July 1, 1863. Luckily for Grear, the minie ball that had struck him had missed the artery…unlike the bullet that had hit Billy. Solomon remembered back to when they'd returned to the woods and found Billy's body. They buried him only a few yards away from where he'd died, like so many others they'd found from the Nineteenth Indiana.

Now, though, William Williams's grave was only two rows away from James in the National Cemetery. Yesterday, Solomon saw Grear standing at Billy's grave. When Solomon introduced him to Clara, Solomon noticed Grear's eyes were wet and that he'd been crying. He'd never seen Grear cry before, not even after he'd found out Billy had died.

Solomon teared up too when Grear told them why he was so upset. Billy's son, whom Billy had never met, had died just last year. His name was also William Williams. Like his father, he was only twenty-two when he died. It was tough standing over a man's grave and having to tell him *that*.

But now, as they approached Grear at the monument, he seemed to be in better spirits again—like the Grear of old.

"Good to see you again, Clara," Grear said with a smile. "And you too, Mr. Williams."

"It's amazing to see so many people make the long trip," Solomon said, reaching out and shaking Grear's hand.

"I wouldn't miss it for the world," Grear replied.

Just then, a politician Solomon had never seen before stepped in front of the crowd and started giving a speech. The speaker offered a brief account of what occurred here in 1863 and spoke of the sacrifices the men of the Nineteenth had made during the war. He then talked about the hardships the veterans and their families had suffered even after returning home.

After a few minutes, the speaker paused, and the veil over the monument was pulled away. As the crowd applauded, Solomon immediately realized the monument was a beautiful tribute to the men who had fought here. The speaker continued, and Solomon's mind drifted to what had happened here along the creek and in these woods. Solomon tried focusing on the speaker's voice, but still, he could see the men's faces and even hear their screams.

Solomon felt a tear and, trying to block out the nightmarish scene of 1863, closed his eyes. He then felt a sprinkle of rain and looked up at the overcast sky.

The wind had picked up again, and the tops of the trees whooshed and swayed. More leaves fell, and his eyes followed them down to the trampled grass.

The speaker finished, and after a polite applause, many of the people near the monument began to walk away. Solomon knew he'd never see this place again, although he also knew that he'd never forget it either. Even all the way from Oregon, it was important he'd come. Feeling his wife's hand on his back, he looked at her and smiled.

"Thank you," he said, raising his arm and placing it around her.

"I'm glad we came, Sol."

"Me too."

Looking down again, he saw raindrops landing on the fallen leaves. Autumn was here, and winter was close behind. For some reason, he thought of all those leaves that would soon be lying under the snow.

Solomon felt a chill and pulled his wife close. He looked up at the monument again. It seemed so...*timeless*...and *immortal*.

As he stared, he thought of all the seasons and years that had passed. Time never stops, he knew. His eyes watered again. This time, though, it wasn't sadness that caused it...just the cold wind.

After wiping his eyes, he glanced at his wife. He then looked at their horse and carriage up on the road. The woods were just beyond the road, and he took one final, long look before turning away.

Then, he thought of home.

Author's Notes

The Battle of Gettysburg was the largest battle ever fought in the Western Hemisphere. During the three days of July 1–3, 1863, the two armies suffered over 51,000 casualties, including killed, wounded, missing, and captured. Late in the afternoon the following day, the Confederate Army began its retreat from Gettysburg back toward Virginia.

That same day, July 4, 1863, the Confederacy was dealt another major blow at Vicksburg, Mississippi, when Ulysses S. Grant's Army of the Tennessee captured that city and essentially gained control of the entire Mississippi River, effectively cutting off several states and an important supply line of food and materials from the rest of the Confederacy.

By the time General Lee's army crossed the Potomac back into Virginia in the wee hours of the morning of July 14th, they had lost nearly one third of their men. The Army of Northern Virginia would continue to fight for two more years, however, finally culminating with General Lee's surrender to General Grant at Appomattox Court House, Virginia, on April 9, 1865.

At Gettysburg on July 1, 1863, the Iron Brigade arrived on the northwest outskirts of town with approximately 1,850 men. The soldiers who fought with the Iron Brigade that horrible day fought bravely despite overwhelming numbers and having to defend inferior ground. By the end of the first day's fighting, they had suffered an estimated 1,212 casualties, resulting in the highest percentage of casualties of any brigade during the entire Civil War.

The Nineteenth Indiana brought 308 officers and men to Gettysburg and suffered 210 casualties, a loss of just over 68 percent. Of the thirty-two men in company B who started the morning on July 1ˢᵗ, only five remained with the regiment when they reached Culp's Hill that evening.

Among those wounded at Gettysburg was Brigadier General Solomon Meredith, the Iron Brigade's commander and the Nineteenth Indiana's original colonel. Solomon Meredith, who as a young man had walked from North Carolina to Indiana to start a new life, was reportedly referred to by President Lincoln as his "only Quaker general in the Army."

At Gettysburg, after General Meredith's horse was shot from underneath him and the general himself was struck by a shell fragment, Meredith was trapped under his horse and unconscious before being removed from the battlefield. He suffered a severe head wound, broken ribs, and a broken leg. All three of his sons also served with the Union Army during the Civil War, two of whom died from wounds suffered during battle. General Solomon Meredith died in 1875 at the age of sixty-five and is buried with his family in Riverside Cemetery in Cambridge City, Indiana. Above Meredith's grave, there is a large monument with a bronze likeness of the general standing high atop it.

Young Abe Buckles, while still suffering from his wound at Gettysburg, was shot again a year later while leading a charge and carrying the Nineteenth's flag at the Battle of the Wilderness. After Abe's actions at the Wilderness, for which he later received the Congressional Medal of Honor, he was wounded again at Hatcher's Run. The wound there resulted in the amputation of his right leg just below the knee. Abe Buckles, still only nineteen years old, was discharged in March of 1865 as a second lieutenant in the Twentieth Indiana.

Abe then returned to Muncie, Indiana, where he obtained his law license. A few years later, Abe Buckles became a prominent lawyer in Indianapolis and eventually moved to California, where he became a judge before being elected the Los Angeles County district attorney. Abe Buckles died in 1915 at the age of sixty-eight and is buried in San Bernardino, California.

Burlington Cunningham, the color sergeant who was wounded at Antietam and twice at Gettysburg, mustered out in 1864 and survived until just a few months short of his ninetieth birthday, dying in 1930. Cunningham is buried in Wayne County, Nebraska.

One of the true heroes of the Nineteenth Indiana was Sergeant Major Asa Blanchard. After rallying the survivors and waving the national flag above the Nineteenth's reformed battle line near the rear of Herbst Woods, Blanchard was mortally wounded with a minie ball passing through an artery in his groin.

Asa Blanchard is credited with two of the most famous quotes of the Battle of Gettysburg... "Rally, boys!" and, after being shot, "Tell my mother I did not falter." Asa Blanchard is buried in the Congressional Cemetery in Washington, DC.

Lieutenant Colonel William Dudley, who was shot in the right leg while carrying the Stars and Stripes on July 1st, was carried into town and placed in a house across the street from the courthouse. On July 4th, Dudley was moved to Littlestown, Pennsylvania, where doctors performed the amputation of his leg. Dudley remained in the service, however, as a member of the Veterans Reserve Corps and was breveted to the rank of brigadier general.

After the war, William Dudley returned to Richmond, Indiana, where he was appointed as the county clerk from 1867 to 1870. He also served in President Garfield's administration as Commissioner of Pensions. Dudley died in 1909 and is buried in Arlington National Cemetery in Washington, DC. Interestingly, William Dudley's signature is on Solomon Whitlow's marriage certificate with Solomon's first wife, Mary Jane Nation, in 1867.

On July 5th, the day the Nineteenth's survivors walked out to where the Company B skirmishers initially fought, they found many of their fallen. Among them, still alive but severely wounded, was First Lieutenant Samuel Schlagle. Although he was able to return to Indiana alive, he never fully recovered and died in January of 1866. He is buried in Earlham Cemetery in Richmond, Indiana, atop a small hill overlooking the old National Road.

As for the civilians at Gettysburg, approximately 2,500 residents lived in the town during the time of the battle. After three days of fighting by the two armies, those families were confronted with the care of approximately 25,000 wounded soldiers left behind in their homes, barns, churches, courthouse, and even in their open fields.

Although fictional, the story of the McLaughlin family is representative of so many families in Gettysburg after the battle. The lives of those who lived in and around Gettysburg had been changed forever. Wounded soldiers were hospitalized in nearly every structure that had a roof, and the farmers' fields were full of shallow graves.

Most of the African American families living in and around Gettysburg had fled before the battle, many of them fleeing even prior to Jubal Early's invasion June 26th, five days prior to the battle. Once the Confederates captured the town late in the afternoon on July 1st, any free blacks still in town would have been desperate to make their escape. The story of the fictional black family Solomon came across leaving their house just prior to nightfall on July 1st was intended to give the reader a sense of the fear and desperation that African Americans felt during the American Civil War.

Writing about the Whitlow brothers in this story was an enjoyable experience. The oldest brother John, who wasn't at Gettysburg (or was he?), fought with the Third Indiana Cavalry in the western theater of the war and lived the longest of the three Whitlow brothers. He died in 1926 and is buried in Kentucky.

King S. (Solomon) Whitlow moved with his family several times after the Civil War. He eventually settled in Oregon with his new wife Clara. In addition to Solomon's daughter Maime, Solomon and Clara had one child together, Ernest Whitlow. Solomon died in 1890 at the age of forty-eight and is buried in Hillsboro, Oregon. His child Ernest lived to be only six years old.

James, as mentioned in the final chapter, rests in the Indiana section of the Soldiers' National Cemetery and is identified as a member of the Nineteenth Indiana's Company B. Seeing James's grave there many years ago is what set me off on this journey. Being a distant cousin, I immediately wanted to learn his story and share it with as many people as I could. Clara and Solomon were both right about Gettysburg National Cemetery. It is a beautiful place.

As for Henry, Hawk, and Sergeant Boller...they were incredibly enjoyable to write about. If they seemed almost unreal, then you were right... I made 'em up. I now believe that seeing a fictional character coming to life in the mind is one of the most satisfying feelings a writer can have. I hope you were entertained by their stories and their personalities as much as I was while writing about them.

Acknowledgments

It takes a lot more than one person to complete a story of this magnitude, and I was blessed to have a wonderful team of people with me throughout the process. At the risk of unintentionally leaving someone out, I want to acknowledge several of the organizations and people who deserve mention here for their assistance.

First off, I want to thank all the historians who have previously written about the Nineteenth Indiana regiment, the Iron Brigade, and the Battle of Gettysburg. There are way too many great writers to try to acknowledge all of them here. But I would like to mention a few of them who have had an influence on me and have written about the Iron Brigade or, in particular, the Nineteenth Indiana.

Alan Nolan's *The Iron Brigade* was one of the first books I had in my collection and is a timeless work of writing that I refer to often. *The Flags of the Iron Brigade* by Howard Michael Madaus and Richard H. Zeitlin contains a treasure chest of photos of the Iron Brigade's flags and great stories of the men who fought beneath them.

Lance Herdegen has produced several great books on the subject, and his books are packed with amazingly detailed stories that seemingly bring the men of the Iron Brigade back to life. I have found several of Mr. Herdegen's books especially useful in the writing of this historical fiction novel. A few of his books that have given me inspiration are *Those Damned Black Hats! The Iron Brigade in the Gettysburg Campaign, The Iron Brigade in Civil War and Memory, The Men Stood Like Iron: How the Iron Brigade Won Its Name, In the Bloody Railroad Cut at Gettysburg,* and *Union Soldiers in the American Civil War.* Mr. Herdegen's lifetime of work has memorialized forever the brave men of the Iron Brigade.

William Thomas Venner's *The 19th Indiana Infantry at Gettysburg: Hoosiers' Courage* told a magnificent, emotional story and is a must-read for any fan or student of the Nineteenth Indiana regiment. The book's first chapter was the gripping and heart-wrenching account of the Nineteenth's survivors claiming their dead and wounded two days after the battle. *Iron Men, Iron Will* by Craig L. Dunn is an incredible regimental history of the Nineteenth Indiana and is packed with superb photos and detailed accounts by the men of the regiment.

Alan Gaff is a superb writer and has written many great historical books. Gaff's *Brave Men's Tears: The Iron Brigade at Brawner Farm* is an enjoyable book concerning the Iron Brigade's first major engagement just prior to the Battle of Second Manassas. One of my favorite books and an incredible resource for this novel was Mr. Gaff's *On Many a Bloody Field,* which focused not only on the Nineteenth Indiana in general, but also on Company B in particular—the same company containing several of the characters in *Brothers of War.*

For maps of the Battle of Gettysburg, I frequently reference Philip Laino's *Gettysburg Campaign Atlas* and Bradley Gottfried's *The Maps of Gettysburg.* Both are wonderful reference books that any student of the battle should have at their side while reading any Gettysburg book. Gregory Coco has written several books on the battle, and the books by Mr. Coco that I frequently refer to are two of his works on the aftermath of the battle, *A Vast Sea of Misery* and *A Strange and Blighted Land.*

For an incredible resource on the casualties of the battle, I can find no source greater than the works by Travis W. Busey and John W. Busey. Their three-volume *Union Casualties at Gettysburg* and four-volume *Confederate Casualties at Gettysburg* are not only great, comprehensive resource materials but are also packed with incredible stories of the men who sacrificed during the Battle of Gettysburg.

For one of the best records of what happened to all the men of the Nineteenth Indiana, I often refer to Phil Harris's wonderful website NineteenthIndianaIronBrigade.com. Mr. Harris has put an amazing amount of work into compiling the stories of the men and also documenting and photographing the graves of the brave men of the Nineteenth.

I would also like to thank the great historical fiction writers whose works have given me much joy over the years. I would feel remiss if I didn't mention the novel writers Michael Shaara, Jeff Shaara, Ralph Peters, Bernard Cornwell, Newt Gingrich, Alex Rossino, MacKinlay Kantor, Jim R. Woolard, Stephen Crane, and so, so many more that are too numerous to list here. Mr. Sinex, thank you for the 1980 Christmas gift, *The Red Badge of Courage*. That wonderful gift helped set the course for this adventure.

Several organizations have also been extremely helpful for the completion of this work. Among those are Find-a-Grave.com, Ancestry.com, the Indiana Historical Society, the Adams County Historical Society, Gettysburg's Seminary Ridge Museum, the Gettysburg Battlefield National Military Park and their wonderful team of interpretive rangers, and the Association of Licensed Battlefield Guides at Gettysburg.

I owe a sincere thank-you to the publisher, Fulton Books, and their associates, who not only agreed to take on this project and help me with the enormous task of completing this work but have also been incredibly supportive throughout the process.

I would like to give a special thank-you to Gettysburg National Park ranger and historian John Heiser for access to Gettysburg National Park's incredible library and archives. I also want to thank Mr. Heiser for the wonderful maps he has produced for this book and for graciously allowing me to include them with the story.

The cover art for *Brothers of War* was the work of professional historical painter Mark Maritato. Working with Mr. Maritato on the painting for this book was an incredible experience, and I want to offer him special thanks for painting the picture that I couldn't do with only words.

Throughout the journey of completing *Brothers of War*, I had the support and encouragement of many of my friends and relatives. These marvelous people graciously read chapters, often out of order, and offered their opinions, advice, and encouragement. There are too many to list here, but without their support along the way, completion of this book would not have been possible.

I was fortunate to have the support of Phil Spaugy, one of the most knowledgeable historians of the Iron Brigade and particularly the Nineteenth Indiana. Not only is Phil the foremost historian of the Nineteenth, but he is also an expert on Civil War era firearms. Phil has graciously assisted me during this journey and helped me prevent the boys of the Nineteenth from wandering too far astray of their true history. I give Phil my sincerest thanks for all his assistance and for keeping me honest.

I would also like to thank Annemarie Shomber for her immeasurable assistance and enthusiasm for the book. Annemarie not only offered encouragement and support but also paid attention to the smallest but most important details and helped make this book a success.

I owe a special thanks to Teresa Mason. Early on, she took on this project and became a writing coach and teacher to someone who really needed one. Teresa has a better understanding of words and the English language than anyone I have ever known. She made me see words in an entirely new and deeper perspective and taught me how to bring characters to life. This book would have never been possible without her, and I will be forever thankful.

I must also offer a sincere, heartfelt thank-you to my good friend Al Condit. Al is a true historian whose opinions I have always trusted and whose ideas appear throughout *Brothers of War*. I have spent countless hours walking the hallowed grounds at Gettysburg with Al...in the rain, snow, sleet, sun, and heat. Discussing the battle with him has allowed me to "see" what happened there and translate the story into words. Writing this book was a monumental task for a first-time author, and I couldn't have done it without Al's assistance and support.

Max...yes, that was you. Throughout this journey, you were my Moses and will be remembered forever.

Lastly, I want to thank my wonderful family. My wife Kara and my two children, Trevor and Allison, always offered a listening ear and were with me every step of the way. I will be forever grateful.

About the Author

Michael Eisenhut has studied the American Civil War his entire life. While researching for *Brothers of War*, he spent several years focusing his study on the Battle of Gettysburg and the Nineteenth Indiana Volunteer Infantry regiment, part of the famed Iron Brigade. Michael is a pilot for a major airline and lives in Monrovia, Indiana, with his wife Kara and two children, Allison and Trevor. *Brothers of War, The Iron Brigade at Gettysburg* is his first novel.

CPSIA information can be obtained
at www.ICGtesting.com
Printed in the USA
LVHW110827010622
720195LV00001B/70